MW01287406

BLESSINGS IN
FEATHERSTONE VALLEY

FEATHERSTONE VALLEY SERIES

LONDON JAMES

ONE

SARAH

"*T*rust in the Lord with all your heart and do not lean on your own understanding. In all your ways acknowledge Him, and He will make your paths straight." *Proverbs 3:5-6*

New Year's resolutions often fail. It's not because the person making the promises to themselves or others wants to fail. But sometimes, the motivation just isn't there. What makes them want to promise and what makes them keep the promise are two different things. Neither is right. Neither is wrong.

It's just how it is.

Sarah hadn't missed a New Year's resolution in years. At least not until the year her husband died. Then it all fell apart. She didn't do any of the things she'd planned on. She hadn't seen the beauty of every day for what it was. She hadn't laughed every day, at least once, as she said she would. She hadn't cooked much beyond what the guests needed at the inn or the inn's café. And she hadn't woken up each morning with a sense that today was a new day and another chance.

Another chance for what?

Being a widow? She'd been one for two years now. Being a better version of herself? She'd long since given up on that.

Sure, she didn't wish to be a bad person or someone a friend couldn't count on. Everyone could always count on her, no matter what she had going on in her life. She'd do anything to help the people of Featherstone Valley, that was for darn sure. But a better version of the woman she saw in the reflection of her bedside mirror?

She didn't even really know what that meant anymore.

"Miss Holden, this is the finest breakfast I've had in a long time." Ruppert Clemons, a salesman who had come to Featherstone a few days into the new year, sat in one of the dining room chairs, beaming from ear to ear as he held up a fork full of scrambled eggs. "If my wife cooked like this, I swear I would be three hundred... no, four hundred pounds."

"Well, it's probably best she doesn't then. Not to mean any offense to her, but being four hundred pounds wouldn't be good for your health."

"No, I guess it wouldn't. Still, I would love to come home to cooking like yours instead of hers."

"I wouldn't tell her such, though, Mr. Clemons." Sarah paused. "By the way, do you have a date set for when you're heading home?" She cocked her head to the side, trying to remember where Mr. Clemons had said he was from. For the life of her, she couldn't remember.

Was it Boise?

I think it's Boise, she thought.

"I'm not sure yet," the salesman said.

While she had enjoyed having Mr. Clemons staying in her inn, she couldn't deny that his presence had not been as easy-going as other guests in the past. Everywhere she'd turn most days, he'd be there—in the parlor while she was trying to clean, in the dining room well before the meals were served, in the hallways when she would be dusting the picture frames, or even just outside while she was tending to the animals that helped supply the inn's kitchen with food or collecting firewood for the cold winter nights.

He was always around, and she wondered how many bicycle seat gadgets he had sold since he arrived. Given his time at the inn, her guess was less than two. Of course, even if he'd been out talking to people all day, he probably wouldn't have sold many. Not too many people in Featherstone Valley had bicycles. There wasn't a need for them. The town was small enough to walk around, and if anyone needed to get to Deer Creek or Bent Fork for supplies the mercantile didn't have, they either rode horses or took their wagons. Not to mention, it was the dead of winter. Why anyone would think someone would want to ride a bicycle around when there were three feet of snow on the ground was beyond her.

The only ones who had bicycles were the children, and they didn't need special seats.

"Well, whenever you're ready. Of course, there is no rush," she said.

"I should think about it, though. I will this afternoon. I need to see a few more people before I consider returning home." He leaned down and tapped his briefcase as though he meant for the movement to indicate his intentions of selling more bicycle seats. She thought about asking him how business had been for a moment, but she stopped herself.

She wasn't all that interested.

He had started his sales pitch with her the minute he walked through the door of the inn, but she wasted no time telling him she wasn't interested, and she wasn't about to even broach the subject again for fear he would think she'd changed her mind. She didn't need the new-fangled gadget any more than anyone else. She had her horse, Bessie, and her wagon, and the pair did just fine to suit Sarah's needs—even if Bessie was getting on in years.

"Well, I wish you luck today," Sarah said, nodding to the salesman and leaving his table before he could say anything else.

Tucking the coffee pot close to her, its scent wafted. She'd always loved the smell of coffee, and every time she'd smell it, she always thought of how Harold would awake before her, sneak out of their bedroom, and brew a kettle, "so the house smells nice when you wake up," he would always tell her when she asked why he did it.

She wove through a few more filled tables, stopping by the few other guests to see if they needed anything.

Early winter and just after the new year had never been a popular time for visitors to Featherstone Valley. Of course, no season ever was. Unlike Deer Creek and Bent Fork, it was a modest town with little to see. The town was always too remote —or at least that is what she'd heard from people over the years who would stop in for a day or two, then quickly leave for 'greener pastures.' Deer Creek and Bent Fork were bigger and more attractive for those seeking entertainment. They had a saloon, not that she cared much for that type of place, but to each their own. They also had a theater, and between just those two things, more settlers had been heading there instead of staying in Featherstone Valley. Sometimes, she wondered if it was a blessing or not that the town stayed small. It was debatable. Still, even with the lack of newcomers and guests staying at the inn, she'd always had enough people either here on business or passing through and waiting for the next stage to keep up with her livelihood. Not to mention, the townsfolk enjoying her small café was a huge help after Harold died. It wasn't much. But it was enough. She lived content.

Papers rustled near the corner, and she looked up to see Mr. Craig Harrison, the owner of the gold mining company in town, throwing his hands up in annoyance. Wyatt Cooper, another young man, sat with him, and Mr. Cooper's eyes widened as he watched Mr. Harrison. The two had been talking as they combed through files of paperwork since they arrived this morning for breakfast, barely looking up from the parchment to eat. She made her way over to the table, refilling their coffee cups.

"I could be wrong, but I think something is troubling you, Mr. Harrison." She chuckled, trying to ease into her joke so it didn't sound rude. She made her way over to his table, and as he looked up at her, a hint of remorse etched through the crease on his forehead.

"Sorry for making such a ruckus, Miss Holden." Mr. Harrison gathered the papers, tapping the sheets on the table to make them line up. "It's just this land deal I'm trying to secure. Mayor Duncan is bent on making everything difficult."

"That sale hasn't gone through? I thought he would have approved it months ago when you first offered to buy Rattlesnake Mountain."

"I know. I would have thought so, too. But no. It hasn't. He's had other bids on the property, and he hasn't seemed too keen on just taking mine, but rather, *he'd like to hear all offers*, or so this letter says." Mr. Harrison's voice twisted as he finished his sentence and pointed to one of the papers sitting on the table in front of him. Sarah couldn't see all the writing, but she did catch Mayor Duncan's seal on the header and his signature in the footer of the paper. It was an official letter from the town, that much she knew.

"Huh. I wonder why he won't accept your offer," she said.

Mr. Harrison snorted with a slight growl on his lips. It was as though he knew the answer but questioned whether or not to tell her. Of course, she wasn't stupid as to why the Mayor would hesitate on the deal. Having two men trying to outbid each other on a piece of land meant only one thing for the town— more money. And the mayor was just greedy enough to try to get as much as he could. Part of her understood the reason even if the other part thought it was wrong.

"Well, surely, Mayor Duncan will come to his senses soon and take your offer so the deal can be done."

"From your mouth to God's ears, I hope." Mr. Harrison inhaled a breath and rested his elbows on the table. "It was a fine breakfast this morning, by the way. I would have to agree with that guest over there. Harold was a lucky man in more ways than one."

"Well, thank you for saying that."

"I want you to know I miss him. He was the best foreman I could have asked for, and I hate that he's gone."

"I miss him too. Every day." She sighed, trying not to get lost in any memories that wanted to sneak into her mind. She'd always allowed them to before, and it was one of her resolutions this year not to do it so much.

This one I plan to keep, she thought.

It wasn't that she didn't want to think about her beloved Harold or bask in the memories of him, their love, or their marriage. It was that every time she did, she'd fall a little deeper into dwelling in a land of despair, and she didn't want to do that any more than she wanted to live without the man she had married twenty-five years ago. There is only so much time one can allow oneself to live in sadness, and she knew if she didn't pull herself out of it, she'd remain there forever, letting it overwhelm her to a point she didn't want to think about.

Blessed are they that mourn: for they shall be comforted. Matthew 5:4, she thought.

She cleared her throat, switching the coffee pot from one hand to the other. "He would be proud of you trying to buy that land and expand your business," she said, distracting herself.

Mr. Harrison adjusted his seat. "I think he would too. Although, I can't say I don't wish I could have his help with it or his opinion. He always had the best advice, and I could always go to him with anything I needed."

"Yeah, he had that quality."

Mr. Harrison furrowed his brow and clicked his tongue. "That gives me an idea." Before Sarah could say anything, he gathered the papers, leaving one out and shoving the rest in his briefcase. He scribbled a few words on the paper and then handed it to Mr. Cooper. "Take this to the mayor."

"Are you sure?" Mr. Cooper asked.

"Yes. Take it to him right now before I change my mind."

Mr. Cooper jumped to his feet, nodded toward Sarah, and darted out the door, nearly knocking into a table in his haste.

"He's eager," Sarah said, chuckling.

"Just like your husband was. He had less experience, though. What I wouldn't give to hear what Harold thought of this whole land deal. He always knew what would benefit the town and what wouldn't. I used to think his mind was wasted on the job he had. He should have been town mayor for the smarts he had."

"He wouldn't have been happy as town mayor. He never liked politics."

"He had a gift for it, though. He would have known how this deal would affect the town—positively or negatively. Mr. Cooper just isn't there yet."

"So, it's true, then? You hired Mr. Cooper for the foreman position."

"Yes, I did."

"I hope he's working out for you."

"He has done well. Part of me was surprised, but then part of me wasn't. He reminds me of me at that age—determined to make a name for himself without mistakes. He's a hard worker like his father, Zeke. But he's also educated."

"You at that age? Listen to you. You're talking like you're an old man or something." Sarah laughed, brushing her fingertips against her cheek.

"Well... I'm older than him. I celebrate my thirtieth birthday next month."

"Really? You'll have to tell me the date, and I'll bake you a cake."

"I would love that. It's the seventeenth."

"I'll make a note of it. Do you prefer chocolate or butter-cream frosting?"

"Chocolate cake with chocolate icing is my favorite."

"Well, consider it done. I'll have it waiting for you when you come in on the seventeenth." She smiled warmly as she stepped forward and laid her hand on Mr. Harrison's shoulder. "And try not to worry too much about Mayor Duncan or his motives. He will come to his senses, and it will all work out. I'll pray for you and the right outcome."

"Thank you. I could use all the prayers I can get, especially when it comes to Mayor Duncan and Sidney Miller." Mr. Harrison rolled his eyes.

"Sidney Miller? From Deer Creek?"

"The one and the same."

"What does he have anything to do with it?"

"He's the one who keeps outbidding me."

"But why would Mayor Duncan even entertain the idea of Mr. Miller buying land in Featherstone Valley? Does he not know the type of man Mr. Miller is?"

Sarah straightened her shoulders, trying to ignore the memories of all the stories Harold used to tell her about his dealings with Mr. Miller. At least once a week, one of the miners would get a wild hair up their backside and think it a smart idea to go to Deer Creek to blow his money on Mr. Miller's *establishments*. The town was lovely; she'd never say it wasn't, but it had a dark side full of booze and women with... questionable morals, and Mr. Sidney Miller was involved in it all right down to their core. She didn't want to think about what that man would or could do to a town like Featherstone Valley.

"I don't see how he wouldn't know. Everyone does. It's not like Mr. Miller keeps it a secret. He's the first one to tell a person about his accomplishments." Mr. Harrison snorted, shaking his head. "I have no idea what Mayor Duncan is up to or thinking. But I will get to the bottom of it."

"Well, I wish you luck."

"Thank you." With a furrowed brow, Mr. Harrison gathered the rest of his papers and flicked his wrist, checking the time on his watch. "I should get to the office. I have a lot of things on my to-do list this morning." He reached into his pocket and yanked out several folded bills. "What do I owe you for the breakfast and coffee?"

"That will be fifty-five cents."

"Here." He handed her a dollar bill.

"Let me get you some change." She turned to leave, but he stopped her.

"I don't need any."

"But this is too much."

"Aside from the fact that I don't think it is, considering how tasty it was, consider the extra as a tip for your service and kind words."

"You don't have to do that, Mr. Harrison."

"Yes, I do, and I will see you for lunch." He grabbed his coffee cup, draining the last gulp before setting it back down and grabbing his hat. He placed it on his head, nodding at her before leaving the dining room and heading for the door. After opening it, he paused and stepped backward, tipping his hat as Mrs. Gables entered the café and made a beeline for Sarah, waving her hand intently to get Sarah's attention.

Sarah inhaled a deep breath, bracing herself. It wasn't that she didn't like the woman; she did. But Mrs. Gables always seemed to be in crisis mode, where everything around her was in the utmost dire of circumstances, and if something wasn't done right then and there, the world would collapse around them. Harold used to say she was the most high-strung woman he'd ever met. She also had a knack for speaking her mind without thinking first.

"I swear that man is always in a hurry. He should slow down more, if not for his health, then to notice the world around him," Mrs. Gables said, glancing over her shoulder as though Mr. Harrison was still in the doorframe. He wasn't.

"It's never a harm to be busy, especially when his mines keep so many of our men working." Sarah chuckled, shaking her head. "What can I help you with, Mrs. Gables?"

"I was wondering if you had time to make a batch or two of muffins and take them to Mr. and Mrs. Fields. The poor dear is still in bed, and Dr. Sterling said she can't get up for anything until after the baby is born."

"Oh no. That's awful."

"Isn't it? Especially when she has Miles Jr. and Millie to tend to. The poor thing. She's just beside herself with worry. Fortunately, Mr. Fields is there to help, but he has his work during the day. I've been running around town all morning, which has been no easy feat with the snowfall last night, asking people to help with meals and even taking the children for one or two nights to help. Dr. Sterling said it could be at least another month and a couple of weeks before she delivers."

"Well, I can certainly help with meals. And the children can stay with me whenever they need. I have a couple of rooms available, and I don't see anyone renting all of them in the next few weeks. Even if they do, I can make up a few beds in my house."

"Oh, bless you, Ms. Holden." Mrs. Gables reached out, grazing Sarah's arm. "I just can't imagine what Mr. and Mrs. Fields are going through. If I were in the same situation, I would be a basket case."

"I'm sure God would give you the strength you need just as He is giving it to them."

"I suppose you're right. Still, we all need to keep them in our prayers." Mrs. Gables bit her lip and folded her arms across her chest. "Thank goodness our new pastor arrives on the afternoon stage. The Lord must know we need him now more than ever."

Sarah inhaled a deep breath. "I'd forgotten the new pastor was arriving today."

"Oh no. You have his room ready, right?"

"Of course. Everything has been taken care of. I knew he was coming; I just forgot what day of the week it was."

"Well, at least you have everything ready. It would be quite a shame for him to arrive and not have a tidy room." Mrs. Gables twitched as she lifted her chin, looking down at Sarah slightly.

"The room is tidy, I assure you." Sarah's jaw clenched as she fought a tone she knew would be uncouth. She'd never been one to match rudeness with rudeness, no matter how much she wanted to. "I should be getting myself into the kitchen, though, if I'm going to make a few batches of muffins for Mr. and Mrs. Fields. Was there anything else you needed, Mrs. Gables?"

"No, that was it. I appreciate your help. I shall be by again should I need anything."

"Of course. I'm always here to help."

Sarah tucked the coffee pot close to her chest as she turned and left the dining room, heading toward the kitchen as she heard the bell above the door chime, telling her Mrs. Gables had left.

"That woman is still high-strung, Harold," she whispered as she glanced up at the ceiling. Although she couldn't hear him, she imagined him laughing alongside her.

TWO

JACK

The only constant thing in life is change.
Although Jack had heard the phrase at least a dozen, if not more, times in his life, none of those times had ever really sunk in. At least not until now, as he sat in the stagecoach while it rolled down the road toward the town of Featherstone Valley. He hadn't known what was in store for him in the dusty little town, but he knew one thing—it was far away from the life he wanted to leave behind in Texas.

And that made the calling to the ministry in Featherstone Valley worth its weight in gold.

Jack had never been much for change. While some thrive on it, dwelling in the unknown circumstances flying around every corner, others avoid it at all costs, fighting like mad for only the familiar to grace their daily lives.

He was of the latter.

Or at least he was for most of his life.

Sure, change happened to him. It was inevitable. Some of the changes were good—falling in love with and marrying Maryann and having his two sons. But then, some of the changes were not so good—Maryann's death and the estrangement between him and his sons. Those events were downright the worst times of his life. He always hated change for just that reason, which he supposed was shocking given his current situation, but even if Featherstone and their church were nothing more than unknown questions without answers, they were at least a safe route. The one he could trust that God put in Jack's path for a reason.

And what could he not like about that?

He was just happy they had offered him the position, given he hadn't been a pastor for long. So, when the letter came in, he didn't question it, nor did he look around at his house, so full of memories he didn't wish to ever think about, and think for a second of refusing.

The only problem was he didn't tell anyone where he was going.

Guilt prickled in his chest as he glanced out the window at the snow-covered mountains and forests passing by. Or he supposed the wagon was passing instead.

"Where are you headed to, Mister?" a voice asked.

Jack glanced at the small boy sitting across the wagon, staring at him. The boy's mother's head whipped toward her son, and she furrowed her brow and shook her head.

"That's not your business, Billy," she said. "You shouldn't ask strangers such personal questions."

"Why not?" The boy looked up at his mother and stuck his finger in his nose.

Jack was nailing this thing called having manners, wasn't he? A smirk inched across his lips.

"Because it's rude." She grabbed his wrist, yanking his hand away from his face.

"I don't think it's rude. I was going to tell him where we were going if he asked." The boy looked at Jack. "We're headed to Deer Creek."

"Billy! I said stop."

"No, you said it wasn't my business where he was going. You said nothing about me telling him where we're going." The boy looked up at his mother, and she closed her eyes, blowing out a breath. Jack had seen the same look on many women throughout his life, and they all had given it just as their children were about to step on the mother's last nerve. Perhaps they'd already stepped on it and were now grinding it into the dirt with their boots.

Jack chuckled under his breath and nodded toward the woman. "It's quite all right, ma'am. I don't mind the boys' curiosity."

She half-smiled and glanced at her son one last time before looking out the window of the stagecoach. A slight crease formed on her forehead. She looked burdened by an unknown emotional weight she carried.

Jack turned his attention back to the boy. "Deer Creek is a fine town. I'm sure it will serve you well. As for me, I'm headed to Featherstone Valley."

"What's in Featherstone Valley?"

"My new job. I'm to serve as the town's new pastor."

"You're a pastor?" The boy blinked, and the mother gave Jack a brief look before turning back to the window. She inhaled slightly as though she'd done something wrong, even though Jack didn't know what it was.

"Yes, I am." Although Jack's gaze moved toward the mother for a moment, he focused back on the boy.

"Mama doesn't like going to church. She said it's pointless." As the boy hooked his thumb toward his mother, the woman's head whipped toward her son once more. Her mouth gaped, and then she slapped her hand against her chest.

"Billy! Why would you say that?" Her shoulders straightened. "I can't believe you would tell him a thing like that!" She looked between her son and Jack, stuttering. "I'm... I'm sorry. I can't fathom where he gets such ideas."

"You say it all the time," the boy said. "Nearly every Sunday when all your friends are getting ready for church with their husbands, and they don't got time to talk to you. You say it's pointless and don't understand why they go." He scratched his nose this time, keeping his finger on the outside instead of the inside. His little voice rang with an innocent honesty that melted Jack's heart. The boy didn't know the damage his mother believed he was causing—not that he was causing any. Jack wasn't about to criticize the woman for having an opinion on how she wanted to live her life, even if it wasn't precisely how Jack would live it.

There was a time he thought the same as her. Of course, he never saw attending church as pointless or a waste of time. It was more that he didn't make the time because he didn't see it as important enough. It wasn't until Maryann died that he thought about stepping inside a church, and even then, he felt... off.

And then he heard something that he knew he'd never forget. A prayer that hit him so squarely in the chest, he knew that such was not only how he wanted to live his life but how he wanted to share it as himself in such a way that he might bring joy, hope, comfort, and peace to anyone who wanted or needed it.

Lord, make me an instrument of your peace: where there is hatred, let me sow love; where there is injury, pardon; where there is doubt, faith; where there is despair, hope; where there is darkness, light; where there is sadness, joy.

It was the Peace Prayer of Saint Francis of Assisi, a prayer he repeated to himself nearly daily.

"Billy, if you don't shut your mouth right now..." Her breath quickened as though panic was starting to set in. "I'm going to make them stop this stage so that I can take you to the side of the road and whip your backside."

The boy's eyes widened, and he scooted away from her, leaning against the other side of the coach.

"It's quite all right, ma'am," Jack said, holding up a hand. "I take no offense to anything the boy is saying. We are all here on this earth with the free will to decide what is best for us. I don't begrudge you for choosing what to make of your own life." He paused, waiting until she seemed to calm. "I'm not the type of man or pastor to force anything on another. At one time, I thought the same way you did. Well, I didn't think going to church was a waste of time, but I did think it wasn't important."

"It's not that I think it's a waste of time." She took another breath, biting her bottom lip for a moment. "I'm not sure I can have faith when so much has happened to us. We've had a lot of struggles."

"I can understand that. I've met plenty of people who felt like you, too. I suppose even I did for a while." A slight chuckle hinted across his lips as he hoped to ease any ill feelings in the woman in case she thought him rude for giving advice or his opinion when she didn't ask. "The beauty of God, though, is no matter how far we stray from Him, He is always with us. You'd be amazed at what He can do with the brokenness of your life. All you need is prayer, and like clay in the hands of a potter, He molds and shapes us."

"Well, you've certainly given me something to think about," she said. Although her words conveyed that perhaps she would consider what Jack said, the stiffness of her shoulders and her tone told him otherwise. Perhaps another time, he might have pressed the issue, asking her more questions or giving her some Bible verses to think about, but this time he didn't. He simply nodded, whispering a prayer in his mind that God would soften her heart.

The mother and son kept to themselves the rest of the ride, looking out the windows as Jack did and watching the trees and mountains passing by. Although he noticed the young boy looking at him from time to time, neither of them said a word, and Jack leaned back in the seat, resting his head as he closed his eyes.

Pausing to wait if he felt another nudge, he didn't say another word.

Perhaps he'd made a foolish choice not to talk to the woman more. He still had moments where he wasn't sure about his pastor duties. Was he supposed to talk to them no matter what? Or was he supposed to let them come to him? He wasn't sure how involved he was supposed to become. Surely, if they came to him, he would get as involved as a sheriff trying to hunt down a criminal...

Boy, was that a bad analogy...

Anyway, in the end, he supposed he could only go with what his heart told him to do, and while he wanted to press the issue, something about the woman stopped him. He knew how she felt, and although he didn't know exactly what she'd been through, he didn't have to. He saw her sorrow and pain through his own eyes in a reflection that still haunted him from time to time.

He never liked thinking about that day by the creek that ran through the cemetery. He'd just buried Maryanne, and the boys had left with their aunt. Alone, mourning, angry, the depth of his emotions had almost been too much to bear, and as he looked upon his reflection in the water with the gun to his head, he nearly made a choice he could never take back. Each time he thought about that moment, he wanted to cringe, yet it was also a moment he never wanted to forget.

"Is she with you?" he had asked as he looked up at the sky—not wanting to admit it was a question for God, but asking just the same. "And is she happy?"

He hadn't expected an answer, of course. Sure, he believed, but why would God respond? Not after the things Jack had done. Wasn't he a lost cause? And then that's when he heard it—

a voice, clear as crystal, as though someone stood behind him and spoke. "Yes."

∾

A knock rapped on the stagecoach's door. "Featherstone Valley," the driver shouted.

His sudden shout jerked Jack's attention, and he sat up, looking out the window. The stage had parked in front of the mercantile, and as the driver opened the door, Jack scooted across the street, nodding toward the woman and her son as he tipped his hat.

"Have a good day, ma'am," he said, not waiting for a response.

As he stepped off the stage, his boots sank into the snow, a crisp contrast to Texas's dry, dusty terrain. The cold air nipped at his cheeks, a reminder that he was far from the sweltering heat of his former home. He glanced around, taking in the sights of what the driver had called Featherstone Valley. Its smallness struck him immediately. A mere handful of buildings dotted Main Street, nothing like the sprawling expanse of his hometown. With its faded wooden sign, the mercantile reminded him of the old general store back in Texas. However, it lacked the wear and tear of years of relentless sun and wind, while the snow-covered rooftops and the gentle smoke curling from chimneys painted a picturesque scene so different from the sunbaked landscapes of Texas. He hadn't known what to expect. The mayor had somewhat described the town in his letter but hadn't included much of the details—especially not its tiny size. It was so small that he could count the buildings on Main Street on two hands.

As Jack's gaze wandered, he noticed the townspeople going about their day. Their relaxed pace and friendly nods were a stark contrast to the hurried, indifferent faces he was used to. It was as if time moved slower here, and he couldn't help but feel a sense of calm wash over him. It was as though, even in the cold, he could still feel the warmth, and not from the sun but from the sense of community around him.

Featherstone Valley might be small, but it held a promise, a chance for a new beginning.

"Pastor Boone?" a voice asked behind him.

He turned to see a man walking toward him in a dapper suit and top hat—an actual top hat. The man smiled from ear to ear, and as he neared Jack, he removed his hat to reveal his bald head and a horseshoe ring of white hair that he combed over to make it look thicker than it was. "Are you Pastor Jack Boone?" the man asked.

"Yes, I am. And who might be asking?" Jack stuck out his hand for a shake.

"I'm Mayor Duncan. Mr. Bartholomew Duncan, to be exact."

"It's a pleasure to meet you, Mayor Duncan."

The two men shook hands. Their hot breath steamed all around them.

"I trust your trip was pleasant?" the mayor asked. He leaned backward, hooking a thumb in the suspenders under his coat as he inhaled a deep breath.

"Oh yes. The stage was comfortable. Much more comfortable than my horse and saddle would have been for such a long journey." Jack pointed toward the horse still tied to the back of the stagecoach, and upon mention of his steed, the driver set Jack's luggage at his feet and ran to untie the gelding. The young man handed him the reins with a nod before wiping a layer of sweat from his brow. "Thank you," Jack said to the young man before turning back to the mayor, who pointed down the street.

"The livery is on the edge of town. Mr. Rutherford owns and runs the place. He does right by the animals, and your horse will be cared for."

"That's good to know." He patted the buckskin horse on the

neck. "We've been through a lot together, him and me, and after eighteen years, I didn't want to sell him or leave him behind in Texas."

"Of course, you wouldn't. Why, I don't know any man who would want to leave a horse behind after eighteen years of service."

"Are you sure Mr. Rutherford has room?"

The mayor nodded. "Of course he does. The miners are up in the mountains during the week, working. It's only on the weekends they come into town to eat at the inn or play poker in the saloon. While most have homes here, a lot live in the mine houses that don't have accommodations for horses."

"Saloon? You never mentioned a saloon in your letter." Jack furrowed his brow, trying to remember Mayor Duncan's letter. Of course, he hadn't cared much if there was or wasn't a saloon. What people did when it came to having a drink was their own business. Still, he couldn't help but wonder if the mayor lied on purpose or if it was a simple oversight.

The mayor's brow furrowed. "It's not a saloon like in Deer Creek or Bent Fork. It's dry. The owner and bartender don't serve anything stronger than sarsaparilla and coffee—the latter of which you might want to steer clear of. It's as strong as it is black, and I swear, with one sip, you'll be awake for three days. I made the mistake of getting a cup one night. I saw noises." The mayor shook his head and motioned down the street. "I can take you there, introduce you to Mr. Harper, and then show you the rest of the town if you want."

Jack followed the mayor's movement and smiled, shaking his head. "I think I'll pass on the tour for now if you don't mind."

"Oh, of course. You probably wish to get settled after such a long journey. Unfortunately, I have yet to secure a house for you to rent. But I'm aware of a few that should be coming on the market soon. You are more than welcome to stay at the town inn for the time being. Miss Sarah Holden, a lovely woman, owns it. She also has a small café."

"Well, that's kind of you. Thank you." He glanced down the street one way and then the other. "Is the inn near the stables?"

"The inn is on the other end of town. You can't miss the place, though." The mayor lifted his hand, pointing his finger toward the sky and wiggling it for a second before he shoved his hand into his pocket and dug around. "Before I forget. Here is the key to the church. It's near the inn, across from the pond. You can't miss it either."

"Oh. Thank you." Jack took the brass key from the mayor and slid it into the inside pocket of his blazer.

"The school teacher is Miss Rachel Evans. She'll be happy to show you around."

"Sounds good."

"It's not much of a building, but we keep it cared for as best we can."

"That's all anyone can do, and I'm sure it will suit me just fine."

"Well, if you need anything, just holler." The mayor stuck his hand out to shake Jack's one more time. "I look forward to hearing your first sermon next Sunday, too."

"And I look forward to giving it."

Jack watched as the mayor strode down the street, looking around as he walked. A few of the people along the way nodded and smiled at their town leader, while a few others ignored the man, looking as though they did so on purpose for one reason or another. If it wasn't just the way they acted that caused Jack to pause, it was certainly the faces they made after the mayor tried to gain their attention that did.

Was the mayor disliked in his own town?

Jack shook the question from his mind. He didn't have the time to think about it, not when he had to get both him and his horse settled after a long trip.

THREE

SARAH

Sarah pulled the hot muffin tin from the stove and set it on the counter, tossing the towel she'd used to grab the tin to the side. Scents of flour, butter, and chocolate wafted around her, and she closed her eyes. She'd always loved the scents of baking in her kitchen. Pancakes were perhaps her favorite to smell, but cookies, brownies, cakes, and muffins were always a close second—especially when they had chocolate in them.

The breakfast crowd had dwindled in the dining room in the time it took her to make the muffins for Mr. and Mrs. Fields, and a calm, serene atmosphere seemed to fill the room. She always enjoyed the lull of the late morning when everyone was off to work, and guests were off to their adventures or business. Ever since Harold died, it was hard for her to be alone at times, yet there were times, like this morning, she loved it.

With a soft hum to her lips, she grabbed the hot muffins from the tray and placed them in a basket she lined with a cloth. Steam rose from the baked goodies as she stacked them, and she bent down, inhaling their delicious scent.

The back door swung open with a force that nearly knocked

it into the wall behind it, and as Sue Ellen rushed inside, Sarah flinched.

"Boy, do I have news for you, dear friend," Sue Ellen said. Her cheeks were flushed a bright shade of pink, and Sarah didn't know if it was from the cold outside or the fact that her lungs heaved like she'd run all the way from her house to the inn.

"And good morning to you, too." Sarah straightened up and folded the cloth over the muffins. It would help keep them slightly warm without making them soggy from the moisture and heat.

Sue Ellen waved her hand. "Oh, don't even start with me this morning. I've got news."

"News? Or gossip?" Sarah flashed her friend a grin and winked.

Sue Ellen jammed her hands into her hips. "It's not gossip. I don't fiddle with that sort of thing."

"Oh really?"

"No, I don't."

"So, telling me about Mr. and Mrs. Benson's fight at the mercantile two weeks ago wasn't gossip?"

"No. I was simply telling you why the mercantile was closed that afternoon."

"Yes, but I didn't ask why, and I also didn't need to know the details. You could have just informed me it was closed and left it at that."

Sue Ellen tucked her chin down and lowered her voice, slowing her speech. "It wasn't gossip."

Sarah glanced over at her friend, giving her another smirk. "Toe-MAY-toe, Toe-MA-toe."

"Whatever. Believe what you want. I know that *this* isn't gossip, though. *This* is news. Big news. Perhaps the biggest news you'll hear all week."

"So what is *this big news* you have?"

"The new pastor has arrived."

"Yes, I know. Mrs. Gables was by this morning and mentioned that he was arriving by the stage this morning. Plus, Mayor Duncan came by a couple of weeks ago to reserve the man a room. He hadn't secured him a house to rent, and the pastor needed a place to stay for a while."

"Well, did Mrs. Gables or Mayor Duncan also happen to mention that the pastor is a rather handsome, stoic man?"

"Sue Ellen Randall. I'm shocked." Sarah turned toward her friend and cocked her head to the side. "And just what would Hank think of you saying such a thing about another man?"

"After taking one look at Pastor Boone, he would probably agree with me." Sue Ellen folded her arms across her chest and chuckled.

"I suppose that's true. But still. Just because your husband has a sense of humor and your marriage is perfect doesn't mean you must always test it."

Sue Ellen cocked her head to the side, lifting an eyebrow. Sarah had seen that look she didn't know how many times; it screamed that Sue Ellen was asking the person if they could hear what they just said because it was beyond foolish.

"All right. All right. Enough about Hank and me," Sue Ellen said. "I want to talk about the new pastor."

"Why?"

"I heard that he's not married."

"That's... nice." Sarah twisted her last word, confused about where this conversation was headed.

"I don't think it is. A man of his age... why isn't he married?"

"What if he doesn't want to get married?"

Sue Ellen opened her mouth but shut it, grimacing her lips into a frown. "I doubt that. Perhaps he's a widower like you, or perhaps he never met the woman he wanted to spend the rest of his life with."

"Well, if he is a widower, then I feel sorry for his loss. But I still don't know why his marital status is of any concern to you."

"Oh, it's not a concern of mine. I was only thinking..." She paused and gave Sarah an odd smile as though she wanted Sarah to take her hint.

Sarah looked at her friend for a moment before it dawned on her, and she brushed her hand against her chest. "You can't possibly think I would be interested in his marital status," she said.

"Why not? If he's not married, and you're not married... it would be perfect."

"Just because two people aren't married doesn't mean they should marry each other. Why do you always have to be trying to find me a man to court?"

"Because I want you to be happy."

"I am happy."

Sue Ellen folded her arms across her chest. "I don't think you are."

Sarah inhaled a breath. It had been the same conversation she'd had with Sue Ellen at least a dozen times before. There was always some man who Sue Ellen thought would be perfect. None of them were, though, not even a single one. Not that Sarah cared. She wasn't looking for anyone to replace the man she lost, and she doubted she ever would. "Not to mention, Hank and I worry about you—all alone in this inn day in and day out. It's not safe—especially at night."

"I'm hardly alone. I always have at least one guest renting a room."

"But they are strangers, and some are men traveling without their wives. It's not safe."

"Nothing has ever happened to me, and I've never felt unsafe."

"That doesn't mean that it can't. But it's not just that you are alone, it's... don't you miss being married and having a husband?"

There it was.

The one question Sarah hated the most, and not because she couldn't answer it or didn't want to, but because she could. She just didn't want to admit it.

Of course, she missed being married and having a husband. She longed to hear Harold's voice, feel his arms wrapped around her, or feel his lips on hers. But the reality was that it was never going to happen. He was gone, and nothing would bring him back, no matter how much she dreamed and hoped.

Sarah opened her mouth, but before she could speak, the backdoor opened again, and Hank, Sue Ellen's husband, rushed inside the kitchen.

"Guess who I just saw?" he asked, looking between the women. He opened his mouth to continue but saw the jar of cookies Sarah kept on the counter, and for a moment, the thought of something sweet seemed to distract him. He reached into the jar, yanked out a cookie, and took a big bite. "The stage just got into town, and I saw the new pastor get off. He talked to the mayor briefly, then headed toward the livery with what I think was his horse. Must be a nice horse if he's bringing it from..." Hank paused, clicked his tongue, then looked at his wife. "Where did you say he was coming from?"

"Texas."

"That's right. Texas. Must be a nice horse to bring it from Texas." Hank finished the last bit of the cookie, and finally noticing his wife's expression, he shrugged and lifted his hands. "What did I say that was wrong?"

"Nothing. I was just telling Sarah that I saw him too."

"Yes, and she mentioned he was good-looking." A soft, whispered laugh left Sarah's lips, and she looked between the husband and wife.

Hank chuckled. "She's right. I mean, I suppose if I was a woman... I might think he was good-looking."

Sue Ellen looked at Sarah, cocking her head to the side as she pointed toward Hank. "See? I told you."

Sarah laughed, shaking her head. "I don't understand you two. I hope you know that."

"Never mind us." Sue Ellen waved her hand. "So, aren't you even a little curious about his appearance?"

"I can't say that I am. But I'm sure I'll find out what he looks like any moment. Remember, he's supposed to stay at the inn until the mayor finds him a house to rent."

"He's staying at the inn?" Sue Ellen's mouth gaped, and she blinked several times.

"Do you not hear me when I talk? Yes, I told you twice in the last five minutes. Where else would he stay without a house to rent?"

Sue Ellen shrugged. "I don't know. I wasn't listening because I was thinking too much about him arriving. That, and I thought the mayor had found him a place to rent."

"I thought he would have too, but I guess he had problems with the one place he had in mind. I don't know. I was only half listening to Mayor Duncan. That man can prattle on and on when he wants to."

"And it's usually about nothing important." Hank grabbed another cookie, shoving half of it in his mouth with the first bite.

Sarah opened her mouth to agree, but the sound of the bell above the inn's front door chimed, and she stopped herself before she said a word. She looked at Hank and Sue Ellen and held her hand up, knowing Sue Ellen was about to assume that the person who had entered the inn was the handsome pastor everyone seemed to be talking about.

"You two stay here," she whispered. "I mean it."

Of course, Sarah wasn't stupid. She thought the same. Well,

that it could be the new pastor, not that he was handsome. She hadn't laid eyes on him yet, so she had no way of knowing if what they said was true or not.

"But I guess I'm going to find out," she whispered to herself.

She continued down the tiny hallway, moving into the foyer, and as she rounded the corner, a tall man standing near the door turned toward her and took off his cowboy hat. She stopped, sucking in a breath.

"Good morning," he said. His voice was deeper than she thought it would be, and he stepped toward her, running one hand through his salt-and-pepper-colored hair while he reached out with the other to shake her hand. "Are you Miss Holden?"

"Yes. I am. You may call me Sarah if you like." She shook his hand. Sue Ellen hadn't been wrong, but it wasn't just his looks that caught Sarah off guard. It was his mere presence, as though to be near him instantly brought a sense of calm even to the most frazzled, and he had a quiet confidence about him, a stark contrast to the pastors who had come and gone in Featherstone Valley before. He stood nearly a foot taller than her, and when he smiled, it lit up his whole face, brightening his blue eyes. She found herself unexpectedly intrigued by this man who had left Texas in search of a new beginning.

"Well, Sarah, I'm Pastor Jack Boone. You may call me Jack. Did Mayor Duncan tell you I was coming?"

"Yes, he did. I have a room all made up for you. I'll just fetch the key and show it to you."

"Thank you. I'm sorry to say I think I tracked in the snow when I came inside." He glanced down at his boots, lifting one foot and then the other.

"It's quite all right. It happens a lot in the winter."

She ducked her chin toward her chest, moving around him and heading toward the desk in the corner of the room. Her heart thumped slightly, and her fingers trembled on the desk drawer's handle as she wrenched open the drawer and searched for the key.

"You have a lovely inn," Jack said, turning in a few circles as he looked around. "It's... bright."

"Yes, fortunately, the windows let in a lot of light throughout the day, especially with the sun shining off the snow. Thankfully, it cuts down on the lamps and lamp oil I need." She found the tiny brass key she'd saved in the corner and closed the drawer, glancing up at the man standing in front of her desk just as Sue Ellen and Hank entered the foyer. Hank was holding the basket of muffins Sarah had made for Mr. and Mrs. Fields— why, Sarah didn't know; perhaps they figured it would be a good reason to excuse them barging into the room—and the two of them skidded to a stop as they looked upon the pastor and Sarah.

"Oh, there you are, Sarah," Sue Ellen said, smiling as she approached. "I'm sorry. I didn't know you had company."

Sarah cocked her head to the side, snorting a laugh. "Lying in front of a pastor. Why, Sue Ellen, that's not a good look for you."

"I wasn't lying." Sue Ellen's face flushed a hinted shade of pink as she brushed her fingertips across her neck. "I didn't know you were still with someone. Whoever opened the door and rang the bell could have left before I came into the room." Although she glanced at Sarah, Sue Ellen kept her gaze on the new pastor. She chuckled a few times and stuck her hand out to shake his. "Sue Ellen Randall. It's a pleasure to meet you. This is my husband, Hank Randall." She motioned toward her husband, who stepped forward to shake the pastor's hand, too.

"It's a pleasure to meet you, sir," Hank said.

"It's nice to meet you both, too. I'm Jack Boone."

"We heard the rumors you were arriving today. We hope your trip was pleasant, riding all that way alone." Sue Ellen's gaze fluttered from the pastor to Sarah, then back to the pastor, and as she smiled, Sarah could feel her cheeks warm. Sue Ellen was nothing short of utterly obvious in her attempts to dig for any information she could.

"Yes, it was. Long, but pleasant."

"We can't imagine traveling from Texas to Montana. But we are glad you are here, safe and sound. Featherstone Valley is a close-knit community, if Mayor Duncan hasn't told you already. We look out for each other here."

Jack nodded, a smile tugging at the corners of his mouth. "I can already sense that. I must admit it's one of the reasons I felt called to come here. Back in Texas, things were... well, let's just say they were different. But I'm looking forward to being part of a community where people truly care about their neighbors."

Sarah watched him, noting the sincerity in his eyes. It was clear that Jack was more than just a handsome face; he had a heart for service. She couldn't shake the feeling that Jack Boone would be an interesting addition to their small town.

"Texas is quite a ways from here," Hank said, shaking his head. "I can't imagine what a trip that was. What made you decide to leave?"

Jack paused, a distant look crossing his face for a moment. "Well, I suppose I just felt a need for a change. A new beginning, you could say. And when I saw the advertisement for a pastor in Featherstone Valley, it felt right. I believe God has a plan for me here."

The pastor glanced at Sarah. She could see the battle inside of him through his eyes. He so desperately wanted to be kind to the Randalls, but he was tired.

"Well, Jack, I should show you your room." She skirted around the desk, motioning for him to follow her. "I'm sure you want to rest after your trip."

Jack turned to follow her, pausing as he pointed toward the basket in Hank's hands. "Is that for me?" he asked with slight hesitation.

Hank gaped at the pastor as though unsure what to do or

say, and Sarah spun, reaching out and blocking the pastor from touching the basket. "No!" she said before she had a chance to think about it first. Jack flinched at her tone and volume, and Sue Ellen slapped her hand over her forehead as though utterly embarrassed at Sarah's behavior.

Sarah cleared her throat. "I'm sorry. I didn't mean to raise my voice. Those muffins are for Mr. and Mrs. Fields. Mrs. Fields is with child, and Dr. Sterling put her on bed rest this morning. The whole town is making them food and helping out with their children."

"Oh, that's... well, it's unfortunate she is on bed rest, but it is good that the town is stepping in to help."

"Yes, it's quite disappointing, I'm sure, for them. I made those muffins to take over to them this afternoon."

"Well, that is nice of you. I'm sure they will be grateful." Jack paused, glancing at the muffins and then at the bags carrying his belongings sitting at his feet. "You said you were going to visit this afternoon. Do you know when?"

"I was going to head to their home after you were settled in your room. If you don't wish for anything to eat."

"No, I don't. I had a large breakfast, so I probably won't need anything until dinner. But since you're headed over there... and I am the town pastor... would you mind if I went with you?"

"No, I wouldn't mind. I'm sure Mr. and Mrs. Fields would appreciate the prayers, and of course, I'm sure they would love to meet you."

"How about you show me to my room, and I'll put my bags up? Then we can leave."

"Sure. Follow me."

Sarah turned, glancing toward Sue Ellen, who had rocked back on her heels and folded her arms across her chest. An odd smirk spread across her lips, and although Sarah wanted to tell her just to get whatever thoughts her friend had in her head to stop, she didn't. Instead, she just shook her head, hoping Sue Ellen would take the hint and forget what she was thinking.

Handsome or not, Jack was the town pastor and nothing more.

And that was precisely how she wanted it to stay.

Of course, she appreciated Sue Ellen's concern, but the last thing Sarah wanted was to be the subject of the town's gossip—especially regarding the new pastor.

Little Miss Matchmaker could just shove her ideas back into her pocket.

FOUR

SARAH

Sarah tucked the basket tight into her waist as she trotted down the steps of the inn and meandered down the pathway to the gate and out onto the street. Snow crunched under her feet as she walked. She didn't want to think about the man who followed her, or at least she didn't want to think about him in any other manner other than he was the town's new pastor and he was only following her so he could meet Mr. and Mrs. Fields and pray over them, their family, and their unborn child.

As he should. He is their new pastor, after all.

Still, though, even with the thought of him walking with her...

She didn't want to think about it.

"So, how long have you lived in Featherstone Valley?" Jack's voice jerked her thoughts, and she glanced over her shoulder, trying to play off that he hadn't caused her to flinch.

"Huh?" She shook her head. "Oh, um, six years now, I think. Five or six, somewhere in between."

"And have you owned the inn the whole time?"

"No. I opened the inn about two years ago after... " She

paused, unsure if she wanted to finish her thought. The problem was she didn't know why. It wasn't a secret that she was a widow, and surely the pastor would find out. "After my husband, Harold, died."

Jack took in a deep breath and lowered his voice. "I'm sorry for your loss."

"Thank you."

"Do you mind me asking what happened?" He moved up alongside her, glancing at her. The kindness in his eyes made her look at him twice before she looked away. Her cheeks flushed with a bit of warmth.

What is wrong with me, she wondered. *Stop. Just stop. He's the new pastor, for corn's sake.*

"I don't mind," she said, trying to distract herself. "It was his heart."

"I'm sorry to hear that."

"It was sudden. He clutched his chest and fell to the ground. He was gone before he landed in the dirt. At least he didn't suffer. I can thank God for that."

Jack's brow furrowed at her words, and he cleared his throat. It seemed as though a thought crossed his mind, and it was one he didn't like. Her words had touched a nerve. Sarah glanced at his left hand, knowing he wouldn't be wearing a ring because Sue Ellen had already mentioned he was unattached. She had to look anyway.

He walked a few steps in silence, looking at a house they were passing. His body shook, and he tightened his coat around his neck, blowing out a breath that clouded his face. "I didn't think it would be so cold here. Nor did I expect so much snow."

"Does it not snow in Texas?"

He shook his head. "Not much. Occasionally, we will get a few inches. Maybe a foot. But not like this." He pointed toward the mounds of white powder all around them.

"Well, I'm afraid we still have a couple more months of snow."

"Something to look forward to, I guess. How far do Mr. and Mrs. Fields live from town?"

"Not far. They live in that house just over there." She pointed toward the cottage just a little ways down the street from them, and upon looking at the place in dire need of a new coat of white paint, she couldn't help but quicken her pace a little. Between talking about Harold and feeling nervous around the pastor, she'd never been so happy to see a house. It wasn't that she didn't wish to speak with Jack; it was just the topic. Talking about Harold was never easy, but talking about him with another man made her thoughts churn in her stomach.

Jack matched her speed, lengthening his long stride to keep up with her shorter, choppier steps.

"It's nice what the townsfolk are doing for the couple," he said.

"It's what we do around here in Featherstone Valley. As Sue Ellen said, we take care of each other, and it is a wonderful little town."

"It seems to be. However, I haven't been here long." He chuckled, and Sarah couldn't help but notice how his gaze lingered on the snowy town, a look of wonder mixed with a hint of apprehension in his eyes. It reminded her of how she felt when she first moved to Featherstone Valley, a mix of excitement and uncertainty. "I admit that I already like what I've seen. I hope that I'll fit in."

"I'm sure you will."

They continued down the lane, passing through the tiny hole in the fence that led to the Fields' house. The door opened before they could cross the porch and knock, and Mr. Fields looked between the two of them. A crease formed on his forehead as he wiped his hands on a dishtowel and then threw half of it over his shoulder.

"Good morning, Miss Holden," Mr. Fields said, nodding as he gave her a weak smile.

"Good morning, Mr. Fields." She motioned to Jack. "This is Pastor Boone. He's the new pastor in town; he just arrived."

"Good morning." Jack reached out, and the men shook hands.

"So, what can I do for you two this morning?" Mr. Fields asked.

"We just came by to see how you and your wife were doing and to give you these muffins," Sarah said, handing the man the basket.

"Thank you. That's very kind of you." Mr. Fields stepped aside and motioned toward the inside of the house. "Won't you two come in?"

"Are you sure?" Sarah asked. "We don't want to impose."

"It's not an imposition. I'm sure Anne would love to say hello and thank you."

Sarah went inside the house, followed by Jack and Mr. Fields, stopping just inside the door as she looked around. The morning's dishes were still on the table, with half-eaten food next to glasses half full of milk. Laundry baskets were piled near the chairs, and a mess of wooden blocks lay scattered all over the living room floor. It looked like no one had cleaned in months.

"You'll have to excuse the mess," Mr. Fields chuckled as he tucked his chin down. "Anne hasn't been able to do much by the way of chores lately, and well, I'm afraid I lack the skills of a wife and mother."

"It's quite all right, Mr. Fields. Would you like some help with anything you need done this morning?"

"Mrs. Gables is sending her daughter to clean the place this afternoon. I just wanted to finish what I could before I had to take Miles Jr. and Millie to school. Miss Evans said they could be a little late."

At the mention of the two children, one of the bedroom doors opened, and the young boy and girl came running down the hall. Millie screamed as she rushed toward her father while her brother chased her.

"Take it back, Millie," the boy shouted.

"Hey! Hey! Hey!" Mr. Fields knelt, stopping them both. "What did I say about shouting in the house, especially when your mama is trying to get the rest she needs?"

The kids both skidded to a stop and looked up at their father. Millie clamped her mouth shut while Miles Jr. pointed at his sister. "But she took my baseball."

"No, I didn't. It was under his bed, just like I told him."

"Yeah, because you stole and hid it on purpose."

"No, I did not. You dropped it, and it rolled under there on its own."

"Stop it, both of you," Mr. Fields straightened back up and laid one hand on his son's shoulder while the other rested on his daughter's. "Please, no fighting this morning. There's no need for it, and we have guests."

The two children took notice of Sarah and Jack, and their eyes widened.

"Who is that?" Miles Jr. asked, pointing at Jack.

Jack smiled and nodded at the children. "Good morning. I'm Pastor Jack Boone."

Millie reached up, scratching her nose. "Are you the new pastor that everyone has been talking about?"

"Well, I'm not entirely sure, but probably. Although, I don't know how I should feel knowing everyone is talking about me," Jack chuckled as he looked at Mr. Fields. "But I can't say I'm not surprised that people are talking."

"Of course, everyone is going to," Mr. Fields said. "It's big news around here. It's not every day we get a new pastor all the way from Texas. It must have been a long trip for you, Pastor Boone."

"It was. But I think it was worth it."

"Well, I wish you luck here, Pastor. I'm looking forward to service on Sunday and your first sermon."

"Thank you. I am, too. I would also like to pray for you, your wife, and your children."

"We would appreciate that... more than you know." Mr. Fields patted his children on the shoulders. "Are you both ready to go to school?"

"Yes, Pa," they both answered at the same time.

"All right. Why don't you say goodbye to your mama, and then I'll take you to school?" He patted them both on the head again, and they ran down the hallway toward the bedrooms. Sarah heard them open the door, and then Mrs. Fields said hello to them. Mr. Fields watched his children, then heaved a sigh. He turned back to Sarah and Jack, and with a look of defeat in his eyes, his shoulders slumped. "They mean well. But it's been hard on them not having their mama around like normal. She always knows what to make for supper and how to help them with their homework. I'll tell you, I never thought of myself as useless, but I got to say, that's exactly how I've been feeling lately."

"You are hardly useless, Mr. Fields," Sarah said. "Anne always talks about how wonderful of a husband and father you are. You're just overwhelmed, and anyone in your shoes would be."

"I suppose you have a point. But still, I should know more than I do. It's not just the children who need to be taken care of, either. My wife is struggling, and she needs more attention. But I can't care for her how I want between work and the children."

"Of course, you can't, and I'm sure Anne isn't holding anything against you. I'm sure she knows how hard you're working."

"I was so thankful when Mrs. Gables offered to have people in town cook our meals and help with the children."

"Speaking of which, she mentioned you might need

someone to take them for a night or two. I have plenty of room, and they are welcome to stay with me."

"That would be wonderful." Relief washed over the man's face, and he heaved another deep sigh. "But are you sure you want to do that?"

"Of course. Miles Jr. and Millie are delightful children, and I don't think my guests would mind." She glanced at Jack. "Do you mind?"

"Not at all."

"And I know I wouldn't mind in the least," she pressed her hand against her chest, "honestly, I would rather enjoy the company. It's been far too long since I've had the patter of children's feet in that dusty old inn." She cocked her head to the side and winked.

Mr. Fields smiled. "I would be indebted to you, Miss Holden."

"It's no trouble."

"Well, you might think differently after a night with them." Mr. Fields laughed as the children trotted back down the hallway. "Perhaps we can plan for a night later this week?"

"That is fine with me."

"We're ready, Pa," Miles Jr. said.

"All right. Grab your books and your lunch pails. It's time to go to school."

While the two children trotted into the kitchen to fetch their lunch, Sarah and Jack turned toward the door. She glanced over her shoulder at Mr. Fields, who followed behind them.

"Just let me know what night you would like help, and I can pick up the children after school... if that would help," she said.

"It would." Mr. Fields skirted around them, opening the door. "I'll speak with Anne tonight and let you know."

～

JACK

Jack followed Sarah across the porch, down to the gate, and out onto the street, glancing at her as he moved alongside her. Of course, he'd noticed her size as soon as she stepped into the foyer at the inn, but seeing her walk beside him gave him a profound awareness of how tiny she was.

She inhaled a deep breath, looking as though she was conversing with herself in her mind. For a moment, he wondered what she was thinking about.

"Is everything all right, Miss Holden?" he asked.

She opened her mouth but closed it, waiting a few moments before speaking. "Are you sure you don't mind the children staying a night or two at the inn?"

"Of course, I'm sure. I don't mind."

"Good. I don't think any of the other guests will mind, either. I just hope I'm right about that."

"If they do mind, that is their problem, and I'll talk to whoever you need me to talk to if that is the case."

"I don't think it will come to that .. I hope."

"Well, if it does."

She shook her head as if to shake whatever she was thinking from her mind and sighed. "One thing for sure is it will be nice to have children around again, and for longer than just a meal in the café when their families come in to eat."

"You sound as though you have children of your own."

"I do. Oh, but they are grown adults now. Luke lives in San Francisco and works for a banker while Elena... I don't know where Elena is living. She moves around the country a lot, following her dreams."

"What dreams are those?"

"To be honest, I'm not entirely sure. They change all the time. Harold and I always hoped she would settle somewhere, fall in love, and start a family, but... that kind of life just doesn't seem to suit her." Sarah looked at him, half smiling. "Sometimes I fear for her, and I don't know what to make of her adventurous spirit, and other times I envy her more than I can imagine."

Jack couldn't help but notice the slight twinkle in Sarah's eyes. It was the same twinkle any mother would have for a child, yet there was a subtle difference. At first glance, Sarah looked like any other wife and mother on the frontier, bound to an oath she pledged to herself and her family to love and care for her husband and children as best as she knew how. It was a commendable act, full of dedication and sacrifice. Yet, behind that, almost hidden in the depths of this outward appearance, he caught a glimpse of a wild spirit that was never allowed to run free. He imagined her as a younger woman, happy and content to play the role she was expected to fulfill, yet also dreaming of open trails and the endless possibilities of a life lived outside of what society—or anyone—placed on her. It was as though she wanted to dwell in two worlds but couldn't.

And he knew exactly how that felt.

"I should probably write to them one night this week—well, at least write Luke. He seems to know where Elena is from time to time better than I do. I usually send my letters to her, to him. But I haven't heard from either in months, and I used to be better about sending them letters."

A twist of guilt prickled in Jack's chest. Not only had he not written or spoken to his sons in years, but he hadn't even told them he'd left Texas. It wasn't by his choice, though. He would have seen them every day if it were up to him. But it was their choice to cut ties, fueled by what happened to their mother and the disparaging words their aunt poisoned them with.

Lord, if there was ever a person to hate in this world—which Jack knew there wasn't, but if there was—Beatrice Laveau would be the first on the list. Jack never liked his wife's older sister, not even from the moment he met Maryanne, and he was pretty sure that the feeling had been mutual from the start. He and Beatrice were like oil and water, two beings that should never be within feet of one another for long.

Or at least they had been.

He knew he was called to forgive and move on. He couldn't deny that no matter what she'd done to him, she had helped him in raising the boys, and even if she'd taken them away to do it, she'd done what was best for them. Of course, he didn't exactly fight her, either. Far too distraught with his grief, he figured it would be better for them.

And it was until it wasn't.

Still, even with everything that had happened between them, Jack knew Patrick and Kit had a right to know he'd left and moved to Montana, even if they never did anything with the knowledge but toss it in the back of their minds without giving it another thought.

"Where is the post office?" he asked Sarah. "I would like to send a couple of telegrams."

Sarah shook her head, glancing at him. "I'm sorry, but Featherstone Valley doesn't have one. However, you can get your mail and send and receive telegrams at the mercantile."

"Where is the mercantile again?" He remembered seeing it when he first arrived in town, but after going to the livery, the inn, and Mr. and Mrs. Fields' house, he was all turned around and wasn't quite sure what direction he was even walking.

"It's just over there." She pointed to a mint green building with white trim. Several wagons were parked outside, hooked to sleeping horses while they waited for owners to load the supplies they would carry back to their homes. With fuzzy fur coats, their breaths made billowing steam waft around their noses.

"Thank you." He started to walk away from her but paused, feeling the tug of guilt about what was proper and what was not. "I'm sorry, I shouldn't have been so rude. I should walk you back to the inn before I go to the mercantile."

She chuckled, shaking her head. "Pastor Boone, I've been walking alone all over this town for two years, and I can do it today. Thank you for the offer, though. I will see you later."

He tipped his hat, giving her a whispered, "Ma'am," before setting off for the mercantile. He didn't know what he would say in the telegrams to his sons, but he hoped that by the time he got to the store, God would help him.

FIVE

SARAH

Sarah had heard the saying that those who love gossip like to flap their lips. Or was it when they gossiped it made their lips flap? Sarah didn't know exactly what the saying was, and although she wanted to think of it, the way that Sue Ellen was staring at her at the moment left her little time to think of anything else.

"And then what happened?" Sue Ellen leaned her backside against the table as she popped bits of cookie into her mouth and chewed. Her eyes were round and blinking, and she stared at Sarah while eating.

"Nothing. He walked off to the mercantile to, I assume, send whatever telegram he wanted to send."

"And that's it? You didn't ask to whom he was sending a telegram?"

"No, I didn't ask him." Sarah furrowed her brow. "It's none of my business."

"And he hasn't said anything that would hint who it was since?"

"No."

"Do you mean to tell me that he's been staying at the inn for two days and hasn't said anything, and you haven't asked?"

"No, I haven't asked. I told you it's none of my business."

Although Sarah wholeheartedly agreed with her statement, she couldn't deny that for the rest of that afternoon and night, she thought of how he'd left her so suddenly and acted as though something was wrong. She wanted to believe she was only making something out of nothing, but a twist in her gut said otherwise, and she must have repeated the conversation at least a couple dozen times.

What had she said that was so awful?

She hadn't talked about anything other than her children and writing them letters.

Was that what the problem was?

Did he have children that he missed? Or worse, did he have children that he lost?

Her heart sank with that thought. She'd been so focused on getting to the Fields residence and making small talk to ease her erratic mind that she hadn't given much thought to the things she was saying. No one had known much about the new pastor after the mayor hired him. They were told he lived in Texas and would be here in the coming weeks, but that was it. He did not mention if he was married or had a family. Sure, some wondered, like Sue Ellen, who had informed Sarah he was unattached, but no one knew anything beyond that. Had he been married? Had his wife left him? Or worse, died? Did they have children?

Obviously, he had something in his past that he held onto.

Otherwise, he wouldn't have reacted the way he did.

Right?

"Even if you think it's not your business, you could still ask him. Just do it casually."

"A casual way? As in how?"

"You could ask him if he was able to send off whatever telegram he wanted and see if he will say anything."

"And what if he just says yes and ends the conversation?"

"Then I suppose you would just walk away."

Sarah pressed her lips together and glanced at Sue Ellen from the corner of her eye. A hint of guilt washed through her. The last thing she wanted to do was make the man feel bad, or worse, unwelcome in this new town.

She opened her mouth to tell her friend just those words, but before she could speak, the café door opened, and the bell interrupted her thought. It was relatively early for someone to arrive for breakfast, and she peeked down the hallway before asking who it was.

"It's Mr. Fields, Ms. Holden," Mr. Fields answered.

Sarah glanced at Sue Ellen again as she grabbed her apron strings, untied it, and made her way down the hallway toward the dining room.

"Good morning, Mr. Fields."

"Good morning." His face was red, and his lungs heaved slightly as though he'd been running. "I... the children are still asleep, but I thought I would come here before I had to wake them for school. Does the offer for Miles Jr. and Millie to stay at the inn for a night... does it still stand?"

"Of course it does."

Relief spread across his face, and he exhaled deeply, laying his hand on his chest. "Oh, thank you. It's been a rough couple of days, and I didn't know who to ask. Mrs. Gables said other families had said they could take them, but when I asked yesterday, no one said yes."

"I'm sorry you had such trouble, but they are more than welcome to stay here."

"Thank you." He hooked his thumb over his shoulder. "I'm going to head back home to wake them and get them ready for school. Then I need to get to work."

"Do you want me to pick them up from school this afternoon?"

"That would be helpful."

"All right."

"I'll inform Miss Evans when I drop them off, and after work, I'll bring some of their things they will need for the night by the inn."

"I'm sure they will appreciate that."

"Thank you so much, Ms. Holden."

"You're welcome."

The forlorn-looking father heaved another sigh and turned, leaving the café. Although his shoulders still carried a heavy burden, he seemed to walk with a lighter step than he'd come into the café with.

Sue Ellen came into the dining room, chewing on another biscuit. "Poor man. He has a lot on his mind."

"He does." Sarah clasped her hands together. "Well, I should start making breakfast. Townsfolk will be coming in soon for the morning rush, and I need to get as many chores done as I can before I have to pick up the children from school."

Snow crunched under Sarah's feet as she made her way to the schoolhouse. She'd thought about what Sue Ellen had said for most of the morning as she prepared breakfast, served whoever joined her that morning, and then went about the rest of her late morning and afternoon chores. Her thoughts were like an endless loop, and the conversation repeated so many times she wondered if she'd go mad. They were also made worse when Pastor Boone came downstairs from his room to eat. Each time she looked at him, she swore she heard Sue Ellen whispering in her ear, "Ask him."

She didn't listen, of course, but the voice was still there, just the same.

"So, who do you think it is?" a voice asked. It jerked her attention, and she glanced up, noticing several women huddled around Mrs. Gables.

"I have no idea. But it certainly is... interesting, to say the least. Why Mr. Jenkins thought it appropriate to have such an article in the newspaper is beyond me. I mean, just who would think a gossip column would be a good idea? It's such a small town, and I think it's quite the invasion of privacy." Mrs. Gables looked at all the women before noticing Sarah. "Oh, Miss Holden." She folded the newspaper in her hands and tucked it under her arm. "Good afternoon."

"Good afternoon, ladies."

"Are you looking for one of us, Miss Holden?" Mrs. Gables asked.

"No. I'm here for Miles Jr. and Millie. They are going to stay with me at the inn tonight so Mr. Fields can take care of what he needs."

"Oh, that's so wonderful." Mrs. Gables moved around the other women and made her way over to Sarah. "I have been asking around town for the last few days, and while I have a few families able to help with the children, none of them could take them until the weekend. This will be such a blessing for Mr. and Mrs. Fields."

"I hope so. I took another batch of the muffins yesterday morning, after the ones I took a couple of days ago, and I just want to help in any way I can."

"Well, I'm glad to hear you say that." The two women looked toward the schoolhouse, waiting for the doors to open and Miss Evans, the teacher, to excuse the children. Mrs. Gables heaved a deep breath. "I take it the new pastor has settled in after he arrived?"

"Yes. He has. He's a nice man, and I think he will do a respectable job for the town."

Mrs. Gables untucked the newspaper from her arm and handed it to Sarah. "So... would you say that this article is true, then?"

"What article?"

"It seems Mr. Jenkins, the newspaper editor, has added what I can only describe as a seedy gossip column out to destroy this town."

"What?" Sarah furrowed her brow and unfolded the paper, scanning the pages until she found the headline in thick black ink—The Arrival of Pastor Jack Boone: A Man of Mystery in Our Midst. "Who is Prudence Chatterton?"

"No one knows. But as you can read, whoever it is has chosen to take a fake name, and the name of the article is the Parlor Patter. Can you believe it? The nerve of whoever is writing this. I plan to formally complain to Mr. Jenkins in the morning."

Sarah read the first paragraph, and with every sentence about his looks and marital status, implying that a string of women would soon be standing in line to get to know him better—if he was interested in such matters—her stomach twisted more and more. She didn't know what was worse—this article or knowing that it was spreading around town like wildfire. It made her skin crawl. She had always valued privacy, and the idea of anyone becoming the subject of town gossip was unsettling. She didn't want to read another word, yet she couldn't stop. She needed to read what was written so she could refute Mrs. Gables' questions.

"Who would write such things about a stranger... and a pastor, no less? Have they no regard for a man of the cloth? Even if it is true." Mrs. Gables cocked her head to the side and clicked her tongue. She leaned in, lowering her voice to a whisper. "I have to ask, though, you've met Pastor Boone. Is what she wrote true? Is he handsome and unattached?"

"I don't have much of an opinion on that, Mrs. Gables." Sarah cleared her throat, trying to suppress the laugh itching for freedom behind her tight lips. Of course, she would expect no less from Mrs. Gables or any other women standing nearby. Pretending to be appalled by something they could only wish they had thought of seemed just about right, knowing them. Sarah wouldn't even be surprised if one of them was the writer in the flesh. Although she would never point fingers without knowing for sure. Accusing someone of something without evidence was never good.

"Well, I suppose it will be interesting to see how everything plays out."

"I suppose. However, I must say... I don't think Pastor Boone deserves to be the subject of idle chatter."

Before Sarah could say anything, the schoolhouse doors opened, and Miss Evans stepped out onto the porch, ringing the bell in her hand. Children filed out, running toward their mothers as they each shouted about different things that happened that day. One little girl was holding her tooth, yelling at her mother that she'd lost it in her sandwich at lunchtime. Another little boy ran to his mother, telling her about how he got all the words correct on the spelling test that day, and finally, a third young lady—one of the older children—told her mother about how a boy shared his taffy stick with her, giving her the larger piece. The girl glanced over her shoulder, smiling at the young man who waved before motioning toward his little brother and sister to follow him so the three could walk home.

Miles Jr. and Millie trotted out of the schoolhouse, stopping to say goodbye to Miss Evans before heading toward Sarah.

"Ms. Holden! Ms. Holden!" they both shouted. "Are we going back to the inn?"

"Yes, you are."

Both children jumped up and down, and Millie clutched her books tightly to her chest. Her smile beamed across her lips.

"Do you have all your things?" Sarah asked, holding out her hand for the little girl to take.

"Yes, ma'am," Miles Jr. said. "May I ask you something, Ms. Holden?"

"Certainly."

"Do you have food at the inn?"

"I'm sure I can find you something to eat while you do your homework and I make dinner."

"Good, because I'm hungry. We had a test today, and my brain didn't have enough food."

Sarah chuckled, patting Miles Jr. on the shoulder. "Well, don't worry. When we return to the inn, we will give your brain plenty of food. I think I can even be talked into making some hot chocolate, too. We all need something to warm up from the cold."

"Yay!" both children shouted.

JACK

Jack could hear the children downstairs in the kitchen as he buttoned his clean shirt and tucked the ends into his pants. Their laughter made him smile and reminded him of the sounds of his own house when the boys were young and in the kitchen with Maryanne.

"I don't care if they are boys; they will learn to cook," she would always say.

Of course, she got no complaints from him. His mama had thought the same thing and forced him to learn to cook, too. He couldn't make anything fancy like she could, but he could at least make enough that he wouldn't starve or need to rely on a saloon or café whenever he wanted to stuff his face.

He fastened the last button and secured his belt before making his way to the door and heading downstairs. More laughter echoed through the hallways, and as he passed the parlor, he spied a disgruntled-looking man sitting in one of the chairs, glancing over his shoulder with every sound the children made.

Jack snorted, shaking his head as he continued past the parlor, through the dining room, and into the kitchen.

"It sounds like quite the party is going on in here," he said as he pushed open the door. Ms. Holden flinched, and the children whipped their heads toward him. They both smiled.

"Hello, Pastor Boone," the little boy said.

"Hello, Pastor," the girl added. She sat next to her brother, holding a big red, juicy apple with several bites taken out of it.

Jack nodded toward them and then looked at Sarah. "I hope it's all right for me to come in here," he said.

"Of course. May I get you anything? Water? A snack?"

"No, I'm quite all right for now. I can wait for supper. Speaking of which, it smells good in here."

"It's only stew. But it was my mother's recipe."

"Stew is just fine by me. In fact, I would say it's one of my favorite dishes, and I think it's perfect for a cold winter night."

"We got cornbread, too, Pastor Boone," Millie said, giving him a big smile.

"Well, that makes it even better." He moved toward the counter, clasping his hands together. "Do you need help with anything?"

Sarah blinked at him. "You... you want to help?"

"Sure. I know my way around a kitchen. What do you need help with?"

"Well, I could use the apples sliced for the pie I wanted to make for dessert."

"I can do that." He looked around, finding a bushel of apples next to a cutting board and a knife. He pointed to them. "I'll just get started." He grabbed a couple of the apples and turned them over. "These are lovely. I've never seen them with these amazing yellow and red patterns."

"They are Honeycrisp apples. My tree had a lovely crop this year, and I still have several bushels down in the root cellar. I was also able to can lots of apple sauce and pie filling that will last me well into winter."

"You grew these?" He glanced at her, his mouth slightly agape for a moment before closing it.

She nodded. "I try to grow most of the food I use at the inn. It cuts down on what I have to buy from the farmers and the mercantile. I also have chickens and two cows in the barn behind the inn. They provide me with fresh eggs, milk, and cream that I serve and use to make cheese."

"I didn't even notice." He chuckled, shaking his head as he moved to the window and looked toward the backyard. "I don't know why. I should have."

"You had quite a lot to see this afternoon, Pastor Boone—lots to look at. It doesn't surprise me that you missed my barn."

"Still." He paused, and a shiver seemed to wash over him. "I don't know if I'll ever get used to how cold it is here."

"You will. Especially when you have chores to see to and animals to care for even in the winter months." She chuckled.

"May we help you milk the cows tonight, Ms. Holden?" Miles Jr. asked. "Ma always lets us help her."

"Maybe. But I tend to the cows after the guests have all turned in for the night, so I'm not interrupted. It might be too late for you to help me tonight, but you can help me in the morning before school."

Both children let out shouts of excitement, and Sarah flinched and laid her finger against her lips. "Not so loud, remember. Mr. Clemons is probably still in the parlor, and we don't want to make him mad again." She held up her hand, wiggling her finger at the children.

"Yes, Ms. Holden," they both said.

"I take it not all your guests were as accommodating about the children staying at the inn for the night?"

"All but Mr. Clemons." She rolled her eyes. "I have to say I was shocked when he threw such a fit about it. I know he doesn't have children of his own, but he is married. I have to wonder what he's going to do when his wife..." Sarah bit her bottom lip. "I shouldn't speak that way about him or his marriage. It's not my place."

"Just as it's not his place to tell you who you can and can't have stay at your inn."

"And that was exactly what I reminded him of when I spoke to him. He still wasn't thrilled with the situation. I felt bad, but it's just one night."

"He didn't seem like it when I passed. But he'll get over it. If he doesn't, he can leave."

Sarah looked at Jack, moving her eyes while she kept her head still. "Normally, I would try to find a compromise that everyone could live with, but this time... I won't be told what I can and can't do. Not when I'm trying to help out a neighbor in need, and it's only for one night."

Jack glanced at her, sensing something deeper troubling her about the situation she'd let on. It felt as though Mr. Clemons hadn't exactly been the best guest during his time staying at the inn, and she was getting fed up with his behavior.

"If you wish for me to try to speak with him, I will," he said.

"Thank you. I don't think that will be necessary, but I will let you know if it comes to that." She exhaled a deep breath and shook her head, glancing at him with slight hesitation as she dumped pie dough out of a bowl onto the counter. She mashed it with her palms before grabbing a rolling pin to finish the job. "So... did you get what you needed at the mercantile?"

His body stiffened at her question. "Yes, I did."

She stared at him momentarily, then dropped her gaze, tucking her chin toward her chest. "Forgive me if I asked something I shouldn't have."

A lump formed in his throat, and although he tried to swallow it, he couldn't.

When Jack was a sheriff, he lived by the safety of secrets. No one outside of those who really knew him knew he had a wife and family. They lived far out of town, and aside from gatherings with the trusted souls he had befriended over the years, Maryanne stayed quiet about her identity, spending more time at home than in town with the other wives and mothers. Of course, he liked it that way; he preferred it. But he never forced her. She did it on her own and never complained. He once asked if it bothered her, but she said it didn't. Could she have lied? Possibly. Although he doubted it.

A homebody, through and through, that's what she always called herself.

Of course, the secret grew with the birth of his first son, Patrick. It also got a little harder to keep. Infants don't say much, and even toddlers don't know what is happening. However, when young boys start school and make friends, they can sometimes—or all the time—run the risk of saying something they shouldn't. It was natural for boys when they wanted to make themselves better than one another, like bragging about their fathers' jobs or something their fathers did, which often led to slips-ups, like after his second son, Kit, had just turned three years old and told his friends more than he should.

In a matter of a few days, the whole town of Fort Worth knew he had a wife and two boys, and it wasn't just the simple townsfolk but the undesirables, too. The criminals. The thieves. The murderers. The men who would stop at nothing to get the revenge they sought for one reason or another, and without the secrets protecting them, his world was like a mirror that fell to the ground, shattering into thousands of pieces.

After all that, one might think he would keep secrets close to his chest, guarding them with his life in ways he couldn't before. It was true; he had them, and keeping them never bothered him. But something about arriving in this new town made him uncomfortable with the thought that no one around him knew anything about him. It wasn't that he wanted to be an open book, but he also didn't want to hide anything.

At the same time, he wasn't sure how much he wanted everyone to know right now. He was still a stranger to them, and they were strangers to him. Strangers can't be trusted. At least not when he didn't know who lived here and where they had ties. The only one he felt comfortable with was the tiny woman beside him.

Jack couldn't help but glance at Sarah. She hadn't been what he had expected, not in the slightest, and he couldn't help but be taken aback the minute she walked into the foyer earlier today after he entered the inn for the first time. It wasn't just her size that caught him off guard, but it was just the mere sight of her. Beautiful, sure, but even that aside, something was different about her—something that told him he wouldn't meet another woman like her even if he tried.

"You didn't," he finally said, ignoring how his gut twisted with the truth sitting on the tip of his tongue. He wanted to tell her, yet no matter how hard he tried to force himself to say the words, he couldn't. Instead, he held up the apple, looking at Miles Jr. and Millie. "I think we are going to make a delicious pie. What do you two think?"

As the children nodded, Jack returned to peeling the apple's bright red skin. Sarah opened her mouth but shut it without a word and continued rolling the pie crust. While it had been a conversation he needed to have, he wasn't ready for the story any more than he was prepared for the why and how questions the woman was surely thinking about.

At least not yet.

For now, though, he wouldn't think on the matter. Instead, he would focus on the apples and pie. Instead, he would focus on the inn, the new town, the church, and the people he would meet in this new adventure. *Matthew 6:34* says, 'Therefore do not worry about tomorrow, for tomorrow will worry about itself. Each day has enough trouble of its own.' And that would be just what he did. He would not worry about tomorrow any more than he would worry about today. And he certainly wouldn't worry about what he imagined Patrick and Kit would do when they received the telegrams. Of course, he would like to think they would be happy to hear from him. But no matter how much he doubted they would be, he wouldn't worry about it.

He wouldn't worry about anything.

SIX

PATRICK

Patrick scanned the morning newspaper, looking through the reports of stock market prices rising overnight. A slight warmth spread through his cheeks, and he dragged his finger across the paper, looking through the list of company investments and their numbers.

"Anything interesting this morning?" a voice asked behind him.

He glanced over his shoulder as Julia, his pregnant wife, made her way around the table and sat across from him. She brushed her hand over her swollen belly as she struggled to take the seat.

"I'm just looking through the stock market listings," he answered.

"Ah. Rechecking the investments." A slight chuckle hinted at her lips as she placed her napkin in her lap and reached for a cheese and berry Danish. "Didn't you just check them in yesterday's newspaper?"

"I did. And I will continue to check them tomorrow, the next day, and the next. I want to keep an eye on them every day so I can determine when it would be a good time to buy and sell what we already have."

"Don't you have a man doing that for you? The same guy who helps Papa? I thought he set you up with a meeting."

"He did, but I like to check them myself anyway. It is my job, after all, and one should never leave their money in the hands of someone else." Patrick picked up his knife, cutting a pat of the sweet creamy butter off the stick and spreading it on his morning toast before pointing the end of the blade at her. "You shouldn't leave anything in someone else's hands—especially important things."

"Money isn't everything." Julia winked and took a bite of her pastry.

Patrick smiled and snorted. "You wouldn't say that if you lived on the street."

She raised one eyebrow and straightened her shoulders to lean against the back of her chair. "I saw a beggar woman standing on the corner last week. She didn't look all that miserable."

"You'll forgive me if I don't believe you." He finished buttering the toast and set the knife down as he took a large bite of the toasted bread.

Julia giggled. "Perhaps I am wrong about her. But I do know a few women who don't have a lot of money, and they are happy. I also know several women who have all the money in the world, and they are melancholy day in and day out."

"Like your mother?" He cocked his head to the side, twisting his tone to make a joke more than to say something serious.

Julia laughed and rolled her eyes. "I don't know if anything could make my mother happy. If she were rich, she'd be sad. If she were poor, she'd be sad. If she were tall, she'd be sad. If she were short, she'd be sad. If she were overweight, she'd be sad. If she were skinny, she'd be sad." Julia rolled her eyes again. "It's a wonder I was ever able to find anything that made me happy, given how everything always made her unhappy."

"Yes, well, don't get me started on our parents' mistakes and how we turned out the way we have." Patrick groaned, leaning back in his chair, taking another bite of toast, and trying to distract himself with the richness of the butter.

Julia stared at him, and although she looked like she wanted to say something, she didn't. He was glad for it. Sure, he had made the comment, but just because he said what he did didn't mean he wanted to discuss it further.

"So, is there anything else interesting in the newspaper?" she asked. It was just one of the things he loved about her—her ability to discern when to press an issue and when to drop it. She was amazing at it.

"Not that I read. There were a few robberies on the other side of town. But it looks like the sheriff caught the person responsible." His eyes skimmed over the front page. "Other than that, there isn't much."

Julia took another bite of her pastry and glanced out the window, smiling as a bird landed on the bush just outside. Patrick saw the blue jay, too, watching as it jumped from branch to branch a couple of times before flying off.

"I want to take a walk after breakfast. Do you want to go with me?" she asked.

"A walk? Do you think it's best to take one in your condition?"

"Yes, a walk. It would be good for me. Dr. Sherman even said it was. He said stretching my legs and getting sun and fresh air would help me. Besides, I still have a couple of months before the baby is born. Don't try to keep me locked away in the house just yet."

Patrick chuckled at her mocking tone. "Whatever you say, dear. If you wish to take a walk, we will take a walk." He finished off the last of the toast and fetched his coffee cup, taking a sip. The hot liquid warmed his mouth.

"I can't believe that man!" a voice shouted from the foyer.

Before Patrick could glance over his shoulder, his aunt stormed into the dining room, waving her arms. "How dare he even send this telegram! I ought to send him one back, giving him a piece of my mind."

"What is going on, Beatrice?" Julia asked the plump, older woman. She looked at Patrick, giving her husband a sideways glance as if to silently ask if she should stay in the room or find a safe place far away from whatever it was that had set Beatrice on edge.

He shook his head as if to tell her no and to stay.

Beatrice marched over to the table and slammed a piece of paper down next to Patrick's plate of half-eaten eggs and sausage links.

"I can't believe his audacity."

"Whose?" Patrick glanced from his aunt to the paper, grabbing it and reading it before she could answer. His eyes traced over his father's name, and he inhaled.

"Who is it from, darling?" Julia asked.

"It's from my father." His voice deepened with his answer as dread washed through his chest.

"I can't fathom why you call him that," Aunt Beatrice threw her hands up, letting them slap back down against her sides. "He hasn't behaved as a father should. Not for a long time." The older woman moved around to the other side of the table, taking the last seat with a huff on her breath. Her face was blotchy, and although there was no other outwardly disheveled look about her besides her cheeks, Patrick knew she was upset on the inside. He'd seen it before—and usually when it had something to do with his father.

"Geez, Aunt Beatrice, tell me how you feel." Patrick heaved a sigh and rolled his eyes as he fetched the telegram off the table and held it out to read.

Sending word to let you know I'm in Featherstone Valley, Montana. STOP.

I got a new job as the town pastor. STOP.

I hope you and your brother are well. I will write more when I can. STOP.

Your father. STOP.

"What does it say, Pat?" Julia asked, placing her hand on his arm. Her touch did little to calm the tension bubbling in his chest as he read the telegram three more times.

"My father has moved to Montana, to a little town called Featherstone Valley."

"Montana? Why?"

"He's got a new job. He's the town's new pastor."

Aunt Beatrice threw her head back, roaring with laughter. "Jack Boone is a pastor? That is the stupidest thing I've ever heard." She laughed even harder. "Does he think he can just pretend to be someone faithful to God and everything will be forgiven?"

"But he was forgiven," Julia said.

Patrick didn't know if Julia's words or just the suddenness of her voice made him flinch, but he looked at her, blinking a few times. "What do you mean? I haven't forgiven him."

"God has."

While Aunt Beatrice huffed and threw her hands in the air, shaking her head, Patrick clenched his teeth. Religion had always been something for him to avoid rather than embrace. It wasn't that he didn't believe, but he just didn't know if he wanted to. Far too much evil resided in the world for him not to doubt that God wanted what was best for everyone. If He wanted what was best for Patrick and Kit, then why did their mother have to die? And in the horrible manner in which she did?

He closed his eyes. "So, because God has, then I should?"

She looked at him, blinked, and said, "Yes."

"Just like that? Forget everything that happened and all he did wrong?"

Julia cleared her throat. "I realize it's not my place, Pat, but... if God forgave him, who are you to not to? Do you think you are owed something that gives you the right to hang onto your feelings when God has chosen to forgive?"

"I think I do."

"You do, over God?"

"You have no idea what happened."

"No, I don't." She paused, cocking her head to the side. "Because you have never told me. And since you have never told me the details, you've left me no choice but to always wonder about your relationship with your father and why you don't think you could repair it."

"It's not that simple."

"But it is. *Ephesians 4:31-32* says, 'Let all bitterness and wrath and anger and clamor and slander be put away from you, with all malice, and be kind to one another, tenderhearted, forgiving one another, as God in Christ forgave you.' I'm not saying it's not work; it is. But it's also simple."

"And why tell me this now?"

"Well, I've been wanting to say something to you our whole marriage, but I... I know how you feel, so I have bit my tongue."

Although a flicker of annoyance beat in Patrick's heart, so did a hint of regret. She was his wife and the love of his life. He never wanted to hurt her or cause her turmoil. "Dear, I... if I have ever made you feel as though you couldn't talk to me about anything—including God and church—"

"You haven't. It was my own reservations. I didn't want to make you feel uncomfortable. But, well, I suppose with the baby coming... it's just been on my mind. You'll be a father in a few months, which means he will be a grandfather."

"Like he cares," Aunt Beatrice said, interrupting their conversation. She grabbed a pastry from the plate in the middle of the table and set it on the plate sitting in front of her. "If he had no desire to be a father, what makes you believe he wants to be a grandfather?"

"People can change, Beatrice." Julia looked between her husband and his aunt. "And who knows what he was thinking at the time. He'd just lost his wife."

"And his boys had just lost their mother."

Julia glanced at the woman, scowling slightly as she blinked and turned her attention to Patrick. "What are you going to do, darling?"

"What do you mean?"

"Are you going to write back to him?"

Beatrice ripped off a bite of pastry, chewing and swallowing before she spoke. "If you ask me, the only thing you should do with that telegram is toss it in the trash and forget you ever received it."

Patrick folded the telegram, a sense of unease settling in his stomach. He had always respected Aunt Beatrice. Her words shaped much of his past and present, and she had been there for him when his father wasn't, comforting him after the tragedy. Yet, as he sat beside his wife, her gentle questioning prodded at a curiosity he had long since buried.

Julia laid her hand on his arm. "Surely not all your memories of the man are terrible. Surely there was a time when he was a father, and you were a son."

Patrick nodded, and a flicker of nostalgia warmed his chest. "Yes, but that was a different life. One that's a distant dream now."

"But it wasn't a dream. It was real. And your father was part of that reality."

Patrick shifted in his seat, torn between his loyalty to Aunt Beatrice and his growing curiosity about his father. "He was," he admitted, the words tasting like betrayal. "But it's hard to think about how I can reconcile that with the man who taught me to ride and fish. He wasn't around when I needed him the most."

Julia gave Patrick a weak smile. "People aren't perfect. Maybe there's more to your father than Aunt Beatrice told you."

"I beg your pardon?" Aunt Beatrice huffed a breath. "I have never lied to either of the boys about what their father did or the man he is."

"I never said you lied." Julia glanced at Aunt Beatrice and then at Patrick. "But I am saying that I think perhaps it's time Patrick discovers who his father is for himself."

Patrick closed his eyes briefly, then glanced around the room, focusing on everything he could—the table, the couch, the hutch filled with their wedding china—bought by Julia's parents. It had been one of the rooms Julia had loved the most when they looked into purchasing the house, and he remembered hearing all her talk about the parties and family celebrations they would host. At the time, he had thought of his brother and father, wondering if he could see them in his house, in his life. He had thought he didn't need them. He had Julia and her family. But deep down, he couldn't deny that their absence left a wound that had never healed, no matter how much he told himself it had. Now, the dining room felt like another room that housed a memory he wanted to forget. He hoped for a distraction, but all he found were the reminders of what his life had been and what it hadn't. Sure, he'd gained so much, growing into a young man with a lovely woman at his side and money in the bank. But what had he lost in the process? His father? His brother?

There were times he wondered if it all was worth it, and then there were times when he regretted nothing. He couldn't change the past, and he certainly couldn't change their actions.

He slid the chair away from the table, listening to the sound of the legs sliding across the hardwood floor. "Will you please excuse me? I need some fresh air."

"Did you still want to take our walk, darling?" Julia asked. She reached for his hand, but he moved before she could grab it.

He cocked his head to the side, touching her face as he rose to his feet. He didn't want to disappoint her, but at this moment, he had to. "I'm not sure I would be good company right now. I hope you understand."

"Of course, I understand. I can ask Stanley to go with me instead."

Patrick didn't like that his wife would take a walk with the butler, but he also knew that Stanley would be a far better choice for her.

JACK

Early morning sunlight filtered through the lace curtains draping the window. Jack squinted as he looked down at the buttons of his shirt and looped them in the holes. After tucking the bottom into his pants and buckling his belt, he slipped on his shoes and headed downstairs. The salty, rich scent of bacon and eggs wafted in the air, and as he rounded the corner to the dining room, Miles Jr. and Millie, sitting at one of the tables, looked up from their plates.

"Pastor Boone!" Miles Jr. called out. "Over here. Come sit with us."

"Yes, come sit with us." Millie nodded and smiled, and as Jack approached the table, she squirmed a little in her seat.

"Good morning, children," he said, looking down at them sitting at the table.

"Look, Pastor Boone, Ms. Holden made pancakes just like she promised last night she would." Miles pointed to a plate in the middle of the two with a stack of pancakes. The tower leaned a little to one side and looked as though it was on the verge of toppling over at any moment. Thankfully, the pancakes stuck together, holding one another upright. The young boy cut off a bite and stabbed it with his fork before shoving it in his mouth. He closed his eyes as though he wanted to show Jack how delicious the pancake was.

"Are you going to sit with us?" Millie asked.

Before Jack could answer, Sarah came out of the kitchen with a kettle in one hand and another plate of stacked pancakes in the other.

"Good morning, Pastor Boone," she said, giving Jack a nod.

"Good morning."

"Are you hungry?"

"Yeah, I think I am. I'll take some of those pancakes, too, if you don't mind."

"Do you want anything else? I also have eggs and bacon on the stove."

"A couple of pancakes will do just fine." He sat at the table with the children as Sarah left the dining room. A few minutes later, she returned with another plate and a coffee cup with a saucer. She set the dishes in front of him and poured Jack a cup of coffee.

"Do you want cream or sugar?" she asked.

"Nah. Black is fine." He grabbed several of the pancakes off the plate, tossing them on the one Sarah brought him before grabbing the butter dish and the small pitcher of syrup sitting in the middle of the table.

"Do you think that's enough for the three of you, or should I make more?"

"You should make some more," Millie said, laughing.

"Yeah, I'm going to eat a ton more, too," Miles Jr. laughed.

"I think there's plenty to go around." Jack smiled at Sarah, and she nodded. "Why don't you eat what is out here, and if you need more, I'll make them?" She winked at the two children. "In the meantime, I'm going to finish your lunches so we can get you to school." She turned toward another table, but Miles Jr. called after her, stopping her.

"Are you going to pick us up again this afternoon so we can stay another night at the inn?" the boy asked.

"I don't know. Your father only asked if you could stay for one night. If I see him around town, though, I will ask him if they need another one."

"Really? We can stay again if our parents say we can?" The two children exchanged glances, their mouths wide open in excitement.

"Of course. You both are welcome to stay again if your parents say you can."

A loud thump echoed throughout the room, jerking Jack's attention. He looked at another man Sarah had called Mr. Clemons, sitting at the next table with his hands clenched in fists. He pounded on the tabletop a second time, causing everyone in the dining room—guests from the inn and people at the café eating breakfast—to look at him.

"Is there a problem, Mr. Clemons?" Sarah asked. She turned toward him, cocking her head to the side.

"I would like to say there isn't, Ms. Holden, but I'm afraid I would be lying if I did."

"Is something wrong with the food? Is it cold? Does it not taste good?" She moved over to his table, cradling the kettle of coffee in her hands—a concerned crease formed on her forehead.

"Nothing is wrong with the food. It's good, as always. It's the children."

"The children?" She glanced at Miles Jr. and Millie, then back at Mr. Clemons. "What about them?"

"They have been nothing but a nuisance since they walked through the door yesterday, and I won't have it for another second." He lifted his hand, wiggling his index finger in her face.

"I'm sorry you feel that way. But the children have been quiet and respectful. I admit they were loud a few times when they arrived, but they have not misbehaved since."

"I don't care. They could, at any moment, disrupt my peace. And I will not have it any longer. You cannot have them for another night. They will have to go back to their parents. I don't even know why they are here to begin with."

"Not that it's any of your business, Mr. Clemons, but their mother is on bed rest per doctors' orders, and everyone in town is helping them with meals and caring for their children."

"If they can't care for their children, they shouldn't have more."

Sarah straightened her shoulders, and her brow furrowed. At the sight of her reaction, Jack's teeth clenched, and his body stiffened. He shifted in his chair, waiting to see how the scene would play out. He didn't want to get involved, but he wasn't about to sit around and do nothing. It wasn't just that the children had been well-mannered; it was that he didn't care for the man's tone or behavior toward Sarah.

"That is none of your business, Mr. Clemons."

"But it is my business when their children are at the inn because you've brought them here. This is an inn, Ms. Holden, a business."

"And do you not think that parents travel with their children? I hate to tell you, but these children aren't the first and only children I've had in my inn." She paused, but only long enough as though she did so to make a point, not to wait for him to respond. "And may I remind you that it is *MY* inn. You are a guest and are more than welcome to check out if you don't like your stay."

"How dare you speak to me that way."

Mr. Clemons stood and puffed out his chest, moving toward

and bumping her. A slight scream left her lips as she backed away from the man's bold advance, and without thought, Jack shoved his chair away from the table and jumped to his feet. He rounded the table, moving toward the man. His old sheriff instincts took control, and he wouldn't sit around and do nothing. He grabbed Mr. Clemons by the shoulders, shoving the man backward and away from Sarah. She gasped slightly while the few other guests and dining patrons silenced and gaped at the situation unfolding.

"Is there a problem with what Ms. Holden said to you, Mr. Clemons?" Jack asked the man. A slight growl rumbled in his throat. A few other men in the dining room stood from their chairs too, but although Jack saw them from the corner of his eye, he kept his gaze focused on Mr. Clemons. Years of training had helped him be aware of his surroundings while staying hooked on his target.

Mr. Clemons looked between them, focusing longer on Jack. He opened his mouth as if to say something, but looking at Jack again, he clamped it shut and shook his head.

"Shall she expect you to check out, then?" Jack asked him.

Mr. Clemons nodded; his eyes were the size of the plate on which half of his uneaten breakfast still sat. A slight tremble wormed through his body, and he cringed away from Jack.

Jack narrowed his eyes and lowered his voice even more. "Then I suggest you pack your things so you can be on the afternoon stage."

Without another word, the man spun and trotted from the dining room before heading upstairs to, what Jack could only assume, pack his belongings.

As Jack turned to face Sarah, she closed her eyes and took several deep breaths. Her grip around the kettle tightened.

"Are you all right?" Jack asked her. Although he wanted to reach out and lay his hand on her shoulder to comfort her, he didn't.

"Yes." She opened her eyes. "I just don't like confrontation like that."

"Well, you handled yourself appropriately. I was impressed." Jack chuckled. "I'm sorry if I butted in, but I couldn't just stand by and let him speak to you like that."

"You don't need to apologize." She shook her head, inhaling and exhaling another deep breath. "I honestly was at the end of my nerve. I didn't know what else I was going to say or do after he lunged toward me the way he did..." She backed away from Jack, dropping her gaze to the ground as her voice cracked. "I should get the children's lunches made. They need to leave for school soon. I just hope Mr. Clemons is packed before I leave to take them."

"I can take them to school. I was going to go there this morning anyway to meet Miss Evans, the teacher, and to see the church and schoolhouse."

"You don't mind taking them?"

"Why should I mind?"

"I don't know. You didn't agree to care for them."

"That doesn't matter." He turned slightly toward the table, then faced her again. "If I see Mr. Fields, I'll let him know the children may stay at the inn another night."

"Thank you."

"You're welcome."

"Well, I should finish their lunches." Before Jack could say another word, she strode off toward the kitchen. He watched her leave the room, and his chest tightened as she vanished down the hallway.

You're going to have to watch yourself, he thought to himself, *you will only bring her pain.*

SEVEN

JACK

"*God sees for all time—from the beginning until the end.*" Jack had heard those words at least a dozen times from a man he once knew. Joseph Mayweather had a knack for quotes. He often spoke them so much that Jack used to think that was all that ever came out of the man's mouth. Nothing but quote after quote after quote, and while Jack would often find himself not listening most of the time, some—like this one— seemed to hit him right when he needed it the most, like the other time he quoted *Isaiah 43:18-19,* 'Forget the former things, do not dwell on the past. See, I am doing a new thing.'

Jack was never one to dwell in the past. At least not until Maryanne died, and then that was all he did. For so long, he had wandered the streets of the town of memories in his mind. Part of him had wanted to, yet the other didn't. Why live in the past when there was a present and a future to look forward to? Unless it was because he didn't know if he could look forward to it—which was a notion that burdened him more than he cared to admit.

Growing up, he had loved every part of his life. Sure, there were times he hated, like when he got in trouble for doing something he shouldn't, and his Pa took it out on his rump. After the first time it happened, though, he tried not to do anything to make it happen again. In the end, he failed three other times. But that was beside the point. He loved his childhood. He had wonderful parents who provided what they could, and even though he probably didn't have as much as other boys had, Jack knew he never wanted for anything. He had clothes on his back, a roof over his head, toys to entertain him, animals to take care of, a pony that bucked him off a few more times than he cared for, but he still loved the stubborn thing, and a full belly anytime he asked for a meal. What more could a kid want?

Nothing.

As he got older, it didn't change either. His young man years were spent equally as happily. He got the schooling he needed and could follow his dreams of being a sheriff. By the time he married Maryanne and they had their two sons, he had a home he'd built himself and had made a name for himself—a name he was proud of. Nothing about his long days as a hard-working man made him question what he'd done or wanted from his life. It could have all stayed the same, and if it had, he would have laid on his deathbed, happy and without regret.

Of course, then it all changed.

"God sees for all time—from the beginning until the end," Joseph had told him at Maryanne's funeral. "Starting over is never easy. But give your concerns to God. He will be your guiding light in this darkness." At the time, Jack had snorted at those words. Guiding light? What did that even mean when all that surrounded him was never-ending darkness?

And then it all changed again.

Or at least he thought it had.

It was true; starting over took work. It was harder than anything one could face in one's life, and it challenged whoever dared travel down its long road. But he had rather liked this bend in that road. Being a pastor had brought him more peace than anything else he had sought—which luckily started—and stopped—with a bottle of booze.

Lord, he would have had his head if he had done anything else that was worse than drinking.

"Pastor Boone, why was that man so angry with us?" Millie looked up at Jack as she, her brother, and Jack walked toward the schoolhouse. Sunlight glinted off her baby-blue eyes, and their shape showed a hint of sadness. They looked as though they could fill with tears at any moment.

"I don't think he was angry with you. I think he was just angry with the situation. More than likely, he doesn't have much tolerance for children, and you two were just the closest ones to him, so he took out his feelings on you."

"Why doesn't he like children?" Miles Jr. asked.

"I'm not sure, and sometimes I wonder if people themselves know why they do the things they do or think the things they think."

"What does that mean?" Millie asked.

"Well, say, for instance, your father doesn't like... chicken."

"Chicken?" Millie laughed. "Pa likes chicken. He likes it a lot." She giggled.

"Yes, I'm sure he does. But for my example, let's say he doesn't. All right?" Jack paused, and the children both nodded. "All right. So, say your father doesn't like to eat chicken, so you two never eat it growing up. All you hear about is how disgusting chicken is and how much your father hates it, so you start to believe that you don't like chicken either."

"I love chicken," Miles said.

"I do, too," Millie added.

"Well, that's good, but again, stay in my example." Jack chuckled and then continued. "When all you've ever thought is that you don't like something, then you believe it, even if it's not true, or at least the whole truth."

"The whole truth?" Miles Jr. raised one eyebrow.

"Well, if you've never had something, you can't say you don't like it. So, that's not the whole truth."

"Oh, now, I understand."

"Does that mean Mr. Clemons likes children but doesn't know it?" Millie asked. She looked up at Jack again, scratching her nose. Her little voice cracked slightly.

"Perhaps. But I'm not sure if we will ever find out. I'm not sure if he will either. That's up to God to show him or not."

"Well, I hope God shows him because we are good children, and he should know we are." Millie reached out, grabbing Jack's hand as she skipped a few steps. Her quicker pace jerked on his arm, and he took a few faster steps to keep up with her.

"I couldn't agree more, Millie," he said.

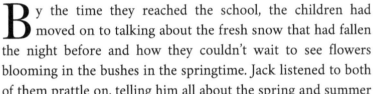

By the time they reached the school, the children had moved on to talking about the fresh snow that had fallen the night before and how they couldn't wait to see flowers blooming in the bushes in the springtime. Jack listened to both of them prattle on, telling him all about the spring and summer in Featherstone and how they couldn't wait until winter was over—even if they loved playing in the snow.

"Pa likes those seasons too," Millie said. "But he doesn't like winter much, so he's not always happy when the leaves start falling in the autumn." Millie tucked her lunch pail tighter into her chest and squeezed Jack's hand.

"I didn't know much about the winter here in Montana before I arrived, and I still don't. Winter in Texas can be cold, but not this cold." Jack tightened his coat around his body, shivering slightly. He'd been through ice storms where thick layers of ice covered everything, and while it got cold, it was nothing like the temperatures he'd seen here.

"Does it snow in Texas?" Miles Jr. asked.

"Not a lot."

The little boy sighed and rolled his eyes. "We get lots of snow, even more than we already have."

"Well, I can't say I'm looking forward to more than this." Jack motioned all around them.

"I like the snow," Millie said. "It's fun to play in."

"I'm sure it is."

Jack looked around as the brother and sister argued back and forth about whether or not snow was fun. He saw both sides of the coin. Snow could be fun and an excellent source of water for the rivers and lakes, but it is cold—and given that he didn't have much experience with the snow, he wasn't sure what to make of the thought of it.

As they neared the church and schoolhouse, Millie released his hand.

"Daddy! Daddy!" She ran toward a figure walking toward them with his arms outstretched.

"Pa!" Miles Jr. took off after his sister, and the two children landed in their father's arms. Each one of them squeezed each other tight.

"I missed you two," Mr. Fields said. "Mama missed you too."

"How is Mommy?" Millie asked.

"She's fine. Did you have fun at the inn with Ms. Holden?"

"Lots of fun. We had pancakes this morning."

"Pancakes? So, that's why I can smell the syrup on your breath." Mr. Fields chuckled.

"Uh-huh. It was real maple syrup, too. It was so good."

"I bet it was." Mr. Fields glanced up at Jack, rising to his feet as Jack reached them. "Good morning, Pastor Boone."

"Good morning, Mr. Fields."

After shaking Jack's hand, the father pointed at the church and schoolhouse. "I hoped I would catch them before they started school, and I had to be at work. I'm glad I did."

"Me too."

"I hope they weren't too much of a bother last night for Ms. Holden."

"Not at all. She had planned to bring them to school but got caught up dealing with a guest who was checking out. I offered to take them since I wanted to visit the church anyway." Jack paused to pat Millie on the top of the head. She looked up at him and smiled. "Oh, and Ms. Holden asked me to tell you the children are welcome to stay another night at the inn if you and your wife need them to."

"Oh, well, that was kind of her. My wife was just talking today about how nice it was to have a break. But she also missed them something fierce. Please thank Ms. Holden for the offer, but I think the children will stay in their own beds tonight."

"I will let her know. But I'm sure it can go without saying that the offer stands anytime you need."

"Thank you. I'll keep her in mind. I should get to work." He patted his children on the head. "You two have a wonderful day. I'll see you after school."

As Mr. Fields walked away, glancing over his shoulder to give one last wave, the front door opened, and a young woman stepped onto the small porch. She held out a large bell in her hand and started ringing it.

"Miss Evans! Miss Evans!" Millie shouted. She waved a second before giving her father one last hug and rushing toward the teacher. "We spent the night at the inn with Miss Holden and Pastor Boone! It was so much fun. And then this morning, we had pancakes with real maple syrup."

Miss Evans smiled as the little girl approached. "You did? It sounds like you had quite the adventure."

"We did. And even though we don't get to stay again tonight, we might another night."

"Well, that sounds like you'll have lots of fun when you do." Miss Evans clasped her hands for a moment, then patted the little girl on the head. "You can tell me all about it later, all right?"

"All right." Millie turned and waved to Jack before skipping into the schoolhouse. Her lunch pail slapped her hip with her movement, making a tin-ping sound.

Miss Evans watched the little girl, then turned to welcome a few other students before focusing on Jack. "You must be Pastor Boone," she said, sticking out her hand. She was short and tiny and looked more like a child attending school than a woman teaching it.

"I am. It's nice to meet you."

"It's a pleasure to meet you, too."

"I hope I'm not bothering you. I just wanted to come by and see the church this morning."

"Oh, you're not a bother at all. You're welcome to go inside and have a look around. If you wanted to talk to the children, I'm sure they'd love to meet you."

"Thank you. That sounds wonderful."

Jack and Miss Evans continued welcoming children, who gave Jack funny looks after saying good morning to their teacher.

Once all the children were in their seats, Jack helped close the doors before following Miss Evans up to the head of the classroom.

"Boys and girls, as you have seen, we have a special guest with us this morning. I want to introduce you all to the new pastor of Featherstone Valley, Pastor Boone."

"Good morning, Pastor Boone," they all said together.

"Good morning, boys and girls. Thank you for welcoming me into your school this morning. I just wanted to come by and meet all of your bright faces and introduce myself." He looked around the room, smiling. The ages ranged from child to child. Some, he guessed, were as young as five or six, while the older ones in the back, he figured, were sixteen or seventeen, and they all greeted him with a warm 'good morning.'

One little girl raised her hand.

"Yes, Emily?" Miss Evans said, pointing at her.

"Pa said that Pastor Boone was from Texas. Is that true?" Emily asked.

"Yes, I am. I was raised in Fort Worth and lived there until I moved to Featherstone Valley."

"Why did you move here?" an older boy asked. "Was it just to be our pastor?"

"Don't forget we raise our hand when we want to ask a question, Elijah," Miss Evans reminded him. The boy nodded, and his cheeks turned slightly pink as a couple of the other older boys snickered. Miss Evans shot them each a glare, and they straightened in their chairs and cleared their throats. Elijah smiled at the unspoken warning the teacher gave them.

Jack ducked his chin for a moment to hide his amusement before he glanced back up at the classroom and looked at the boy. He wasn't quite sure how much he wanted to dive into the question. Sure, he could go on about wanting to start a new life far away from the one he left behind. But did they need to know that? And did he want to tell them?

"I'm not sure I can tell you why I moved here, young man," Jack said. "I guess it was a calling I felt."

Miles Jr. raised his hand. "Do you miss Texas?"

"I suppose a little. But I love this town so far, and Montana is beautiful. Some might even think it's prettier than Texas."

Another young boy sitting next to Miles Jr. raised his hand. "What about a family? Do you have a family in Texas? What about a wife or children?"

"My mom says that he's unattached. Whatever that means," one of the older girls said as she brushed her long hair behind her shoulders. Before Miss Evans or Jack said anything, Elijah whipped his head toward the girl.

"It means he's not married," he said to her, looking at her first and then at Jack. "So, is it true, Pastor Boone? Are you married or not?"

"If he were married, then his wife would be with him," the older girl shot back with a slight glare in her eyes.

"Mary, we don't take that tone with others," Miss Evans said. "And remember to raise your hand first, please."

As the older girl stared at the teacher, Jack cleared his throat. *Oh, the honest questions from children that they don't see as a problem. Of course, truth be told, they shouldn't.* They weren't trying to be mean or force him to hash out feelings and memories that brought him pain. It was merely a simple question that children ask because they are curious. They didn't know the truth. How would they? Jack opened his mouth to answer, but the boy who had been arguing with Mary couldn't hold it in any longer.

"That's not true. His wife could still be in Texas, and she plans on coming later. Perhaps she needed to stay behind for one reason or another. Perhaps they have children who need to stay there, too."

The little girl who had first asked him a question turned to the sparring boy and girl, wrapping her arms around her shoulders as though to hug herself. "I never want to move away from my mommy and daddy."

"You have to. You have to leave home when you get married and live with your husband," the boy beside her said.

"But why can't we live with my parents or next door? We can live next door. Can't we, Miss Evans?" The girl blinked at the teacher, who smiled and nodded.

"I suppose you could, Emily, if you and your husband agree to live so close."

Emily beamed, liking the answer her teacher gave her.

For a moment, Jack liked the back-and-forth banter between the children. It gave him the much-needed distraction to not face the questions he didn't want to answer. But as the children finished, they stared at him, waiting, and his heartbeat kicked up. He knew what they expected from him, and he cleared his throat again, glancing at Miss Evans, who unfortunately didn't seem to see the desperation in his eyes.

He cleared his throat a third time. "I don't know that I can say I miss Texas all that much," Jack told the young boy, hoping the answer would suffice. "But I know I'm needed here, so here is where I want to be. I can't wait to make my home here with the residents of Featherstone Valley."

Miss Evans stepped up beside him. "And we can't wait for your Sunday sermons, Pastor Boone." She paused, smiling at him before winking. Perhaps she had noticed after all. "Thank you for speaking with them today."

"You're welcome." He hooked his thumb over his shoulder toward a door in the corner. "I'm going to check out the office."

"Sure. No problem." She turned toward the students. "Everyone, thank Pastor Boone for visiting with us this morning."

"Thank you, Pastor Boone," the children said together.

As Jack made his way to the door, he heard Miss Evans tell the children to get out their readers and pencils because they were starting their English lessons this morning. The collective sighs of displeasure caused him to smile, and he shut the office door with a slight chuckle on his lips.

The office was tiny and modest, but it was more than he would ever need. A small desk sat in the middle of the room with an oil lamp in one corner, a stack of Bibles in the other, and a copy of this morning's edition of the Featherstone Gazette in the middle. There were three chairs around it, too, and a few paintings on the walls, along with two windows with sheer curtains that let in a fair amount of light. He wasn't quite sure what he would do in this space, but for a moment, he couldn't help but wonder if a bed would fit.

You can't live here, you fool. Just find yourself a modest house and be happy, he thought.

Happy.

He almost snorted at the word.

Was there such a thing for him anymore?

He wanted to believe that there was—especially in this town.

"I just need to have faith," he whispered. "Faith that this was the right choice to make."

He sat in one of the chairs and scooted it toward the desk, glancing around the room before his gaze fell upon the morning newspaper. A couple of different headlines popped from the page, but one caught his attention, and he furrowed his brow as he focused on the words printed on the white paper in black ink: The Puzzling Past of Pastor Jack Boone: Telegrams and Family Secrets Unearthed.

He grabbed the newspaper and unfolded it, reading the article titled Prudence Chatterton's Parlor Patter. His stomach twisted as he read the details of the apparent scandal brewing over him, being seen sending secret telegrams.

He had come to Featherstone Valley seeking a fresh start, a chance to leave behind the shadows of his past. But now, it seemed that his past was catching up to him even in this remote town. The column hinted at hidden truths and whispered rumors, casting a shadow over his new beginning.

And just how was the town supposed to trust him after this?

He had hoped to provide them with guidance and spiritual leadership, and now, even before he could give them one sermon, he felt it was all threatened to be overshadowed by whispers of scandal and mystery. He refolded the newspaper, taking several deep breaths. He didn't know what to do or what even to think. He thought of everyone in town reading this article and the whispers they would surely speak behind his back. Would they be angry? Would they ask Mayor Duncan to relieve him of his post as the town pastor?

How was he supposed to have faith now?

~

CRAIG

C raig had just about as much faith as any man.

Or perhaps he thought he did.

However, there were times he wondered about that. Sure, faith saw him safely to California, where he found his passion for gold, but a lot of grit got him there, too. Not to mention what he lost in the process. He saw men do things to other men he never wanted to see again. Brutality, certainly, wasn't for the weak, no matter how badly you think you can stomach something out of desperation.

And his stomach couldn't take any more than it already had.

With the same faith that saw him to California, it saw him out with enough money and knowledge to start his own mining company far away from the cruelty that some called just part of life and death, making their actions somehow excusable. Arriving in Montana had been a breath of fresh air and the land he'd secured.

Now, he just needed the chance to buy more.

Rattlesnake Mountain had caught his eye from the moment he'd stepped off the stage, and the only thing that stood in his way was a greedy mayor he wanted to punch in the face.

If this deal doesn't go through and he sells to Sydney Miller...

Craig closed his eyes, exhaling a breath. He couldn't even finish his own thought.

It would anger him too much.

The office door opened, and Wyatt rushed inside, carrying a few envelopes. "Mr. Harrison! Mr. Harrison! The mayor responded! He left this for you at the mercantile!"

"Settle down, Wyatt." Mr. Harrison furrowed his brow. The

young man had been a hard worker, but sometimes, his eagerness was too overwhelming.

"Sorry, Sir." Wyatt slowed his pace to a walk and walked to Craig's desk. He handed over the envelopes. "There were a few other letters in the post as well."

"Thank you."

"Do you want me to head up the mountain now? I'm sure the men are waiting for me, and I have a job to do up there." Wyatt spun as though he was heading back to the door but paused, waiting for the answer. Tension seemed to wash through his shoulders, and Craig suddenly realized the reason for his haste. He was eager to return to the mountain and manage his men like he was hired, not to play errand boy for the owner.

"Of course. I'm sorry, Wyatt. Handle the men. I will take care of all of this office stuff myself."

"Thank you, Sir."

Craig nodded, ignoring how Wyatt rushed from the office, grabbing his coat and hat from the rack so quickly the thing teetered, rocking back and forth and teasing it would fall over. The door shut as Craig grabbed the letter opener, and he slid the blade into the envelope, ripping it apart before he slid the letter out and unfolded it.

He inhaled a deep breath as he read the first sentence.

Dear Mr. Harrison,

I regret to inform you...

EIGHT

SARAH

Sarah tucked her basket close to her chest as she walked to the mercantile. Anxiousness still prickled along her nerves as she tried not to replay the scene with Mr. Clemons in her mind.

She failed.

Several times.

Over and over again, she thought of what the traveling salesman had said and done. She pictured how he had risen to his feet and lunged toward her, bracing himself as though to bully her with his sheer size. Not that he was a large man by any means. He wasn't like Pastor Boone. Now, *he* was a large man. But still, even a man of a smaller size, like Mr. Clemons, was larger than her. Being small had been the one thing she'd dealt with all her life. Harold called her petite and a tiny package that God meant for him.

How wrong he'd been.

But that was beside the point. She shook her head, focusing back on Mr. Clemons and his audacity to approach her in the manner in which he did.

Oh, the nerve of that man.

She shook her head just thinking about it. She wanted to say so much else to him after he'd packed his things and she was checking him out, but she didn't say anything. Instead, she bit her tongue and thanked him for his stay as she handed him the receipt for his payment and returned the room key. It was the side of the business she never liked and one she had only faced a few times—unruly guests she had to ask to leave. Confrontation was never her thing, but she could still hold her own for the most part. At least, she thought she could to a certain extent. But still, even with the bit of confidence she held, it wasn't something she wanted to do or liked doing. There were hardly any times in her life when she didn't like the inn, but in those situations, she wanted to close her doors and never open them again.

She couldn't do that, though. She needed the money too much.

At least Pastor Boone had been there to help, she thought. *I don't want to think about what would have happened if he hadn't been there.*

Her throat closed, and her stomach twisted with that thought. She never wanted to need a man and had prided herself on her independence. It was a quality Harold used to brag about.

"She's with me because she wants to be with me, not because she has to be," he would always tell people.

Of course, it still rings true today. However, she couldn't deny there was a part of her that missed the security that came with having a man around the house... or inn. Even with that, though, she couldn't let her thoughts slip into that frame. She had to forget what happened; otherwise, it would eat away at her for the rest of the afternoon.

"Good morning, Ms. Holden," a voice greeted her as she entered the mercantile.

Sarah glanced up, meeting the smiling face of Mr. Arthur Lockhart, the owner. "Good afternoon, Mr. Lockhart."

"May I help you with anything?"

"I'm just here to have a look around."

"A shipment of pumpkins arrived yesterday, and they look like a great crop. Mrs. Hickman bought a couple and has plans to make a few pumpkin pies and a couple of loaves of pumpkin bread."

"Oh, that sounds good. I bet my guests would like that."

"They are in the corner if you want to look at them."

"Thank you. I will."

The bell above the door chimed, and Sarah glanced over as Mr. Harrison strode inside. He removed his hat, tucking it under his arm with his gloves as he greeted her and the mercantile owner. "Good morning, Ms. Holden. Mr. Lockhart."

"Good morning." The two both acknowledged his greeting with their own.

"What can I help you with today, Mr. Harrison?" Mr. Lockhart asked.

"First, I'm here to send a telegram, and then I was wondering if you might know where Mayor Duncan is."

"I haven't seen him since I dropped off a few letters for him to hand out. But we can take care of that telegram."

As Mr. Lockhart grabbed a notepad, Mr. Harrison leaned toward the counter, tossing his hat on the wood slab as he exhaled. His brow furrowed as he glanced at Sarah, and she inhaled a deep breath. Knowing the business dealings between Mr. Harrison and the mayor, she could not only see the unease in the gold mining company owner, but she could feel it from his straightened posture.

"Here you are, Mr. Harrison," Mr. Lockhart handed him a pencil, and as Mr. Harrison began jotting down what he wanted the telegram to say, Sarah took a few steps away from the two men. She wasn't about to stick her nose into someone else's business unless they chose to include her, and as she turned her attention toward several candles stacked on the counter near the register, Mr. Harrison slid the paper over.

"The address is below the message. Please see that this goes out today."

"Of course, Mr. Harrison. I will get this right out for you."

Mr. Harrison nodded and smiled before he looked toward the door as though looking out onto the street through the oval window. Although Sarah couldn't see his face, she imagined him closing his eyes while he took several deep breaths.

"And you're sure you don't know where the mayor is, Mr. Lockhart?" he asked.

"I'm sorry, but... wait... come to think of it, I think he mentioned going to the barber after he left here to get his hair trimmed."

"Did you say he was headed to the barber?" Although he asked the question, Mr. Harrison didn't wait for the answer. Instead, he left the mercantile, letting the door slam behind him. Mr. Lockhart and Sarah exchanged glances.

"I do hope it wasn't anything I said or did that offended him," Mr. Lockhart said.

"Knowing Mayor Duncan, I'm sure it wasn't."

"Well, I should get back to stocking the inventory shipment. Let me know if you need help with those pumpkins, Ms. Holden."

Before she could say another word, he turned and made his way toward the back room, vanishing behind a set of thick, hunter-green curtains. Sarah watched the fabric's movement before her gaze drifted to the counter and the cash register. A thick layer of black tarnish eclipsed a little of its beauty in places. Just like everything and everyone in this town, it had its shiny half and blemished half, and it felt as though she was looking through an old window into the years that the counter had been its home. Out of everything that came and left the store, it stayed—a part of the building more than anything else.

There was a small part of her that knew how it felt.

With a deep sigh, she continued on her way through the store, and as she rounded the corner, she came face to face with Mrs. Gables and Mrs. Newman standing in front of the jars of pickled fruit from the shelf with their heads so close together they could be one person.

"Can you believe it?" Mrs. Newman gasped.

"No, I can't. Well, perhaps I can. The audacity of that man and a pastor, no less!"

Sarah halted in her steps. "Good afternoon, ladies," she said.

Both women spun, and while Mrs. Gables brushed her hand against her chest, Mrs. Newman let out a slight gasp.

It was the exact reaction Sarah had been going for.

"Oh! Ms. Holden. You surprised us." Mrs. Gables tucked the newspaper she'd been holding under her arm.

"I see that, and I'm sorry if I interrupted something." Although Sarah didn't want to let on, she knew something was up because she didn't want to embarrass either woman; she also couldn't help herself.

"Oh, you weren't interrupting anything. We were just talking."

"I see." Sarah motioned toward the wadded-up newspaper. "Something interesting in the newspaper this morning?"

"Oh, it's nothing." Mrs. Gables glanced at Mrs. Newman and shrugged. Mrs. Newman bit her bottom lip.

A slight chuckle whispered across Sarah's breath, and she couldn't help herself. She had to press the issue just a little. "It doesn't sound like nothing. But I won't ask any further."

The two women looked at one another, and then Mrs. Gables stepped closer, lowering her voice to a whisper. "Do you remember that column I showed you yesterday? The gossip column that Mr. Jenkins has added to the daily newspaper?"

"Yes. Something Chatterbox... Parlor... I can't remember the name."

"It's called Prudence Chatterton's Parlor Patter." Mrs. Gables leaned in even closer. "They published another article about Pastor Boone in this morning's paper."

"Oh really? And what does it say?"

"Well... it says that he sent two telegrams to Texas the afternoon he arrived."

Sarah's stomach twisted. She knew where this was going, and while Jack mentioned he'd sent the telegrams, he hadn't mentioned to whom they were for. She had wanted to press the issue last night, but he seemed as though he wasn't comfortable with telling her, so she didn't want to pry. "That doesn't sound like anything scandalous. We all send telegrams now and then." It was one of the worst attempts to deflect a conversation, and she hoped it would work.

"Yes, but apparently, the recipients made it a story." Mrs. Gables leaned back, putting a few inches between her and Sarah. Sarah's hope that she'd managed to distract the woman deflated. "Has the pastor said anything about his life in Texas?"

Sarah shook her head. "Not really. But I haven't asked." It wasn't exactly a lie. Perhaps she could still get out of this conversation without fibbing. Sure, she'd have to get creative, but she could do it.

"For heaven's sake, why not?" Mrs. Newman asked. Her sudden voice caused Sarah to flinch, and the woman's eyes widened, and she blinked at Sarah for a moment.

"Because it's none of my business."

"He is the town pastor." Mrs. Gables' eyes widened, and she cocked her head to the side.

"And what does that have to do with anything? It doesn't mean we have the right to his private life."

"If he is counseling us in matters of our faith and what God desires for us, then he shouldn't have any secrets—especially when it involves him having secret children!"

Sarah's stomach clenched. Secret children? What on earth was Mrs. Gables talking about? She shook her head and closed her eyes for just a second. "Who said anything about secret children?"

"He has two sons, to whom he sent the telegrams. Apparently, they both live in Texas."

Although a small part of Sarah wanted to react—who wouldn't, given the surprise that was just dropped at her feet about a man she thought she was beginning to know—but she knew it was best not to. Reacting would give Mrs. Gables the attention she so desired, and Sarah wasn't about to feed the beast dwelling in the gossiping woman. Not even for a moment. "I'm sorry, but I fail to see what the problem is, Mrs. Gables," she lied.

"There are several problems, Ms. Holden."

"Such as?"

"Such as how old are these two sons? Are they children, or are they adults? Was he married to their mother? Why didn't he tell the mayor about them? Is it because they don't have the same mother?" Mrs. Gables rattled off her questions, pausing to bite her bottom lip as though her thoughts were almost too inappropriate to say, much less think. "Surely, a man... no, a pastor wouldn't have a string of children all across the country by different women. Would he?"

The last question hit Sarah the hardest.

Once again, she wanted to react to what Mrs. Gables had said but didn't at the same time. Mrs. Gables loved knowing she shocked people and loved getting a rise from seeing someone respond to what she told them. She fed off it like a starving person arriving at a banquet, and Sarah didn't want to give her the satisfaction today.

"Perhaps we should just wait and see what he says on

Sunday. You don't know that he intended to keep his children a secret. Perhaps he just wanted to tell us while we were all together." It was a stretch, but it was one Sarah had to make.

Mrs. Gables folded her arms across her chest, and the newspaper crinkled. Her brow furrowed. "Is there something you're not telling me about Pastor Boone?"

"No."

"Because you are the only one in town who has spent time with him."

"He's told me nothing, and he hasn't because I haven't asked. It's not my place."

Mrs. Gables' eyes narrowed. "And how do we decipher the truth without all the details? For all we know, *you* could be Prudence Chatterton, and you're using this mystery surrounding a man with whom you are the only one to have contact to start your career."

"My career? What are you talking about? I own the inn. That is my job. And I certainly don't partake in the mindless gossip around town." Sarah wanted to add to the statement, pointing out that she wasn't the one who started this conversation or the other at the school, but she wasn't the type to do such things.

"Well, I think that we all—and you especially—should demand that this *pastor* come clean with everything he is hiding or lying about."

"I don't understand; why, especially me?"

"Because he's staying at your inn... with you... alone."

A flicker of annoyance whispered through Sarah's chest. Never once had anyone, specifically any woman in this town, ever questioned how she was a woman living alone and running an inn where male guests stayed.

"We are not alone, Mrs. Gables. And may I remind you I don't spend my nights in the inn. My cottage is behind it, where I live alone."

"Well, yes, but the inn is close."

"Just what are you implying, Mrs. Gables?"

"Nothing. She's implying nothing." Mrs. Newman stepped between the two women. "Are you, Mrs. Gables?"

Mrs. Gables sucked in a breath, brushing her fingertips along her collarbone again, this time not in shock but in a mindless way, as though she was thinking about whether or not she should say what she wanted to do next. "No, I'm not," she finally answered. "I'm sorry if I implied that you are a woman with questionable morals, Ms. Holden. That wasn't my intention. I just don't like that Pastor Boone is keeping something from us. It's not right."

"And that's your opinion, Mrs. Gables, which you are allowed to have, just as I am allowed to have a different one." Sarah paused, but only for a moment before speaking again. She didn't want to give Mrs. Gables the idea she could say anything. "If you ladies will please excuse me, I ought to return to the inn to prepare dinner for the guests and the café. I hope you have a lovely afternoon."

She turned and strode back to the counter, handing Mr. Lockhart a nickel before grabbing a copy of The Featherstone Valley Gazette. She wasn't about to read Prudence Chatterton's article in front of Mrs. Gables, but that didn't mean she wasn't interested in seeing what it said. She tucked the paper under her arm, and as she opened the mercantile's door, a booming argument echoed from outside.

CRAIG

"And just what is the meaning of this?" Craig waved the letter he'd opened just moments ago in his office in Mayor Duncan's face. It was another rejection for the purchase of Rattlesnake Mountain—the fourth one he'd received in the last couple of weeks. "You have rejected my offer again, and I demand answers as to why." His breath clouded around his face in the cold air.

Mayor Duncan's eyes widened, and he glanced around at the townsfolk gathering around the scene. "Keep your voice down, Mr. Harrison. People are watching."

"I don't care if they are watching. I want to know why you keep rejecting my offers! I've offered more than enough for what that mountain is worth. I've probably even offered triple the land value. So what is it? Why do you keep saying no?"

"Who told you what the land was worth?" He paused but shook his head and hand as though he wasn't looking for an answer. "Never mind. It doesn't matter. That said, I assure you, you haven't come close to the amount."

Craig pointed at the mayor and poked his finger into the mayor's chest. "I want the truth, Bartholomew Duncan. Don't even think of lying to me."

"I don't know what you're talking about, Mr. Harrison. I've done nothing but good things for this town. This town has prospered because of me and my decisions." The mayor clenched his chubby hands, resting them on his hips as he puffed out his chest. Or at least he tried to. Instead, it was more of his belly that puffed. "Now if you wish to discuss the matter, then I suggest we take it to my office. Otherwise, I will bid you a good day and be done with you and this conversation." The mayor moved around Craig and headed down the street at a brisk pace.

Craig followed after him, trotting up alongside the round, waddling man. "You will do nothing of the sort, Mayor Duncan. You will talk to me about this matter. Right here. Right now."

"Fine. You want the answer as to why your offer was rejected? As I stated in my letter," he pointed at the letter in Craig's hand—the one Craig waved in his face only moments ago, "the offer was rejected because someone outbid you again."

"Oh, they did, did they? And just who is this someone?" Although he asked the question, Craig already knew the answer. He just wanted to hear Mayor Duncan say it out loud.

"You know I'm not at liberty to tell you who it is. That's a private matter between who makes the offer and the town mayor."

Craig stepped toward Mayor Duncan. "Cut the façade, Mayor Duncan. You aren't fooling anyone."

Mayor Duncan stepped backward in the same number of steps that Craig had taken. "Again, I don't know what you're talking about."

Craig wasn't sure what he was growing tired of more: Mayor Duncan refusing to be honest with everyone in town or just refusing to sell him Snake Mountain. He stepped forward again, lowering his voice. He wasn't the type to give any more chances than just the one, but he also wasn't the type to throw a man to the wolves. At least not yet. That part of him could change. "Don't push me, Bartholomew. I'm sure you know what I'm privy to—things that would put your career as mayor of this town on the chopping block."

Mayor Duncan sucked in a breath. "Is that a threat?"

"Only if you make it one."

"Well, then, let me remind you that it's only me who stands in the way of you and that precious mountain, so if I were you, I would tread lightly."

"Why? Another mayor could accept my offer just as easily as you could."

"Not if I sell it to the other man before I leave office."

The two men stood toe to toe, or at least somewhat did. Considering the plump mayor was about four inches shorter than Craig, it wasn't a fair match.

"Selling to Sidney Miller from Deer Creek would be the biggest mistake of your career. Are you aware of the type of man he is?"

"I'm not sure how you discovered the other party's identity, but it doesn't matter."

"Oh, but it does. Do you think any of the townsfolk will say yes to letting a man like that buy any land in Featherstone Valley?"

"They don't have the choice. Not to mention, I think perhaps they might change their minds once they learn about all the growth Mr. Miller wants to bring to our little town. The economy is booming in towns like Deer Creek, and it's because of businessmen like him."

"No one will want him here."

"You cannot predict how everyone will feel."

Craig opened his mouth but stopped himself only a moment before blurting out. "I don't know why I'm arguing with you when you obviously have the intelligence of a rock."

"Well, that is rather an offensive thing to say."

"Perhaps to rocks, it is. But not to you."

Mayor Duncan wiggled his finger in Craig's face. "If you think I'm going to stand here and let you talk to me like that, you've got another thing coming. This conversation is over." He turned to leave, but Craig moved around him.

"How much was his offer?" Craig asked, ignoring how the mayor had tried to leave.

"I'm not at liberty to say. But he matched yours and offered a sizable chunk extra."

Sizable?

Just what on earth did that mean?

"Tell me how much."

"I can't, and even if I could, I won't."

"I live in Featherstone, Mayor Duncan. I don't understand why you wouldn't want that mountain to go to someone who lives in the town. What if I matched Mr. Miller's offer? Then you could still have your money."

"You will have to make an offer just like he does."

Although Craig couldn't prove it, part of him felt that Mr. Miller didn't have to work this hard. Just why was the mayor being so difficult? Craig grabbed the bridge of his nose and blew out a breath.

"Have you already given him your answer?" he asked.

"Not yet. But I had planned on sending him a wire soon."

"Can you do me a favor and at least give me a few days before you do?"

Mayor Duncan inhaled a deep breath and folded his arms across his chest. Craig sensed the hesitation washing through the mayor's mind. His only hope was the mayor would agree to give him a few days to come up with more money—or at least an idea of how to obtain it.

"Please, Mayor."

"Fine. Today is Tuesday. You can have until next Monday."

"Thank you."

As the mayor walked away, a growl whispered through Craig's chest. He'd already put up as much as possible in the last offer. He wasn't sure how he would come up with more than that. One thing was for sure, though; he would have to think of something.

NINE

SARAH

I f there were ever a time of day that was her favorite, Sarah would have to pick the late evening when all the guests had gone to bed, the chores were done, and she could sit in the parlor and enjoy a nice cup of tea while she read her book. It was the last hour before she went to her cabin to get what always felt like much-needed sleep. She looked forward to this time more than anything. It was a time to relax, forget the world around her, and dive into another place populated with people unlike anyone she knew.

Tonight, however, wasn't like the rest. The chaos of the events at the mercantile and reading the article from Prudence Chatterton had left a knot in her gut that hadn't eased. She hadn't known what to make of the accusations made in the Parlor Patter, and as she sat in the parlor chair and grabbed that morning's newspaper again, she inhaled a deep breath. She had wanted to talk to Jack about what the article said, but she hadn't seen him. After returning from visiting the schoolhouse, he went to his room and didn't come back downstairs, not even for supper.

The floor creaked as though someone entered the parlor,

and as she looked up, Jack smiled. Secrets or not, she couldn't help but feel a twist of relief spreading through her body at seeing him enter the room. He'd been such a presence in her life in just the few days he'd been there that suddenly, his absence this evening had left a hole in her world.

"Good evening," he said, lowering his voice to just a hair above a whisper.

"Good evening."

"I hope I'm not bothering you." A slight sheepish grin inched across his lips, then vanished.

"You aren't."

He hooked his thumb over his shoulder. "I was going to make myself a sandwich, but I didn't want to impose or do something I shouldn't."

"You are not imposing, and you're welcome to use the kitchen and what I have. However, I did keep a plate in the oven for you just in case you came down for supper."

"You did? Thank you."

"You're welcome. Let me get it for you."

"I can get it."

"No, no. It's fine. Why don't you have a seat, and I'll bring it out to you?" She pointed toward another chair in the parlor before setting the newspaper down next to the cup of tea and standing. Before he said anything, she slipped from the room, fetched the plate from the oven, returned, and handed it to him.

"It should still be warm enough."

"Thank you." He paused, looking at the newspaper she'd set on the table. "I'll leave you to your reading."

"You're not going to stay?"

"I don't want to impose."

"You're not. You're more than welcome to eat here." She moved over to the chair and sat, letting out a deep sigh. "I hoped we could've chatted tonight, but you never came down for supper."

"Yes, I'm sorry about that. I just... I just have a lot on my mind." He adjusted his seat, and although he spoke to her, he didn't make eye contact with her—not even once. His voice was soft and light, but not because he was happy. Instead, he had a sadness to his tone, as though sorrow pained him.

"Did things not go well this morning when you visited the church?" Although she was sure that wasn't the reason for his melancholy, she asked anyway. A slight part of her almost wished that was the case since that was a lot easier of a problem to face than what she believed it truly was—the gossip columnist who had made it their mission to drag his private life into the street for everyone to talk about.

"No, it went fine. I met the children and spoke with them for a little bit. It was... something else that happened." He furrowed his brow, pausing to pick up his fork and cut a chunk of meatloaf off before shoving it into his mouth and chewing until it was gone. Sarah could sense not only that something was on his mind, but she also had a gut feeling that she knew what it was. "I saw the newspaper this afternoon," he continued. "And I found out I've been quite the hot topic for the last couple of days."

Her gut had been right. He knew about Prudence Chatterton's Parlor Patter articles. "I know you have."

"So, you've read the columns?"

"I have." She hated admitting it, but she didn't want to lie.

His brow furrowed again, and he shook his head as he stared at the ground. His shoulders hunched, and the notion she'd read them seemed to not sit well in his mind. Guilt prickled in her chest. She almost wished she hadn't read them. Yet, she also knew if she hadn't seen what they'd said, she couldn't help him.

"Do you know who Prudence Chatterton is?" he asked, furrowing his brow again.

"From what I gather from a few women around town, no one knows who she is. Well, I suppose Mr. Jenkins knows since he hired her to write the column."

"No, he doesn't."

"How do you know that?"

"I asked him." Jack took another bite of meatloaf, chewing before taking a couple of bites of mashed potatoes and carrots.

"You asked him?"

"I had to. After seeing the article, I went to his office and asked him who this woman was. He told me he's never met her. She sent him a letter proposing the column, and he wrote back agreeing because he thought it would be interesting for the newspaper. It seems the sales are less than he had hoped as of late, and he thought it would help." Jack rolled his eyes. "She sends him what she wants to print, and he prints it and sends her the money."

"But that can't be how he wants to run his newspaper. What about checking facts?"

"It's a gossip column. He hardly has the desire to walk up to people and ask them about whether or not the information is true. He'd rather print what is written and let the chips fall where they may. Truth or not, scandal sells newspapers."

Her heart thumped. Did this mean the gossip wasn't true? Had she been unsettled all day over nothing? "So, it wasn't true what she wrote about you? You don't have secret children, and you didn't send them a wire telegram?"

Jack leaned forward, resting his elbows on his knees as he stared at the food. It looked as though he'd suddenly lost his appetite and was wondering if he'd be able to finish the meal on the plate or if he should take it back to the kitchen and throw it in the trash—the food, not the plate. "I didn't know that it was so important for a town full of strangers to know such personal things about me."

"That was what I told Mrs. Gables."

"Who is Mrs. Gables?"

"She's just a woman in town. She seems to think that your

past should be our business because of how important pastors are to a person's walk with God and faith."

Jack cleared his throat and stared at his food a little more. "I suppose she has a point. It's not that I planned not to tell anyone. I just wanted to get to know people first."

"I can understand that. I think perhaps people are feeling blindsided because you didn't tell Mayor Duncan. He told us everything he knew about you, and none had anything to do with a wife or family. People are confused as to why and ask if it's because..." She bit her lip at the accusations resting on the tip of her tongue. How was she supposed to say them?

"Because why?"

"Because there is a reason you didn't want anyone to tell anyone about them. Like perhaps you aren't married to their mother, or perhaps they don't have the same mother." Her gut twisted with her words. She hadn't wanted to think them, much less say them. But she knew if she didn't, she would regret it.

He looked up at her for the first time since he entered the parlor, and his eyes pierced hers. His voice deepened into a stern tone. "Neither of those are true."

Although a sense of relief washed through her, her heart still hammered, and her palms were slick with sweat. She tried to ignore how she suddenly felt foolish for even saying the words.

Jack glanced down at the plate and then looked at her again with the same intensity. "I have two sons, Patrick and Kit. They are both grown men, and they have the same mother... or I should say they *had* the same mother." Although he chuckled at the first part of his sentence, his smile vanished by the time he finished the last part, and his voice deepened.

Sarah hesitated, then decided to ask anyway. "So, your... wife..."

"She died several years ago, and yes, she was my wife. Our first son came along a short time after we were married. It was all proper, I assure you."

"I believe you, and I'm so sorry to hear that she passed away."
Sarah tucked her chin toward her chest. Although it felt better
to have something in common between them, it was the worst
thing that could be. "Do your sons live in Texas?"

"Yes. They do."

"I bet you miss them terribly."

"I do. But... " After staring at his food for another minute, he
hesitated and finally took another bite of meatloaf, speaking
again after he chewed the bite and swallowed it. "I haven't seen
much of them as of late."

"I don't understand."

"I haven't had the best relationship with them for quite some
time."

"Why not?"

"After their mother died, I struggled with a lot of things.
Being a parent to them was one of them. Her sister, their aunt,
finally took them from me. She said she would care for them
better than I would, and in their anger and her anger, we lost
touch with one another. They didn't want to have much to do
with me now."

"I'm sorry to hear that, too."

"I've tried to reach out to them, both before I left and then
again yesterday when I sent the telegrams, but they never
responded to my letters. I don't believe they will after they
receive the telegrams, either. But even if I don't think they will, I
had to send them word for my peace of mind."

"Perhaps they still will respond. Perhaps they just need some
time."

"I hope so. But I don't want to hang on to the hope for fear
of disappointment. With that, however, I felt they deserved to
know at least where I am."

"Of course they do. And you deserve for them to know."

Jack inhaled a deep breath, blowing it out slowly as he

puffed his cheeks. "I'm sorry for not telling you, or anyone for that matter."

"You don't have to apologize, or at least I don't think you do. But I also still don't understand why you didn't."

"Pride, maybe." He chuckled slightly and smiled. He finished a couple more bites. "I must admit that I am interested in discovering who this Prudence Chatterton is."

"I am, too, and I think the whole town will be soon if they aren't already." She couldn't help but roll her eyes. She knew several women who loved to gossip so much they would be prime suspects. But she'd also known them for so long that it was hard to see them doing anything like this. Sure, they liked talking about people, but they were still kind women who wouldn't be so cruel.

At the same time, one of them was just that mean.

The only problem now was finding out who that one was.

"Well, I should get to bed. I didn't mean to interrupt you."

"You didn't."

"Still. I'm quite tired after today." He rose to his feet and turned to leave the room.

"Jack?" She called after him. He turned but didn't say a word. "I have faith that your sons will find their way back to you. You should have faith, too."

"Knowing that I should and actually doing are two different things. But I will try. Good night, Sarah."

"Good night, Jack."

PATRICK

Ephesians 4:31-32 Get rid of all bitterness, rage and anger, brawling and slander, along with every form of malice.

Be kind and compassionate to one another, forgiving each other, just as in Christ, God forgave you.

Patrick sat at his desk, thinking about the Bible verse Julia mentioned again last night. They'd been getting ready for bed, talking about the telegram he'd received from his father when she climbed under the sheets and muttered the verse.

He had asked her to repeat it, but after just a few words, he'd regretted his request. Of course, she would pick the right one, knowing just what to say to prickle at his guilt. Not that he wanted to put much stock in living by the Bible. He hadn't in most of his twenty-eight years on this earth and had done rather well for himself; why should he start now? He didn't need it. Just like his brother told him, or perhaps he'd told Kit. He wasn't sure, and it didn't matter anyway.

His mother and aunt loved attending church, and even Julia tried to get him to go after they were married, but it didn't matter. He knew it wasn't for him. He had thought it wasn't for his father, either, given his father's life after his mother died.

Apparently, he'd been wrong.

A pastor, Patrick thought. *How can a man like him become a pastor?*

It almost seemed laughable, only Patrick wasn't in a laughing mood.

What had changed in his father to cause him to make such choices? What brilliant thought process led him to decide to become a man of the cloth? Was he trying to somehow make up for the wrongs he'd done in his life, thinking that if he became a pastor, everything would magically be good again? Did he believe that in telling Patrick about his sudden change of heart, Patrick would come flocking back to him, wanting to have him in his life?

That was almost laughable, too.

And yet, it wasn't at the same time.

He couldn't deny that while part of him wanted to tear up

the telegram and throw it in the trash, the other part didn't, and that part was feeding into the notion that he could, if he so desired, travel to Montana and see for himself what his father had done with his life.

"But why do I want to know about him?" he asked himself. "Why does it matter?"

"Because it does," a voice said.

Patrick looked up to see Julia standing in the office door-frame. Her large belly occupied most of the space, and she exhaled deeply as he looked at her. "How long have you been standing there?"

"Long enough." She shuffled into the room and sat in the chair across from him, holding the bottom of her belly as she plopped into the seat.

"I don't know what to do with this telegram."

"Well, if it were up to your aunt, it would be tossed in the trash." Julia rolled her eyes. "I don't understand why she hates your father so much."

Patrick glanced down at the desk, letting his gaze trace around the swirling pattern of a knot in one of the wooden boards. "There's just a lot that has happened between them. And it wasn't always pleasant."

Julia's eyes narrowed. "What happened all those years ago after your mother died?"

"It's not important."

"Obviously, it is if she still harbors such ill will for the man."

Patrick shook his head, trying to forget how his aunt had never liked his father, not even when his mother was alive. He never understood why, although he also didn't know if there was any other reason than the simple fact she just didn't like him. "I don't want to talk about it."

"I can understand and respect that." She paused, looking from the piece of paper to him and then back to the telegram. "Do you want my thoughts on the matter?"

"Don't I already have them? You want me to forgive and forget."

"I suppose I do, but there's more to it than just that."

"What else is there?"

"Going to Montana to see him and speak to him."

Patrick's mouth fell open, and he stared at his wife. Of all the ideas she'd had over the years, this one had to be the craziest—even more so than the time she thought they should travel to the southern coast, rent a boat, and take it out into the middle of the ocean.

"Are you crazy?" he asked, more out of just saying something than getting an answer from her because he knew the answer was already yes.

"What is so crazy about it?" She cocked her head to the side and raised one eyebrow. "I happen to think it's a wonderful idea."

"You would."

"And what is that supposed to mean?"

"I can't believe that you would just think I would leave my pregnant wife—who only has a few months left before she delivers our child—and travel across the country to visit my father, whom I haven't spoken to in years."

Her brow furrowed, and her head slightly jerked with movement. "Who said anything about leaving me behind?"

Patrick sucked in a breath and rose from his chair. The anxiety of their conversation was suddenly too much for him to sit still. He had to move; otherwise, his head might explode. Just what on earth was Julia thinking? He knew that she was an adventurous woman. It was one of the things he loved about her the most. But this? This was just too much.

"You can't seriously be thinking that you should travel across the country in your condition."

"Why not?"

"Julia, you have only a couple of months left. It's too risky. What if we couldn't return home in time?"

She shrugged. "Then I shall have the baby in Montana."

He cocked his head to the side. Guilt prickled in his chest. "You can't do that."

"Why not? I'm sure they have doctors in Montana just like in Texas."

"But your parents."

"Can see the baby when we come home... if he or she is born in Montana."

Although he appreciated her casual stance on the matter, he couldn't help but wonder if she was being a little too nonchalant about the idea. What if something happened? And not in Montana but along the way there? "I can't ask you to do this. It won't be an easy trip, and it's dangerous."

"We will be taking the train, Patrick. It's not like we have to do it in a covered wagon the whole way." She chuckled and waved her hand as though to dismiss the concern she knew was on his mind. Before he said anything, she struggled to her feet, rubbing her hands over her belly as she waddled over to him and placed her hands on his shoulders. "Everything will be all right. I don't want to worry. I'm not worried, and you shouldn't be either."

"Of course, I should. That's my job."

"Well, you shouldn't worry about a trip." She took a few steps away from him. "But you should worry about telling Beatrice."

"Telling me what?"

Before Patrick could even take a breath, his aunt walked into his office. Her pungent perfume filled the room, instantly giving him a headache. He wished she'd never bought that bottle of that stuff, as he hated the scent more than any other scent in the world.

He cleared his throat, glancing at Julia, who twisted her lips to the side and shrugged as if to say that she wasn't sure how he should tell his aunt the news either and wished him silent good luck because he was going to need it.

"Um. I was going to tell you that... well, I don't know how else to say this, so I'm just going to come out and say it."

Beatrice exhaled a deep breath, glancing between the two of them. "Say what?"

"We are planning a trip."

"For when?"

"We will leave in the morning."

"In the morning?" Beatrice raised one eyebrow. "And just where do you plan on going with your wife months from her due date?"

"We're traveling to Montana to visit my father."

Beatrice froze, staring at Patrick until he began to wonder if he'd shocked her into becoming a statue. He was about to ask her if she'd heard him, but before he could, she threw her head back, roaring with laughter.

"Aunt Beatrice?"

She continued laughing for several more minutes until she finally calmed and blotted her eyes with her fingers as though to brush away tears. "I'm sorry. But I think I misheard you. I thought you said the two of you were traveling to Montana to visit your father."

"That's exactly what I said."

She froze again and then scowled. Her eyes narrowed, and her hands clenched into fists. "Why on earth would you do such a stupid thing?"

"Stupid? It's not stupid."

"Yes, it is. It's the stupidest thing you have ever done. What are you even thinking? How can you even think to not only take a pregnant woman across the country but also to take her to meet and see that man?"

Anger flickered in the warmth that radiated up the back of

Patrick's neck. "The decision isn't up to you, Aunt Beatrice. The choice is mine and Julia's, and we will make it together."

Beatrice glanced between them again. She inhaled a deep breath, puffing her chest. "Fine. If you two are so bent on being fools, I suppose I shall go with you."

"What? Why?"

"Because someone has to be around for Julia if she goes into labor."

"I'm sure they have a doctor in Featherstone Valley, Aunt Beatrice."

"Yes. A country doctor who probably also treats the residents' farm animals."

Before Patrick could speak, Beatrice spun on her heel and stomped from the room. Julia watched the woman leave, turning toward her husband as soon as they were alone. "I must admit that went better than I thought it would."

He snorted. "I have to admit the same."

TEN

SARAH

I n the days since Jack shared his secrets with Sarah, the town shifted its prying eyes from the new pastor to the very public fight between Mr. Harrison and Mayor Duncan. Word spreading about the screaming match in the street outside the mercantile had helped a great deal, and, of course, it was only fueled by another article by Prudence Chatterton, describing the event as she tried to figure out not only what the fight was about but what the outcome would be.

"Stay tuned, dear readers, as Prudence Chatterton pledges to keep you abreast of all the juicy details and clandestine dealings in our beloved town. The saga continues, and the suspense is positively electrifying!" Sarah chuckled as she finished reading the article.

"Electrifying?" Jack chuckled, too. "Does it really say that?"

"In black and white." Sarah showed him the newspaper, handing it to him as he sat across from her at one of the dining tables with his breakfast in front of him.

He took it from her and read it, laughing by the time he reached the end. "I would pay a month's salary to whoever finds out who this woman is."

"Who says it's a woman?" Sarah straightened her back, shaking her head so her soft, greying curls were pushed back over her shoulders.

Jack cocked his head and leaned forward in his chair. The front of his shirt was dangerously close to his plate of eggs, bacon, and hash browns, but he ignored it as he lowered his voice. "Are you saying that you think Prudence Chatterton is a man?"

"It could be, or it could not. But you can't just assume it's a woman."

He laughed and leaned back in the chair again, grabbing his fork. "I suppose you're right," he said.

"So, who do you think it is today? Got any other suspicions?"

"Well, let's see. We've both thought of Mrs. Gables."

"But she wasn't in the mercantile when you sent the telegrams."

"Not that I'm aware of. Although, at the time, I didn't know what she looked like, and for all I know, she could have been in the store. I just didn't see her."

"Hmm... she does like to gossip. But she was also against the column, or at least she said she was when I picked up Miles Jr. and Millie from school when you arrived at the start of the week."

Jack clicked his tongue. "Have you ever wondered about Mr. Lockhart?"

"The owner of the mercantile? Whatever gives you the impression it's him?"

"Think about it. He is the one sending and receiving all the telegrams and postcards. The mercantile is in the center of town, which means he has a bird's-eye view of everything that goes on in the streets. Not to mention, I'm sure he hears all the conversations that go on in the place. It would make sense that he knows more than you think he does."

"But to write about it?" Sarah shook her head. "I just don't see him doing something like that. I've known Arthur for years and years."

"Is he married? What about his wife?"

"Claire? I don't believe she's the type to behave in such a way." Sarah's interest was piqued at the thought of Mrs. Lockhart penning the letters that had kept everyone's eyes glued to the newspapers or huddled in groups on the sides of the street or front porches throughout the town. She had only known the woman to be quiet, often remaining in the back of the store where she stocked the supplies and took care of inventory checklists. It was always Mr. Lockhart and their daughter Grace who helped the customers. "But I do suppose anything is possible."

Jack smiled and winked. "For all I know, it could be you."

For a moment, she thought of smacking his arm and telling him to bite his tongue. Instead, she had something funnier in mind. "Hey, it could be."

His smile vanished. "I was joking."

"And who said I wasn't?"

He laughed, pointing his finger at her. "You shouldn't joke."

"Oh, come on, it's not every day I get to laugh."

"Yeah, I suppose I could agree with you on that... for me, not you."

"Well, why don't we both resolve to change that? Every day, we find something to laugh about and something that brings us nothing but joy."

"Sounds like a plan to me."

Looking into Jack's eyes, her stomach twisted, and she looked away. Heat prickled along the back of her neck, and the dining room walls suddenly closed in on her. She hadn't meant for it to sound like they should be happy together. She had meant they should each find it in their own way. Unfortunately, the way it came out wasn't the way she'd planned for it to be. She stood and reached for her teacup, knocking it over instead of grabbing it. Tea spilled on the tablecloth, soaking the cream-colored material with a light brown tint.

"Oh! I did not mean to do that. I should get it cleaned up." She jumped to her feet, grabbing the cup and saucer with one hand and throwing her napkin on the stain with the other. She grabbed her breakfast plate and darted from the room.

She rushed into the kitchen. Her heart thumped as she set the dishes in the sink and grabbed another hand towel. She headed back to the dining room even though she only wanted to cling to a corner and hide from the world.

"I got it cleaned up as best as I could," Jack said as she returned. He handed her the napkin, stained with the same color as the tablecloth.

"That's all right. You didn't need to do anything. I guess I just wasn't paying attention to what I was doing." She took the napkin and pointed to another table. "Would you mind moving so I can clean the table off?"

"Oh, sure. No problem." He glanced over his shoulder, and although he moved, he kept his eyes on her. His brow furrowed. "Is everything all right?"

"Yes, of course. I just need to get this tablecloth under cold water before the stain sets in. I've come to know that tea can be difficult to remove." When Jack moved over to a different table, she went to work on gathering the tablecloth, folding it into itself to keep the stain from spreading before she threw the napkin on top.

She left the dining room again and returned to the kitchen, unfolding the cloth and reaching for the bucket of water she'd gathered before cooking. There was still enough left, and she dunked the tablecloth, closing her eyes and blowing a few breaths. Her mind was a mess of thoughts, and her hands trembled as she reached for the soap and used it on the cloth. Pungent-smelling suds bubbled around her fingers, and the material slipped from her grasp and fell to the floor.

"No. No. No. Don't do that," she whispered, hissing a breath through her clenched teeth. "I haven't swept the floor yet."

"May I help you with something?" a voice asked behind her.

Although she knew who it was, the sound still made her flinch. She glanced over her shoulder, chuckling. "Nah. I've got it."

"Wow. That's quite the pile of dishes." Jack pointed to all the breakfast dishes she'd taken from the guests after they finished eating and stacked them on the counter. "Do you need help with them?"

Her stomach fluttered. "Oh, no, you don't have to offer... this isn't any more than I have every meal. I'm used to it. I usually do them before I head to the barn to feed the animals and milk the cows."

"Well, I can help you with those chores too. I've got nothing else to do today. My sermon for Sunday is prepared, and I don't like interrupting Miss Evans while she's using the church for the school." He stared at her for a few seconds, waiting for her to say something. Before she could, though, he unbuttoned his cuffs and rolled up his sleeves.

"You don't have to do this," she said.

He shrugged. "I know I don't have to. But I want to." He grabbed the buckets next to the wash basins and headed to the water pump outside the back door.

Watching him fetch the water, a lump formed in Sarah's throat. Of course, the help would be appreciated. It was the one thing that she hated the most about running the inn alone—everything fell on her shoulders. Everything. The cooking. The cleaning. The laundry. Tending to the animals. Even fixing things that broke often fell upon her. Well, if she could. She had learned over the years how to fix a few things on her own. But she couldn't deny there were things that she had to ask Hank to do. Still, washing dishes wasn't one of those things, and she didn't want Jack to feel he had to help her.

"It's no trouble to do the dishes on my own," she said as he returned to the kitchen.

"I know you can do them. That was never my reason for wanting to help." He poured the water into the kettle, and after lighting the stove, he made his way over to the wash bins, laying the bars of soap in the bottom before organizing the plates and cups into stacks. "And don't even think about telling me that a woman should do this. Men can wash dishes. Or at least according to my mother, they should." He let out another chuckle.

It didn't take long for the water to heat, and steam rose all around Jack as he poured the water from the kettle into the wash basins and over the soap, creating puffy suds that bubbled and popped. He grabbed a plate, a cup, or a utensil one by one, washing the scraps from them before setting them in the other bucket to rinse them later.

Sarah watched him for several minutes, then continued working on the stain on the tablecloth until it was finally gone.

"I'm going to hang this to dry," she said, moving around Jack.

"It's freezing outside," he said. "That thing will freeze into a solid sheet of ice."

"I wasn't planning on taking it outside." She motioned toward a rack near the wood stove. "I was going to hang it near the stove. It shouldn't take long to dry there."

"Oh. Good plan." He cleared his throat, focusing on a cup in his hand.

After hanging the tablecloth and smoothing any wrinkles, she made her way over to the wash bins, grabbing the top plate on the stack before he could. "I can take it from here."

His brow furrowed, and for a moment, Sarah wondered if he would protest. He didn't, though. Instead, he half-smiled. "How about you wash, and I'll rinse and dry?"

"Are you negotiating with me?"

"Of course. And you should know I'm a master at it."

"Oh really? And where did you pick up such a skill? Were you a lawyer before you were a pastor or something?"

"No, I was a captain with the Texas Rangers."

She sucked in a breath, nearly choking on some spit that tried to go down her windpipe. After several deep coughs, she patted her chest and cleared her throat, trying to blink away a few tears before they streamed down her cheeks.

"Are you all right?" he asked. He reached for her but stopped as he glanced down at his dripping-wet hands.

"I'm fine. I'm fine." She coughed a couple more times and took several breaths. "I... I'm sorry, I just... you were a Texas Ranger?"

He nodded and shrugged but didn't say a word.

Sarah grabbed another plate, dunking it in the sudsy water as her mind traveled through distant memories of newspaper articles she had read throughout the years. Of course, most of the daily printed pages were full of local stories about a business opening or closing, a gold mining accident, something that had to do with the railroad, or an advertisement for a town gathering. However, occasionally, when a story was big enough to travel across the United States, Mr. Jenkins would print it. For the most part, these stories would be about the capture of a notorious murderer who had been on a robbing and killing streak, evading law enforcement until finally, the Texas Rangers got involved.

"But I left that life long ago," Jack finally said. "I'm a pastor now."

"How long ago? If you don't mind my asking."

"I retired about twelve years ago after a rather hard case with a gang led by a man named Sam Bass. He used to rob trains and banks, and it took us a while to get them, but my men and I got them. It wasn't without sacrifice, though."

His tone suddenly changed, and she couldn't help but feel a sense of unease, like there was more meaning behind his words.

Of course, she wondered what the story was, but she wasn't about to ask. "I'm sorry to hear that."

Jack shrugged again. "It's over and done with. Nothing I can do about anything that happened except forget about it and move on."

"Can you forget something like that, though? Capturing men like that... it's brave and heroic."

"There's nothing heroic about it." Jack's voice deepened, and he cleared his throat. He kept his chin tucked toward his chest, and his brow furrowed again. "I was just doing my job."

"Well, if that's what they call it in Texas, I can respect that. But—and I mean no offense by this—but in my mind... a man who risks his life to put a criminal behind bars is a hero."

He made a slight grunting noise, and although Sarah could tell he wanted to disagree, he didn't say another word. She wanted to press the issue further but didn't, deciding it was perhaps another conversation for another day. He had his reasons, and she wasn't about to pry. Even if she did want to, it wasn't her place.

Of course, she didn't know why he would think differently. Who would? Who would tell someone who made it their job to keep people safe they weren't a hero? Had something happened to make him feel otherwise? And if that were so—which seemed to be the case—what was it?

"Have you ever considered what you want in life? And whether or not how you're living now fits into your desires?" His sudden voice jerked her attention, and she paused before reaching for another plate.

"What do you mean?"

"Well, like running this inn, for instance. Is it everything you want?"

"Everything I want or everything I need?" She chuckled, glancing at him. The seriousness in his eyes caused her to pause and clear her throat. "I suppose it's everything I want. But if you're asking if I thought this was how my life would turn out, I would have to tell you no."

"I understand that. I have to wonder if that's normal, though. We can't all know what the future holds, just like we can't predict what will happen."

"Do you mean like with our spouses dying?"

He nodded.

"I would have to agree. And yes, that's mostly what I meant when I said this wasn't how I thought life would be. I think any widow or widower would agree."

"Has anyone asked you whether you wish to remarry?"

Her heart thumped—hard. Blood drained from her face, warming the shells of her ears as it traveled down her neck. She cleared her throat again. "Perhaps a few have asked me throughout the years, but not as of late. I think people around here have an idea."

"Have an idea that you don't wish to remarry?"

"It's not that I don't wish to. I just haven't thought about it."

"Why?" He held up his hands, promptly continuing the rest of the sentence. "If you don't mind my asking. I'm just curious."

The reason behind his question seemed innocent enough, even if the question itself wasn't. She'd thought of all the other times people had asked her the same thing and how she'd answered them. Of course, none of her answers were lies. She'd spoken the truth each time. However, the more she said the words—whether to others or herself—the more she wondered about them.

No bride ever walks down the aisle toward her forever, thinking about how there was a chance she would have to face anything alone. She had never once thought of how life would be without Harold, never imagined how she would feel or what she would do.

The thought had never crossed her mind.

Not until it had to while looking down at his coffin in the ground.

Sarah furrowed her brow at the pictured image in her mind. She scrubbed at the plate, watching the suds slip through her fingers like fleeting memories. The mention of remarriage stirred a dust storm of emotions within her, each grain a sharp reminder of her loss. Harold had been her dream and her hope, guiding her through life. At times, the thought of riding alongside someone else felt like a betrayal, a dagger twisting in the wound left by his absence. Then, other times, she would find herself longing to share the trials and triumphs and to have the companionship she had lived without for so long. It was a battle between the icy grip of loyalty to a love that had been her everything, which was now gone, and her longing for the warmth of a man's arms.

"If you think it's because I don't wish to think about it, you're wrong. I don't have the time with running the inn... it's all day and all night work."

"I'm sure it is, and I wasn't thinking anything. I assure you." He gave an awkward chuckle as though he hoped to smooth any ruffled feelings he'd stirred in her mind.

She wanted to think he hadn't unsettled her at all, but the truth of the matter was that he did. Although she'd made it a secret to most—other than Sue Ellen—she did often think about marrying another. It wasn't always pleasant thoughts. In fact, most of them made her squirm. The idea of kissing someone other than Harold or sharing a bed...

It made her legs prickle just thinking about it now.

Harold had been the only man she'd ever known or loved. He'd been her everything. And suddenly, he was gone. How was she supposed to just share those feelings with another man? Surely, other widows found happiness in the arms of another. But could she? Sometimes, she thought perhaps she could, and others, she didn't. It scared her too much.

Still, even with those fears, she also couldn't help but feel a sense of longing for the love and connection of a husband. She would watch Sue Ellen with both happiness that they had each other yet a hint of envy while she dwelled in her loneliness. Wouldn't it be nice to have love again? Wouldn't it be nice to have a marriage again?

The thought, certainly, was appealing.

"Have you ever thought of remarrying?" she asked him, trying to distract herself.

His head jerked slightly as though he hadn't seen the question coming, even though he should have.

"I suppose I have." He shrugged. "When the boys were younger, I didn't think about it. Not even after they left to live with their aunt, but as they got older, I didn't think it would bother them." He snorted. "Of course, I don't think anything I would or wouldn't do would bother them since they want nothing to do with their old man." His face twisted with his words as though it pained him to say what he did.

"I don't know how my children would feel about it. They probably wouldn't mind—Elena especially wouldn't, I think. I'm not sure about Luke. He and his father were close." She took a deep breath. "In the end, though, I would like to believe they would want me to be happy."

Jack turned his head toward her. "Are you not now?"

Her stomach fluttered. "I am. That's not what I meant. I meant if I decided that I wanted to fall in love again and remarry, I would hope they would both want that for me. But that doesn't mean I'm not happy now."

"I understand. Perhaps it was foolish of me to ask such a thing."

"Are you happy now?" She smiled as she glanced at him, hoping he would understand the mocking undertone of her voice. She grabbed another plate and dunked it under the water, scrubbing the food from it.

"Yes, I am." He chuckled. "I have enjoyed starting this new life as a pastor. It has brought a lot of healing and joy. I suppose I could say that I wonder if something is missing in not having a wife or a marriage. But I am fulfilled, or at least I feel as though I am. Perhaps God would say otherwise. We don't know His plans."

She handed him the plate, and as he reached for it, their fingers brushed against one another. His touch made her stomach flip, and she caught her breath. Her heart pounded like the hooves of a runaway horse. She glanced down at his fingers, strong and steady yet gentle in their grasp. They paused, suspended in time, as if the world had stilled around them, and after what felt like minutes, he finally took the plate and rinsed it, setting it aside so they could dry it with the rest later.

"No, we don't," she whispered.

Jack glanced at her and inhaled a deep breath. "I should head upstairs. My first sermon is tomorrow, and I should prepare."

"Do you know what you're going to say?"

He shook his head. "Not yet. But I'm sure the right words will come to me."

ELEVEN

JACK

Voices carried through the office door even though it was shut. Townsfolk had started arriving for church this morning, and while Jack had gone over his sermon at least a dozen times, he suddenly felt like he hadn't even looked at it while writing it. This wasn't the first sermon he'd given since leaving the Texas Rangers. But it was the first time in Featherstone Valley—a town that had spent the good part of the first few days after he arrived talking about him behind his back.

If he weren't already intimidated enough, just moving to a new town without knowing a soul would have pushed him over the edge, and it did. He would never admit to anyone—it was bad enough he had to admit it to himself—but his confidence had been shaken. Of course, that had happened to him a time or two before. He was never like this. Not until Maryanne died. It's hard to be sure of yourself when you are the cause of something so horrible it is beyond words.

But that was his burden to bear.

And one that he'd live with for the rest of his life.

The problem was deciding how much of what had happened he wanted to divulge. Did he want to tell the good people of

Featherstone Valley the truth? Or did he want to give them a vague account, leaving out details he didn't think they had a right to know?

"You tell them whatever you wish to tell them or don't tell them anything at all. It's none of their business," Sarah told him last night when he broached the subject. She had been rather adamant about it too, standing her ground in the opinion that her own town should only know what he wanted them to know and nothing more.

There was a time he would have wholeheartedly agreed with her.

But he couldn't deny that as soon as he thought about it, the guilt would wash through him, tightening his chest. He never wanted to lie to anyone, and he never wanted to hide anything either. And he'd already done the latter with Sarah a few times. First, he did not tell her about his sons, then he did not tell her about his wife, and lastly, even though he told her about his family, he still hadn't told her what happened.

A knock rapped on the office door, and before he could say a word, the knob twisted, and the door cracked open. Sarah poked her head inside and smiled. "I'm not interrupting anything, am I?"

"Not at all. Come in."

"I didn't see you before you left the inn this morning, and with the door shut, I must admit I was worried."

He snorted. "Did you think I left?"

"I'm not going to lie. The image of you jumping out of that window behind you did cross my mind. As did you in your suit, running through the field away from the church and glancing over your shoulder to ensure no one was running after you."

"You think someone would run after me?"

She shrugged. "Probably. It's been a few months since we've had a pastor in town. I think everyone is determined to keep you."

"Perhaps they shouldn't write gossip articles about me then."

She smiled and nodded. "It's probably better that I not say anything regarding that."

"It's probably better if I don't either." He cocked his head, smiling as he blinked at her and hoped she would take his movements for the mocking joke he meant them as.

She laughed, and then her smile faded. "Are you going to say anything to any of them?"

Jack inhaled a deep breath. He'd given that question much thought in the last few days. He shrugged, then glanced over his shoulder, staring at the scraps of paper on which he'd written the notes for his sermon. He hoped that he would approach the congregation the way Jesus would, that he wouldn't lecture or be confrontational, but that he would advise with kindness and support. He would never make the one mistake he swore he never would. He would never judge or confront again. That was the old Jack. Not the new one.

That was not the man he wanted to be in this town.

It was not the pastor he wanted to be either.

At the same time, he would not be forced to play a hand he didn't want to play either. He cleared his throat. "You should find your seat. I think the service is about to start."

SARAH

"How is Pastor Boone feeling?" Sue Ellen barely let Sarah take her seat before she leaned in and whispered in Sarah's ear. Mrs. Newman, who was sitting in front of them, glanced over her shoulder, giving Sarah a sideways look before turning her attention back to the empty pulpit standing at the front of the room.

"He's all right." Sarah eyed the woman, trying to ignore how, although she couldn't see Mrs. Newman's face or hear her thoughts, she could read them like they were the book sitting on the end table near her chair in the inn's parlor. Of all the women she'd thought about this week when trying to figure out who Prudence Chatterton was, Mrs. Newman hadn't crossed her mind. Now, Sarah wondered why.

It would make sense.

She was always around Mrs. Gables. In fact, most days, those two were attached at the hip. Sometimes, Sarah even wondered if their husbands minded how much time those two spent together. The only difference between them was that Mrs. Newman was also more of a quiet type, keeping next to Mrs. Gables but not saying much whenever the two conversed with anyone other than each other.

"He said to take my seat because he was about ready to get started. I think he's excited." Sarah raised her voice a little, and as Sue Ellen furrowed her brow in confusion, Sarah moved her eyes from her friend to Mrs. Newman and then back to Sue Ellen, repeating the dance until Sue Ellen seemed to understand.

"Ah. Well, I'm sure he will do a fabulous job."

"I think so too."

The two women exchanged another glance, and before anyone could say another word, the office door opened, and Jack stepped out. Everyone around the room silenced and stared at him. Sarah's chest tightened, and her heart pounded. Nervous for him, she fidgeted with her hands.

"Good morning, everyone," he said, moving toward the pulpit. Light filtered through the church's windows, illuminating the room in a warm glow. It had always been the prettiest little church, or at least Sarah thought so, fitting to the town with its bright white painted walls and chocolate-colored stained pews. Having the children use it for their schoolhouse only seemed to give it a warmer feel, as though more love than it could hold pulsed through its veins.

As Jack laid his Bible on the pulpit, a collective assortment of 'good mornings' was said throughout the small church, and he looked around the room, meeting a few sets of eyes before finding Sarah's. A lump formed in her throat. He'd seemed so confident when she left him in his office, and she hoped he still felt the same. She knew she shouldn't worry, yet it was all she could do.

"I have to say what a joy it is this morning to stand before you today as your new pastor in this beautiful community of Featherstone Valley. Reflecting on my initial days here, I have been pleasantly surprised by the warmth and welcoming spirit each of you has extended to me. Indeed, Featherstone Valley is a wonderful town filled with wonderful people, and I am grateful to be part of this family of faith. As we gather here today, let us turn our hearts and minds to the Word of God, seeking wisdom and guidance for our journey together. Now, if you will, please turn to *Proverbs 16:28*."

He paused, opened his Bible, and waited for everyone to take theirs out and find the right page before he started reading. "*Proverbs 16:28 says,* A perverse person stirs up conflict, and a gossip separates close friends." He looked around the room, staring into the faces as they stared back at him. The tension throughout everyone's shoulders stiffened, and Sarah tried not to smile.

"So, what is this verse trying to say?" He continued. "Well, it is my belief the wisdom of Proverbs provides insight into the impact of our words and the understanding of the power of the tongue. It describes how a seemingly small action, like gossip, can stir up significant conflict. Despite its size, the tongue holds immense power to build or destroy. Gossip, like a perverse action, can separate close friends and disrupt the harmony within relationships. It doesn't just harm individuals either. It corrupts the very fabric of relationships, and the toxicity of gossip can lead to the separation of close friends and create discord within the community. Words spoken in gossip can sow seeds of doubt and mistrust, causing fractures in the bonds we hold dear."

As Jack paused again, Sarah glanced at Sue Ellen and then looked at the backs of Mrs. Neman's and Mrs. Gables' heads. A tiny part of her wished she could see their faces.

"So, what can we do from now on? First, we must recognize that we are all prone to faults; then let us approach one another with grace and humility, creating an environment where love covers a multitude of sins. Let our words be a source of encouragement, edification, and blessing. Choose words that build up rather than tear down. We must also forgive. The Bible is rich with verses that speak to the transformative power of forgiveness, urging us to extend this grace to one another. In *Colossians 3:13*, we are reminded to bear with each other and forgive one another, just as the Lord forgave us, and the Lord's Prayer in *Matthew 6:12* encourages us to forgive others as we have been forgiven.

"Gossip has no place in the kingdom of God, and we are called to be people who bring life and healing through our words. Many argue, 'But Pastor Boone, if only those who wronged me expressed remorse, I might consider forgiveness.' And when they say that, I say to them, 'However, such contrition is rarely forthcoming, and we often use this as a pretext to harbor bitterness, anger, and the desire for retaliation.' If we stop and contemplate Jesus on the cross, we will find that no one expresses regret. Even as he spoke those words, the crowd scoffed, mocked, and reveled in his suffering. Those who passed by hurled insults, challenging him to prove his kingship by descending from the cross. The forces of darkness appeared victorious, and the Son of God was about to be laid in the tomb. No one admitted culpability, yet Jesus said, "Father, forgive them, for they don't know what they are doing." This is precisely the sentiment we must embody to follow Jesus. We must extend forgiveness to those who deliberately and persistently harm us, to those who maliciously attack us, and even to those who inadvertently inflict wounds upon us. This includes those closest to us—spouses, children, parents, friends... and even neighbors."

He paused again, drawing in a deep breath. Not a single sound echoed. Sarah looked around the room. Several townsfolk began shifting in their seats, and she smiled as she caught Jack's eye. The two of them stared at one another, and while she wasn't sure what he was thinking, she had a pretty good idea. Would he tell everyone what they wanted to hear, or would he keep silent?

"I hope that I encourage you to be builders of hope and bearers of blessing. In the words of *Ephesians 4:29*, let us choose expressions that uplift and inspire rather than tear down with the weight of negativity. As we navigate the challenge of combating gossip, let us not forget the overwhelming gift of forgiveness bestowed upon us by our gracious God. The Scriptures overflow with verses emphasizing the transformative power of forgiveness, urging us to extend this divine grace to one another. In *Colossians 3:13*, we are gently reminded to bear with each other and forgive, just as the Lord forgave us. The Lord's Prayer, found in *Matthew 6:12*, echoes the call to forgive others as we have been forgiven. In drawing this time of reflection to a close, dear congregation, let us ponder the profound impact of our words and recognize the weighty responsibility we carry as followers of Christ. Gossip has no place in the kingdom of God, and we are commissioned to be a people who bring life and healing through the spoken word. May we be ever mindful of the influence our tongues wield and strive to use them in a manner that glorifies God, building one another up. Amen."

"Amen," everyone said in response.

Jack closed his Bible and gave Sarah one last fleeting look before stepping away from the pulpit and walking through the pews toward the doors. He opened them up, letting the sunlight filter in, and a gentle breeze brought in a wash of fresh air. Everyone in the church glanced at one another before standing and walking toward the doors.

Jack smiled and nodded at each couple, shaking the men's hands as they passed.

"T'was a fine sermon today, Pastor Boone," Mr. Fields was the first to say a word.

"Thank you. I'm glad to hear it."

A few more men echoed Mr. Field's sentiment and shook Jack's hand as they passed him, telling him how much they enjoyed it and were thankful he was here.

Sarah skirted out of the pew behind Mr. and Mrs. Gables and Mr. and Mrs. Newman. Sue Ellen and Hank followed her, and Sue Ellen wasted no time elbowing Sarah. Sarah nodded toward her friend, inching closer to the two couples as they neared Jack.

Mr. and Mrs. Gables stopped first, and after Mr. Gables introduced them and shook Jack's hand, Mrs. Gables hooked her arm through her husband's and brushed her collarbone with the other hand.

"It was a beautiful sermon, Pastor Boone," she said. "I must admit it was a little short for my taste, but it was effectual."

Effectual?

Sarah jerked her head, scrunching her nose as she listened to Mrs. Gables stumble through the words she was trying to say. Sue Ellen covered her mouth with her hand as though she meant to stifle her laughter, and although Jack caught Sarah's eye for a moment, he kept his attention on Mrs. Gables.

"That was the point, Mrs. Gables," he said. "I thought it best not to lecture too long but just to let everyone think and pray on the matter in their own time."

"Well, I hope they do! What you said was much needed around here as of late. I haven't the slightest idea what Mr. Jenkins is thinking, printing such an ad in his newspapers."

"It's quite all right. I am no stranger to words being said behind someone's back. It's unfortunate, but it happens."

"Well, whether it happens or not, I did complain to him, but whether anything will be done is anyone's guess. He's not often the sharpest tool in the shed, if you know what I mean. No matter that, though, I still told him exactly what I thought of the column."

"I did, too," Mrs. Newman said. She straightened her shoulders as she stood arm in arm with her husband, who introduced himself and his wife after she spoke.

"I thank you both for the support. Although, I have to say, should Mr. Jenkins decide to keep the column, that is his choice. I will not say anything more on the subject. Thank you both for coming today. I hope I will see you next week."

"Yes, of course." Although only Mr. Gables spoke, the rest of the three nodded to agree with him, and with another few goodbyes said to the two couples, Jack glanced toward Sarah, smiling.

"It was a wonderful sermon, Pastor," she said, winking.

"Thank you."

"Are you pleased with your choice?"

"I am. We shall see what comes of it."

"Yes, it will be interesting." She chuckled, but only slightly, and as she noticed Mrs. Gables and Mrs. Newman looking at her just before they left the church and Jack, she cleared her throat. "Well, I guess I shall see you back at the inn."

"Yes, of course. I should return around lunchtime." He tipped his hat at her, and her cheeks warmed. She hadn't seen him dressed up in his Sunday best before today, and she couldn't help but notice it suited him rather well.

After Sue Ellen and Hank said their goodbyes, the three made their way out of the church and down the stairs. The early morning hour had already given way to the early afternoon, and although the sun shone high in the sky, the snow left a chill in the air and caused their breath to cloud their faces.

"So," Sue Ellen moved up alongside Sarah, glancing at her a few times before she continued, "are you going to tell me what that was all about?"

"What was what all about?"

"That look between you and Pastor Boone." Sue Ellen wiggled her eyebrows and cocked her head to the side. "And don't even say that you don't know what I'm talking about because that's a lie."

"There wasn't a look."

"Yes, there was. And I saw it. I'm sure Hank saw it, too." She pointed at her husband, who looked at both women. His eyes widened. "You saw it too, didn't you?"

He clamped his mouth shut and dropped his gaze to the ground.

Sue Ellen let out a sigh and turned back to Sarah. "He saw it. He just doesn't want to say. But I know what I saw, and I *will* say it. Is something going on between you and the pastor?"

"What? No. He's a nice man, and I've enjoyed having him at the inn. We've had a few lovely conversations, but that's all it is. Once Mayor Duncan finds him a house to rent and he moves out of the inn... I will probably only see him on Sundays."

"It's all right if you like him or want to have feelings for him. You are allowed to fall in love again."

Sarah clenched her teeth. She didn't want to have this conversation, not now, not ever, and she deepened her tone in the hope that Sue Ellen would take the hint. "I'm aware of that, and I never said I thought otherwise. Although it's kind of you to say it, I don't need the reminder because nothing is going on."

While she didn't tell her friend a lie, she couldn't say it was the truth, either. She wanted to forget the hint of longing she felt while they were washing dishes and how much she enjoyed his company whenever he was in the room. It wasn't that he reminded her of Harold either. They were two different men. Still, something about him made her stomach flutter, and her knees weakened every time he smiled.

As Sarah left the church, a sea of emotions churned within her. The brief exchange of smiles, the subtle touch of their hands—each moment was etched in her mind, stirring feelings she thought had long been buried. She found herself stealing glances at him whenever she could, admiring how his presence commanded the room and how the conviction in his voice always made her feel safe. It was more than just admiration; it was an undeniable pull, a connection that excited and terrified her.

Sitting in the pew this morning, Sarah's thoughts wandered into questions she didn't know if she wanted answers to. What was it about Jack that drew her in so? Was it his strength, his kindness, or the way he seemed to understand the weight of loss?

Or was it just him?

She couldn't deny that the walls she had built around her heart since Harold's passing had started to crack, and it both thrilled and scared her. Opening her heart to someone else felt like a betrayal of Harold's memory. Yet the loneliness that had been her constant companion whispered that it was time to let go, and as she thought of his words about forgiveness and moving forward, it was as if he were speaking directly to her, urging her to release the past and embrace the possibility of a new future.

But could she?

Was she ready to take that leap, to allow herself the chance to love and be loved again?

She longed for a sign, a nudge in the right direction. The brief moments of connection with Jack had sparked something within her, a flicker of something she couldn't quite name. It was a feeling she knew she couldn't ignore, no matter how much it scared her.

"Sue Ellen, I don't know what you're talking about. Nothing is going on."

Sue Ellen inhaled a deep breath. "When you want to admit it, you will."

"There's nothing to admit." The lie felt bitter on her tongue, but she said it anyway. For the truth of it *was* that there was something to admit. The problem was that she wasn't about to say anything to anyone.

Not even Sue Ellen.

She could barely say it to herself.

TWELVE

JACK

The late afternoon sun had begun its arch over the sky as Jack stared out his bedroom window at the inn. His interest was piqued through the frosted glass, and his gaze followed Sarah while she did her chores around the barn. Chickens ran around her feet as she threw them dried corn; the golden kernels littered the white snow while the birds pecked at them and squawked. Although he couldn't hear the inn owner, he imagined her talking to the fowl, either telling them about her day or the rumors around town. Perhaps she said nothing like that at all. Perhaps she merely lectured them on not giving her enough eggs or how she disliked taking care of them in the winter. He didn't know, but it didn't matter. It all still made him smile.

She made him smile.

He folded his arms across his chest, and *Jeremiah 31:3* came to his mind. 'Love yesterday, today, and forever,' the verse says.

Although he wanted to snort at the idea of love—and a few years ago, or even months ago, he would have—he couldn't. Not now. It wasn't that he had suddenly found it again. He honestly didn't know what his thoughts were at the moment. But there was still something different inside him. He hadn't looked for love in the years since Maryanne's death. It wasn't that he didn't want to find it. It just wasn't important to him. Of course, he would meet lovely women in the churches he spoke at. But none of them had ever sparked his interest enough to pursue any courtship.

They weren't like Sarah.

She was different. He just couldn't put his finger on why.

Perhaps it was just her kindness. Or perhaps it was also the slight roughness she had about her, like she wasn't about to take anything from anyone, at least not without a good reason. She seemed like the first one to be willing to help someone in need, yet she wouldn't let anyone walk all over her or even step on her toes. Her brains, beauty, and a little brawn gave her this overwhelming sense of independence. He felt drawn to it, and even more so when he also saw hints that she was a woman who needed someone at times, even if it was just for a warm hug and the comforting words that everything would be all right.

We all have those moments, no matter how strong we are, and he saw that Sarah was no different.

Another smile inched across his lips as she shut the gate to the chicken coop and grabbed the pitchfork next to a hay bale in front of the cows' pen. Both cows moved toward her, belting sounds so loud they echoed through the closed window. She shoved the forked tool into a pile of hay, throwing several scoops over the fence to the awaiting bovines, who happily began munching away, not caring that a flake flew back onto her, covering her with a layer of hay that, although she tried to dust off, stuck all over different parts of her coat and in her hair. Jack covered his mouth to stifle his laugh even though he knew she couldn't hear him.

The overwhelming urge to help her hit him square in the chest, and before he thought about it, he turned away from the window, slipped his feet into his boots, and headed downstairs and outside.

A soft breeze cooled his skin, and he yanked the collar of his jacket up around his neck before tying his scarf tighter.

"May I help you with anything?" he asked as he approached. She spun to face him, looking as though he'd caught her off guard, and he smiled, chuckling slightly to himself. "Sorry. I didn't mean to scare you."

"It's all right. I'm just about done." She pointed toward the hay and the cows.

Hay stems still littered the front of her from her hair down to her waist, and as she brushed them off, a few from the top of her head fell in her face. She blew at them. It didn't help, and they clung to her hair like they were beings adrift in the ocean, clinging to a lifeboat.

He chuckled again, this time a little louder. "Here. Let me help you." He moved toward her, picking each stalk of hay from her greying curls. The strands moved through his fingers, and for the first time, he noticed how little she was. Surely, he'd seen she was short since the moment he met her, but as his body towered over hers, there was something different about looking down into her eyes this afternoon. He wanted to wrap his arms around her, enveloping her in an embrace that protected her from anything and everything.

"I think I got them all," he said, picking out the last stem.

"Thank you."

"I can imagine that happens a lot."

"Every time I feed them." She let out a slight laugh. "Sometimes I find hay on my pillow when I wake in the morning. I try to get it all out, but when I don't have someone helping… I miss pieces." Her voice softened as she finished her sentence, and by the time she said the last word, it was a mere whisper.

Although she tried to hide it, Jack sensed a hint of sadness in her.

"Well, I will help you with that. I can help you feed, too, while I'm here. Honestly, not having something to do each day is wearing on me. I'm used to having a home that needs work. There was always something to do on the ranch in Texas."

"Was it a big ranch?" She moved around him, setting the pitchfork against the fence.

He glanced at the tool, then at her. "Not for Texas." He chuckled. "Most ranches there are hundreds of acres. I only owned ten. I bought it right after I married, and we built the house." He paused, needing a distraction and a change of subject. "What other chores do you have to do?"

"I just have to gather the firewood." She pointed toward a large pile near the back door.

"How much do you need?"

"I need a basket in the kitchen, a basket in the parlor, and a basket for each guest. It's just you and Mr. Schneider tonight since Mr. Clemons left." She paused, looking toward the little house several yards from them near the barn. It was small and needed work, but it was a quaint, modest little place with a dark red door and white shutters. "And I need a basket in my cabin. But I can fetch it all. It's no trouble."

"No, please, let me." Jack turned, and as he looked upon the wood, a chill that wasn't from the weather washed through him. He paused, inhaling a deep breath. He hadn't thought about what he'd just volunteered to do, and the sudden realization of the task in front of him hit him square in the chest.

Just what had I agreed to?

A thin layer of sweat spread across his forehead as he neared the stack of wood, and as he closed his eyes, he tried to fight the pictured images of his wife lying dead in the dirt from flashing in his mind.

"Don't do it," he whispered to himself.

He'd found her near the stack of firewood behind their cabin, with her arms and legs sprawled as though she'd been running when someone jumped on her, throwing her to the ground. Claw marks on her face and neck, as well as her whole body covered in dirt stains, spoke of a struggle, and from the finger-shaped bruises around her neck, her death hadn't been quick, like a gunshot to the chest or head.

She had looked her killer in the eyes.

She had known she was going to die.

He grabbed a couple of chunks of wood and set them on the stack. The sound echoed in his mind. It was the same one his wood had made as he bumped into the stack of wood outside his home, rushing toward his wife. A few pieces were knocked loose and tumbled to the ground, rolling around him as he dropped to his knees and grabbed Maryanne. Her body was limp in his arms as she looked up at the sky, lifeless.

His body tightened, and he stepped away from the wood stack. His breath quickened. The thin layer of sweat worsened, moistening the collar of his shirt. He grabbed the material, tugging it away from his skin. The world around him started to spin.

"Jack?" Sarah called out.

Although he heard her voice, he couldn't respond.

"Jack?" she asked again. "Are you all right?"

Frozen, he shook his head. He knew he had to say something, anything. But no matter how often he opened his mouth, nothing came out.

Sarah rushed to him, moving around to face him. "Jack? Are you all right?"

He looked at her, and for a moment, the image of his dead wife changed. It wasn't Maryanne's face he saw, but Sarah's, and it was her lying dead in the dirt.

His body jerked in reaction to his thoughts, and Sarah's eyes widened. She took a step back and laid her hand on her chest.

"Jack? What is wrong?"

He shook his head again. "Nothing. It's nothing."

"It doesn't feel like it's nothing. Are you all right?"

"Of course." He cleared his throat and set the basket of wood onto the stack. "I'm sorry, Sarah, I need to... I'm going to have to excuse myself."

Before she said a word, he spun and strode off. His heart hammered in his chest. He didn't know what to be madder at—for leaving Sarah in the manner in which he did or allowing himself to fall prey to his own mind. He'd always tried to separate the emotions of his life and work. He'd also always tried not to let himself get caught up in the past. Why should he think about it? It wasn't like it was going to change.

Maryanne would still be dead.

And Sam Bass' men would still be the ones who killed her.

He couldn't let it happen again.

He couldn't let his past kill another innocent woman.

He needed to stay as far away as he could from Sarah Holden, and she needed to stay just as far away from him.

SARAH

No matter how much Sarah wanted to call after Jack, she didn't. Instead, she stood near the wood pile, watching him disappear through the inn's back door. She laid her hand on her chest, trying to replay the last few minutes in her mind.

Had she done something wrong?

Had she said something, she shouldn't have.

She repeated the conversation. She hadn't said anything other than simply telling him he didn't need to help her. He was fine until he approached the woodpile. Then he wasn't.

What was it about the woodpile that freaked him out?

She furrowed her brow and scratched her head before bending down to fetch the basket. She threw several chunks of wood inside the woven pieces of wicker, carrying the first load to her cabin, where she piled them near the stove. Then she returned to the woodpile to gather more wood chunks for the inn's guests and the kitchen.

A thin layer of sweat stuck to the back of her neck, and she wiped the back of her hand across her forehead, blowing out a breath.

"Ms. Holden?" a voice called out.

Sarah turned to see Miss Evans, the schoolteacher, walking toward the inn. Miles Jr. and Millie walked alongside her, and she waved as she saw Sarah. "Ms. Holden?"

"Good afternoon, Miss Evans," Sarah said as the three of them passed through the gate and rounded the corner of the inn. "How are you this afternoon?"

"Oh, just fine." The schoolteacher blew out a breath before raking her fingers through the curls piled on top of her head. "I'm glad I caught you. Mr. Fields asked if I could bring the children to the inn this afternoon after school. He needs them to stay for the night if the offer still stands."

"Of course, it does. They are both more than welcome." Sarah glanced down at the young boy and girl. "You know," she bent down and tapped Millie on the tip of the little girl's nose. "In fact, I was just thinking I need to make cookies. But the problem is, I didn't know who would eat them. What do you two think about taking on the job? Do you think you have what it takes?"

The children smiled and nodded, and as Millie lifted her finger to her face and scratched her nose, her forehead scrunched.

"Ms. Holden, why did Pastor Jack leave?"

Sarah cocked her head to the side. "Leave? I don't understand what you mean."

"We saw him while we were walking toward the inn, and he

looked sad about something." She scratched her nose again. "Did you guys argue about something like Miles and I do?"

Sarah glanced at Miss Evans, watching the young teacher's eyes widen as she placed her hands on Millie's shoulders.

"It's not polite to ask people if they are arguing with someone else," Miss Evans said to the girl.

"We weren't arguing." Sarah's gaze darted from the two children to the teacher, then back again, and she lightened her voice, almost giving it an amused chuckle. She blurted out the words before she had a chance to think about them, and in her haste, she feared she'd only made their suspicions worse. She cleared her throat. "He just had a thought that made him sad for a moment. But he will be fine. I'm sure he will come down for dinner, and you'll see the same happy Pastor you have come to know."

Sarah's stomach clenched as she told her lie. She hated telling them, however big or small. Harold used to laugh at her, telling her that sometimes small ones were needed and not to worry. No matter what, though, she always worried.

"Shall we go inside and start making the cookies?"

"Yes!" both children shouted.

Sarah laughed, waving to Miss Evans before she led the children to the inn's kitchen.

"Don't touch. It's hot." Sarah fanned the pan as she set it on the counter. The children rushed toward it, each reaching for a cookie. She blocked them with her arm, and they retreated at her words.

"Sorry, Ms. Holden," Millie said. The girl jerked her hand away and stuck out her bottom lip.

"It's all right. You're not in trouble. I just don't want you to get hurt. Let me take the cookies off the pan, and then you can have one after they've cooled."

"Yes, Ms. Holden."

Sarah grabbed each cookie and placed them on a plate. The hot treats burned the tips of her fingers, and she blew on them after several cookies as though she thought it would help. It didn't. After taking all the cookies off the pan, she scooped more raw dough into small balls, placed each ball onto the pan where the cooked ones had been, and slid the pan back into the oven. After she repeated the process two more times, putting the new cookies on the plate on top of the others, the kitchen filled with the scent of brown sugar, vanilla, and chocolate.

The children took cookies from each batch, arguing back and forth about which was better—hot or cooled. Millie argued that a cooled cookie was better, while Miles Jr. wanted them hot.

"But when they are hot, you can't enjoy them because all you can think about is how hot they are," Millie said.

"But when they are hot, the chocolate melts in your mouth." Miles Jr. shook his head. "Hot is the best."

The two continued back and forth while Sarah placed a few cookies on a small plate. She glanced up at the ceiling, taking a deep breath as she thought about going to Jack's door or leaving him alone. She certainly didn't wish to bother him, but she also didn't want him to feel he had no one to talk to if he needed someone.

"Don't touch anymore until I return, all right?" she said.

"Where are you going, Ms. Holden?" Millie asked.

"I'm just going to see if Pastor Boone would like some cookies."

While the children continued their argument over hot and cooled, Sarah grabbed the plate and made her way upstairs, meandering down the hallway until she came upon Jack's door.

She bit her lip, hesitating, before she clenched her fist and knocked.

"Yes?" Jack asked from the other side of the door.

"Millie and Miles Jr. are staying with me tonight, and we made cookies. I brought some up in case you wanted to try them. They are chocolate chip."

She held her breath as she waited for him to open the door.

He didn't.

"I don't want any."

"Are you sure?"

"Yes, I'm sure." He paused. "Thank you for thinking of me, though."

"You're welcome." She turned to leave, but an idea twisted in her stomach. Just leave the plate, she thought to herself.

Before even considering whether it was the right choice, she set the plate on the floor in front of the door and headed back downstairs. Even if he didn't want to come down, perhaps he would understand them to mean what she hoped—that she was there if he needed a friend.

~

JACK

Jack heard Sarah's footsteps as she left the door and returned down the hallway toward the staircase.

He closed his eyes, trying to remember the tone he'd just used and praying he hadn't sounded as rude as he thought he had. The last thing he wanted to do was treat her worse than he already had. Standing out by the pile of firewood, he had been screaming at himself to stop the damage he was creating, yet no matter how much he had, he lost all control. He allowed his past and his memories to overthrow his own mind and body, and he had walked away from her.

He closed his eyes, rubbing his forehead with his fingertips. How could he be so foolish? He wanted to do better not just for himself but for others. He wanted to be there, wherever needed, not allowing his own pain and strife to cause hurt and confusion in others.

Which is perhaps precisely what he'd done.

At least, he thought he had.

He didn't exactly know for sure.

He raked his hands through his hair, blowing a deep breath and letting it puff his cheeks. He needed to make this right, to be the better man he wanted to be.

Before he could even ask himself another question, he turned and headed for the door, opening it. As he took a step, his boot kicked at a plate, and he looked down, watching as the few cookies on the dish shifted. One of them fell to the floor. He bent down, picking up the plate and cookies, and while he threw the one that had fallen off in the trash, he grabbed another one and took a bite.

Man, that woman can cook, he thought to himself as he headed down the hallway and descended the stairs.

L ittle voices carried through the inn's dining room as he approached the kitchen and hesitated at the threshold. Listening to them, a smile tugged at the corners of his lips despite the turmoil churning inside him. He couldn't deny that a part of him wanted to turn around and retreat to the solitude of his room to hide from the happiness that seemed foreign to him now. But another part, a part he thought he had lost, yearned to be part of this simple, joyful moment.

Taking a deep breath, Jack forced himself to step forward, to push aside the shadows of his past and embrace the light of the present.

Millie and Miles Jr. were laughing about something, and as Jack pushed open the door, the two children silenced and paused, looking at him for a moment before they realized he was there.

"Pastor Jack!" Millie squealed. "Do you want to help us make cookies?"

Sarah glanced at him as he let the door shut behind him, noticing the empty plate in his hand.

"Here," he said, handing her the plate. "They were delicious. Thank you."

"You're welcome." She gave him another smile as she took the plate and set it in the sink to wash later.

"So, are you going to help us with the cookies?" Millie asked again, scratching her nose.

"Sure. I can help. What do you need help with?" He moved toward the counter, grabbing another two cookies from the cooling plate and popping one in his mouth whole. Millie's eyes widened, and Miles Jr. laughed.

"I wish I could do that, but Pa always tells me it's not good manners."

Jack chuckled, nodding as he chewed and swallowed the cookie. "He's right. Forgive my lack of manners just now." Instead of eating the second cookie whole, he ate it in a few bites.

Sarah glanced up at the ceiling and giggled before she turned toward the oven and grabbed her apron, using the material to protect her hands. She opened the oven door and looked at the cookies baking inside.

"Are they done, Ms. Holden?" Millie asked.

"Not quite. I think they need a few more minutes."

"Can we have another cookie, Ms. Holden, now that Pastor Boone is with us?" Miles Jr. pointed toward Jack and smiled as though he hoped the sudden appearance of another adult would be a great excuse for them all to enjoy one more cookie.

Sarah cocked her head to the side, raising one eyebrow. Jack sensed the hesitation in her mind, and he wondered how much the children had enjoyed before he came downstairs. Surely, it was several. How could anyone not eat Sarah's cookies until their stomachs burst? Jack himself even wanted about a dozen more.

"Please..." Miles Jr. let the 's' in his word hiss for a second, then clasped his hands together.

"All right, fine. You can have one more. But then, no more until after you've had some dinner. The last thing I need is you two getting a tummy ache while you're staying here."

The children exclaimed with delight, and while Millie grabbed one of the cookies, Miles Jr. hesitated.

"Don't you want a cookie?" Jack asked. "Isn't that why you asked for another one?"

"He wants one of the hot ones," Millie said, hooking her thumb over her shoulder as though to point at the oven. "He thinks they are better even though they aren't."

"Yes, they are." Upon his argument, Miles Jr. grabbed a handful of flour and threw it at his sister. The white powder covered her head from her hair to her face, and she screamed.

Sarah whipped around, but before she could tell either child to stop, Millie grabbed her own handful of flour and threw it at her brother. Her aim wasn't as great, and because he expected it, Miles Jr. stepped away, barely getting hit. Displeased that he'd gotten away, Millie grabbed another handful and stepped forward, launching the second at a closer distance. This time, although Miles Jr. tried to move, she was closer, and she hit him square in the chest.

He jumped backward, then lunged forward, grabbing another handful of flour just as Sarah lunged for them. The scene played out in slow motion, and as Miles Jr. threw the flour at his sister, Sarah stepped between them. The flour hit Sarah, spraying her dress with white powder. Miles Jr. and

Millie gasped, and Millie covered her mouth with her hand. Jack just stood there, paralyzed as to what to do or say.

Sarah looked at both children, and while Jack thought she would start yelling, her mouth twisted into a smile instead. Before anyone said anything, she hurried to the counter and grabbed two handfuls of flour, throwing one at each of the children.

The children began laughing and running around the kitchen, and Sarah ran with them. All three laughed as they grabbed handfuls of flour, tossing them at one another in a war that made the kitchen look like it had snowed.

Jack laughed, and as he took in the scene, he couldn't help but remember a time when his sons chased Maryanne around the kitchen with the fish they'd caught from the pond that morning. Maryanne never liked fish. She never liked eating it. She never liked cooking it. And she never liked it when the boys brought their daily catches into the house.

Jack continued watching the scene and laughing until someone cleared their throat behind him. The sound also silenced Sarah and the children, and everyone turned to see who had entered the kitchen.

"Mrs. Gables," Sarah said, brushing the flour from her apron. Her lungs slightly heaved from running around the kitchen, and she made her way over to the woman, trying to act as though she was pretending the nosy woman didn't just witness her throwing flour and making a mess. "What can I help you with?"

Mrs. Gables' mouth hung open as she looked around the kitchen and at everyone's faces. "Um... I... " She closed her mouth. Her eyes were wide. "I just came by to ask if you would make some pies for the social after church next Sunday."

"Social? What social?"

"A few of the wives and I got together and decided that we would like to have a town social next week after church as a way of welcoming Pastor Boone." Mrs. Gables looked at Jack. "If that's all right with you."

"Of course," he said. "It would be nice to get to know the people of this town."

"Great." Although she smiled, it was a forced one, as though her mind was still reeling from the mess in the kitchen. She looked at Sarah. "Can you make a few pies?"

"Sure. I would be delighted. Do you just want a few pies, or would you like me to make anything else?"

"Just pies are fine." She continued to look around the room, still showing her teeth as though she was smiling when she wasn't. "Yes, just a few pies should be fine." Mrs. Gables backed away, nodding at Sarah. "That was all I needed. I shall let you get back to your... afternoon."

"You have a lovely afternoon, Mrs. Gables," Sarah called after her.

Although Mrs. Gables nodded, she left the kitchen without another word. Jack and Sarah looked at each other.

"I think it's safe to say that she won't be eating at the café for a while," Jack said.

Sarah laughed and then waved her hand in the direction where Mrs. Gables had vanished. "If ever again. Oh well. I hate to say it, but part of me thinks it was worth it." She inhaled a breath and smiled as she looked around the floor. "I'll fetch the broom and dustpan and clean up this mess." She pointed to the children. "You two can have one more cookie, and that's it until after dinner." She winked.

THIRTEEN

SARAH

Trust in the Lord with all your heart and lean not on your own understanding. *Proverbs 3:5*

Sarah didn't know how many times she'd heard this verse in her life any more than she knew how many times she'd uttered it. It was one she often used when she thought about all the rough times dealing with a daughter who thought it nothing to move around the country, never staying in one place too long as she pursued every dream and whim that tickled her mind.

In the last two years alone, she knew of ten different cities that her daughter called home, and she never understood the how or the why when it came to Elena. How could her daughter not want to settle down and have stability? Why didn't she just find a nice man to love and marry? Of course, Sarah knew she would never receive the answers, just as much as she knew she had to let go and trust that the Lord knew what He was doing.

Which is what she'd also done this week with Jack.

Jack had spent the last several days since the afternoon at the woodpile doing chores around the inn and acting as though nothing had happened. Sarah had thought to broach the subject a few times, but she'd chickened out each time. It was shameful of her—or at least she thought so—but it was what she'd done, giving in to the fear and clamping her mouth shut.

It wasn't like he wanted to talk about it, either, though, so she tried not to feel too guilty about it.

"Well, I think we have enough eggs if you want to take the boiled ones to the social." Jack shut the back door and set the basket on the counter. She moved over to the counter, holding a ball of freshly made pie crust. She peered into the basket, looking at the white and brown eggs.

"That's a lot for this time of year," she said.

"I thought the same. But as long as they are laying, I'll take them and eat them." He chuckled.

"You can put them in the corner. I'll boil them tonight and slice them in the morning before church." She returned to the counter with the dough, tossing it on the countertop with a layer of flour sprinkled over it. Her hands went to work, pressing and flattening the dough until she could use the rolling pin to finish turning the once thick, round ball into a flat sheet no thicker than the slices of tomato that Harold liked on his sandwiches. "Did you see this morning's newspaper?" she asked. Although she should be furious with what a certain town busybody had to write, she also couldn't help but feel slightly amused.

"I did not." Jack cocked his head to the side. "But I had planned to read it with my lunch."

"Are you sure you want to be eating when you read it?" Sarah rolled her eyes toward the ceiling, slightly chuckling at the thought of the article she'd read over her morning coffee.

What was the headline again? A Flour Fiasco at the Café: A Tale of Mischief and Mayhem.

"Is this it?" Jack asked, pointing toward the single sheet of parchment sitting on the edge of the counter.

"Yes, that's it."

"So, what is it today? Was I caught stealing something from

the mercantile? Or perhaps I was sending another mysterious telegram to some unknown person—a woman this time perhaps." Jack chuckled as he grabbed the paper and flipped it over. His mouth moved as he read the headline of the Parlor Patter.

A grin spread across his face. "Did she really..." He let his voice trail off as he took in the first paragraph.

"Oh yes, she did," Sarah said, knowing exactly what he was trying to ask and say with his question.

Jack laughed. "This is just too good. I might reread it aloud just to gain the full effect."

"Oh, please do."

"Greetings once again, cherished readers of Featherstone Valley! It's your ever-vigilant observer, Prudence Chatterton, bringing you the latest scoop from our delightful town. This week, I have a rather... floury tale to share with you, one that has left the community buzzing with whispers and chuckles.

The scene of our story is none other than the beloved café at Ms. Sarah Holden's inn. It appears that a playful afternoon took a turn for the chaotic when Sarah and the lively Fields children decided to engage in what can only be described as a flour-throwing extravaganza! Yes, you read that correctly. Our usually serene café was transformed into a veritable snowstorm of flour, with white clouds billowing and laughter echoing through the kitchen.

Now, while the thought of such merriment warms the heart, it does raise a few... concerns. The word on the street is that the aftermath was a sight to behold—a flour-coated kitchen from floor to ceiling. As someone who takes great pleasure in dining at Ms. Holden's establishment, I must admit that this news has left me feeling a tad uneasy. After all, cleanliness in a place where food is prepared is paramount.

Now, don't misunderstand me, dear readers. I am not insinuating that our esteemed inn or its café is on the brink of a rodent invasion. However, one can't help but wonder about the thoroughness of the cleanup. A mess of such magnitude, especially involving foodstuffs, could indeed be a siren call for unwanted guests of the scurrying variety.

So, while I cherish the joy and laughter that fills our town, I find myself compelled to gently remind Ms. Holden that cleanliness is next to godliness, especially in the culinary domain. And to my fellow townsfolk, I urge you to keep a watchful eye on our beloved café. Let us ensure that our haven of hospitality remains a beacon of hygiene and delight.

Rest assured, I, Prudence Chatterton, will monitor the situation closely, ever ready to report on the developments. For now, let us hope that the only flour in our future is the kind that leads to the creation of delectable pastries and bread, not culinary chaos.

Until next time, may your days be filled with tidiness and your meals free of mishaps. Keep your ears to the ground and your spirits high, for in Featherstone Valley, every day is an adventure waiting to unfold!

"She really knows how to give those last lines a punch, doesn't she?" he asked, clenching his hand into a tight fist and then punching the air.

"Yes, she does. I wonder where she learned to write like that."

"Does anyone in town have experience writing for a newspaper?"

Sarah shook her head. "Not that I know of. Except Mr. Jenkins, of course."

"Well, one thing is for sure: this does mean we could be a step closer to figuring out who Prudence Chatterton is."

"How?"

"Mrs. Gables was the only one who knew about the flour fight because she was the only one who saw it."

"It's true, she was, but that doesn't mean she's Prudence

Chatterton. Given how she likes to talk, she could have told half the town within an hour."

Jack's smile faded, and his brow furrowed. "That's true. Whoever Prudence is could have heard it from Mrs. Gables or someone else entirely." He tossed the paper back onto the counter. "It was worth a shot to try and figure it out, though."

"I agree; it's too bad it didn't work."

He glanced at Sarah and then at the newspaper and clicked his tongue. "We might still be able to figure it out."

"How would we do that?"

"It wouldn't be exactly honest, though. And we might have to tell a few white lies in the process."

Sarah paused as she lifted the sheet of dough off the counter to turn it over. "Why, Pastor Boone, I never thought you would be for telling lies."

"Only little ones." He chuckled as he held up his hand, pressing his finger and thumb close together yet not quite touching. "And only to see if we can figure out who is writing these articles."

"I don't know." Sarah exhaled. "Part of me wonders if finding out who Prudence Chatterton is even matters. Getting rid of her—or his—articles in the newspaper will not stop gossip from spreading around town. Far too many ladies like to talk. The only thing this article has done is print such gossip in black-and-white ink for people to read. People would still talk even if the newspaper didn't have the articles."

"Yeah, I suppose you're right. It would still be nice to know who it is." Jack rested his hand on his hips and looked around the kitchen. "Do you need any help with the pies?" Jack asked, pointing toward the dough.

"Well," she bit her lip, "if you can fetch me the two pie tins from the counter, that would help." She motioned toward the tins she'd left near the sink, and he marched over and grabbed them, bringing them to her and setting them down.

"Here you are."

"Thank you."

"What flavor will those be?" he asked.

"Berry." She motioned toward the jars of berries she canned last fall. "I have two pumpkin and two apple, too." Jack looked around the kitchen, finding the other four pies on the cooling racks.

"I can't believe you've made six pies today."

"Well, I've made four." She chuckled. "These aren't baked just yet."

"It's still a lot of pies."

"Nah. I've made way more than this in one day. Last year's bake sale, I think I made twelve."

"Twelve pies? In one day?"

She nodded. "It's not that hard. And it's for the town."

"Folks seem to do a lot of things like this, don't they?"

She nodded again. "It's a good little town, full of a lot of people who care about one another."

"I can see that."

She looked at him, cocking her head to the side. She wasn't sure if she should ask the questions resting on her mind, but at the same time, she knew she wouldn't be able to continue with this mindless small talk either.

"Did you not live in a nice town in Texas?"

He shook his head. "Fort Worth isn't what I would call a town. It's a lot bigger than Featherstone Valley."

"How much bigger?"

"A lot. Probably twenty... thousand."

She inhaled, blinking several times as the number resonated in her mind. "Oh." Her word was more of a whispered breath, and if her hands hadn't been covered in dough, she would have laid one on her chest. "That's... I wouldn't have thought a ranch would be so big."

"Yeah. We lived on the outskirts and only went into the city when we needed supplies. After the boys were born, Maryanne didn't even go into town. She stayed home with them while I bought everything we needed."

"So, her name was Maryanne?"

He furrowed his brow for a second. "I didn't tell you that before, did I?"

"No, you didn't."

"I thought I had. Yes, her name was Maryanne."

"It's a pretty name."

"And she was a pretty woman." He glanced down at the ground. His shoulders slumped slightly, and he cleared his throat. "You know, I... I have to be honest; watching you and the children the other day baking the cookies and throwing the flour made me remember this one time when the boys chased her around the kitchen with fish in each of their hands."

"Fish?"

"Maryanne didn't like fish. She didn't like to cook it. She didn't like to eat it. She didn't like to catch it. She didn't ever want anything to do with fish. Patrick and Kit always thought it was funny." He snorted a laugh as a distance seemed to wash through his eyes. It seemed as though for a moment he wasn't in the kitchen anymore, or at least not Sarah's kitchen, but one thousands of miles away and in another time. "It seems like such a long time ago, yet it wasn't."

"How old were your boys when she died?"

"Kit was twelve years old, and Patrick was ten."

"It's a shame they lost their mother so young." She paused as she grabbed the jar of canned berries and unscrewed the lid. "Losing their father was hard on Luke and Elena, but I think adults have it in their mind that the time is coming. Don't get me wrong, it was a shock, but they weren't young children." She dumped the berries into the pie tins, smoothing the tops with a wooden spoon before grabbing the other two balls of dough and flattening them before covering the fruit. "Is that why you retired from being a Ranger? So you could stay closer to home and raise them?"

Jack's brow furrowed. "Something like that." He shook his head and snorted as though he was trying to change the thoughts in his mind. He shrugged. "It was just fun watching you with the children. It made me smile."

"Sometimes it's when we least expect it that the best memories seem to come out of nowhere." She laid the top crust on one of the pies, crimping the edges together before reaching for the last ball of dough and sprinkling flour on the counter. "Someone once told me after Harold died that we should always be mindful of the everyday memories and not just the special ones because those are easy, whereas the day-to-day are harder. They are muted in the grind of chores, naptimes, suppers, and the worries that everyone carries. But they shouldn't be overlooked." She paused, turning toward him as she leaned her hip against the counter. Words rested on the tip of her tongue, but she wasn't sure she should utter them. "I've always tried to appreciate all the memories, not just the special ones, but the ones people might think were boring. I can also appreciate the not-so-good ones, even if sometimes I don't wish to do so." She glanced at the ground, praying he would understand the deeper meaning behind what she said. "But I know not everyone shares my opinion on that."

Jack inhaled a deep breath, letting it out slowly as he stared at her. "I think they do think the same," he said. "It just might be harder for them to admit."

Although she waited for a moment for him to say something else, after a few moments of his silence, she went back to finishing the last pie. It wasn't exactly the conversation she'd hoped for, but it was a step in the right direction—at least, she thought it was.

Perhaps one day, he'd tell her what bothered him.

~

PATRICK

The train whistle blew as the train pulled into the station. Patrick jerked at the noise and cleared his throat as he glanced out the window. People meandered all around the station in several directions, chatting with one another as they weaved around. He didn't know whether they were saying hello or goodbye, but in the end, the interactions seemed to have the same emotions—smiles, laughter, hugs, and tears.

He hadn't ridden a train in a long time, and as the memory of the last time he'd set foot on the platform of a train station hit him square in the chest, he sucked in a breath.

Memories always seemed to do that to him.

Or at least the ones that involved his mother or father did.

Of course, memories were like that, were they not?

Nothing more than silent whispers of our pasts, they echoed through the corridors of time, reminding us of moments both monumental and mundane. Some memories are as vivid as the day they were born, etched into our minds with the precision of a master artist. Others are more like faded photographs, their edges worn, their colors dulled by time. Yet, whether clear or clouded, each memory holds a piece of who we are. They are the building blocks of our identity, the foundation upon which we build our present and future. In the quiet reflection of memory, we find laughter and tears, joy and sorrow, love and loss. They are the reminders of our triumphs and our trials, the lessons learned, and the roads traveled. Memories are the precious keepsakes of the heart, to be cherished and held close, for they are the legacy of our lives, the story we leave behind.

"Patrick, darling?" Julia touched his arm, and he flinched. His head whipped toward her, and her eyes widened. "I'm sorry, darling. I didn't mean to scare you."

"You just startled me, that's all." He shook his head, furrowing his brow. "It's nothing."

Before she could say another word, he scooted out of the seat and stood, stretching his legs from the long train ride. "Let's get you to the hotel where you can rest."

"Must we stay? I had hoped to get on the road to Featherstone Valley after the train arrived."

"Well, we have to wait for the stage, and I don't know yet how long that will take."

"What about buying a horse and carriage?"

"And what should we do with it when we no longer need it?" He shook his head. "I'd rather wait for the stagecoach."

He motioned for her to turn around, and as she did, he pressed his hand on her lower back to lead her out of the train car. "Whatever we do, we first have to find Aunt Bea."

"I still can't believe she came along." Although Patrick couldn't see his wife's face, he could hear how she rolled her eyes. "All she's going to do is just get in the way of you and your father talking and healing whatever it is between you."

"I'm sorry, but healing? Just what is that supposed to mean?"

"Yes, healing." Julia turned around and faced him. "Talk to him, clear the air, resolve whatever tore you apart."

"You make it sound so simple."

"That's because it is."

If there had ever been anything he hadn't wanted to hear Julia say, it would have been her telling him the rift between him and his father was simple. Especially when he felt it was anything but. However, once Julia set her mind on something... well, she wouldn't change it. Not for anything. It was the main reason she was even here. Had it been up to him, a woman in her condition would be lying on the couch at home. He motioned for her to turn around again. "Well, I'll cross that road when I get to it. For now, let's find Aunt Bea and see about finding a hotel."

"All right. All right." She spun, waving her hands. "But don't think this conversation is over, darling, because it is not."

He glanced up at the ceiling, muttering under his breath. "I never would have thought otherwise. Unfortunately."

"And that is the soonest the stage leaves for Featherstone Valley?" Patrick pointed to the time etched on the slip of paper.

The stagecoach ticket attendant glanced down, twisting his neck slightly as he tried to read the words from the side. "Yes. There is another stagecoach if you would rather go to Deer Creek."

"How far is Featherstone Valley from Deer Creek?"

"Oh, I would say about a day's wagon ride."

Patrick stared at the man. Was he trying to make a joke? "If I'm traveling to Featherstone Valley, why would I take a stage-coach to a town that is a day's wagon ride away?"

"Well, I suppose I just can't fathom why anyone would want to go to Featherstone Valley. Have you ever been there before?"

"No. Why? Have you?"

"Yeah."

"And is it an unsafe town?"

"Oh, no, not Featherstone Valley. It's a quiet and safe little town. But it's little. It's not exactly a place for tourists to see or visit."

"I'm not going because I'm on vacation. I'm going to visit someone."

"Oh. Well, that's the only time we have a stage going to Featherstone Valley. Do you want a ticket?"

"Yes. Three, please."

After paying for the tickets and securing the slips of paper in his jacket pocket, Patrick returned to the hotel where he'd left

Julia and Aunt Bea. Weaving down the street, he nodded toward the men who greeted him as he tried to think of anything else other than the reasons why he was in Montana.

Truth be told, Patrick wasn't sure about this trip or why he'd decided even to take the adventure, and he couldn't help but wonder if this was a chance to confront the past and seek answers to questions that had haunted him for too long, or if this was nothing but a fool's mission. Each step he took was heavy with the weight of uncertainty, and while there was a part of him that longed for reconciliation, to bridge the gap that had widened with each passing year, the thought of reuniting with his father after such a long time filled him with a sense of unease that made his stomach twist. That, coupled with a lingering fear of rejection and of opening old wounds that had never truly healed, only worsened the knowing feeling in his gut.

What kind of man had his father become in the years since they'd talked?

Would he even recognize him?

Worse, would he even be happy to see him at all?

FOURTEEN

SARAH

For where two or three come together in my name, there am I with them. *Matthew 18:20*

Sarah didn't know whether Jack had planned the sermon because of the social gathering or if he had the verse on his mind before the plans had even been set. Of course, when she asked him, he only playfully gave her a wink and a simple, 'that's for me to know' answer.

The thought of his words made her smile as she sat in the pew, watching him stand in front of the congregation. It was only the second sermon he had given since arriving in Feather-stone, yet as he stood there, Sarah couldn't help but feel as though he'd been in the town for years.

That was how he made her feel—so comfortable that it felt like she'd known him for longer than she had and that he'd been in her life forever. Having him around had been a blessing she hadn't seen coming, and the thought both warmed her soul and inched fear into her chest all at once.

"When a very dear friend asked me today what message I would give you all, I have to admit that I was coy with my answer." A few of the townsfolk chuckled, making Jack smile. "It wasn't that I didn't want to tell this person. But I just wanted it to surprise everyone, including them."

As Jack looked at Sarah, he smiled, and heat flushed her cheeks. She glanced down at her hands, watching them fidget in her lap as Sue Ellen nudged Sarah with her elbow.

"As your new pastor and someone who hasn't been in this town long, I have to tell you all that I have found great comfort and joy living here. I take walks around town, and I can't help but be reminded of how close you are all as a town. When I learned that the social had been planned, I couldn't help but think of the Gospel of *Matthew 18:20*: For where two or three come together in my name, there am I with them."

Jack paused, watching different men and women nod in agreement. "This verse isn't just for Sunday service. This verse is a beautiful reminder of the power of gathering in His name. At any time. For any event. For any purpose. It assures us that no matter how small our group may be, Christ is present among us. As I begin my journey with you all, I am filled with hope and excitement, knowing that in every prayer, in every conversation, and in every shared moment, Christ is with us, whether we are in this church or just walking through town.

I believe our gatherings, whether in this church, in our homes, or even under the open sky, are sacred. They are opportunities for us to connect, to support one another, and to grow in our faith. It is in these moments of togetherness that we can truly feel the presence of our Lord and experience the depth of His love.

I am eager to speak with each of you, to hear your stories, and to walk alongside you in your spiritual journey. Let us embrace the promise of *Matthew 18:20* and seek to come together in the name of Jesus, not just as a congregation but as a family in Christ.

As we move forward, let us cherish our times of fellowship and remember that Christ is with us in our unity, guiding us and blessing our community. I am hopeful for the beautiful journey ahead in Featherstone Valley and grateful to be part of this family of faith.

May we always find strength and comfort in His presence as we gather in His name. Would you bow your heads, please?"

Everyone bowed their heads.

"Lord, we thank you for the chance to not only come together as a town to listen to your word but to also just be together as a community... as a family. May you bless the people of this town, keeping them safe and healthy. May you be with them all as they live their daily lives, enjoying the simple pleasures of a life lived through you and for you. I humbly ask that you continue to wrap this whole town in your arms, helping them, giving them hope, and providing them with the guidance and strength they need to face any challenges that come their way. May your love and grace be evident in all we do, and may we always remember the importance of coming together in your name. We are grateful for your presence in our lives and our community, and we ask that you continue to bless Featherstone Valley with your peace and prosperity. In Jesus' name, we pray. Amen."

"Amen," everyone said in unison.

"Before I dismiss you," Jack raised his hands as though motioning everyone to pause before they stood to leave, "I'd like to invite you all to head over to the saloon, where I've been told quite the banquet of refreshments is waiting for all of us. I'm sure we all will have a wonderful time, so I hope all of you can come."

With the last of his words, everyone in church stood and began gathering their things. An echo of several conversations sounded off the church walls, and as Sue Ellen stood and grabbed her coat, she looked at Sarah and raised one eyebrow. "So, who do you think this dear friend was that he spoke of?"

"I couldn't say," Sarah said without looking at her friend.

"I don't believe you."

"You can say that, but it doesn't change my answer."

Sue Ellen looked at her again. "Why are you so determined to deny what I can plainly see?"

Sarah opened her mouth, but no matter how much she wanted to find something to say, her words failed her. Life had never not been easy for her to explain, nor had her feelings. She'd always been the one who could speak her mind, or at least speak it when warranted. She also knew when to say nothing, which was the truth. "Let's get to the saloon before all the good desserts are taken," she finally said.

I t didn't take long for everyone in town to reach the saloon, and as people filed into the building, gasps of excitement filled the air. Tables laden with different treats lined the far wall while the echoes of gentle music played in the background. Mr. Harper had allowed Mrs. Gables to decorate somewhat, and the brightly colored streamers she'd hung everywhere lit up the brown hues of the tables, chairs, walls, and hardwood floor with splashes of color.

Townsfolk meandered about the room, chatting with one another about different topics—work at the gold mines, a new recipe to try, a horse with a limp that doesn't seem to be getting better, and a cow that had recently gotten loose through town were all stories she heard as she weaved her way toward the table with the cookies and cupcakes.

Sue Ellen was hot on her heels, sticking close to Sarah as they headed for the punch bowl, each grabbing a glass.

"It looks like everyone in town is here," Sue Ellen said, glancing around the saloon. "Even Mr. Hayes is here." She motioned toward the young Colton Hayes, who had just inherited his grandfather's cattle ranch on the outskirts of town last summer. He hadn't set foot in town much since he arrived, finding solace in the animals instead of people. Of course, that only seemed to fuel more gossip surrounding the man, whom Sarah only knew to be kind and hardworking. "I wonder why he is here. He normally doesn't attend town events like this."

"Maybe he felt compelled to this morning because of the sermon," Sarah said. "After all, he seems to be misunderstood in this town. Or perhaps Jack talked him into coming. For all you know, he could be the *dear friend* Jack was talking about."

Sue Ellen shot Sarah a glare and rolled her eyes. "Don't even try to play it off."

"Play what off?"

"The lies you are telling yourself this very moment." Sue Ellen grabbed the ladle and poured some punch into a glass before picking it up and taking a sip. She continued to look around the saloon.

"What lies?" Sarah asked.

"I'm not even going to dignify the answer I'm sure is sitting on your tongue by repeating the words."

"Just what do you want me to say, Sue Ellen?" Sarah set down her own glass and folded her arms across her chest. She leaned toward her friend, lowering her voice. "Do you want me to say that I like him? That for the first time since Harold died, I see a glint of hope that perhaps I'm not dead inside, and I could, maybe just maybe, find love again?"

"That's exactly what I want you to say." Sue Ellen matched Sarah's stance. "And now that you've said it, why do you deny it?"

"I have to."

"Why?"

"I don't know why. But I have to."

"Do you want my thoughts?"

"You mean besides what you've already told me at least a dozen times?"

Sue Ellen waved her hand as if to dismiss Sarah's words. "I think he feels the same way about you as you feel about him, and if you both would admit it to each other, then you two could go on living a happy life with one another."

"And what if he doesn't feel the same? What if all I am is a dear friend?"

"That is just a risk you'll have to take. You'll have to talk to him and wait for the story to unfold."

Sarah inhaled deeply, glancing at Jack standing across the room and talking to Mr. and Mrs. Cooper. As much as she didn't want to hear Sue Ellen's words, she knew she had to. It was as simple as her friend made it sound—talk to him and wait for the story to unfold.

But what if the story isn't one I want to read? Or worse, what if the story doesn't have a happy ending?

JACK

Jack shook Mr. Cooper's hand, and as he nodded at Mrs. Cooper, he caught sight of Sarah over the woman's shoulder, staring at him.

His heartbeat kicked up.

What he wouldn't give for insight into her thoughts.

Of course, that would only be worth it if it was the same thing he was thinking.

If it wasn't...

Well, he just didn't know how he would feel about knowing she only thought of him as the dear friend he had called her.

He probably shouldn't have used those words. He didn't want her to think that is what he saw her as—just a friend, even a good one. That wasn't enough for his liking. He wanted to tell her he thought of her as more, even if there were voices in his head that told him he should tell her to stay away; he was damaged goods, deserving of nothing but a life lived alone without love in payment for the crimes he committed against it.

He'd left his wife without his protection, and look what happened...

"Are you enjoying your new life in Featherstone, Pastor Boone?" Mrs. Cooper asked, her voice jerking his attention.

"Huh? Oh, yes, I'm enjoying it very much."

"Well, we are so happy to have found you. Zeke and I discussed your sermon last week and thought it was wonderfully said. I've never been much for the gossip of others. I don't think it's right for Christians to pass such judgments... well, unless they know the person or are coming from a place of authority."

Her son, who had introduced himself as Wyatt Cooper, the Head Foreman of the Harrison Gold Mining Company, snorted and looked away as though he disagreed with his mother's words.

Jack's gaze darted from the son back to the mother, and he smiled at her, hoping to deflect that he'd noticed the young man's reaction.

"Finding and traversing along the thin line of judging and discerning is hard, Mrs. Cooper, and often it's not followed as one should. But I'm glad you enjoyed the sermon. Hopefully, this morning's was even better."

"Oh, yes, it was. That is the one thing we love about Featherstone Valley. Even if we have the gossips, everyone does what is best by each other and for the town. We've made our home here and hope our children will stay, too." She beamed at her son and daughter, Emma, who had only smiled at Jack as she was introduced. "We are both so proud of Wyatt getting promoted to Head Foreman, and Emma has quite the interest in fashion. All she talks about is opening a dress shop in town one day."

"Well, that sounds like a lovely dream to have."

Although the young woman smiled and nodded as though to acknowledge what her mother had said, she didn't say a word.

"We think so. Hopefully, we can see it come to pass one day." Mrs. Cooper glanced at her husband and children once more, then inhaled. "Well, we probably shouldn't keep your attention away from others more than we have. It was a pleasure talking to you, Pastor Boone."

"The pleasure is all mine. If you or your family need anything, please ask."

"Thank you, we will."

With the last of her words, the four of them meandered off to the table of cookies near the window, chatting amongst themselves. While Wyatt waved to other young men throughout the saloon, Emma kept her head down, hiding behind her long, blonde curls as she wove about the crowd as though she didn't want anyone to take notice of her.

Jack watched her for a moment, then turned toward the bar, making his way to a group of men, including Mr. Arthur Lockhart, the owner of the mercantile, and Mr. Frank Rutherford, the owner of the livery. They stood around the stools, holding glasses of water and iced tea. Their laughter boomed throughout the saloon.

"You seem to be having a fun time, gentlemen," Jack said, approaching them.

"How can anyone not have a good time in a room filled with delicious treats made by the lovely wives of this town?" one of the men asked. He stuck his hand out to shake Jack's. "The name is Mr. Theodore Whitmore. I'm the owner of the bank in town."

"It's nice to meet you, Mr. Whitmore."

"It's nice to meet you, too."

"I must say, I enjoyed your sermon today."

"Thank you." Although Jack knew why that was always the first subject broached when meeting new people, he still often found that people starting a conversation with him about his job or a recent sermon he gave were usually not interested in getting to know him as a person. Of course, at the same time, he wasn't sure how he'd feel if they walked up to him, shook his hand, and asked him if he'd sent any recent telegrams to his secret sons lately.

He resisted the urge to smack his hand against his forehead with his thought.

I had made a mess of it all, keeping the secrets that I did, didn't I?

He glanced around the saloon, finding Sarah again still over by the punch bowl, talking to Sue Ellen. Hints of burdened thoughts seemed to brew in the lines of her furrowed brow, and the two spoke to one another as though they were discussing something Sarah wasn't the least bit interested in.

"You should come by the bank, Pastor Boone," Mr. Whitmore said, jerking Jack's attention away from Sarah like Mrs. Cooper did.

I really need to pay attention to the conversations in front of me.

"I could show you around the office, and we can chat about your future plans in Featherstone Valley." The banker smacked Jack on the back of the shoulder. "Have you been looking for a home or land you want to buy?"

Jack shook his head. "Not yet. I'm sure I will want to find something soon since I have plans to put down my roots here, but I haven't been looking."

"Well, when you find the place, I can get you a great interest rate on a loan." Mr. Whitmore leaned forward and patted Jack on the shoulder. A slight chuckle whispered through the man's voice, and although the other men around them chuckled too, Jack didn't. He didn't know if it was the tone the banker had used or the words he'd said, but something was off about the whole thing.

Why were they suddenly talking about loans?

Jack stared at the man, thinking of the money hidden in the depths of his luggage at the inn. It probably wasn't much by Mr.

Whitmore's standards, given he owned a bank, but after selling his ranch in Texas, he was sure he could buy a place in Featherstone Valley outright without needing Mr. Whitmore or his bank.

As Jack stared at the banker, two women approached, and Mr. Lockhart smiled, motioning toward Jack.

"Pastor Boone, have you met my wife and daughter?" the mercantile owner asked.

Jack turned his attention toward the women and stuck out his hand. "I haven't. It's a pleasure to meet you."

"It's a pleasure to meet you, too," Mrs. Lockhart said. "I'm Claire, and this is my daughter, Grace."

"It's nice to meet you, Grace."

"You too, Pastor."

"I believe I've seen you around the mercantile a time or two when I've been there."

The young woman nodded. Her raven curls bounced with her movement.

"Grace works there when she doesn't have her nose stuck in a book." Mr. Lockhart moved to his wife, wrapping his arm around her waist while Mr. Whitmore and Mr. Rutherford shifted to the bar, slightly away from the women. Jack's ears perked as they continued talking about the livery and whether Mr. Rutherford was interested in expanding. At first, it seemed the stable owner was, but as the conversation turned to the dealings of borrowing money, Mr. Rutherford straightened his shoulders and began rethinking his previous 'perhaps' answer.

Surely, it was good business for Mr. Whitmore to secure loans. That's how banks stayed in business. But something about the man's approach to people didn't seem right.

"There's nothing wrong with one's nose being stuck in a book," Mrs. Lockhart playfully tapped her husband's shoulder. "Just because you are not a fan of books."

"I'm a fan of books. I'm just more a fan of business and

helping our customers." He rolled his eyes but then smiled at his wife and daughter.

"So, you love to read?" Jack asked the young Miss Lockhart.

She nodded, and her eyes darted toward her father, then back to Jack. "Yes, sir."

"Well, I think that is wonderful." Jack smiled, hoping to give the woman a little bit of encouragement. "You know, Benjamin Franklin once said, 'The person who deserves most pity is a lonesome one on a rainy day who doesn't know how to read.' I would say I would have to agree with him."

"I agree with him, too," Mrs. Lockhart said, glancing at her husband.

Mr. Lockhart smiled and tucked his chin toward his chest. He chuckled as he shook his head. "All right. All right. I get what you're all saying... or not saying, but are hinting at. Reading is important too. Just not when a customer wants to buy some supplies."

Mrs. Lockhart softened and patted her husband on the back, leaning her body into his as a sign of affection. "That is true, dear."

Watching the couple, Jack caught sight of Sarah over their shoulders, and as he focused on her, she focused on him. His heart thumped. Even from across the room, she stole all attention—or at least his—and something stirred within him as a gentle smile played on her lips. Although he wished it was an unknown emotion he couldn't name, he knew that even considering that notion would be a lie. He could name it because he had felt it once before the first time he laid his eyes on Maryanne. Looking at Sarah, even in the slight distance between them, it was as if her laughter echoed in the hollows of his heart, filling it with a warmth that, although he had known he was missing, he wasn't aware of how much, at least not until now.

"If you three would please excuse me," he said, laying his

hand on Mr. Lockhart's shoulder as he reached to shake the man's hand. "I'm feeling quite parched, and I think a nice glass of punch is just what I need."

"Of course, Pastor." Mr. Lockhart shook Jack's hand, and the three nodded as Jack moved around them and made his way toward Sarah.

"Hello again," he said to her as he approached.

"Hello, Jack. Are you having fun?" she asked.

"Yes, I am. Are you?"

"Of course." She glanced at Sue Ellen, who had momentarily shifted her attention toward Hank, walking toward the three of them with a plate laden with cookies in his hands.

"What on earth will you do with all those cookies?" Sue Ellen asked. She shoved her hands into her hips.

"I'm going to eat them," her husband answered.

"No, you are not. If you eat all of those cookies, you'll make yourself sick."

"I am not." Hank's head jerked back, and his brow furrowed.

"Yes, you are." Sue Ellen stepped closer to him. "Don't you remember what happened at the Christmas party?"

Jack looked at Sarah as she looked at him, and then both smiled, turning slightly away from the husband and wife to hide their laughter. She wiggled her finger, motioning him to follow her to a pair of chairs in the corner of the saloon near the front door. Sunlight filtered through the window, warming the cushions.

"I see you've been meeting more of the townsfolk."

"Yes, I've met a few people I haven't had the pleasure of meeting until now."

"Mrs. Cooper spoke to me after talking to you. She thinks you're a kind soul."

"Well, that was nice of her to say."

"Did Mr. Whitmore talk to you about a loan?" Sarah chuckled.

"Yes, he did."

"He does that with everyone. I have never had a conversation with that man that doesn't either start or end with him asking if I'm interested in a loan or suggesting a loan for something I may or may not need. He does that with everyone. Most of us just ignore the mention of money and change the subject." She leaned forward, crossing her legs and resting her elbows on her knees. Her hands fidgeted.

"Is something wrong?" he asked.

"No." She shook her head, straightening up in the seat as she sighed. "I was just thinking about what we should do for supper tonight."

"Oh. Well, whatever you decide is fine with me."

"I'll have to see what I have in my pantry when I return to the inn." She looked around the room, fidgeting with her hands even more as she picked at her nails. "I wonder how many I should expect at the café."

Sunlight filtered through the windows, flecking her face with a soft light. Her blue eyes changed into a lighter shade, sparkling with a hint of nervousness behind the hue. She had always looked pretty in his eyes, but in this moment, another layer of her beauty unfolded, and a sudden wave of gnawing fear washed through him.

Something was off.

Something was different.

Something hung between them, and although he hoped it was something he couldn't explain, he knew better.

He wasn't a fool.

He'd always known he was a man with more shadows than light, a man who had walked through storms and emerged with scars. How could he, with all his imperfections, ever be worthy of her radiance?

He opened his mouth, and his voice caught in his throat, his words failing him. At that moment, he understood that this was more than a mere attraction; it was a connection that threatened to unravel the very fabric of his being.

And he was irrevocably, undeniably scared.

"Sarah, I... I..." Jack paused, letting his silence echo against the sound of the saloon door opening behind him.

Before he could continue, a voice said, "Father?"

FIFTEEN

SARAH

Sarah watched as Jack stood and turned toward the young man and pregnant woman standing in the saloon's doorframe.

"Patrick?" Jack said. His eyes narrowed, not in anger but in confusion, and he furrowed his brow. "What... what are you doing in Featherstone Valley?"

"I received your telegram. I... I don't know why I came."

"Well, I'm glad you did." Jack moved toward him, opening his arms to hug his son. As Patrick's body stiffened, Jack hesitated and looked toward the young woman. "I'm Jack Boone."

"Julia Boone."

Jack looked between them, finally seeming to notice the woman's round belly. "Congratulations. You have a beautiful wife."

"Thank you." Patrick clenched his jaw and stepped closer to his young bride. His chest puffed slightly as though he was positioning himself to protect her from unknown harm.

Sarah glanced around the room, noting how more and more townsfolk had taken notice of the young man just the same and had silenced to overhear the conversation. She stood, moving toward the two men.

"Perhaps you two should talk outside where you can have some privacy."

Jack looked over his shoulder, noticing everyone turning to watch him, and he nodded. "Yes, we should." He motioned toward the door. "Shall we go outside?"

"Outside? It's freezing out there, and my wife needs to rest. She's had a long trip."

"How about we go back to the inn?" Sarah asked, moving toward the young woman. She smiled and outstretched her hand. "My name is Sarah Holden, and I own the inn in town."

"It's nice to meet you. Julia Boone."

As Sarah shook Julia's hand, the saloon door opened again, and another woman strolled inside. She halted as she saw Jack, and her face contorted. Her jaw clenched, tightening and slimming a little of the roundness in her face. Her skin flushed with a shade that almost matched the deep red material of her dress, and she looked as though she held her breath for several minutes, finally exhaling.

"What are *you* doing here?" Jack asked her.

"I came here to make sure that Patrick and Julia are taken care of."

"Taken care of? They are adults and are about to be parents."

"Yes, and they will be better than you ever were, no thanks to you." With her words, the woman lifted her chin so that she looked down her nose at Jack.

More of the townsfolk silenced behind them, and Sarah glanced over her shoulder, meeting a few concerned and confused gazes.

They had to get out of the saloon before anything else was said.

"I think you're quite right, Mr. Boone," she said to Patrick as she laid her hand on Julia's shoulder. "I'm sure your wife would love to rest after her long trip. How about I take you to the inn myself and see that you are settled into your rooms?"

Although Patrick looked like he wanted to argue, he exhaled a deep breath and nodded instead. "Fine."

S arah had always thought that either a change of scenery or a change of subject would ward off any awkwardness in which one would find themselves. Whether it was a conversation they didn't want to have or one they stumbled into through either no fault of their own—or doing something stupid—if they would alter whatever they could to regain their composure or any little control they could, then the awkwardness would disappear.

She didn't know how wrong she'd been.

Neither the cold January air nor the warmth of the inn starved the unease or tension between the father and son as they followed the women, and as she shut the door of the study, leaving Jack and Patrick alone to talk about whatever they needed, she leaned against the door and exhaled a deep breath.

Her mind stumbled around all the questions without answers. She didn't want to think about how Jack must be feeling any more than she wanted to think about how Patrick was feeling.

"You have a beautiful inn." Julia exhaled her own deep breath, and as she looked around the room, she ran her hands over her belly. "Isn't it lovely, Beatrice?"

The older woman looked around the room, too, and although she smiled, a hint of annoyance spread through to the scowl on her lips.

Just who was this woman, Sarah thought. *Was she Julia's mother? If she was, why wouldn't Julia just call her mother?*

"We should go in the study," Beatrice said, her tone sharp as she moved toward the door. "We should not let Jack speak to Patrick alone."

Julia reached out and stopped her. "Patrick asked us to leave. And we need to respect that."

Beatrice opened her mouth, looking as though she wanted to argue. Even if she did, though, she said nothing and turned away from Julia, pacing in front of the door instead.

Sarah looked between them, noting the exhaustion on Julia's face. "We should get you upstairs where you can rest." She pushed off the door and made her way around the desk, opening the top drawer and fetching two brass keys from the corner. "Do you think you can manage the stairs?"

Julia nodded. "The stairs won't be any trouble."

"I can't imagine how uncomfortable you must have been traveling from Texas to Montana. I don't think I could travel more than across town with either my son or daughter."

"It wasn't all bad. The train was comfortable. It's just the stagecoach was not." Julia laughed, rubbing her belly again. She let out a slight noise as though she had a shot of pain and closed her eyes. "One thing I will not miss about being pregnant is how hard this baby can kick."

"When is the baby due?" Sarah asked, grabbing two of the suitcases. She motioned for the women to follow her upstairs.

"In a couple of months. Patrick wasn't sure about me making the trip here, but I didn't want to be left at home."

"I can understand that. It would have been hard for me, too."

"Hard or not, you should have stayed home," Beatrice said. While Sarah and Julia meandered up the stairs slowly to give Julia rest between the steps, Beatrice's footsteps thumped against the wood planks, and she charged up the stairs like a bull loose in a barn.

"I wasn't about to let Patrick do this alone, Beatrice, and even my doctor said it would be all right."

Beatrice spun on the last stair and pointed at Julia. "No, he didn't. He told you he didn't think it was a good idea, but," she paused, letting her voice thump on the letter 't', "since you were bent on doing it anyway, he thought you would be all right."

Before Julia could say anything to defend herself, Beatrice spun back around and headed down the hallway toward the room doors.

"You'll have to excuse Patrick's aunt," Julia whispered. "She doesn't care for Patrick's father, and she doesn't think we should have come."

"It's all right. Everyone is entitled to their feelings."

"That is true." Julia lowered her voice to a whisper. "But she doesn't have to be so vocal about them."

"Which one is my room?" Beatrice yelled from down the hallway.

Sarah and Julia looked at her, both taking a deep breath as they finished walking up the stairs and made their way down the hallway toward the last door on the left.

"This is one of my best rooms. You should be quite comfortable in here." Sarah unlocked the door and opened it, motioning Julia inside. Beatrice followed close behind but stopped just inside the doorframe.

"It's one of only two rooms with two windows, so it has more light," Sarah said.

Julia turned a few circles, taking in the sight of the canopy bed with light blue blankets and pillows, two bedside tables, and an oversized dressing cabinet in the corner. "It's beautiful, just like the rest of the inn. You have a wonderful place, Miss Holden."

"It's Mrs."

"Oh. I'm sorry. I... I'm not sure why I didn't think you were married."

"It's all right. I was married. My husband passed away a couple of years ago."

"Oh, so you aren't married."

"Well, no, I suppose I'm not. But proper still is proper, so I'm Mrs. Holden."

Julia stared at Sarah and then cocked her head to the side and clicked her tongue. "Patrick's father is a widower, too. Did you know that?"

"What does it matter if she knows he's a widower?" Beatrice glared at the young pregnant woman, and a slight growl hitched to the tail end of her question.

"It's just a question, Beatrice. Why don't you go across the hallway and look at your room?" Julia motioned for Sarah to give Patrick's aunt her key, and although Sarah always liked showing their guests to their spaces, as Beatrice stepped forward and held out her hand, Sarah handed the key over without so much as a hinted refusal. The woman snatched it from Sarah's grasp and grabbed her suitcase from the floor before leaving the room.

"Sorry if I overstepped," Julia said, waving her hand as she rolled her eyes. "I haven't had more than a minute of peace from that woman since we left Fort Worth."

"It's quite all right." Sarah paused, trying to keep herself from laughing. "And to answer your question, yes, I knew Jack was married and his wife died."

Julia sat on the bed, studying Sarah for another few minutes. "How close are you and Jack?"

"I beg your pardon?"

"How close are you and Jack? Are you courting?"

"No. No, we're just friends."

"But he stays here at the inn, right?"

"Yes."

"And neither of you are married."

"Yes."

"And he's attractive." Julia waved her hands. "I say that as in my husband is attractive, and they have the same qualities."

"I know what you mean, and yes, I suppose Jack is attractive. But... I... we..." Not knowing how to answer Julia's question, Sarah let her voice trail off, and the two women stared at one another.

"It's all right, Mrs. Holden. You don't have to say anything, and I would like to apologize to you if I've overstepped. I can be quite blunt when I want to speak my mind. It was something Patrick had to get used to, I'm afraid." She offered a smile, rubbing her belly again before yawning.

"Don't worry about apologizing." Sarah motioned toward the pillows. "You should get some rest. We can talk more after supper."

Although Sarah sensed that Julia wanted to talk more, the young woman nodded before reaching around and grabbing one of the pillows. She lay down as Sarah made her way out of the room and shut the door behind her.

The soft click echoed, and Sarah closed her eyes.

What was with everyone—friends and strangers—asking about her feelings toward Jack?

"He's not a good man," a voice said behind her. The sudden sound made Sarah jump, and she spun to find Beatrice standing in her room's doorway.

"You scared me," Sarah said, laying her hand on her chest.

"You should know that Jack is not a good man."

Stunned, Sarah just stared at the woman. Was she serious about what she'd said? "I beg your pardon?"

"Jack is not a good man."

"I... I'm sorry, but I don't understand why you're telling me this."

Sarah moved to leave, but Beatrice shifted as though she wanted to stop her. "Because I can see that there is something between you. He looks at you like he's falling in love with you. I saw it when he looked at my sister. He was looking at you the same way when we walked into the saloon."

"I don't know the man you knew, but the one I know is good."

"Men like him don't change. They are selfish. They take and take and take. They don't listen to anyone, and they don't care about anything but themselves."

Sarah clenched her hands into fists at her sides, and her nails dug into her palms as she fought to keep her composure. Her pulse beat in her ears, drowning out the echoes of the woman's words. How dare this woman come into Sarah's home and cast such aspersions on Jack's character?

"Jack isn't like that. He cares about everyone. He's been a wonderful pastor to this town and a wonderful friend to me."

"It's all a lie."

With every word that spilled from Beatrice's lips, a fire ignited in Sarah's chest, burning hotter and brighter. Her jaw tightened, and her teeth ground together as she struggled to contain the anger bubbling up inside her. Her cheeks flushed, and it felt as if Beatrice's words were poison, attempting to taint the pure image of Jack that Sarah held dear.

"I'm truly sorry for the loss of your sister. I can't imagine your pain. But hating Jack for whatever reason you do won't bring her back."

Beatrice's eyes narrowed until it seemed as though a thought suddenly dawned on her. "He never told you, did he?"

"Told me what?"

"How Maryanne died."

"No, he didn't, and I didn't ask. It's not my business."

"She was murdered because of him. He's the reason she is dead."

JACK

J ack sat in the chair, watching Patrick pace along the wall of the inn's study. He hadn't said anything since they left the saloon, and although Jack wanted to be the first to speak, something told him it was best to wait.

Kit had always been like him, but Patrick... Patrick was all Maryanne, even from the moment he started walking and talking, and if there was one thing he'd learned in the years they had spent together, it was that when Maryanne got worked up, it was always best to say nothing until she spoke first.

Patrick stopped pacing and blew a breath, running his hands through his hair. "I thought I would know what I wanted to say when I saw you. But I was wrong. So wrong." He chuckled as he tucked his chin toward his chest and shook his head. "All the times I rehearsed on the train... they all mean nothing now. Everything I had wanted to say is gone."

Jack swallowed at the lump in his throat. "I suppose I could say the same."

Patrick whipped toward Jack with his brow furrowed. "And why am I here? Why did I even think this would be a good idea... especially with my wife—my pregnant wife who shouldn't even be traveling, even though her doctor said it would be all right. Well, he said it would only after he knew no matter what he told her, she was going anyway, so he told us it would be all right, I think mostly to appease us... but there's nothing I can do about any of this now. We're here. In Montana. Visiting you. And I have no idea why."

"I can't answer the question of why, myself, but... I'm happy you're here."

Patrick snorted. "You can't answer my question of why." Although one might think he was talking to Jack, from the way he whispered and how he kept his gaze focused on the floor,

Jack knew he wasn't. "It's funny that you would say that like I asked you. I didn't ask you anything."

Tension seemed to build in Patrick's shoulders, and he began to pace once more.

Jack wanted to respond, but he got the impression his son still wasn't ready for him to.

"Montana?" Patrick shook his head and faced Jack. "Why did you move to Montana?"

"I was offered a job."

"Didn't you have a job in Texas?"

"Well, yes, but I... I thought a change would be good for me."

"So, you just thought you'd leave Texas without saying a word."

Jack took a couple of deep breaths. He didn't want to match anger with anger. It never solved anything. It only escalated it. The pastor in him stood on one shoulder while the Texas Ranger stood on the other. "I'm sorry. I didn't know that you would have wanted me to tell you."

"Why is that?"

"Because we haven't spoken all that much as of late. I mean, I didn't even know you were married, much less that you were going to be a father."

Patrick inhaled a sharp breath and nodded. "I suppose you're right. We haven't spoken... and why is that again?"

Jack closed his eyes and leaned forward, resting his elbows on his knees. He clasped his hands together and tucked his chin, repeating several Bible verses in his head. *Matthew 5:4*: Blessed are those who mourn, for they shall be comforted. *Revelation 21:4*: He will wipe away every tear from their eyes, and death shall be no more, neither shall there be mourning, nor crying, nor pain anymore, for the former things have passed away. *Psalm 147:3*: He heals the brokenhearted and binds up their wounds. *1 Peter 5:7*: Casting all your anxieties on him because he cares for you. *Psalm 34:18*:

The Lord is near to the brokenhearted and saves the crushed in spirit. *Matthew 11:28-30:* Come to me, all who labor and are heavy laden, and I will give you rest. Take my yoke upon you, and learn from me, for I am gentle and lowly in heart, and you will find rest for your souls. For my yoke is easy, and my burden is light.

"Are you... are you praying?" Patrick asked.

Jack looked up, meeting his son's gaze. "I'm just repeating some verses to myself to help me."

"I don't understand you. I don't understand Julia. I don't understand why she or you think that book will undo everything that happened."

"I don't believe it will undo anything. I only believe it will help get me through it. It might help you, too, if you gave it a chance."

Patrick snorted again. "Becoming a pastor won't make up for the wrongs you did and the pain you caused." He turned around and lifted some of his hair, pointing to a long scar in his hairline. The slash made his hair grow in a different direction. "You see this?" He turned back around. "Becoming a pastor won't make that scar go away."

The acknowledgment of the disfigurement on the back of his head seemed to ignite another flare of anger, and his shoulders squared.

"I don't know why I even came here," he continued. "Aunt Bea was right. Nothing good can come of this."

"I don't believe that. I believe if we talked about everything and listened to what the other has to say... we could find some common ground to start over."

"Start over? So, we're back to that again, huh? Forgetting everything that happened." His voice bubbled with even more annoyance.

"Not forgetting. Never forgetting. But forgiving. Letting it go and forgiving."

Patrick laughed. "Ah, yes. Your God and your forgiveness. It was the same stupid line Julia gave me."

"I don't think it's stupid, and I doubt she does either."

"Don't you dare speak for her!" Patrick lunged across the room, pointing his finger in Jack's face. A fire burned in his eyes. "She is not yours to speak of. She is mine. You had your wife, and you let her die!"

The study door flew open, and Sarah rushed inside. Her eyes grew wide, and she trotted over to the two men.

"I don't mean to interrupt, Mr. Boone, but I have to kindly ask you to keep your voice down."

Patrick turned toward her. "This is none of your business!"

Jack might have allowed his son to yell at him, but he wasn't about to let him yell at Sarah. He jumped to his feet, stepping toward his son. Although Jack was about twenty years older than his son, he still towered over him. "You will not yell at her."

"And you will not tell me what I can and can't do!" A look of pain seemed to rip through Patrick's anger, and while Jack wanted to wrap his arms around his son, he didn't. Now wasn't the time for that. It would only make things worse.

Beatrice rushed into the study, halting near the doorframe. She inhaled a deep breath, laying her hand on her chest. Her wide eyes blinked as she took in the scene.

"When it comes to yelling at a woman—and one who is not only innocent in all of this, but one who is allowing you into her home—yes, I will tell you what you can and can't do. This is her inn. You are here as a guest, and you will not yell at her."

Patrick opened his mouth but closed it without a word. He backed away from Jack, shaking his head. "We shouldn't have come," he whispered.

Jack said nothing, just staring as Patrick continued backing out of the room and shaking his head. There was so much he wanted to say, yet no matter how much he wanted to speak, his mouth wouldn't work.

As Patrick reached the door, passing Beatrice, he glanced at Sarah. "My apologies for yelling, ma'am." He turned and left before anyone could say another word.

"Aren't you going to go after him?" Beatrice asked, hooking her thumb over her shoulder. The shrillness in her voice scratched across Jack's last nerve.

"No," he said.

"Of course." She threw her hands in the air, letting them slap her sides as they fell back down. "I don't know why I even asked."

"There is a time and place for everything, Beatrice," Jack snapped. "And now is not the time for me to go after him." He paused, but only momentarily, for as she lifted her hand and opened her mouth to respond, he continued. "However, it is the time for you to butt out of my business, so I suggest you retire to your room or at least leave this one and leave me alone."

She narrowed her gaze and clenched her jaw. Jack didn't know if she'd listen, and while he hoped she would, he wouldn't be surprised if she didn't.

In fact, he almost braced himself for it.

Instead, she spun and left the room. Her stomping footsteps echoed from the staircase until he heard a door slam from the second floor.

SIXTEEN

SARAH

*S**he's dead because of him.***

Beatrice's words repeated in Sarah's mind until she thought she would go mad. She lay in bed, replaying the moment as the words ate away at her frayed nerves. How a happy afternoon full of laughter at the town social could have erupted into the mess it had, she didn't know.

Aside from what had happened after Jack's son, daughter-in-law, and sister-in-law arrived, she also couldn't help but think about how she had gotten the feeling that he had wanted to talk to her about something important.

The trouble was that she wasn't sure what that something was.

She chewed on her cheek as she stared at the ceiling.

Sleep had evaded her, and as she rolled over for what felt like the hundredth time, she groaned, threw the covers off, and got up, making her way into her tiny kitchen in her cabin. She glanced at the inn from her window and saw lantern light peeking through the curtains of the kitchen window.

Someone was in the kitchen.

She turned and grabbed her dressing coat, sliding her arms

through the sleeves and tying the sash around her waist as she trotted out the door and toward the inn, praying the person was someone in particular and not someone she didn't want to see.

~

The inn's back door creaked, and as she opened it, she saw Jack standing by the stove. He glanced over his shoulder, exhaling as his gaze met hers.

"I would ask if I woke you, but I doubt I made enough noise for you to hear me from your cabin," he said. A slight chuckle whispered through his words.

"You didn't." She shut the door behind her and made her way to the stove. "I couldn't sleep and noticed the light in the window."

He looked down at the milk swirling around the pot on the burner. "I couldn't sleep either. I thought some warm milk might help." He snorted. "It's unlikely, but I thought I would try."

"I'm sorry you can't sleep."

He glanced at her once more. "And I'm sorry you can't. Would you like some milk, too?"

She nodded.

Without saying anything else, he poured more milk into the pot and continued to stir the creamy white liquid. Sarah moved over to the cabinet, reaching for another mug. Thoughts and questions plagued her mind and twisted in her stomach, each repeating until they begged to escape.

She spun, facing Jack, and her sudden movement caught his attention.

He took another deep breath. "We have a lot to talk about, don't we?" he asked.

"Yes, we do."

~

By the time the milk was warm and Jack had poured it into the two mugs, Sarah's heart had worked into quite the imaginary lather. She thought of the horses that drove the afternoon stagecoaches in the summer with their chests white with a frothy film and pictured that very image happening in her chest. Overworked and tired from the nervous pace it had to endure for the last ten minutes, she wished for a reprieve.

"I don't think it's too hot, but you might want to sip slowly." Jack handed her the mug, which she grasped tightly, ignoring how the ceramic cup seemed to want to slip from her clammy hands. "Shall we have a seat?" He motioned toward the small dining table and two chairs nestled in the corner.

"We shall."

Her heartbeat kicked up even more, and she blew out a breath as she sat, trying to distract herself by concentrating on how the chair felt against her backside.

Hard.

Just like this conversation was going to be.

"Before I say anything else, I just wanted to apologize for Patrick's behavior. He shouldn't have yelled at you."

"You don't have to. It was a heated moment, and I knew what I was walking into. I wasn't surprised by his reaction."

"Still, he shouldn't have acted the way he did."

While Sarah stared at Jack, he stared at his mug of warm milk. His brow furrowed as hesitation seemed to pulse through him.

Since Jack arrived, she had never burdened him with questions. Sure, she had them, but often believing the answers to be none of her business, she had never asked them. What point would they have served? She was the inn owner. He was the pastor. That was it.

She wasn't owed anything, just like he wasn't about her life.

While other people might have different thoughts about whether that was the right or wrong way to think, it was the stance she'd taken because of all the questions that people asked after Harold died. In hindsight, she knew they weren't being nosy or trying to offend her. Curiosity often gets the better of people, causing them to press for answers when under normal circumstances they might wait until the person they are asking answers on their own. She was as curious about Pastor Jack Boone as the next person; only she decided not to do anything about it.

And now it seemed perhaps she'd made the wrong choice.

Who was the man sitting at the table next to her?

He'd been married, and his wife had passed away. He had two adult sons that he didn't speak with much, and he was once a Texas Ranger, riding through the vast lands of the state, chasing criminals and bringing them to justice. While he had led an exciting life, he'd thrown it all to the side, choosing the life of a pastor in a small town far away from everything and everyone he knew. Aside from those details, that was it.

Had it all been a lie?

Had it all been a fabrication to hide a past he wasn't proud of or, worse, a past she would find so bitterly terrible she wouldn't want anything to do with him? Had she been wrong to think of him as a man she could fall for? Had she been too blind to see the truth?

"So, which question do you want to ask first?" he asked. His tone was inviting to her even though his voice cracked on his words. "Because I'm sure you have many."

"I don't know which one to ask first," she whispered.

He closed his eyes, and when he opened them, he stared at his mug once more, nodding slightly. "I understand. Do you remember the afternoon with the children when you made the cookies and the three of you got into that fight with the flour?"

She smiled. "Yes, I remember."

"I think about that day all the time."

"Why? Are you ashamed that you didn't step in and help me

by throwing flour on the children?" She wasn't sure where the mocking tone had come from. This wasn't a joking matter, nor was she in a joking mood. But a tiny part of her warmed and settled as she said the words, and she knew that the rhyme or reason didn't matter.

He let out an awkward chuckle and took a deep breath. "Yeah, you were on your own with that one. I wasn't getting mixed up in all that." He cleared his throat again. "But it was something else. I mostly think of that day because of what happened earlier—out by the firewood."

At the mention of the firewood, a slight wave of warmth inched through the back of her neck and up her cheeks. "Oh," she whispered. "I remember that, too."

He groaned and leaned forward, resting his elbows on the table. "I don't know where I should begin..."

Was that an invitation for questions?

Or was he just saying it because he needed a moment to think?

The awkward pause between them hung in the air, and it only made even more warmth creep up the back of her neck, making the little hairs on her skin stand on end.

He furrowed his brow, taking several deep breaths. "Maryanne didn't just pass away like Harold. She wasn't ill, nor was it an accident." He paused again. "Do you remember when I told you I was a Ranger?"

"Yes."

"And that I had been chasing that bandit and his gang, Samuel Bass?"

She nodded.

"When I first joined the Rangers, I was just a young buck, thinking I had scored the job of a lifetime. I thought I would single-handedly make a difference in all the cases, solving them and bringing men to justice. Boy, was I ever the fool." He chuckled, glancing at the floor as he shook his head. "It took me all of three days to discover how wrong I'd been, and that's when I met the one man who had been on the job for more years than I think he wanted to count and the one man who changed my life. His name was Mr. Brock Thomas, and he beat the foolishness and arrogance out of me—figuratively and literally." Jack chuckled again, this time a little harder, as he pointed to a scar on his chin. "I deserved it, though. Trust me. Out of all the advice he gave, he was adamant about one piece in particular, and it was the one piece I ignored. He used to say it all the time until one night, I told him off and told him to shut up because no matter what he said, I wouldn't listen. Part of me wishes I had. Even if that means my life would be very different right now."

"What was the advice?"

"To not marry anyone." Jack took a couple of breaths. "It wasn't that he didn't believe in marriage or love or want it for himself. He told me several times how he regretted making the choice he did and living his life alone. The Lord only gives you so many days on earth, and he was the first to tell you that while he enjoyed most of his, there were times he wished he had done things differently."

"Why did he think you shouldn't marry?"

"Because we deal with a lot of bad men—men who think nothing of murdering anyone who gets in their way and men who think that the easiest way to exploit a situation is to threaten what the lawman holds most dear."

A nervous flutter inched through her chest. "His men killed her, didn't they? Sam Bass, the man you captured, it was his men."

Jack nodded. "They found out who I was, where I lived, and attacked the ranch in broad daylight. The boys tried to protect her, but they were injured. I was told she told them to leave, and Kit, my oldest, forced Patrick to run. I found her near the wood-pile outside of the cabin, lying on the ground, dead."

He furrowed his brow again, spinning the mug in a few circles before lifting it to his lips and taking a sip.

Sarah watched him—at first, too stunned by his admission to say a word, but as the imaginary dust settled, she could not hold back. "Beatrice told me that you were to blame for her sister's death."

"I figured she would... eventually at least. I suppose I was wrong on the timing."

"I didn't know what to make of what she'd said at first. She's so angry."

"She blamed me... my job."

"I don't see how she is justified in blaming you."

"How could she not be? I blame me, too."

"But you didn't force those men to come looking for you any more than you forced those men to do what they did. You are not responsible for another man's actions."

Jack glanced at her, then his gaze moved around the room, darting in all directions as he seemed to contemplate Sarah's words. After a moment, he looked back at her and shook his head. "Even still, if I hadn't been a ranger, Maryanne wouldn't have been a target. The boys blamed me, too, for their mother and for what happened to them. I didn't do right by them after Maryanne died, which is why they went to live with her." He leaned back in the chair and fiddled with his mug a little before looking up at the ceiling. "And why neither of them will talk to me."

∽

J ACK
Jack didn't know which was worse: using the words he'd chosen or hearing them. Sure, he'd thought to himself the same thing—over and over again, admitting that his sons

wouldn't talk to him. But at this moment, and saying it to Sarah, their meaning struck him like a kick from a mule.

And a nasty kick at that.

He wanted to look at Sarah, yet the shame stopped him.

He'd always known he'd made mistakes in his life, and lots of them, but while some were nothing more than stupid moments he could sometimes look back on and laugh, others cut far too deep to ever be overlooked.

Being the reason for his wife's death was at the top of the list.

Sarah reached for his hand, taking it in hers. Her fingers squeezed his, and he laid his other hand on hers. Their gazes met, and he cleared his throat.

His life had always been forked with two paths, whether it was living the life of a Ranger or living the life of a husband, or returning to the job after his wife died or choosing to follow God's calling to the church. Admittedly, the last one wasn't as hard, but the rest were like choosing whether to try to save his relationship with his sons or to respect their choice never to see him. He would never force them, no matter what he wanted in life.

Sitting here, staring at the woman who had captured more than just his attention, he also stared down another forked path, and while he had decided earlier today which side he would take, the arrival of Patrick had changed everything, altering what he believed to be right and wrong.

"I wanted to speak with you about something before Patrick and his wife came into the saloon." He paused, not knowing if he could say the things he'd wanted to earlier. While he still doubted that he deserved to find happiness in a woman like Sarah, he had a sliver of hope that had vanished in the hours after Patrick's arrival.

He wasn't sure he was brave enough to tell her all that he

wanted to. "But I suppose it's not important anymore," he whispered.

He moved to pull his hands away from hers, but she held on, tightening her grip.

Their gazes met again.

"You might think that what you have to say isn't important anymore, but I have something to say, and it still is important."

His stomach twisted, and his breath quickened. "What is it?"

"I never thought I would find happiness after Harold died. The reasons varied from not thinking I could fall for another man to thinking that life alone was just how it was supposed to be. I had the one chance at love, and that was all I got."

Jack couldn't help but nod. Everything she said spoke with a ring of truth in his heart. There was just one extra reason he had that she didn't—he didn't deserve it after the mistakes he'd made.

"I can understand how you feel," he said.

She inhaled a deep breath, closing her eyes for a moment as though she needed courage. "I want you to know those feelings... They've changed since I met you. I don't know where we go from here, but I know I want you in my life, not just as my pastor... and not just as a friend."

There it was.

The truth he'd wanted to say but couldn't.

The truth he'd wanted to hear.

The only problem was it was also the truth he wasn't sure if he could allow himself to hold onto. "But you deserve better than me."

"Why would you think such a thing?"

"Because it's true. I'm the reason for Maryanne's death. I don't want to be the reason for another woman getting hurt—least of all you."

She straightened her shoulders and shook her head. A crease

formed on her forehead. "But you aren't the reason for Maryanne's death."

"She died because I arrested a criminal, and his men wanted revenge."

"Yes, his men. You didn't choose to go to the house that day. You didn't choose to fire the weapon or do the harm they did by whatever means they did."

"But it wouldn't have happened if I hadn't done my job. She would still be alive."

"And how would Maryanne have seen the circumstances?"

Sarah's question twisted in his gut, and he straightened in the chair, leaning against the back until the wood pressed into his shoulder blades. "I beg your pardon?"

"Say they hadn't gotten to her, but they'd gotten to someone else. Perhaps another Ranger's wife. Would she tell you that the Ranger was to blame?"

"No, I don't think she would. In fact, I know she wouldn't."

"Then why do you?" Sarah paused but continued before he said anything. "Did she wish for you to quit your job? Did she ever tell you it was a risk and one you shouldn't take?"

"No. She didn't."

"Again, I have to ask, why do you?" Sarah leaned toward him, grabbing his hand once more. "What happened to your wife was horrible, and I do not wish it upon anyone. But it wasn't your fault."

So much of his heart ached to believe what Sarah said was true. Still, even with this desire, he wasn't sure he could. Doing so would erase the pain and guilt he'd lived with for so many long years, and it felt wrong, as though he washed his hands of any responsibility.

He didn't think he could do that.

"I don't know if I can see it that way."

"Then I suggest you start praying about it."

~

J ack's thoughts lingered on Sarah's last words as he made his way back upstairs. His mind swirled with not only the advice she'd given but also the thoughts of the future and the what-ifs that seemed to haunt the edges of his heart.

As he reached the top of the stairs, the creak of a door opening caught his attention, and Julia, Patrick's wife, stepped out into the hallway with a restless look in her eyes. She flinched. "Oh!"

"I'm sorry to startle you," Jack whispered.

"It's quite all right." She brushed her collarbone with her fingertips, and her shoulders softened.

"Couldn't sleep?" he asked gently.

"No. I can't seem to get comfortable." She rubbed her belly. "I thought perhaps a snack would help. Is Mrs. Holden still awake?"

"She is. She's in the kitchen. But I suspect she will retire to her cabin soon. You might want to hurry downstairs if you want to catch her." He hooked his thumb over his shoulder and took a step to leave and return to his room.

Julia reached out to stop him. "Wait, Mr. Boone."

"You may call me Jack. We are family, after all. Or at least in my eyes, we are."

A smile inched across Julia's face. "We are in mine, too." She paused, glancing down at the floor before looking back at him. "You did a good thing, sending Patrick that telegram and letting him know you'd left Texas."

"You think so?"

"You don't?"

"I'm not sure."

"I know your talk didn't go as well as you hoped, but I think Patrick just needs time, and we all need prayer."

"Yes, we do. Lots of it."

"He misses you." She paused, chuckling slightly. "He'd probably have my head if he ever learned I told you that. But it's true. He misses you."

Jack's chest tightened. He hadn't known how much hearing those words would affect him. "I hope you're right. I miss my sons, especially when I think about how I haven't been around for moments like your wedding or the birth of that baby."

"I'm sorry you missed it."

"I am, too. You're a lovely woman, and Patrick is lucky to have found you."

"And he's lucky to have a father like you, even if he doesn't realize it yet. I promise I won't let you miss out on anything else."

"It might be harder with me in Montana and you in Texas."

"We can still write... and visit." She glanced around the hallway. "It really is lovely here in Featherstone Valley—the town, the inn, and Mrs. Holden. She's been so wonderful to us all. I can see why you are happy here—or why you seem happy."

"It is a wonderful place indeed, and Sarah makes it more so."

A pause loomed between them until Julia laughed softly. "I didn't know she was a widow, just like you."

"Yes, she lost her husband a few years ago."

"She is pretty, too. And so kind."

Jack chuckled, the sound more wistful than he intended. "I've had similar thoughts myself," he admitted, his gaze drifting down the hallway toward the staircase leading downstairs to the kitchen. "Speaking of Sarah, you should head to the kitchen if you want a snack before she returns to her cabin."

Julia nodded, following his motion toward the staircase, her expression thoughtful. "It was nice talking to you," she said.

"You too. I hope you get some rest."

"Thank you, Jack. That means a lot."

As Julia waddled away, Jack's heart ached with a mix of sorrow and budding hope. His growing feelings for Sarah were a light in the fog of his loneliness, yet the shadow of his estrangement from Patrick loomed large. Missing his son's wedding was a regret that gnawed at him—a missed moment that he would never get back.

He thought of his other son, Kit. Had he married too, without Jack knowing?

He wondered about the paths not taken and the choices made in the name of duty and sacrifice.

Had he made nothing but mistakes?

While Sarah had shown him that perhaps there was a chance for redemption, for new beginnings, he still wondered if he could find a way to mend the fences with his sons, to bridge the gaps that had widened over the years.

He wasn't sure.

But he knew he wanted to try.

SEVENTEEN

PATRICK

"Have you been awake all night, darling?"

Patrick looked up from his papers to find Julia sitting upright in bed. The blanket was draped over one shoulder, and she cocked her head to the side with one eyebrow raised.

He shrugged and looked out the inn's window next to the small table where he sat. "Most of it, I suppose."

"Why don't you try to come back and get some rest?" she asked.

"I might later. But I'm going to get some work done."

"But the sun is just barely rising. It will be daytime soon."

"It's all right. I'm not that tired."

She stared at him for a good minute before laying back down and covering her shoulders with the blanket. He watched as she yawned, closed her eyes, and drifted back to sleep. A small part of him envied her, yet he knew no matter how much he longed for sleep for himself, it wouldn't come. He had too much on his mind.

He'd spent the good portion of the night tossing and turning beside her before sheer annoyance overwhelmed him, and he got up. He'd spent the rest of the night reading through his client's files, searching for anything that needed tweaking. It wasn't exactly a job he had to do, but being away from the office with only a few files left him without much of a distraction other than going over their investments with a fine-tooth comb and making notes on how to invest his own money.

He glanced back at Julia and then out the window, watching as the sun began to peek over the mountains in the distance. The light flecked across the tops of the pine trees, casting shadows where it couldn't touch. Featherstone Valley was even prettier than Butte, and while he wasn't sure about his reasons for visiting or that he even wanted to stay another day, he couldn't deny the town's attraction. It wasn't a mystery as to why his father took the job.

He thought of the conversation in the study. He had left in the heat of his anger, and when he returned last night after cooling off, he retreated to the hotel room, where he didn't talk to anyone about what happened.

He would never say coming to Featherstone Valley was a mistake, but he was starting to wonder what the point was—had he allowed Julia's words of forgiveness to get the better of him, giving him hope that speaking to his father would solve things? He almost wished he had listened to Aunt Bea and tossed the telegram in the trash without ever reading it.

His head pounded with an ache he had hoped would go away. Instead, it only seemed to worsen as the hours ticked by. His stomach growled. He hadn't eaten supper last night, opting instead to hide away. Not that he would have had the appetite last night, anyway. Food had little meaning to him last night, but this morning was a different story.

And it spoke of hunger.

He stood and stretched his arms above his head before slipping on his shoes and making his way to the door. The hallways and staircase were deserted, and not even the slightest sound came from any of the other rooms. He headed down the hallway and staircase to the first floor, and as he stepped off the last stair, the scent of coffee, eggs, and bacon filled the air. Sniffing at the salty smells, his stomach growled even more, and he followed his nose to a door on the other side of the dining room, where he stopped and leaned toward the wood to listen.

The sounds of spoons tapping on pans drowned out the slight hint of someone humming an early morning tune, and he knocked before opening the door a crack and peeking inside.

"Hello?" he said.

"Hello?" a female voice responded.

He opened the door a little more and poked his head inside.

"Good morning, Mr. Boone," Ms. Holden said. As his gaze met hers, she smiled and waved slightly as if to invite him into the kitchen. "I didn't wake you, did I?"

"Oh, no, no. I was awake... I had to get some work done."

"And what do you do for work, Mr. Boone?"

"I deal with investments for people."

"Investments. Like a banker?"

"Not really. I don't work with private people. My clients are companies—railroads, mining companies, and sawmills. Investment banks don't work with notes or deposits. I mainly serve as a broker, bringing investors with money into companies that need it."

She raised one eyebrow and slightly nodded. "Well, that... that sounds interesting."

"It has its moments." He chuckled and looked around the kitchen. "May I have a cup of coffee?"

"Oh, yes. I'm sorry." She brushed her fingertips against her forehead. "Where are my manners? Please excuse my rudeness."

"You weren't rude."

She moved around him and withdrew a mug from one of the cabinets. "The kettle is on the stove. Would you like cream or sugar?"

"Black is fine."

"Just like your father." She let out a slight chuckle, then after looking at Patrick, her smile vanished as though she realized what she'd said, and it suddenly occurred to her that he probably wouldn't like the comparison. She handed him the mug. "Sorry. I shouldn't have said that."

"It's all right. It didn't offend me." He took the mug and made his way over to the stove, grabbing the kettle and pouring himself a cup of coffee. "Breakfast smells good. Are you expecting everyone to wake up soon?"

She nodded. "The miners will be headed back up to the mines this morning, and they stop in for an early breakfast before they go. It's their last home-cooked meal until they return on Friday nights."

"What do they eat up at the mines?"

"Mostly beans and cornbread."

"All day, every day?"

She nodded. "They don't get much by way of eggs and bacon up in the mountains, so they always like to stop by the café before they leave, and since it's quite the trek up the mountain, they leave as the sun is coming up." She shifted her stance and looked out the window. "Speaking of which, I should get some plates served and ready."

She moved to the stove, grabbing the corner of her apron to protect her hand from the pot's hot handle. She scooped several spoonfuls of eggs onto several plates she'd laid out on the counter. Steam rose from the fluffy yellow food, and Patrick licked his lips.

"Do you think I can steal one of those plates?" he asked, not fully considering whether the question was rude.

"Of course, you can." She set down the spoon and grabbed a fork, stabbing a couple of pieces of bacon and setting them next to the eggs before handing him the plate. "If you need seconds, just ask."

"Thank you. I might take you up on that." He chuckled, feeling a bit of relief wash through him. "I am quite hungry."

"Skipping supper can do that."

They exchanged glances, and although she raised one eyebrow, she didn't say another word. Trying to ignore the hinted meaning behind her words, he shoveled a rather large bite of eggs into his mouth. Guilt prickled along the back of his neck, and after chewing and swallowing, he cleared his throat.

"Ms. Holden," he said, pausing until she turned and looked at him. "I want to apologize for yesterday. I shouldn't have behaved in such a manner, yelling the way I did. Although I was angry and had every right to be, I shouldn't have taken such a tone with you in your home and place of business. It won't happen again."

"Thank you for saying that." She offered a kind smile that eased the guilt in Patrick's heart, even if it was just a little. "For what it's worth, I think you have every right to be angry, too. But I will say I'm also a big believer in forgiveness."

"You, too, huh?" He ripped off a bite of bacon. "It seems like that's the point that everyone makes."

"Well, perhaps that means something."

Her words twisted in his stomach, and for the first time since he'd walked downstairs, his hunger seemed to vanish. Trends of the market, he would always hear men in his office say. People follow market trends, buying and selling into what others are buying and selling because that was an easier way to make money. He'd always prided himself on his ability to make deals from the sole point of 'if everyone is getting into whatever business or product he was trying to sell at the time, then they should too'. Wasn't that the easiest way to convince people? There will be a profit for a hot commodity, no matter what it is.

Only this time, the commodity wasn't something to profit from.

Well, monetarily, anyway.

He'd given forgiveness quite a bit of thought throughout the years, and while he couldn't deny that it now annoyed him, he couldn't help but still wonder about it. How would it feel? Would it change anything? Would it make it easier? Or would it be nothing short of a pointless endeavor that would only cause him more pain in the end?

"Forgiving and forgetting is not easy," he said.

She faced him once more, tilting her head to the side. "I don't recall saying that it was. Life isn't easy, Mr. Boone, and some make it more difficult than it should be because of their choices. It's up to you to decide how hard and easy you want your life to be."

"Has my father told you everything that happened?"

"He did."

"So, you can see how hard it would be for me?"

"I do. I see both sides, his and yours. I see pain. I see heartbreak. I see mistakes... but I also see a past you two could walk away from. I see forgiveness. I see hope in a future where a father and son can rebuild what they lost because deep down, they didn't lose it; they just think they did."

Patrick opened his mouth to respond, but the door opened behind him, and Aunt Bea entered the kitchen. Her eyes narrowed, and she strode toward them.

"Don't listen to that nonsense, Patrick," she said.

SARAH

A soft answer turns away wrath, but a harsh word stirs up anger. *Proverbs 15:1*

Sarah must have repeated this verse to herself at least a dozen times in her life. But in all the years she'd ever said it, none of them counted as much as this one time.

"I'm sorry, but nonsense?" She stared at the woman standing in her kitchen.

"Forgiveness. Forgetting. It's all nonsense. It's all dreamed up by those who did someone wrong and want to be excused for their actions or behavior." Beatrice folded her arms across her chest, squaring her shoulders.

A soft answer turns away wrath, but a harsh word stirs up anger. Proverbs 15:1

"I'm sorry you feel that way."

"And I'm sorry you don't."

Sarah inhaled a deep breath through her nose. "I beg your pardon?"

"I'm sorry you feel as though you must live the lie that all should be forgiven and forgotten. How awful it must be to not stand up for yourself like that." Beatrice narrowed her eyes again. "If you wish to lie to yourself, that's fine, but do not think I will stand by and allow you to taint my nephew's mind with your foolish notions."

"Aunt Bea, there's no need—"

"You don't have to say anything, Patrick. I can do just fine defending you from this woman's crazy notion that you have to forgive your father for all the wrong he's done."

"Defending him?" Sarah's head jerked back slightly. "He's a grown man. He's not a child."

"I know he's not a child. But he still is somewhat in my eyes. You obviously aren't a mother, or else you would know that no matter how old your children are, they will always have your protection."

The inn's front door opened, and several men filed inside before making their way to the dining room. Their chatter echoed through the doorframe into the kitchen. Sarah closed her eyes for a moment, then opened them and reached for a couple of plates, taking one in each hand. "I have to serve breakfast. Please excuse me." She moved past Beatrice, pausing as she passed the woman. "Before I leave, I would like to say a couple of things. First, I am a mother. I have two children who I brought into this world. You are right that mothers will protect even when their children are adults. However, that does not mean we treat them as children for the rest of their lives, and second, Patrick is not your son. He is your sister's son, and he is Jack's son. Lastly, if you wish to continue to speak to me or talk about Jack in the manner you have in my own home and place of business, I will have to kindly ask you to leave. You are welcome to take the stagecoach to the Deer Creek Inn."

Before Beatrice had a chance to say a word, Sarah left the kitchen, catching sight of Patrick's opened mouth gaze just before leaving the room.

After exiting through the door, she made her way to the first table of men, setting the plates in front of them.

"Good morning, gentlemen, sorry for the delay. I'll be right back with more." She turned to walk back into the kitchen, and her gaze met Jack, who was leaning against the wall near the door. A smile inched across his face, and the sight of his expression caused her to wonder if he hadn't just heard every word of her conversation with Beatrice.

"Good morning," he said as she passed him.

"Good morning. Are you hungry?"

"I could eat, but..." he pointed toward a table in the corner of the dining room. "I'll eat in the dining room if you don't mind."

"I'll bring you a plate in just a bit."

PATRICK

Patrick didn't know which had made his morning—the shock of seeing Mrs. Holden stand up to Aunt Bea in the manner that she did or the enjoyment of merely talking to her.

He couldn't help but smile when he thought of the older inn owner. She seemed like a genuine person, full of heart and soul. He almost envied the children she spoke of. Surely, she was a fantastic mother.

Just like his own mother.

Or at least what he remembers of her.

He was young, after all, and his memory wasn't what it was.

"So, did you get any sleep last night at all? Or were you up all night trying to distract yourself with work?"

Julia's voice jerked his thoughts and attention, and he glanced at her as they strolled down the street toward the tiny town. The slight breeze they'd felt when they left the inn, telling Aunt Bea they wanted to check out the sites of Featherstone Valley, had picked up, and a few of her red curls blew into her face, catching in her eyelashes as she blinked. She brushed her hair away.

"I got some," he defended. "A few hours at least."

"Are you sure?"

He furrowed his brow, trying to think of how last night had been. He knew he went to bed and tossed and turned awhile before finally getting up. Surely, there was some rest between the dreams that didn't want him to sleep.

"No," he admitted.

"I'm sorry you had a bad night." Julia tightened her grip on his arm and exhaled a deep breath. "It's been quite the trip for you, and we haven't had a chance to discuss it."

"What is there to talk about?" He shrugged.

"There is a lot to talk about." She blinked at him, and she continued before he could say anything. "For one, I would like to hear how you've felt about seeing your father again after all these years. I would also like to know how you felt after your conversation."

"I'm sure you heard how it went."

"Well, yes, I did. But that doesn't mean I know how you felt about it. Do you think you will try talking to your father again?"

Patrick shrugged a second time. "I don't know."

"Do you want my opinion?"

"I'm not entirely sure I do, but I know I will hear about it anyway."

She flattened her lips, giving him a stern look out of the corner of her eye. "I think you should speak to him again, and I think you should leave your anger in another room while you do it."

He stopped and turned to face her, wiggling his arm from her grasp. "My—"

She held up her hand. "Hear me out before you argue... when you come into a conversation with anger, you don't listen. All you feel, see, hear, and want to speak is your anger, and doing so doesn't allow you to hear the other person."

"But I don't want—"

She held up her hand again. "You are proving my point, Patrick."

"It just sounds like you're making excuses for him."

"I am not making excuses for anyone. You have every right to feel your anger; I have never said otherwise. But that doesn't mean you shouldn't listen to his side. Just as he should listen to your side."

Why did she have to hit me with logic? Of all the times...

"Fine," he growled. "I suppose if the opportunity presents itself for us to talk again, I will do so, and I will try to remain calm and not talk with my anger."

"That's all I wanted to suggest."

Patrick wanted to roll his eyes but thought better of it. He knew her advice came not only from a place of love but from wisdom and patience—three qualities he never seemed to have regarding his feelings about his father. Did he enjoy that it was such a flicker for him? No. But did he want to actively change it? He wasn't sure.

Why was it always easier to let go of love than to let go of anger?

Why did people seem to take more comfort in holding grudges than forgiveness?

He thought of his Aunt Bea and how she'd held so much hatred for his father all these years. Her bitterness had cost her so much time and energy, and he thought of all the times she would go on long rants, barely breathing through her words while she dragged Jack Boone's name through the mud.

Had it made her feel better, talking in the manner she did?

Patrick didn't think so.

In fact, he knew so. He knew it didn't ever make her feel better, and if it did, the validating feelings she sought when she ranted were short-lived.

Or at least that's how he felt when he went through those kinds of moments.

He thought of Mrs. Holden, too, and the interaction this morning set another smile on his face. She'd been so calm yet firm. Convicted in her stance, she put her foot down, immediately moving on from the moment. Once she returned from delivering a few breakfast plates to the miners, she changed back into the welcoming and comforting woman she'd been since they arrived. There was no grudge. No

"What are you thinking about?" Julia asked, raising an eyebrow at his amusement after such a serious conversation.

"Oh, nothing."

"It's not nothing."

"Well, this morning, while I was enjoying breakfast, Aunt Bea entered the kitchen. She hadn't exactly had anything nice to say about my father, and Mrs. Holden… well, she didn't waste a moment putting Aunt Bea in her place. It was the first time I've seen anyone stand up to that woman."

"I bet that was a sight to see," Julia chuckled.

"It was."

"How did your aunt take it?"

Patrick chuckled. "I think she was just as shocked as I was." He pointed toward a few buildings in town as they approached them. "Well… what would you like to see first?"

"Everything."

EIGHTEEN

PATRICK

Patrick watched as Julia's eyes lit up. She smiled at everyone who passed them along the road into town, nodding a greeting while he struggled even to tip his hat. That was her, though. Always the ever-cordial one, she made everything better. He hadn't ever known how he'd gotten so lucky to not only meet her, but for her to fall in love with him and agree to marry him. Her father certainly wasn't always keen on the idea—although he eventually changed his mind.

"Shall we check out the mercantile?" she asked, pointing toward a prominent building in the center of town.

"If you wish. Although, I'm not sure why you want to."

She shrugged. "I'm just curious about this little town your father moved to. It's intrigued me from the moment we arrived." A little sparkle glinted in her eyes as she looked around the town, and a smile spread across her face.

Patrick shook his head, slightly laughing at her admiration as he followed her up the stairs and into the mercantile. A tiny bell chimed over their heads, and a balding man wearing spectacles greeted them as they entered.

"Good afternoon," he said.

"Good afternoon." Julia smiled again and waddled over to the counter.

"What can I help you with today?" the man asked.

"We're just here to look around. My husband and I are visiting family, and I wanted to look around the town." She glanced at the shelves on the wall behind the counter, noticing all the different bottles of whatever products were inside them.

"Well, I'm glad you decided to come in today. Welcome to my store. I'm Arthur Lockhart."

"It's nice to meet you, Mr. Lockhart. I'm Julia Boone." She hooked her thumb over her shoulder. "This is my husband, Patrick Boone."

Mr. Lockhart reached out to shake Julia's and then Patrick's hands. "Boone, huh? I suppose you're related to our Pastor Boone."

"Yes," Julia answered while Patrick remained tight-lipped. It wasn't that he wanted to be rude, but he also preferred to ignore the man's question and not answer it. "Pastor Boone is my husband's father."

"You don't say." Mr. Lockhart nodded. "Well, I think that's just wonderful. Both my wife and I love having your father—and your father-in-law," he said right to Julia, "as our pastor. He's been a wonderful addition to our town."

"That's lovely to know." Julia glanced at Patrick and smiled. "Isn't it, darling?"

"Yes. Quite." He turned away from his wife, closing his eyes as he inhaled deeply. He wished he had her ability to see the wonderful side of everything.

You can, you know, he thought to himself. *You just have to do it.*

He spun back toward her, smiling. "I'm sure my father is equally happy living in this fine town as you are of having him."

"That's good to hear, given his rocky start." Mr. Lockhart chuckled, twisting his face as he rolled his eyes.

"Rocky start?" Julia raised one eyebrow and cocked her head. "What do you mean, Mr. Lockhart?"

"Well, it seems that the town's new gossip columnist for the newspaper took quite the interest in finding any bad press she could on your father. Whoever it is authored some pretty nasty articles if you ask me." The store owner shook his head, glancing down at the counter. "It's been about the only bad thing about living in this town as of late."

Julia pressed her hand against her chest. "Oh my. That's terrible." She paused and asked, "What do you mean, whoever it is?"

"No one knows who he or she is. Some of the townsfolk have complained to Mr. Jenkins, the owner of the newspaper, about it. I thought he would fire whoever is writing them, but it hasn't happened yet."

Julia blinked as she glanced between Patrick and Mr. Lockhart. "That is... I don't know what to make of that."

"You aren't the only one who doesn't, Mrs. Boone." Mr. Lockhart took a deep breath. "We have all just learned to ignore the articles, and we pray that one day, enough people will complain to Mr. Jenkins that he'll take the column out of the newspaper."

"I shall say a few prayers for you myself."

"Thank you, Mrs. Boone." He nodded his appreciation and took another deep breath. "But enough of such troublesome talk. Is there anything I can help you two with this afternoon, aside from you wishing just to browse?"

Julia exhaled a sigh. "No, not really. We were just looking around." Once again, she started looking around the mercantile.

"Well, I'll let you two to it and not take up any more of your time. If you have any questions, please ask."

"Thank you, Mr. Lockhart. We will."

With one last nod toward the couple, Mr. Lockhart backed away from the counter, turned, and made his way toward the back stockroom, disappearing through a pair of curtains. Julia reached for Patrick, hooking her arm around his as he led her through different parts of the store. She studied the shelves of jarred food—jams, jellies, and everything under the sun pickled for freshness and great taste.

"They have quite the array of products," Julia said. She reached for a row of different jams, letting her fingertips brush against the tops of the jars. "One might think they live in a large city, not a small town."

They continued to several crates of root vegetables, such as carrots, potatoes, beets, broccoli, and heads of lettuce and cabbage. Behind them were even more shelves with loaves of baked bread wrapped in paper. Julia grabbed a loaf, taking it to her nose as she inhaled the deep aroma.

"Oh my. That smells amazing. I wonder if Mrs. Holden would make us sandwiches for the trip home if I bought a few loaves."

"I'm sure she would."

Julia glanced at him from the corner of her eye without moving her head. "Speaking of which, when do you think we will head back to Texas?"

Patrick shrugged. "I'm not sure. But we should think about it sooner rather than later."

"Why?"

"Because of your condition."

"Oh, I'm all right. I assure you. You shouldn't worry at all about me."

"But I do worry, and I should, as your husband. It would be better for you to be home in the city where there is a doctor we know and trust." He paused, furrowing his brow. "In fact, just thinking about it makes me nervous enough that I think I will look into when the next stage is leaving Featherstone Valley."

"But we just got here."

"So?"

"So, I think you should at least try to spend a little more time with your father before we leave. I think you should try to talk to him again."

"I'm not sure if that's a good idea. I think it just might be a lost hope."

"Nothing is a lost hope."

Patrick closed his eyes, inhaled a deep breath, and grabbed the bridge of his nose, pinching it. He wasn't in the mood to argue. He wasn't in the mood to do much of anything, really. Well, except for finding out when the next stage left this town. He was interested in that.

"Can we just not talk about this right now?" he asked, finally opening his eyes to meet her gaze.

She blinked at him for a moment before nodding.

"Good. Where do you want to go now?"

She shrugged. "How about we just keep walking around? Perhaps we could even go to the schoolhouse. I saw it when the stage rolled into town."

"The schoolhouse? Isn't it also the church?"

"So what if it is? It's not a Sunday."

He narrowed his eyes, knowing what she was doing even as she tried to hide behind some justification that just because it wasn't Sunday didn't mean they would run into his father.

"All right. We can visit the school. Although, I don't know why you would want to."

"I suppose that I just want to see where the children of this town learn."

"Why?"

She shrugged again. "No reason."

Before he could say another word, she strode off toward the door, stopping by a table to examine the stack of newspapers on top. Her brow furrowed, and she grabbed the newspaper on the top, unfolding it as she read the front page.

"Patrick?" she called out, and as he approached, she handed

him the newspaper. "It seems your father isn't the only Boone to be the subject of gossip in Featherstone Valley."

"What do you mean?"

"Read it."

A WELCOME PARTY TO REMEMBER

Greetings, beloved readers of Featherstone Valley! It's your faithful correspondent, Prudence Chatterton, here to dish out the latest and most tantalizing tales from our charming town. This week's event, the welcome party for Pastor Jack Boone, turned out to be more than just a mere gathering – it was a night that will be etched in our town's memory for years to come!

The evening began with the usual fanfare – a splendid array of dishes, laughter ringing through the air, and warm handshakes. Mayor Duncan, always the gracious host, was in his element until Mr. Craig Harrison, known for his ambitions concerning Rattlesnake Mountain, stepped in. The air quickly thickened with tension as these two influential men locked horns once again over the future of our beloved mountain. Their heated exchange was the talk of the party, with many guests speculating about the outcome of this long-standing feud.

But, dear readers, the real twist of the evening came with the arrival of three unexpected guests. A young couple – the man with a look of earnest concern and his pregnant wife, radiating a mix of excitement and nervousness – accompanied by an older woman whose gaze could curdle milk. The older woman's eyes fixed on Pastor Boone with a look that spoke volumes of a history fraught with emotion.

Whispers swept through the crowd as the trio approached the pastor. It was clear they were acquainted, but how? The older woman's disdainful glances toward Pastor Boone sparked a wildfire of speculation. Could she be a figure from his enigmatic past? And what of the young couple – were they family or perhaps old friends caught in a tangled web of past affairs?

The pastor, usually the epitome of composure, seemed momentarily taken aback, his face a canvas of conflicting emotions. The townsfolk watched, enraptured, as this silent drama unfolded.

As the night drew to a close, questions lingered in the air, heavier than the scent of Mrs. Holden's apple pie. Who were these mysterious visitors, and what secrets did they bring to Featherstone Valley? The older woman's scornful looks toward Pastor Boone hinted at a story yet untold, a chapter in the pastor's life that perhaps he hoped would remain closed.

Fear not, for your devoted Prudence Chatterton is on the case! I shall leave no stone unturned, no whisper unexamined, to bring you the truth behind these intriguing newcomers and their connection to our pastor.

So, stay tuned, dear readers. Featherstone Valley is abuzz with secrets and stories, and I, Prudence Chatterton, am here to uncover them all. Until next time, keep your eyes wide, your ears open, and your hearts ready for the next twist in our town's ever-unfolding saga!

Patrick didn't just read the article once; he read it a second and third time to be sure he hadn't missed any words, and as he finished the last sentence the third time, a hard lump formed in his throat. He tried to swallow it but couldn't.

"Unfolding saga, huh?" he finally said, jerking his head as he snorted a slight laugh. "Just where does this woman get her nerve?"

Julia lifted her finger and wiggled it. "Now, now, don't just assume it's a woman. Mr. Lockhart said they don't know who is writing it. For all anyone knows, it could be a man."

"You think a man wrote this?" He motioned toward the newspaper, shaking his head. "The wording... it doesn't sound like a man to me." He folded the newspaper and tossed it back onto the table. His stomach twisted as he thought of the words he'd just read. He had enough trouble with the fact that he was visiting his estranged father. Now he had to worry about some woman or man walking around town, watching his every move, judging him, and writing stories about him. He didn't even live in this town, for Pete's sake! "Now, do you understand why we should head back to Texas?" He motioned toward the door. "We should return to the inn."

"No. I still want to visit the school."

"Why? Aren't you worried that this Prudence Chatterton will write more articles about you?"

Julia shrugged. "So what if they do? Besides, you heard Mr. Lockhart. The townsfolk just ignore these articles anyway. Walking into town today, we received nothing but smiles and warm greetings. No one cared about that article, so you shouldn't."

"But—"

"I want to visit the school. Then we can return to the inn." She folded her arms across her chest, resting her forearms and elbows on her belly. Even though Patrick wanted to argue with her, he couldn't. She looked cute when she was acting fierce, and having the belly now gave her even more cuteness, if that was possible.

He couldn't argue with her.

Not this time.

"All right. Let's find the school."

While the schoolhouse and church looked the same as some in the small towns in Texas, Patrick couldn't help but feel a difference that seemed to wash over him when looking at the schoolhouse in Featherstone Valley. Perhaps it was how the small white building with green shutters sat against the mountain backdrop with the pond nearby or how the snow played off the sunlight, surrounding the tiny building with a sea of diamond-like sparkles. Whatever the reason, he just got an overwhelming sense of peace.

Perhaps it's not the schoolhouse at all, he thought. *Perhaps it's the church.*

He furrowed his brow with his thoughts. That was something that his wife would say, not him. He wasn't big on that stuff.

No, it's not the church, he thought. *It's just... something else.*

"What a precious little schoolhouse," Julia's smile beamed across her face, and she tightened the grip on his arm. A slight bounce hinted in her steps, and she quickened her pace, leading him instead of him leading her. "I wonder if we can go inside."

"You want to see the inside?"

"Of course."

"But there are probably children in there, learning."

"So?"

"Are you suggesting we interrupt their studies so that we can see the inside?"

Patrick saw a flicker of hesitation wash through Julia's face, and for a moment, he thought he had finally stuck sense into his wife.

But only for a moment.

"Oh, they won't mind." She waved her hand and quickened her pace a little more, waddling through the snow.

He stopped, pulling her to a stop too, and as she turned toward him, he cocked his head and raised one eyebrow. "Why do you want to go inside the schoolhouse so badly?"

She shrugged. "I just do. Perhaps with the baby coming, I just want to see what small-town schoolhouses look like."

"Why would it matter, though? We don't live here." Questions fired off in his mind about his wife's true intentions. Was it really about the schoolhouse? Or was it about the church? Did she believe that his father was there? Was she hoping they would talk? Surely, she wouldn't think that a schoolhouse full of children would be the best audience for him to attempt to speak to his father again.

"I just want to see it, all right?" She furrowed her brow momentarily and tugged on his arm, bringing him closer to the schoolhouse.

The early afternoon sun brightened the snow around the little building, making the green shutters pop against the colorless hue of the white. As they neared, the doors swung open, and several students trotted out, bundled up in coats and hats; they darted down the stairs, shouting at one another about which game they would play for recess. A young woman followed them all, bringing up the rear as she lifted her hand to shield her eyes from the sunlight and smiled. Her breath clouded her vision as she watched the children search through the snow for different things they could play with. One boy grabbed a ball and threw it at another one, who grabbed it and threw it at a third. Round and round, they threw it to one another, adding more boys and girls into the game until soon nearly all of them were playing it.

"Don't let it hit the ground," the first one who grabbed it said.

Patrick glanced at Julia, who smiled as she watched the children and tugged on his arm even more until they reached the stairs.

The young woman turned toward them. "Good afternoon," she said.

"Good afternoon." Julia smiled again and motioned toward her husband. "We are Mr. and Mrs. Patrick Boone."

"Ah. You must be related to Pastor Boone."

"Yes, he's my father-in-law." Julia motioned toward Patrick again. "And his father."

"How wonderful. I'm Miss Evans, and I'm the schoolteacher. Are you here to visit your father?"

"Is he here?" Julia asked.

"Yes. He's in his office. He's here most days. He says he likes to hear the children while they learn. He says there is nothing like a young mind learning something new. I may be biased, given that I'm a teacher, but I must agree." Miss Evans chuckled, then glanced at the children still playing the game before looking back at Patrick and Julia. "You're more than welcome to go inside and knock on his office door while the children enjoy their recess."

"Actually, we are here to see the schoolhouse," Patrick said. As soon as the words left his lips, a pang of guilt twisted in his chest. He hadn't thought about what he said and how it sounded until after he said it.

Miss Evans blinked. "Oh. Well, I can show you around the schoolhouse. It's not the biggest of buildings, so there isn't much to show." She half chuckled as she approached the door and waved them to follow her. "But it serves the town and the children, and I couldn't hope for a better blessing from God."

Patrick and Julia followed her inside. Their shoes clicked on the lightly stained hardwood floors, and while Patrick stayed closer to the door, not venturing inside more than a few feet, Julia unhooked her arm from his and followed Miss Evans to the front of the room. She circled a few times, pointing at everything from the chalkboards on the walls to the rows of desks that folded down into the backs of the seats in front of them, turning the seats into pews where the townsfolk sat for church services.

"I had once considered studying to be a teacher," Julia said, grabbing a slate off one of the desks and studying the words the student had written in chalk. "But my father didn't think it would suit me."

"Why?" Miss Evans asked.

Julia shrugged. "I don't know. I think perhaps he wanted me to be more like my mother—the doting wife with all her societal responsibilities. Don't get me wrong, she does important charity work, but I was never one for a life of parties and social events. Still, I wasn't allowed, so I did what was proper for my family."

Julia glanced around the room, and as Patrick watched, her thoughts weighed heavy on his mind. He had never heard Julia speak ill of the life they'd created, and while he didn't think that was what she was doing now-—at least not entirely—he couldn't help but hear the slight melancholy in her voice.

Had she been unhappy with the life they shared?

He had a successful job that allowed her the luxury of not worrying about finding one of her own. They had a lovely home, and her days were filled with attending charity events, afternoon teas, and dress shopping trips in the city with her mother whenever she had the whim. He had thought she'd enjoyed her day-to-day life, but he now questioned his beliefs.

And he wasn't sure he liked it.

Not because he wanted her to be that doting wife without dreams to follow or a sense of purpose in life outside of the one she lived, but because he wanted her to have everything she'd ever wanted.

He wanted her to have the world.

"But," she heaved a deep sigh and smiled as she rubbed her belly. "I suppose I will have the pleasure of teaching a child soon, and while it won't be the education he or she will get from school, I can still teach the basics: reading and writing."

"Anything parents teach before a child goes to school is a blessing. A few students are ahead of their studies just because their parents started them before they brought them to school."

"That's good to hear."

Julia took a few more turns, looking at everything in the schoolhouse while gushing about everything from the coat hangers to the shelves where the students kept their lunch pails.

"Where does that lead?" she asked, pointing toward a closed door in the back of the schoolhouse.

Miss Evans's eyes flickered from Patrick to Julia, and she cleared her throat. "That... that is Pastor Boone's office."

"Oh." Julia inhaled and glanced over her shoulder at Patrick.

"Julia, I don't think you should bother—"

Before he could finish his sentence, Julia made her way over to the door, and with a clenched fist, she knocked. Patrick's heart hammered.

This was precisely why she wanted to visit the schoolhouse.

The door opened, and Patrick's father peered through the frame. He blinked as he looked from his daughter-in-law to his son.

"Good afternoon, Julia," he said.

"Good afternoon, Jack." A smile beamed across her face. "We came by the schoolhouse to see it, and Miss Evans mentioned you were in your office, so I thought I would say hello."

"Well, I'm glad you did."

"Are we bothering you?"

"No, not at all." He opened his door a little wider. "Come in and see my office if you wish."

"Thank you." Glancing over her shoulder at Patrick again, she left him standing in the middle of the schoolhouse, not wanting to follow her but knowing he should.

I should have seen this coming, he thought.

NINETEEN

JACK

Jack's heart thumped as Julia and Patrick sat on the other side of his desk. He hadn't had any visitors to his office since he'd arrived. Well, except for Sarah knocking on his door the morning before his first sermon. He hadn't had much chance to decorate it, not that it needed much. It was just a pastor's office, meant for him to counsel members of his congregation, not impress them with stylish trimmings and whatnot that did nothing for the room. Not to mention, he'd never been one to need anything outside the basic furniture. Give him a desk, a couple of chairs, and a lamp, and he would be happy.

"I'm glad you two stopped by this afternoon," he said, trying to ignore how uncomfortable his son looked sitting near the wall.

"This is quite the town you've moved to, Mr. Boone," Julia said, her eyes darting around the office. The excitement that had fueled their entire tour of the town still resonated in her voice, adding a little bounce to her movements.

"Yes, I agree. I've enjoyed my time here and look forward to many years."

"I bet you are. We visited the mercantile earlier. Mr. Lockhart seems nice."

"He is."

"Then I told Patrick I wanted to visit the schoolhouse, and, well, here we are."

"It's one of the finer schoolhouses I've seen in my travels. And churches, too. I've enjoyed it." He glanced between his son and daughter-in-law, waiting for Patrick to add to the conversation. He said nothing.

Julia seemed to notice, too, and after glancing at her husband, she clasped her hands together, giving a slight clap as she prattled on, talking faster than he'd heard someone talk. "And the supplies at the mercantile... I was surprised to find it so well stocked with different canned goods and the bread selection... they all smelled wonderful. I told Patrick I wanted to buy some and ask if Mrs. Holden would make us sandwiches for our trip home."

As soon as she said the word 'home,' Jack's stomach clenched.

They were already talking about leaving.

While he wasn't surprised that his son wouldn't want to stay long, he still couldn't help but feel a bit shocked by the news. It'd only been a few days since they'd arrived. They couldn't leave now, not when he had so much to say to his son.

"I didn't know you were planning on leaving so soon," he said, looking more at his son than his daughter-in-law.

Patrick stared at the floor, furrowing his brow. Julia glanced at him, too, and after waiting for him to speak, she turned her attention toward Jack. "We haven't decided on when we will. Truth be told, I would like to stay for a while. I find this town fascinating."

"But the baby." Patrick finally looked up at her. "And my job. I've already been gone far too long."

Julia merely glanced at her husband without saying

anything. Jack got the impression this wasn't the first time they had had this conversation, and he wasn't sure he wanted to be in the middle of it.

He opened his mouth to suggest a change of subject when a knock rapped against the door.

"Come in," he said.

The door opened, and Sheriff Thorn poked his head inside. "Good afternoon, Pastor Boone," he said.

"Good afternoon, Sheriff. What can I help you with?"

"I'm just going around town and making sure people know there's a storm brewing with dark clouds in the distance, and it doesn't look good. It might be best if you returned to the inn so you don't find yourself caught outside in it."

"Of course. Thank you, Sheriff."

After the sheriff nodded and shut the door, Jack, Patrick, and Julia looked at one another. "Well," Jack said, exhaling a breath. "Shall we return to the inn?"

By the time the three of them reached the inn, the wind had picked up, blowing snow around and causing near white-out conditions. Jack could hardly make out the frame of the inn as they approached, and they relied on holding onto the fence posts to find the gate before making their way to the door. Snow blew into the foyer, dusting the hardwood floor with white powder. Cold air whipped around them.

"Oh, thank heaven." Beatrice darted for them, wrapping her arms around Julia first, then Patrick. "I was so worried. You never told me where you planned to go, and I didn't know if I should look for you two." Her voice cracked.

"We're sorry to worry you," Julia said. "We were just touring the town a little. The sheriff told us we should return to the inn with the storm. It seems we just barely made it." She walked over to the window and pulled the curtain away from the glass. Her body shivered. "I hope no one is out in this."

"Yes, yes. We will pray there isn't." Beatrice motioned toward the young woman. "Come on into the parlor. Mrs. Holden started a fire, and it's nice and warm. She also made a pot of tea." The three entered the parlor while Jack hung back, watching them disappear into the room before heading into the kitchen to find Sarah reaching for a few pots.

"You made it," she said, seeing him.

"I did."

"Did Sheriff Thorn come by the church?"

"He did."

"It was such a beautiful morning. Who would have thought a storm would blow in this fast?" She filled the pot with water, setting it on the stove before going to the nearest window. Like Julia, she moved the curtain and peered outside. "I can't even see the barn."

A sudden thought dawned on him. "The animals," he said.

She glanced over her shoulder and shook her head. "They are fine. After the sheriff stopped by, I went to the barn and penned them inside. I gave the cows fresh hay and water and gave the chickens some more corn and scraps from breakfast. They will be fine until this storm blows through." She exhaled a deep breath and turned toward him. "I was just about to start dinner. I left a pot of tea in the parlor if you want something to warm you up."

"Do you want help with supper?"

She smiled. "You're more than welcome to help me. Or you can enjoy time with your son and daughter-in-law."

Huh. Nothing like being torn in two.

∾

SARAH

As Sarah stared at Jack, his face twisted with the choice of staying with her in the kitchen or going to the study where his son was. She half regretted saying the words she did. She didn't want him to have to choose any more than she wanted to make him feel as though he had to choose.

She would never put anyone in that position, much less him.

She wouldn't want anyone to put her there, and she would never choose someone over her son, Luke, or her daughter, Elana.

"I'm sorry," she said, shaking her head as she brushed her forehead. "I shouldn't have said it that way."

The kitchen door opened, and Julia, followed by Patrick, walked inside. Julia's forehead furrowed in concern, and her voice cracked.

"Have you looked out the window?" she asked.

Sarah turned toward the nearest window. While she could once see the barn from the frosted glass, she couldn't now. Not only had a layer of snow built up on the window, but even through the tiny spaces where snow wasn't clinging to the glass, the wind was blowing so much snow around that everything in the outside world was hidden from view, covered in sheets of nothing but white.

"It's gotten so bad. I've never seen anything like this," Julia strode to the window and stood beside Sarah. "Have you?"

"This isn't bad. This is Montana." Sarah glanced at her, smiling, then laid her arm around Julia's shoulder. She squeezed her and released her. "Don't worry. It will be sunny tomorrow and will look like there wasn't even a storm."

"I've seen weather like this with rain but not snow." She wrapped her arms around herself as if to hug herself, and her whole body shivered slightly. "I can't imagine being outside in this storm right now. I hope everyone made it home safely."

"I'm sure they did."

"What about the miners?" Patrick asked as he approached

the women. His sudden voice made Sarah's head turn, and she faced him as he stood next to his wife. "Those men that came in here this morning for breakfast. You said they were going into the mountains and wouldn't return until the end of the week."

His genuine concern made Sarah smile. She saw so much of Jack in him at this moment, and not just in the shape of his face or his eyes, but in the concerned nature she saw hidden behind his words. "They have a cabin they can hunker down in just in case they need to. It's crowded with them all inside, but they should be all right."

"Can we say a prayer for them at dinner tonight?" Julia asked.

"Of course." Sarah patted Julia's shoulder, inhaling a deep breath. "Speaking of dinner, I should get started." She glanced at the basket of vegetables she'd gathered from the root cellar and pointed to the pot she'd placed on the counter. "I think a nice stew is just what we all need for this cold night."

Julia turned as Sarah walked away from the window and toward the middle of the kitchen. "That's why we came in—to ask if you needed help."

"Aunt Bea went to her room," Patrick said, glancing toward the ceiling as though he were looking toward the inn's second floor. "She said to call her when supper was ready."

"I hope she is feeling all right," Sarah said. She stayed in her room most of the afternoon, only coming down when she noticed the weather outside her window.

"That was probably to your benefit." Julia laughed, glancing from Sarah to Patrick. "But she is all right." Julia then glanced at Jack. "She didn't think it was best to come into the kitchen to help given... how this morning apparently went."

"Ah. I see." Sarah looked at Jack, who ducked his head, tucking his chin to his chest to hide the small smile across his lips. "Well," she inhaled a deep breath, "the stew isn't going to make itself." She pointed toward the basket of vegetables as she looked at Jack. "Can you chop the carrots and potatoes?"

"Of course."

"Why don't you help him?" Julia said to Patrick.

He nodded too and looked at Jack while he moved over to the counter and grabbed a knife. A flicker of longing hinted in his eyes and movements. Was it a connection to his father? Or at least to speak to the man? Or was it merely that he wanted to leave the room? Had Julia forced him to follow her, telling him she was headed to the kitchen and if he didn't join her, he'd be stuck in the study alone? Or worse, she wouldn't talk to him for the rest of the night?

Sarah glanced at Julia, who had also been watching the two men. The women looked at one another as though thinking the same thing—how could they entice Jack and Patrick to talk?

Sarah cleared her throat. "Did you have a nice time in town this afternoon?"

"Oh yes. It was lovely." Julia smiled, and the two women looked at each other and then at the men again. Julia slightly shook her head, wiggling her eyebrows.

They would have to try a different tactic.

Sarah moved alongside Jack, keeping her gaze on the carrots he cut with the knife. "Did you finish writing Sunday's sermon?" she asked.

"I didn't finish it, but I know what I want to say." He paused mid-chop, looking down at her, and as she looked up at him, her heartbeat quickened. The room around them became fuzzy, and heat flushed up the back of her neck. Everything about him drew her in like a moth to a flame. He looked at her again, dropping his voice to a whisper. "Am I cutting this all right?"

"Of course."

"Not too thick?"

She shook her head.

"Not too thin?"

She shook her head again.

"What do you want me to do when I finish with these?"

"Do you want to make the cornbread?" She looked at Julia and Patrick, hoping the excitement coming from her words and smile would ease the uncomfortable stiffness in Patrick's shoulders. "I think his recipe might be better than mine. It's truly delicious."

Patrick closed his eyes and set his knife down. He inhaled a deep breath and backed away from the counter. "I'm sorry," he whispered.

"Patrick, darling? What's the matter?"

"I just need a moment."

Sarah's stomach twisted. She had hoped to start a dialogue between father and son, not drive a wedge farther between them.

"I just need a moment," Patrick repeated. He spun toward the door, taking only a few steps before Julia screamed.

Her shrill sound caused everyone in the kitchen to flinch, and Sarah gasped as the young woman grabbed her belly—a pool of water surrounded her feet.

By the time they got Julia upstairs and into the bed, chaos had erupted throughout the inn. Beatrice was sitting in the corner of the room, chewing her nails while her body rocked back and forth. Her shoulders were hunched over as though she was nothing more than a helpless child lost and scared. Jack stood in the other corner with his arms folded across his chest and his chin tucked, while Patrick paced the floors, screaming that not only was this happening too soon, but he was angry it was happening at all.

"This is why I didn't want to come on this trip!" he shouted.

Each time he opened his mouth about it, Julia rolled her eyes.

Surprisingly calm, she lay in the bed, shaking her head as she watched her husband pace and Sarah gather more blankets and pillows.

"Darling, there's no need to get angry. What's done is done. Now, we must focus on what to do."

"What to do? What to do? We call for the doctor. That's what we do."

"In this weather?" She pointed toward the window in their room, and everyone followed her finger with their eyes.

Even through the curtains, Sarah could see that everything was covered in thick snow. "I don't know that we will be able to fetch Dr. Sterling," she said, half regretting her words even if they were true.

"What do you mean?" Patrick stopped and faced Sarah. His eyes widened. "My wife needs the doctor. She's going to have a child."

"I am aware of that, Mr. Boone. However, I'm also aware of the storm outside. Not only could one get lost in a snowstorm like this, but it could freeze a man in seconds. Dr. Sterling's home is across town."

"I don't care if it was across the state of Montana." Patrick clenched his fists and glanced out the window. "My wife needs the doctor."

"I don't need a doctor, darling," Julia said. "I can do this—" She paused, sucking in a breath and holding it as she leaned forward, closed her eyes, and grabbed chunks of the bedsheets. Every muscle in her body tightened.

"Don't hold your breath," Sarah said, laying her hand on Julia's shoulder. "Keep breathing."

With her eyes still clamped shut, Julia inhaled and exhaled several times before her body softened. She laid back against her pillow. Sarah didn't envy the young woman. She was in for a long, painful night, even if, at the end of the journey, she would welcome her son or daughter into the world.

The joyful moment wasn't without hardship.

"I have Mrs. Holden," Julia said through her breaths.

"She is not a doctor."

"So? What do you think women do who live in places where there is no doctor?"

Sarah's heartbeat kicked up as she glanced between the couple and then at Jack. He looked at her in return. His brow furrowed. "Have you delivered a baby before?" he asked.

She shook her head. "I have helped a couple of women in my day, plus I delivered two of my own."

Beatrice made a scoffing sound, rolling her eyes. "Helping a time or two is not enough. Patrick, Julia needs a doctor."

"It's enough to know what to do." She looked at Julia. "I will do my best to help you through this."

Julia nodded, still panting. "I know you will. We will pray, and everything will be all right."

"You are not leaving this up to God." Patrick rounded the bed, grabbing the headboard behind his wife as he leaned toward her. "Aunt Bea is right. You need a doctor."

"I will fetch Dr. Sterling." Jack moved toward the bed, unfolding his arms. His voice was deep, determined, and he marched toward the door, reaching for the doorknob.

Sarah reached out and grabbed his arm. "You can't go out in this storm," she said.

"It will be all right."

"No, it won't. You could get lost and freeze to death. I've heard of it happening."

"I won't get lost. I will stay close to town and to the buildings." He glanced at Patrick, squaring his shoulders to match his voice. "I will fetch the doctor for your wife."

Patrick closed his eyes, nodding as he opened them. "Thank you."

Without another word, Jack left the room. Sarah listened to his footsteps, and by the time he reached the stairs, she couldn't hold herself back. She looked at Julia, Patrick, and even Beatrice. "You can't let him do this," she said to them all. "He could die."

"And Julia could die if she is not helped by a doctor." Beatrice moved from the corner she'd been standing in and made her way over to the bed. Her unconcern over the danger Jack faced ruffled Sarah's last nerve. Of course, she wouldn't care that he was risking his life when he didn't need to.

She shook her head, taking a few steps backward to the door. "That is less of a chance, and you know it." She spun and trotted down the hallway and stairs. She wasn't sure she had the capable hands to deliver this infant, but she was willing to try. She darted for the foyer, finding Jack standing by the front door, slipping his arms into his coat.

"Jack, you can't do this. You can't go out in this storm."

"I'll be all right, Sarah. I will follow the fence lines and stick close to the buildings. If Julia needs the doctor, then I will fetch him." He yanked the coat together and fastened a couple of the buttons.

"I don't think she does, and I don't think you should go." Tears misted her eyes, and she blinked them away before they could fall down her cheeks.

He glanced at her, laying his hand on her shoulder before he turned toward the door.

She grabbed his arm just as she had upstairs, stopping him—a lump formed in her throat, causing her voice to crack and her nose to burn. "Please don't do this. Don't go."

"I have to."

"Why? I know I can help Julia through this. She will be all right."

"I don't doubt that you will. But Patrick does. He is scared and wants the doctor, so I will get him what he wants. I owe that to him."

A hint of anger flared in her chest. "You don't owe him anything—especially your life. This town... this town needs you."

He grabbed her shoulders, squeezing them before releasing them. "I don't expect you to understand. It's something I have to do. I will return. I promise."

He twisted the doorknob and opened the door. Cold air whipped inside, bringing a layer of snow that littered the floor. The night sky had gone from gray to black, and as Sarah looked out the door, the porch was barely visible, much less her fence line.

"It's not just the town that needs you," she said. A prayer sat on her lips, willing for the courage to say what she wanted. "I... I need you."

Jack hesitated in the doorframe, looking at her with a gaze that weakened her knees and broke her heart. No matter how much she begged, she wouldn't change his mind.

Not even if she told him she loved him.

Which is precisely what she wanted to say.

She didn't just need him.

She loved him.

TWENTY

SARAH

As the door slammed shut behind Jack, Sarah felt a chill that pierced deeper than any winter cold could reach. The wind howled outside, assaulting the small inn with an unrelenting fury that mirrored the tumult inside Sarah's heart.

She rushed to the door, pressing her forehead against the wood. "Lord," she whispered. "Please be with him. Please keep him safe. Please guide him so that he safely returns home... to me." Tears misted her eyes once more, only this time, as she whispered the last of her prayer, she didn't blink them away. Instead, she let them fall down her cheek.

"There you are," a voice said behind her.

Sarah turned to see Beatrice standing on the last stair. She tilted her head slightly to look down her nose at Sarah. "I think it's time you gather the necessary supplies, don't you?"

"Yes. I should. I will fetch the water and blankets. It will only take a few minutes."

Without another word, the two women walked away from one another. Beatrice headed back upstairs while Sarah straightened her shoulders and wiped her face as she made her way to the kitchen. She gathered everything she knew she would need before returning to Julia and Patrick's room. Each step back up the stairs was a fight against the dread welling up inside her. She didn't want to think about Jack, yet she couldn't think of anything else. She tried to picture the town in her mind, focusing on how long it would take him to reach certain places, even if she couldn't know exactly where he was.

A chill ran through her. She had long since gotten to a place where the echoes of her late husband Harold's laughter or his warm, reassuring presence, which she had once thought would be her forever safe harbor, didn't haunt her. The pain of losing him had been a silent torment, a shadow across her heart she thought she'd never face again.

And now, here she was, where she never thought she'd be again. She hadn't expected Jack's departure to stir feelings inside.

She didn't like it.

Not one bit.

Reentering Julia and Patrick's room, the air was thick with anticipation and fear. Beatrice sat at the table near the window, her expression still holding its usual sternness and sourness, lacking anything akin to maternal concern. Patrick stood by the window, his figure rigid, his eyes focused on the white blur.

Setting the hot water on a cluttered side table, Sarah shook her head, refocusing on Julia. "How are you feeling?" she asked, slightly smiling.

"I'm all right. But I should be asking you that, Mrs. Holden. You look like you've seen a ghost."

"It's just the storm." Sarah moved around the bed, avoiding Julia's gaze as she unfolded a few of the blankets and laid them over the edge of the bed. "This weather always makes me uneasy."

"It probably doesn't help we haven't eaten supper either. Surely, everyone is hungry. I'm sorry for interrupting our plans," Julia said. A slight chuckle hinted across her lips, but

Julia's grip tightened on the bedsheets before Sarah could say otherwise. Her body stiffened, and she leaned forward, her breath catching.

"Don't hold your breath, remember?" Sarah said.

"But it hurts," Julia whispered, her voice laced with fear.

"I know it does. But once you hold your son or daughter in your arms, you will forget about it."

"Promise?"

Sarah nodded. "I promise."

"How far is the doctor's place from here?" Patrick's sudden voice caused Sarah to flinch.

"It's on the other side of town. It's quite a walk even on a nice day; in this weather..." She dropped her gaze to the floor, not wanting to think about how to finish that sentence.

Patrick moved away from the window and knelt beside the bed. He grabbed Julia's hand. "Is there anything I can do?"

Julia closed her eyes, laying her head against the pillow as she breathed. Sarah glanced at him. "Just hold her hand. Let her know you are here."

"I am here. Although..." He let his voice trail off for a moment. "Although, I feel like I should have gone with... gone with him."

"No, you shouldn't have," Beatrice said. "You are needed here. However, it would be best if you waited down in the study. You shouldn't be in the room. It's not proper."

Patrick gaped at the woman for several minutes. "What?" he finally asked.

"You should be downstairs waiting in the study."

"Who says?"

"It's what's proper, Patrick. Although I suppose nothing is proper out here in this hick town."

"Proper or not, this is my wife, my child. I'm not leaving this room unless Julia tells me to."

Beatrice exhaled a breath and rolled her eyes. "Figures. After all, you are still your father's son. So, perhaps I shouldn't even be surprised."

Patrick's head whipped toward his aunt. "What did you just say?"

Beatrice blinked at him, hesitating as though she wasn't sure she should repeat what she said. "I... I..."

"What did you say about me being my father's son? What does that even mean?"

She inhaled a deep breath, squaring her shoulders. "It's nothing."

"It's not nothing. What did you mean?"

"Well, when your mother wrote to me about your and Kit's birth, she mentioned that he wouldn't leave the room. Not even the doctor could get him to leave."

As Sarah watched the aunt and nephew, her thoughts drifted to Jack's determined look as he left the inn. His love for his son driving him to risk his life to help. It didn't surprise her that he would refuse to leave the room when his wife needed him the most. It was just another thing to love about the man. Her heart ached, and she left the bedside and made her way to the window. Pulling the curtains back, she looked at the sheet of white sprayed across the glass. His echoed promise that he would return was the only thing she could cling to.

"That sounds like something he would do," she said.

Beatrice snorted a laugh and rolled her eyes just as she had before. "I didn't mean it as a compliment. It was just another reason why my parents and I didn't see him as worthy of your mother." Beatrice rolled her eyes just as she had before. "That's what happens when you don't raise a child properly. You and Julia would do best to remember that."

Patrick furrowed his brow. He looked at his wife as Julia sat up, clutching his hand as she closed her eyes. Another contraction tightened through her body. He looked back at his aunt. "Proper or not, I'm not going anywhere, and I don't care what you think or have to say about it. My father was right for not leaving my mother, and I won't leave Julia."

JACK

The wind rattled the windows as Jack stood near the doctor's house door. His whole body shook. Chilled to the bone, every inch of him felt frozen. He shifted from one foot to the other; the soles of his boots were still covered in snow, and his toes hurt. Surely, he figured they would have gone numb by now, but the pain said otherwise. He could only hope that after returning to the inn, he would still have all of them.

Dr. Sterling appeared at the top of his staircase, his steps quick and sure as he descended with a worn leather bag clutched in one hand. Jack had only seen him from a distance at the Sunday potluck celebration but hadn't had the pleasure of meeting the young man until now.

"I think I have everything I need, Pastor Boone," he said, holding up the bag. "How are you holding up? You look a bit pale."

Jack forced a smile, rubbing his hands together for warmth. "I'll be all right when I return to the inn."

"Are you sure you don't want to stay here and warm up?"

"I'm sure. We should get going; the sooner we return to the inn, the better."

As they stepped out into the frost-laden night, the cold bit at any exposed skin with icy teeth. Jack's breath fogged in the air, a ghostly reminder of the biting wind. Dr. Sterling locked the door behind them and then turned to Jack, his brow creased with worry.

"Are you sure you can make this trek?"

"Of course. But enough worry about me. My son and daughter-in-law need you."

"Then let's go."

A gust of wind whipped around them, sending a shiver down Jack's spine as they left the doctor's house and made their way back down the road toward the inn. He didn't want to think about the cold, didn't want to think about how frozen he felt. He only wanted to get back to the inn, back to his family, and back to Sarah.

The way she had looked at him before he left had nearly stopped him from going. He hated leaving her like he did and hoped she understood why he had to. The last thing he wanted to do was hurt her. Her endless kindness, support, and resilience had been his anchor since he'd arrived in Featherstone Valley, and he knew he had to be hers just as much as she had to be his. No matter what it took, he would stay alive for her and for all the promises he had yet to make in the future days he hoped they would share.

B y the time the inn lights started to flicker in the distance through the thick curtain of snow, Jack couldn't feel half his body. His pants were soaked, his boots were soaked, and every inch of him felt like a thousand needles were stabbing his skin. The frigid air clawed at every inch of exposed skin, and his hands and feet had gone numb. He was certain that, with enough pressure, his nose would break off if twisted. Despite his heavy coat shielding him from the worst of the wind, his teeth chattered uncontrollably, and his steps grew increasingly labored.

He almost didn't know how warmth would feel anymore.

Jack lifted his head as the two men entered the gate. He squinted through the snow-blurred darkness, and as the warm glow of the inn's windows lit the path along the snow-covered steps, hope surged through him, lending strength to his weary legs. The wooden boards creaked under their weight, and just as they reached the door, it swung open, releasing a flood of light from inside. Sarah stood in the doorway, her face etched with concern.

"I saw your lanterns from upstairs. Oh, Jack, I'm so happy you're all right." She rushed out, wrapping her arms around him. His body clenched with pain.

"Did we make it in time?" Doctor Sterling asked.

"Yes, she's about to deliver. You should hurry. She's upstairs in room number two."

The doctor nodded, brushing past Sarah and trotting up the stairs. As he disappeared down the hallway, Sarah turned toward Jack. His legs gave out, and he crumbled to the floor. She gasped, dropping to her knees beside him.

"Jack! You're frozen through! I'm getting the doctor—"

"No," Jack croaked, his voice rough like gravel in his throat as he strained on the word. "Let him... help Julia. She needs him more... than I do right now."

"But Jack—"

Jack rolled onto his hands and knees before he crawled to the wall and used the doorframe to rise to his feet. He leaned against it. Sarah quickly moved to his side, her arm slipping around his waist to steady him. Together, they helped him shuffle into the warm interior of the inn.

"Come on, let's get you to the parlor. There's a fire," Sarah said softly, her voice laced with worry.

With Sarah's support, Jack made it to the parlor. The room was aglow with the light of a crackling fire in the hearth, and the heat brushed against his face. The hairs on his arms stood, and he shivered. She guided him to the couch, where he sank with a weary sigh; his cold, wet clothes clung to him, chilling his bones.

"Here, sit here," Sarah urged, positioning him directly in front of the fire. She grabbed a thick blanket from the back of a nearby chair and draped it over his shoulders. Then she knelt in front of him, her hands rubbing his arms to warm him. "You're freezing," she said.

His teeth chattered as he nodded. "I know."

"You should get out of these wet clothes. What can I fetch from your room?"

"I'll be fine. I just need to get my boots off." He winced as he lifted one foot. His fingers trembled with the laces, and she moved slightly, grabbing them for him.

"No. Let me."

She untied both of his boots and helped him yank them off, dropping them beside the couch. His feet burned, and his skin prickled as though being stabbed with hundreds of needles. Every inch of them hurt with a pain he'd never felt before.

"You shouldn't have gone for the doctor."

Jack shook his head slightly, his eyes fixed on the dancing flames. "I had to. I had to make sure she was all right. They are my family. I'd do anything for them."

Sarah's expression softened, her hands still moving rhythmically to warm him. "I know they are, and I know you would. But what if... what if something had happened to you?"

Jack met her gaze; her blue eyes were intense. He let his eyes linger on her retreating form, and his chest swelled. This woman, this incredible woman, was everything to him. "I'm all right, Sarah. Thanks to you. Just... let me sit here a moment longer."

"I was so worried." Sarah's voice broke, and she paused, swallowing hard. "I didn't want to think about what could have happened to you."

"Nothing happened."

"But it could have. I could have lost you."

"You didn't, and you're not going to. I promise." He reached out to touch her cheek. His hand was still cold, but it carried the weight of his affection.

Sarah leaned into his touch, her eyes closing for a brief moment. "You better keep that promise, Jack Boone. You're too stubborn to let a little cold stop you, but don't scare me like that again."

He chuckled, and a faint smile tugged at the corners of his lips. "I'll do my best."

He stared into her eyes, leaning in as he lifted his hand and cradled her cheek, his lips pressing into hers. Everything about her drew him in. He never wanted to let her go, never wanted to be without her. He wanted to love her every day for the rest of his life.

Someone cleared their throat behind them, and Sarah pulled away, turned, and jumped to her feet. They both looked upon Patrick standing in the doorframe. Tears streamed down his cheeks, and he held a wrapped bundle in his arms.

Jack's heart thumped.

Had something gone wrong? Had they not gotten back to the inn on time?

"Sorry to interrupt," Patrick said.

Both Sarah and Jack shook their heads, and Jack stood, grunting slightly as pain still spread through his body. He hadn't warmed up quite yet. His whole body hurt.

"You didn't interrupt anything, Patrick," Jack said.

"I just... " Patrick moved toward them. He heaved a few breaths and moved closer. "I just wanted you to know I have... I have a son," he whispered.

"Congratulations." Jack closed his eyes. It felt like it was just yesterday when the doctor told him he had his first son. He hadn't known how he would feel, and of course, all he cared about was a healthy child, daughter or son, but still, when he heard the news, his heart swelled nearly out of his chest.

"Thank you for fetching the doctor. He arrived just in time."

"You don't need to thank me. I was only doing what I was supposed to do."

"How is Julia?" Sarah asked.

"She's tired and in pain but will be all right. The doctor said you did everything he would have done. Thank you so much for your help."

"You're welcome. It was an honor. I should make some tea for everyone." After neither man objected, she left the room. Her shoes clicked against the hardwood floor as she made her way into the kitchen.

Patrick watched her leave, then inhaled a deep breath as he turned back to Jack. "May I ask you something?"

"Of course." Although Jack didn't hesitate, a slight part of him wanted to. Not because he didn't want his son to ask him a question but because he feared what the question was.

"Aunt Bea mentioned that you stayed with my mother when she had me and Kit. Is that true?"

"It is. The doctor didn't want me to be in the room and told me to leave several times—especially with you because you were the first. He didn't say much with Kit."

"Why not?"

Jack shrugged as the memories flooded his mind. "I may or may not have threatened him within an inch of his life if he told me one more time to leave the room."

The two men chuckled.

"Did my mother want you to stay? Or did she think it not proper?"

"She wanted me to stay. If she had asked me to leave, though, I would have done it. It was her choice. I always let her have the choice."

"I guess I can understand that." Patrick dropped his gaze to the floor.

Their silence echoed in the room as both men seemed lost in their own thoughts. While Jack wasn't sure what his son was thinking about, he knew his own. He'd missed so much of both Patrick and Kit's lives.

And he hated it.

"Do you want to go see your grandson?" Patrick asked.

"I would love to."

J ack and Sarah followed Patrick up to the room. Although Sarah insisted she carry the tray with the tea, Jack had taken it from her, ignoring how the movement made his cold fingers sore. He had yet to warm up, but when Patrick asked about seeing the baby, he wasn't about to say no.

Only a fool would.

The wind still howled outside, causing the walls and the roof to creak as they scaled the staircase and made their way down the hallway.

Jack glanced at Sarah, who shivered as she looked up at the ceiling before following Patrick into the room.

Dr. Sterling stood near the edge of the bed, shoved his stethoscope into his doctor's bag, and looked up, smiling at the three as they entered.

"Ah. Mr. Boone, I just told your wife that she needs to stay in bed and rest for a few days."

"Is everything all right?" Patrick furrowed his brow, looking from the doctor to his wife, then back to the doctor.

"Yes, of course. Both your wife and your son are in perfect health." Dr. Sterling buttoned up his bag and moved toward the door, pausing as he approached Sarah. He nodded as though tipping a hat he didn't have on. "You wouldn't happen to have a spare room, would you, Ms. Holden? I don't necessarily wish to return home in this storm unless I don't have to, which, to my knowledge, I don't. Besides, I would rather stay close to Mrs. Boone for the night." He lifted his hand before anyone said anything. "Not because I think she will develop anything serious. I just like to be close for a few hours, at least."

"Of course, Dr. Sterling. Follow me, and I'll get you the key to room number four."

Sarah and Dr. Sterling left the room, closing the door behind them. Julia sighed, smiling as Patrick approached the bed and sat at the foot of it. He opened his mouth, but another voice echoed through the room.

"Patrick?" Beatrice asked. Although Jack knew Beatrice was in the room, he ignored her presence, not even looking for her since entering. Her sudden voice sent a slight annoyance through his chest. "Don't you think it's too soon for visitors?" Her question grated on Jack's last nerve.

Patrick opened his mouth, but before he could answer, Julia answered for him. "I don't think it is, Beatrice. Besides, Jack isn't just a visitor. He's the grandfather." She smiled at Jack, making his chest tighten.

He couldn't have asked for a more lovely woman for his son.

"Do you want to hold your grandson?" Julia asked him.

Unable to say anything, he nodded, and as Patrick handed over the baby, Jack cradled the tiny body against his chest.

"He's perfect—so handsome," Jack said. "He's truly a wonder and gift from God."

Patrick smiled, snorting a slight chuckle. "I would have to agree with you on that one."

Jack looked from his son to his grandson. The baby's pink cheeks poked out from the cream-colored knitted blanket, and his mouth puckered with the movement. His face scrunched for a moment but then softened before he started crying. He grunted, then fell back asleep.

"What did you decide to name him?" Jack asked.

Patrick and Julia exchanged glances. "What do you think, darling?" she asked her husband.

"I still like Henry if you do."

"I do. I think it fits him."

"What about a middle name?" Patrick clicked his tongue, and the couple stared at one another for a moment before Julia smiled.

"How about Jack? Henry Jack Boone."

Tears misted Jack's eyes, and he blinked them away as he looked at Julia.

Beatrice let out a scoffed laugh, throwing her head back as if she thought the movement would exaggerate her obvious displeasure. "Do you think that's a good idea, Julia?" she asked.

Julia shot her a glare. "I wouldn't suggest it if I didn't."

Beatrice stood and made her way over to the bed. She cleared her throat, staring at Jack as he held the infant. "And what do you think about it, Patrick?"

Patrick clenched his jaw, glancing over his shoulder. "I think it fits him, Aunt Bea."

Her eyes narrowed, and she folded her arms across her chest. "Well, I don't think it fits him at all. I think it should be Henry James. James was your maternal grandfather's name. It's a good name from a good man."

"I like Henry Jack." Julia matched Beatrice's glare and folded her arms across her chest. Her stance was a little less forceful because she was lying in bed. However, the look on her face told Jack she shouldn't be crossed.

Beatrice moved over to the bed. "Patrick, aren't you going to say something?"

"His name is Henry Jack, Aunt Bea. That is what my wife has chosen for her son."

Beatrice's nostrils flared. She opened her mouth but shut it for a moment before it seemed as though she couldn't control it anymore. She pointed her finger at Patrick, leaning over the bed closer to him as she lowered her voice. "You better be careful, young man. You're acting more like *him*," she pointed toward Jack, "every day."

Without another word, she stormed out of the room, slamming the door behind her. Henry flinched in Jack's arms. His face scrunched again, but instead of going back to sleep this time, he started crying. The sound of the door startled him.

Jack handed him to Julia. "I'm sorry I made him cry."

"You didn't. Beatrice did." She took her son, cradling the baby in her arms.

"I should let you two get some rest. You've had quite the night."

Jack made his way back out into the hallway, shutting the door behind him. Before he moved more than a few steps away, the door opened again, and Patrick followed him.

"Father?" Patrick asked.

"Yes."

"May we have lunch tomorrow? Just the two of us?"

"Of course. I would love it."

Patrick nodded, inhaling a deep breath. "Me, too."

TWENTY-ONE

SARAH

Sarah stood by the kitchen stove, stirring a pot of oatmeal, her movements rhythmic and soothing. With the storm gone, the early morning light filtered through the ice-covered window, casting a sparkle of color and a warm glow across the wooden countertops and the freshly baked bread on the cooling rack.

She hadn't been able to sleep much, not after the excitement of the baby but also after the kiss she shared with Jack; she had woken early, baking several loaves for sandwiches she would take through town to help anyone in need after the bad storm.

The clatter of a plate being set down on the counter made her turn, and as she glanced toward the sound, her gaze met Jack's. His expression held a slight anxiousness that mirrored how her stomach twisted. With the needs of others taking priority, they hadn't spoken since last night.

The memory of last night's unexpected kiss seemed to linger between them, and they both stared at one another as though they both agreed with a silent acknowledgment of something brewing beneath the surface of their friendship.

"Good morning," Jack finally said.

"Good morning. Are you hungry?"

"For your cooking? Always."

Her stomach fluttered.

"I was just about to start on the eggs and bacon. I want to take a tray up to Patrick and Julia."

"Do you need any help?"

She smiled, cocking her head to the side. "Help from you? Always."

Although she chuckled, he didn't. He just stared at her. Her stomach knotted even more, and the smile that had been etched across her face vanished. "What is wrong?"

He took a deep breath, his eyes searching hers. "I love you, Sarah. I probably shouldn't say such a thing, but I can't ignore it, and I don't want to. I love you."

The words hung in the air, heavy and significant. Warmth spread through Sarah's body, and her heartbeat quickened. Surprise washed through her, mixing with the fear that pulsed through her veins. She leaned back against the counter, needing its support.

"Do you... do you not feel the same way?" he asked.

"It's not that simple."

"What isn't?"

"After Harold, I thought that part of my life was over. I didn't believe I could find love again—not like I had."

"I know. After Maryanne, I thought the same. But then, I met you." His brow furrowed, and he moved toward her, grabbing her shoulders. "I know it's not simple. I've got my own past, my own regrets. But I see how we are together, and it feels right. Doesn't it feel right to you?"

Her mind raced with his words. After Harold's death, she had wrapped herself in her work, in the inn, building a wall against the loneliness and the grief that had threatened to overwhelm her. It was her comfort in the sea of the unknown.

But now I have a new comfort, she thought to herself.

As she looked into Jack's eyes, she saw a kindred spirit, someone who had faced his own darkness and was still capable of love.

She nodded. "It does to me, too. I love you, too."

He wrapped his arms around her, drawing her body tight into his. He kissed her again, and she melted into him. Her knees weakened, and she slid her hands around him, hugging him tight.

Someone cleared their throat behind them, jerking their attention. They both turned, finding Sue Ellen in the back door's frame. The door was still wide open, and cold air swept through the room.

"Can you shut the door, Sue Ellen?" Sarah asked.

Sue Ellen did as Sarah asked, shutting the door before walking to the couple. She folded her arms across her chest, cocking her head to the side. She stared at them for a minute. "You mean after all this time, all you two needed was a snowstorm?"

"Good morning to you, too, Sue Ellen," Sarah said.

"I thought I would check to see if you are all right after last night's storm. I see that I worried for nothing."

Warmth spread through Sarah's cheeks. Of course, it wouldn't be long before everyone in town knew she and Jack were courting. But still, it was one thing for people to know. It was another for someone to see them kissing. "Well, we are all just fine. But we did have an interesting night. Jack's daughter-in-law delivered a healthy baby boy."

"Awe. How wonderful." Sue Ellen looked at Jack. "Congratulations."

"Thank you," he said.

Sue Ellen inhaled a deep breath, glancing between Sarah and Jack. While Sarah could see the questions written all over her friend's face, Sue Ellen asked none. Surely, she would eventually, just not when Jack was around.

"Well, since I see that you two are all right after the storm, and you *obviously* have a busy morning with breakfast and a new baby at the inn, I shall let you do what you have to do." She chuckled with a slightly awkward laugh.

"It's all right if you wish to stay, Mrs. Randall. I should get to the church to check on the place, make sure there was no damage from the storm, and that the children will be safe for school." Jack moved around Sarah and headed toward the counter, grabbing one of the muffins from the basket she'd made two days ago.

"What about breakfast?" she asked.

"This muffin will do just fine, and I won't be long. Patrick and I are having lunch this afternoon."

"You are?"

"He asked."

Sarah could see a slight flutter of excitement glinting in his eyes. "Well, that... that is wonderful."

"I hope it turns out that way." A slight chuckle hinted through his breath.

She cocked her head to the side. "Don't worry. It will."

He nodded, giving her one last smile before he motioned toward Sue Ellen. "Have a good day, Mrs. Randall."

"You too, Pastor Boone."

He left the kitchen, closing the door. Sarah heaved a deep breath and closed her eyes, waiting. She knew what was coming.

It didn't take long before Sue Ellen moved toward her. "Tell me everything," she said.

~

JACK

"Tell me everything."

Jack smiled as he heard Mrs. Randall through the door. Of course, he wasn't stupid. He knew those words were coming the moment Mrs. Randall walked into the kitchen and found them together. Hearing the woman only made him smile more as he could tell from her tone that she wasn't asking because she disapproved of what she saw but that she approved.

He glanced up at the ceiling and took a deep breath. Each moment spent with Sarah seemed to stitch a piece of his once-shattered heart back together. He smiled, marveling at how love, like a gentle stream, had begun to erode the jagged edges of his grief.

So much had happened since he stepped off the stagecoach in Featherstone Valley, and he hadn't seen any of it coming. Not that that was a bad thing. Change comes to all; that much he always knew. Sometimes, those changes aren't what anyone wants—the times that challenge us more than we wish, often leaving us so full of questions and dejection that our heads spin.

He'd already been down that road.

And he never wanted to see it again.

But then there are other good times, times that jolt us right back into hope and happiness, making us feel as though the dark days are over and leaving us able to breathe.

That was the road he looked upon now.

And he would cling to it with all his might.

"Well, isn't it just nice to live without the concern of all the damage you've done?" Although Beatrice's sudden voice didn't startle him, the sound twisted in his gut just the same. He'd recognize that annoying pitch anywhere.

He turned toward her as she stepped out of the dimly lit study, remaining in the doorframe. "And just what is that supposed to mean?" he asked.

"My sister lies six feet in the ground, and I see you just making a new life for yourself with someone else." She pointed toward the kitchen door. "Isn't that nice? You get to start all over."

"Is that the reason you've hated me all these years?"

"That's not the only reason."

"Funny. You make it sound like it is. And I don't understand it because I haven't lived a new life. I've been existing in Texas this whole time without anyone—not even my two sons. It wasn't until I came to Featherstone Valley that I started looking after myself."

She snorted. Her voice sliced through the still air, and her gaze was accusatory. "All you've ever done is live for yourself, first choosing your job over the safety of your wife and children and then vanishing from them when they needed you the most. I put my life on hold for your boys, Jack. I never married or had children of my own—all because I was raising yours." She folded her arms, her lips pursed. "And what would you have done, Jack? Left them to wallow in your grief with you?" Her voice rose, edged with bitterness. "I did what I had to do for them."

Her words stung.

"*What you had to do?* You didn't have to do anything, much less take them without asking me. You talk about how you had to sacrifice your life... you made the choice to take them, and you made that decision without me."

"And it was a decision you didn't fight!"

As Jack opened his mouth, footsteps trotted down the stairs, and the kitchen door opened. Patrick stopped at the bottom of the staircase, glancing at Sarah and Mrs. Randall before looking at Jack and Beatrice.

"What is going on?" Patrick asked. His eyes danced from his father to his aunt.

Jack inhaled deeply, glancing down at the floor. He grabbed the bridge of his nose and looked back up at Beatrice. "You're right. I didn't fight you when you came for the boys. It's a regret I hold still to this day. I wish I would have fought you. I wish I had told you no, that you couldn't take them, or at least I wish I would have followed you to the train station and stopped them from getting on that train." His heart ached with guilt and prickled with resentment. He dropped his voice to a whisper. "And I wish... I wish I hadn't been drowning. I know now that if I'd had them with me... maybe I could've found a way out of my sorrows sooner."

Beatrice shook her head. "Or maybe you would have dragged them down with you. Did you ever think of that?"

"Enough!" Patrick moved toward both of them. "This isn't helping anyone. All you two do is fight." He pointed to Beatrice. "And all you do is tell me everything he has done or will forever do wrong." He threw his hands up in the air, turning in a circle as he let his arms slap his sides. "If Kit and I were such a burden, why did you take us?"

"Do you even know what your life would have been like if I hadn't? You both might not have even survived."

Patrick shook his head. "So... you take us without even getting his say?" He pointed toward Jack. "Then you blame us for you not getting to live the life you wanted? Did I hear all of that correctly?"

"That's not how I meant it. I only said what I did to show your father what I was willing to do that he wasn't."

"And how do you know he wasn't?"

Silence wrapped around them, and Jack looked around the foyer, glancing at the ceiling as he whispered a prayer for guidance. "Why don't we go into the parlor and have a seat? I'm sure it would do us good," he said.

While Patrick made his way into the parlor without a word, reluctantly, Beatrice nodded, and she and Jack followed the young man toward the parlor. Jack's heart weighed heavy, and in the quiet of the parlor, the ghosts of his past lingered, reminding him of the roads not taken and the words left unsaid. His mistakes felt like a millstone around his neck, and as they settled into the room, he glanced around at the faces of his family—the son he loved and let down and the sister-in-law who had never made his life easy.

Sarah entered the room last, and she cocked her head to the side as though silently asking Jack for permission to sit with him. He nodded, and she took a seat, brushing her hand against his arm as if to tell him he had her support.

Beatrice's gaze flicked towards the inn owner, sharp and questioning. "She shouldn't be in here. This is not her family."

Jack responded before Sarah could utter a word, his voice firm yet calm. "This is her inn, Beatrice. Moreover, she's with me." He glanced at Patrick, seeking affirmation. "Unless Patrick objects?"

Patrick leaned forward, resting his elbows on his knees. He shook his head, his expression resolute. "No, not at all. She may stay."

Beatrice looked as though she wanted to protest further, but if she did, she didn't say anything. Instead, she sulked in the chair, looking around the room with a scowl. The four continued to sit in silence until Patrick finally inhaled a breath and looked at his aunt.

"I realize taking Kit and me into your home wasn't easy. Especially when you had no one to help. I'm sure it was hard."

"Well, I didn't have no one. I had your grandparents, remember?"

"Yes, I remember. But everything still fell on your shoulders, and I want to thank you for agreeing to it all. It was a blessing to us at the time."

Jack cleared his throat. "He's right. It was. Whether I agreed at the time or agree now, it was commendable of you just the same."

While she smiled at Patrick, she glared at Jack.

Even when he gave an inch, she would still plant her feet on the ground.

"However," Patrick continued, looking at his aunt, then his father, and then back to his aunt, "I can't help but wonder if it wasn't just my father who did the damage you say was done."

Her face hardened, and her lips thinned into a line. "I beg your pardon?"

"You took us away and never spoke a word in his defense. You painted him a villain without letting us figure it out ourselves."

"I did what I had to do to protect you. Your father... his actions led to your mother's death. I can't forgive that, not even if you ask me to—not even if God asks me to."

The air grew heavier as her words were charged with old grief and anger.

Patrick's brow furrowed, and he stared at the floor before looking at her. "If Julia had died giving birth to Henry and I was so broken that my world came crashing down around me... would you take Henry from me?"

"Yes," she replied sharply, her conviction clear and without hesitation.

Patrick's gaze then shifted to Jack. His brow furrowed even more, and he narrowed his eyes briefly before widening them. It was as though a new understanding hit him square in the chest.

Sarah grabbed Jack's arm, squeezing it tight. She stared at Beatrice, and for a moment, Jack could see the words she wanted to say sitting on the tip of her tongue. She didn't like Beatrice's answer. Not in the slightest.

"What is it?" Jack asked, trying to keep his attention on Patrick.

"When Aunt Bea said yes .. perhaps it was the first time I understood the depth of what you probably went through, or at least a little. I'll never know fully as my wife is alive and well, upstairs, sleeping, but... I can't imagine someone taking Henry from me."

Jack cleared his throat. As much as he loved feeling a little support from his son over the woman who had held the cards for all these years—and used them to her advantage. But he also couldn't pass on the blame to her. He wasn't innocent, no matter how much he wished he was.

"It was hard. But it's not all her fault any more than it's all mine."

"I understand. A lot of mistakes were made." Patrick glanced between the two of them. "On both sides."

"I'm sorry, Patrick, but I have to disagree," Beatrice straightened her shoulders, lifting her chin to look down her nose at the young man. "I didn't make any mistakes. I did what was best for you and your brother. I will not be made the bad guy." She rose to her feet and pointed her finger at Patrick. Jack's stomach clenched. Of course, Patrick was a grown adult, but he was still Jack's son and someone Jack would protect against anyone. "If you wish to overlook all he did, that is on you. But I will not dishonor your mother in the way you have."

Patrick inhaled a deep breath, speaking before Jack could even think of anything to say in return. "Dishonor? Are you telling me that my mother would want me to not have anything to do with my father because of what happened?"

Beatrice hesitated. "Well, I'm not sure if I would use those words."

"Then what words would you use?" Jack asked. He was tired of playing the silent one in the room—especially when this woman was putting words into his late wife's mouth.

"What do you care how Maryanne would feel? You have moved on to another woman." She pointed to Sarah.

Jack rose to his feet, matching her stance. He was done. He might be called to forgive Beatrice, but that didn't mean he had to sit around and listen to her insults about him, his son, and the woman he was falling for.

He wouldn't be disrespectful.

But he wouldn't be walked over, either.

"Beatrice, I think it would be best if you left on the first stagecoach out of Featherstone Valley," he said.

"Oh, I would be glad to leave this dirty little town. You just have to tell me when I can leave, and I'd happily oblige."

Jack glanced at Sarah, nodding his silent question.

"There will be one on Monday as long as there is not another storm," Sarah said.

He turned back to Beatrice. "You have until Monday; then I expect you to be on that stagecoach."

Without another word, she stormed from the room. Her footsteps echoed off the walls as she trudged up the staircase and down the second-floor hallway. Patrick stared at the doorframe she'd left through, heaving a heavy sigh as he rested his hands on his hips. He glanced down at the floor, shaking his head.

"Well, I'm going to pay for that all the way back to Texas," he said, a slight chuckle hinting through his breath.

"I'm sorry if I caused you trouble." Jack's shoulders were hunched with guilt. He hadn't wanted to make anything worse for his son, but he also couldn't hold his tongue when it came to Beatrice.

"Don't worry about it. It's nothing I can't handle. I'm more concerned about Julia throwing her off the stagecoach in the middle of nowhere." Patrick chuckled again, shaking his head. "She almost had enough of Aunt Bea on the trip here. I can't imagine she will be in any better mood to deal with much now that she has to worry about Henry."

"Well, if you ask me, I'm on Julia's side." Jack smiled at Patrick while raising one eyebrow. Patrick nodded as though he understood the joke.

"I'll tell her you said that. I'm sure it will amuse her to no end."

"You married a lovely woman, Patrick. I'm sorry I wasn't a

part of any of it. I'm sorry I missed your courtship and your wedding. I'm sorry."

"I know you are." Patrick inhaled a deep breath. "I'm sorry for it all, too. I... I'm still angry with a lot of things, but... I do want us to work on getting acquainted with one another. I want to know what is going on in your life, and I want you to know what's going on in mine. I want you to know me, know Julia, and... I want you to know Henry."

Jack's heart swelled. While he'd known that he wanted to hear those words, he hadn't known how much he *needed* to hear them.

"Are you planning on leaving on the stagecoach with your aunt?" Although he had wanted to hide it, a flicker of disappointment hinted in Jack's voice. He didn't want to make his son feel guilty. Surely, the young family had a life to return to in Texas.

"As much as I want to say no, I can't. I should return to Texas."

"Of course. I understand."

"However," Patrick cocked his head to the side, "I wish I could stay longer."

A calm spread through Jack's chest. "Thank you for saying that."

"I would have liked to have stayed, but leaving only means I can plan another visit—perhaps when the weather is better." He chuckled. "And I do want us to write."

"I would like that, too."

"I should check on Julia. Make sure she is all right."

Sarah rose from the couch, making her way to Jack's side. "Please tell her I will have her breakfast up to her shortly, and I'm sorry about the wait."

"I'm sure she will understand. Thank you." Patrick turned, taking a few steps before turning back toward Jack and Sarah. "I hope you know I don't share Aunt Bea's opinion on your happiness with Mrs. Holden. I am happy you have found someone to share your life with if that is where your relationship is headed."

"It is." Upon his admission, a rush of heat washed through the back of Jack's neck. For a moment, he thought better of making such a statement, but then reality hit him, and he didn't care. He would love the woman at his side even if she didn't love him in return—which he prayed wasn't the case. He glanced at Sarah, meeting her gaze. "Or at least for me it is."

"It is for me, too," she said.

"Well, I do wish both of you the best."

Patrick turned to leave, but Jack stepped forward, calling after him. His heart thumped at the thought of his question. He didn't want to offend Patrick but had to ask it.

He just had to.

"Patrick, would you like to join us for Sunday's service? I would love to introduce you to the townsfolk."

Patrick smiled and nodded. "It would be our pleasure."

TWENTY-TWO

SARAH

The sunlight streamed through the church's stained-glass windows, casting vibrant hues across Jack's office as Sarah adjusted his tie.

"There. Now it's perfect," she whispered. Her fingers deftly smoothed the fabric, and she stepped back to inspect her handiwork, closing one eye as if to check whether it was straight.

"If it's perfect, why are you still checking it?" Jack asked, smiling and chuckling slightly.

"I'm just making sure." She winked, cocking her head to the side.

"So, do you think I will pass muster with the congregation today?"

"Without a doubt." She laughed; the sound was light and easy. "However, I think you could wear a burlap sack, and they'd still listen to every word you say."

"I don't know if I would say that. I'm still the new pastor in town, and I have a scandalous past, according to Prudence Chatterton, remember?"

"Well, you can clear the air a little today when you introduce Patrick, Julia, and Henry."

"I hope you're right." Although he smiled, he glanced at the ground. A slight hesitation seemed to weigh on his chest.

"What is it?" Sarah asked, laying her hand on his shoulder.

"I'm so happy to talk to Patrick finally, but I have another son I miss just as much."

"Perhaps when Patrick returns to Texas, he can speak to his brother and help him see there is a chance to make amends, too."

Jack shrugged. "Maybe."

"God will find a way."

"You're right. He will."

"Just keep praying about it."

"If there is one thing I can do, it's pray." He inhaled, puffing his chest slightly. He shook his head as though trying to shake off his thoughts. "So, I look all right?"

"Yes. Very respectable."

Jack's eyes twinkled with amusement. "Respectable, huh?"

"Why do you sound disappointed?" she chuckled.

"Oh... well... I guess I was aiming for dashing." He raised one eyebrow, giving her a coy smile.

"Dashing, huh? I don't know that I've ever used such a word to describe a man before, but I suppose if asked, I would have to say you look dashing."

He chuckled. "You know, hearing it is kind of awkward. I'm not sure I would choose that word anymore."

"How about handsome?" Sarah asked with a playful roll of her eyes.

"That works."

She glanced at the stack of notes on his desk. "Are you ready for the sermon?"

"I think so." He nodded, furrowing his brow as he turned and reached for the pieces of paper.

"And what is your topic?"

He winked at her, the mischievous glint not entirely

masking the deeper emotion behind his gaze. "Ah, that's a surprise. But let's just say it's something close to my heart."

"Close to your heart, huh? How close are you talking about, and are you sure that's wise?" She raised one eyebrow, cocking her head to the side.

"Are you asking if I will announce our courtship to the town?" He chuckled. "Because while I could, I'm not." His expression softened as he stepped closer to her, his presence reassuringly solid. "However, just because I'm not doesn't mean that I didn't mean what I said. About us. I want to share my life with you for all the days I have left on this earth. And I'll fight for that, no matter what comes."

The sincerity in his voice wrapped around her like a warm blanket. Her heart raced as the old fears of loving and losing surfaced briefly. Yet as she looked into Jack's steady gaze, those fears started to melt away, overshadowed by the deep, resounding truth that she wanted him more than she had ever thought possible.

"It's still scary, you know," she admitted, her voice barely above a whisper. "Loving someone again, after... after Harold. But I do want this. I want us."

"I do, too. I know it's scary. We've both known loss, but we've also seen how beautiful life can be when shared. And I think we owe it to ourselves to fight for that chance."

She nodded. "I'll fight, too. I'm not letting go. Not now, not ever."

The fears, the doubts, and the past sorrows blended into the background, leaving only the sharp, vibrant pulse of the present. Jack leaned in, his lips meeting hers in a kiss that was gentle at first but deepened with the weight of everything unspoken, every promise made silently between them.

At that moment, everything seemed to fall into place.

As they parted, Jack's forehead rested against hers, their

breaths mingling. "This is right," he whispered. "You feel it too, don't you?"

"Yes," Sarah breathed out, her hands resting on his chest, feeling the steady beat of his heart against her palms. "It feels like... like coming home."

Jack smiled, his eyes reflecting the peace settling in Sarah's soul. "Then that's what we'll do. We'll make a home together." He paused. "Well, I'll stay in the inn, and you'll stay in your cabin..." He smiled. "At least for now."

They both laughed.

The clock on the wall chimed, and they glanced at it, noting the time.

"You should get out to the podium," she said, stepping back reluctantly. Her hand lingered on Jack's arm for a second. "I'm sure the townsfolk are waiting."

Jack moved to his desk, grabbing his Bible. "Wish me luck?"

"You don't need it, but yes, always." Sarah smiled, her heart full. "Go inspire them, Pastor Jack."

He grinned, a spark lighting his eyes. "After this, how can I not?"

~

JACK

Jack stepped out from his office, feeling the weight of his sermon notes in one hand and the Bible firmly clasped in the other. The church was filled with the soft murmur of the congregation, their faces illuminated by the windows just as the light that had danced across his office moments before. He scanned the room, his gaze settling on the familiar faces of his son Patrick, daughter-in-law Julia, and his new grandson, Henry, all seated next to Sarah, Sue Ellen Randall, and her husband. A warm smile spread across his face as he acknowledged them with a nod, feeling a surge of gratitude for this moment of family and community.

As he approached the pulpit, the congregation quieted, expectant. Jack placed his notes down, opened his Bible, and looked over the faces before him. "Good morning," he began, his voice resonant in the hushed air of the church. "What a blessing it is today to see all of you are safe and well after the storm. It was my first ever, and I have to say, I've never experienced anything like that in Texas." He chuckled, and several people in the pews did, too. "Today, I want to talk about something that deeply touches our lives—past hurts and the power of reconciliation."

He paused, allowing his words to sink in, then continued, "Many of us carry the weight of old wounds, some so deep that we wonder if they can ever truly heal. But the scripture guides us and gives us hope on this matter." Jack flipped the pages of his Bible to the book of Colossians. "In *Colossians 3:13*, Paul tells us, 'Bear with each other and forgive one another if any of you has a grievance against someone. Forgive as the Lord forgave you.' This isn't easy; it's a divine challenge."

He shifted slightly and gripped the edges of the pulpit. He wasn't sure how much he wanted to divulge, yet he also didn't want to hide from his mistakes. He'd done that far too often in the last decade of his life.

He wouldn't anymore.

"I wasn't always the best father—especially after my wife passed away. My sons paid the price, which I will always regret. My only hope is that they believe, as I do, that reconciliation doesn't mean forgetting the hurts or pretending they never existed. It means confronting those hurts, understanding them, and choosing to forgive, to build anew on stronger, more compassionate grounds. Another passage that guides us in this journey is from *Matthew 5:9*, 'Blessed are the peacemakers, for they will be called children of God.' Being a peacemaker often means being the first to extend a hand, the first to bridge the gap that past hurts have widened."

Jack looked across the congregation, making eye contact with several members, his tone earnest as he paused and took a breath. "For me, this... this is something I have been trying to do and will continue until I make it right. I never disclosed the fact that I was a widower or that I had two grown sons. I had reasons, although I'm not sure they were as important as I believed they once were. The truth is, I've been estranged from my sons for far too long, and I let mistakes and pride keep us apart."

"But here today," Jack's voice grew stronger, his hand gesturing towards Patrick and Julia, "here among us are signs that perhaps reconciliation is possible, and it's a path to greater love and understanding. I'm thankful and blessed to say that my son and I are taking those steps—painful but vital—towards each other. Or at least I pray we are."

He paused, and Patrick nodded silently as if to agree. It was an acknowledgment that he had prayed for and one that swelled his heart with joy.

He let his gaze drift towards Sarah. "And it's not just family," he added. "It's about all our relationships. It's about building a community where we support each other through healing and growing together." He took another deep breath, feeling the weight of his next words. "This journey of reconciliation—it's lifelong. It demands courage, humility, and persistence. But I am committed to it, with my family, with all of you, with... with a special someone who has shown me the strength it takes to open one's heart again.

"As we move forward, let us hold onto the wisdom of *Ephesians 4:32*, 'Be kind and compassionate to one another, forgiving each other, just as in Christ God forgave you.' Let us be kind, let us be courageous, let us be a community where no one walks the path of healing alone. Let us pray."

Everyone bowed their heads; some even closed their eyes.

"Heavenly Father, we gather here today as Your children, seeking Your guidance and Your grace. Lord, You know the burdens we carry—those of past hurts, misunderstandings, and strained ties that weigh heavily on our hearts. We ask You, Lord, to help us embrace the strength found in Your forgiveness as we strive to forgive others and rebuild the bridges that have been broken. Pour out Your spirit of peace upon us so that it may touch every heart here today. Grant us the courage to be peacemakers in our families, among our friends, and within our community. May Your love guide us as we seek reconciliation so that we might see one another through Your eyes—flawed yet beloved, different yet deeply connected. Bless our intentions and our efforts, Lord, as we commit to the path of healing and unity. Keep our steps firm and our hearts open. We thank You for the gift of new beginnings and for the boundless hope that Your forgiveness provides. We pray in the name of Jesus Christ, who reconciles all things to Himself. Amen."

The room echoed with everyone else repeating, "Amen," and as Jack moved to the back of the room to open the doors, everyone stood and gathered their things.

His heart thumped.

Had he done the sermon justice?

Had he stayed true to the message he'd wanted to give?

His gaze locked with Sarah's, and his heart thumped harder.

SARAH

Jack's prayer lingered in the air as the congregation began to stir, rising from their seats so they could shake his hand before leaving the church. One by one, the townsfolk of Featherstone Valley began to file out; many paused to shake

Jack's hand, offering words of encouragement and appreciation. Their faces beamed, their voices gushed, and several men patted Jack on the shoulder with a look of profound respect in their eyes.

"Well," Sue Ellen exhaled a deep breath. "Can I just say that if word gets around about how wonderful Jack's sermons are, the town of Featherstone Valley will need a larger church?" She glanced between Sarah and Hank, who nodded before she moved toward Patrick and Julia, sticking out her hand to shake theirs. "It was a pleasure meeting both of you and this little guy," she motioned toward Henry, brushing her fingertips along his milky plump cheek. "Is about the most adorable baby I've ever seen."

Julia smiled. "Thank you. And it was lovely to meet you, too. It's wonderful to know that my father-in-law has such kind friends here and is not alone."

"Oh, I don't think you have to worry about that," Sue Ellen glanced at Sarah and winked.

Julia chuckled. "I suppose you're right about that."

Sue Ellen wiggled her finger at Henry once again, lightening her voice. "Well, we should probably get to the house. No one is going to do our chores for us. Sarah mentioned you are leaving on the morning stagecoach."

"Yes, we are," Patrick said. He smiled at Julia and wrapped his arm around her waist.

"I guess then this is goodbye." She stuck her hand out to shake Patrick's, and after he returned the gesture, he shook Hank's.

"Goodbye only for now. Julia and I will visit again. Hopefully sooner rather than later."

"That's wonderful to hear. We look forward to getting to know you three better next time." Sue Ellen rested her hand on Julia's shoulder. "Safe travels back to Texas."

After a few more farewell wishes, Sue Ellen and Hank left

the church along with everyone else, leaving Jack, Sarah, Patrick, and Julia alone. Jack heaved a deep sigh as he shut the door and turned toward them, smiling.

"Everyone seemed to like the sermon," he said, a hint of relief and exhaustion whispered through his eyes.

"It was more than liked, Jack." Sarah reached out and squeezed his arm. "From what I heard, people loved it. You should not doubt yourself, not today."

"It was good." Julia nodded as she swayed her body to keep Henry from waking up. The infant slept in his mother's arms, and although his face scrunched a few times from either movement or a dream, he didn't make a sound.

Along with everyone else, Patrick watched the little boy for a moment then glanced at the ground. He inhaled a deep breath. "I thought it was good, too," he said.

"Thank you."

"I know we still have things to sort through, but I'm happy I visited. I meant it."

"I'm happy you did too." Jack looked at Henry and leaned toward the infant, rubbing the boy's tiny head. The thick strands of straight black hair moved through his fingers. "Even if we did have quite the scare with this guy."

They all chuckled.

"Well," Julia adjusted Henry in her arms. "We should return to the inn. We need to pack before we leave in the morning."

Jack's face fell slightly as though the reality of their looming goodbye tempered the joy of the morning's reconciliation. Sarah knew how he felt. She'd come to enjoy Patrick and Julia's company and wasn't looking forward to them leaving. Not to mention, she wanted to soak up every second of Henry's life she could.

"I wish you didn't have to leave," Jack said, his voice thick as though he fought a lump in his throat.

Patrick nodded. "I wish we didn't have to either. But we'll be back. It's not goodbye, just a 'see you later.' Besides, perhaps I can talk Kit into visiting next time, too."

"That would mean the world to me."

Although Jack didn't shed a tear, Sarah saw him blink a few times. She stepped closer to him, hooking her arm in his. "Why don't we stop by the mercantile on our way back to the inn? We can buy a nice roast, and I'll make a huge, wonderful family meal for supper."

As they gathered their things, the air around them was thick with a sense of contentment mixed with the inevitable ache that goodbyes often brought. It was a poignant blend of happiness and sadness, and although the sadness threatened to dominate, Sarah found herself viewing it through the lens of Jack's sermon. Life would undoubtedly have its difficult days, but it would be replete with good ones, too. Sure, there would be people who disappointed you, letting you down in more ways than you would think they were capable, but in the end, nothing they did or could do would measure up to the simple act of forgiveness. Because that was what life was. It was about reconciliation, about moving forward and cherishing the family you have, in whatever form it took.

She glanced at Julia. "We can even pick up a couple of loaves of bread so I can make you all some sandwiches to travel home with."

Julia smiled. "We'd love that, and of course, I would love to help. I want to spend as much time with the both of you as I can."

"Well, then that's what we will do—we will make the most of the time we have left." Jack motioned toward the church door. "And we will make every moment count."

As they stepped outside, the sunlight enveloped them, casting long shadows on the path ahead. Sarah looked up at the sky, considering its vast expanse and endless possibilities. Life, she realized, wasn't just about enduring or moving past hardships but also about embracing each moment as a gift—an opportunity to love, to forgive, and to grow.

"Every day sure does bring its own blessings, doesn't it?" Sarah mused aloud, more to herself than to the others as they strolled down the lane toward town. "Sometimes, they come wrapped in challenges but are blessings nonetheless."

Jack squeezed her hand. "Yes, it does. And the biggest blessing we have besides God is each other, our family. No matter where we go or what we face, we carry that with us."

With a final glance back at the church, she smiled softly. "Here's to the blessings, then," she said. "The blessings in Featherstone Valley."

TWENTY-THREE

CRAIG

Craig's hands shuffled through a stack of envelopes, the crisp paper noises mixing with the soft hum of morning conversations around them. He sat at his usual table in the inn's dining room with Wyatt, his young new head foreman, sipping on his cup of coffee. The light tan liquid smelled of all the cream and sugar he'd dumped into the cup.

Craig wasn't sure how the young man could stand the sweetness, but to each their own.

The morning light filtered through the windows, casting a warm glow in the cozy dining room, and he leaned on the table, feeling the weight of the letter sitting in the pocket of his coat. It had arrived with this morning's post, and he hadn't had a chance to read it yet. The thought of it churned in his stomach so much that he almost didn't order breakfast from Sarah a few minutes after they sat at the table.

Wyatt took another sip, locking his eyes on his boss. "So... what's wrong this morning, Mr. Harrison?" he asked.

Craig stared at his second-in-command. Wyatt had been a hard worker and had proven himself. But he still wasn't Harold Holden, Mrs. Holden's late husband. Could he become as good as the old man who had won Craig's trust within minutes of their meeting? That was still up for debate, but Craig wasn't going to deny Wyatt a chance just because of his apprehension.

"It's nothing. Just trying to get the mayor to sell me Rattlesnake Mountain."

"Why do you want it so bad? Do you really think there's gold in it?"

Craig nodded, inhaling a breath. He clasped his hands together, rubbing them. "I do."

"How do you know?"

"How does a hound know how to follow what it's hunting?"

Wyatt shrugged. "Are you saying you can smell it, Mr. Harrison?"

Craig closed his eyes for a second. "I can't smell it. It's just a hunch. I know how to find it, and it's in that mountain."

"What about Bear Mountain? How long do you reckon we've got before the Old Bear is tapped?"

When Craig first arrived in Featherstone Valley, he'd known Old Bear Mountain wasn't the one he wanted. Forced to buy it anyway—for the only price he could afford—he'd been somewhat happy with the color he'd gotten from the veins underground. He wasn't a millionaire by any stretch, but he'd made a decent enough living. One that kept him living in a nice house with a sizable savings account to his name. Not to mention, his mine was the biggest employer in the quiet town.

And he wanted to keep it that way by buying Rattlesnake Mountain.

Not only that, but while he'd loved Old Bear, it still had yet to produce the mother lode.

"Hard to say, but I fear it won't be long before we aren't getting enough gold from the shafts for it to be worth it. The veins are thinning out. I'd say she's nearly spent, and the lower we dig, the more we will be scratching at shadows and the more risk there is to the men. I won't make them work in unsafe conditions. I will not be the reason there are widows and orphans in this town."

Wyatt's brow furrowed. "Shadows?"

"It's a gold mining term, Wyatt. It means the mountain is nearly depleted, and it's giving its last glimmers of gold before the silence takes over the tunnels."

"Ah. I get it now." Wyatt took another sip of coffee. His shoulders hunched. "So... what are you going to do if the mayor doesn't let you buy Rattlesnake Mountain?"

It had been the question he'd asked himself several times and the one he hadn't wanted to answer.

"I'm not going to think about that." He reached into his coat pocket, yanking out the envelope.

"Well, I know you don't want to, but don't you kind of have to? There are a lot of men in this town who depend on that mine and the paychecks they earn."

"I know there are. But it's not something I want to worry about just yet. Besides," he tapped the envelope on the table, "we won't have to worry if this is what I think it is."

"And what's that?"

"The insurance policy of me getting that mountain..." Craig let his voice trail off as he flipped the envelope over in his hand, whispering a slight prayer to himself as he tore it open and slid the letter from inside. He unfolded the paper, reading the letter enclosed. A smile tugged at his lips as he recognized the handwriting.

Dearest Craig,

We were happy to get your letter and hear you are doing great in your tiny hometown. Roy and I were just talking the other night, telling each other how much we've enjoyed your letters and hearing from you. Of course, a visit would be even better. Perhaps we can look into some plans for one, if it's all right with you, of course. I suppose it's something to consider as the winter months fade into spring. Although I'm not fond of snow, Roy can't help himself. He simply can't stop talking about what it must be like walking around where drifts can be as high as your waist. "We have to see it," he always tells me. Perhaps one of these days, I'll just surprise him by agreeing with him. Of course, my agreeing with him might give him the silly notion that he's right, even if it's only from time to time. I'm not sure I wish to instill that in his mind.

We're sorry to hear about your dilemma with the town mayor and your decision to buy the mountain for your mine. I'll never understand why a man would get in the way of progress for another man. Perhaps if I do make it to Featherstone Valley, I can give this Mayor Duncan a piece of my mind. Anyway, of course we would be glad to invest in the company. Just let us know how much you need, and Roy will get it wired to the Featherstone Bank. I hope you know that while you aren't our real son, you are the closest thing we have to one, and if there is anything you need, know we are always more than happy to help.

Until next time, I'm sending much love your way.

Sincerely,

Edna

"Is it good news?" Wyatt asked. His eyes widened, and both brows were raised in concern.

"Yes, it is. It's excellent news."

"Who is the letter from?"

"A couple of old friends." He paused, scanning the letter again to ensure he'd read it right the first time. "And that's all I will say about it this morning."

"Yes, Mr. Harrison."

As Wyatt tucked his chin to his chest, he took the hint that if Craig had wanted him privy to the details of the letter, he would have made them known. A twinge of guilt prickled in Craig's chest.

"Well, I suppose I can say that I'm hoping the mayor won't be able to say no to my next offer."

The younger man glanced up, and his eyes glinted with

excitement. "Yeah? That's great news. Hopefully, nothing else goes wrong."

Before Craig could contemplate Wyatt's cautious optimism, Mrs. Holden approached the table, carrying a plate in each hand. The steam from the hot breakfast rose above the plates, wafting in the air along with the scent of eggs, bacon, and pancakes.

"Here you are, gentlemen. Breakfast is served," she said.

"Thank you, Mrs. Holden," Craig looked up at her while Wyatt focused on the plate.

The young man licked his lips as she set the food down in front of him. "Thank you, Mrs. Holden," he said, barely getting the words out before he grabbed his fork and dove into the eggs, shoveling a bite into his mouth with the speed of a runaway stagecoach.

Craig raised his eyebrow, turning his attention to the woman, also watching the young man with a mix of confusion and surprise. "So," Craig shook his head. "Mrs. Holden, how is the morning treating you?"

"Just fine." She smiled, wiping her hands on her apron. "Busy as always."

"Has Pastor Boone been down yet? Or is he already at the church? I saw him heading to the church yesterday morning before sunrise. I swear, that man's dedication to work... I wish I could have him for an employee."

"He should be down in a moment. Speaking of which, I better fix him a plate."

She nodded toward the two men and trotted back to the kitchen, vanishing behind the door as footsteps descended the staircase and the town's new pastor entered the dining room. He nodded toward Craig, pretending to tip a hat that wasn't on his head.

Craig had little experience with the man other than head nods and waves from a distance. His sheer size and how he moved around the room told Craig that the man of the cloth hadn't always been in this line of profession, but he couldn't exactly put his finger on what he did back in Texas before giving his life to the church.

Was he a sheriff? A judge?

Craig didn't know.

What he did know, though, was that he'd give his right arm to have a man like Pastor Boone working for him.

The older gentleman smiled. "Good morning." He stuck his hand out toward Craig. "I don't believe we've officially met. I'm Jack Boone."

"Craig Harrison. This is my head foreman, Wyatt Nash."

"Nash." Jack shook Wyatt's hand. "I met your parents at the social last week. They seem like nice people."

"They are, sir." Wyatt smiled then, without missing a beat, shoved another bite of eggs in his face. Craig cleared his throat as Jack chuckled.

"Eat it while it's hot, I always say," Jack said.

Another man came down the stairs, and although Craig had seen him around town and at church yesterday, he didn't know his name. He was just as tall as the pastor, with the same broad shoulders and square jawline. Although the two men were similar for the most part, there was a subtle difference between them.

He must be the son the pastor was talking about.

"Father," the man said to Pastor Boone.

"Patrick," the pastor laid his hand on his son's shoulder. "I'd like you to meet Mr. Harrison and Mr. Nash." Jack paused, pointing his finger at Craig. "You own the gold mining company in town, right?"

"That's right. Mr. Nash is my head foreman."

"Nice to meet you," Jack's son said. "Patrick Boone." He shook both of their hands. "So, you own the gold mining company. That must be interesting work. Hard. But interesting."

"It is more for the men than me now. However, I don't shy away from getting dirty myself. I used to mine up in the Klondike."

"Oh. Wow." Patrick blinked, and his head jerked back. "That's... that must have been work too."

"It was. But it was worth it. Every freezing day." Craig chuckled at his joke. "What do you do for work?"

"I'm in investments. I help my company invest in other companies."

Craig's curiosity piqued. "I'm not sure I understand. How do you help your company?"

"Research mostly. But I do a lot of digging—metaphorically speaking, of course—into the company's assets and financials to determine if they would be a good company to invest in."

Craig's curiosity piqued even more, and he raised one eyebrow. "Really?"

Before Craig could contemplate the conversation unfolding and the interesting turn of events, the inn's front door opened, and Mayor Duncan stepped inside. The man's plump belly moved from side to side, swaying with his short gait, and he stared at Craig, heading straight toward him.

Craig opened his mouth to greet the man but closed it as another man followed the mayor inside and through the dining room. Taller and thinner, this man was the opposite of the mayor and someone Craig never wanted to see striding around town.

"Sidney Miller," he whispered, letting a growl vibrate through the syllables.

Patrick and Jack glanced between the men, and as the mayor approached, Jack stuck his hand out, shaking the mayor's.

"Good morning, Mayor," Jack said.

"Good morning." The mayor nodded, then turned to Craig and waited without saying a word. Silence fell around all the men standing near the table, and everyone looked at one another as if wondering who would speak first. Patrick and Jack looked confused about the tension, and Wyatt leaned toward the table, lowering his head while he shoveled his food into his mouth.

"Mayor Duncan," Craig finally greeted, his voice laced with a growl. "What brings you here this morning?"

"Good morning, Mr. Harrison," the mayor replied, a forced smile on his face. "I wanted to introduce you to Mr. Sidney Miller."

Craig's eyes narrowed as he turned to Sidney. "I know who he is. The question is, why is he here?"

Sidney stepped forward, extending his hand. "Mr. Harrison, a pleasure to finally meet you."

Craig ignored the hand, only glancing at it for a moment before he focused his gaze on the mayor. "Why is he here?"

Mayor Duncan's smile faltered. "Craig, Mr. Miller is here because he has a proposition that could benefit Featherstone Valley."

Craig's jaw tightened. "Benefit?"

Jack cleared his throat as though he sensed the anger bubbling in Craig's chest. "Pardon me," he glanced at Mr. Miller and stuck out his hand. "Pastor Jack Boone," he introduced himself.

"Mr. Sidney Miller." Although Mr. Miller averted his gaze from Craig to greet Jack, he didn't look away long. Craig wanted to punch the look right off the smug man's face, and if they'd been in Craig's office, Craig would have leaped from the table and done so by now, not wasting a second to strike the man so hard he would fall to the floor.

Oh, what a satisfying sight that would be.

"And are you from around here?" Jack asked.

"No, I'm from Deer Creek."

"Mr. Miller owns several businesses in the town of Deer Creek." The mayor smiled and leaned slightly back, patting his stomach as though he were a father telling someone about something remarkable his son did. The utter pride in the mayor's eyes made Craig's stomach turn.

"Several unscrupulous businesses." Craig rolled his eyes.

"What do you mean by that, Mr. Harrison?" Patrick asked, looking between the three men. His father did the same as he clasped his hands behind his back and furrowed his brow.

Although Mr. Miller opened his mouth to answer, Craig did for him. "Saloons and brothels. Businesses that the people of Featherstone Valley don't want in our town."

Sidney chuckled, a smirk playing on his lips. "I think you're overreacting, Mr. Harrison. I'm just a businessman looking to expand my ventures. I assure you, everything will be above board."

"There isn't anything you can do to make those businesses above board. We don't need saloons and brothels. Our town has a reputation to uphold. Can you imagine the families walking down the street while the women of questionable morals stand on the balconies waving to the men? No, Mayor Duncan. I won't stand for it, nor will the rest of the townsfolk."

"I think that when people see how much those places will bring into this town, they will change their minds. Besides, Mr. Miller has agreed to follow any rules that the town sets. If we don't want the ladies on the balcony, then they won't be." The mayor glanced at Mr. Miller, who nodded as though to agree.

"Rules won't matter. And this town has managed just fine without his kind of businesses here. We don't need that kind of money."

"Money is money, Mr. Harrison." Mr. Miller folded his arms across his chest. An air of pride whispered through his voice.

"No, it's not. Money is not money. It depends on where it comes from."

"Is that what you said while you were in the Klondike?"

"I have no idea what you're talking about."

"I know what men did up there, murdering other men for gold and claims along the rivers. Those men drank and enjoyed women more than any man has ever done those things in Deer Creek. I've heard the stories."

"I didn't do any of that."

"And how do we know that for certain?"

Craig jumped to his feet. The legs on his chair skidded along the hardwood floor. He raised his hand, lunging for Mr. Miller and pointing his finger in the tall man's face.

"How dare you accuse me of such things!"

Both the mayor and Jack moved so they stood between the two men, and Mayor Duncan held up his hand. "Gentlemen, please. Let's not let our emotions get the better of us right now. Mr. Miller has assured me that his plans are legitimate and could bring significant revenue to our town."

Craig scoffed. "Revenue at what cost? Our town's integrity? The safety of our families?"

Sidney's smile faded, replaced by a steely gaze. "I understand your concerns, Mr. Harrison, but I'm not here to cause trouble. I'm here to offer opportunities."

Craig took a step forward, his eyes locked on Sidney. "Opportunities? For whom? For you to line your pockets at the expense of our town's morals?" He pointed toward Jack. "What do you think?"

The pastor glanced at him and swallowed.

Before Jack could utter a word, Mr. Miller spoke for him. "I run legitimate businesses, and while I understand that not everyone approves of my line of work, it does provide jobs and revenue."

"Jobs that come with a price," Craig shot back.

Mayor Duncan shook his head. "Mr. Harrison, stop. We need to at least hear him out. The town's finances aren't in the best shape, and we can't ignore potential solutions. Not only would he provide jobs in his mine, but he'd bring these other businesses in to attract tourists."

"Why are our town's finances not in good shape? Have you mismanaged them in some way?"

"You know I haven't." A growl rumbled through Mayor Duncan's chest. "But the size of this town and the lack of tourists visiting will affect how long this town thrives."

Sidney cleared his throat. His voice was low and steady. "I'm not the villain here, Mr. Harrison. I'm a businessman, plain and simple. And I think if you give me a chance, you'll see that I can bring positive change."

Craig glared at him. "Positive change? Do you mean more saloons and brothels? More places for people to lose their money and their dignity?"

"I can assure you, my businesses are well-regulated and provide valuable services."

"Valuable services?" Craig's voice rose. "To whom? Drunk-ards and gamblers? That's not the kind of value we want in Featherstone Valley."

Mayor Duncan stepped between them, raising his hands. "Enough! This isn't getting us anywhere. We need to have a civil discussion about this."

Craig snorted a laugh. "There's nothing civil about bringing Sidney Miller's kind of business into our town. It's a mistake, and you know it."

The room fell silent, the tension thick in the air. Craig's eyes bore into Sidney's. So many questions fired in his mind, and only one man had the answers—the mayor. And unfortunately, it seemed the mayor was more crooked than the man the ques-tions were about.

"Gentlemen, may I offer a suggestion?"

Craig looked at Patrick, who stepped forward, rubbing his chin as he glanced at the ground. All of the men standing around the table turned toward him.

"Who are you?" the mayor asked.

"He's my son," Jack answered. "Patrick Boone."

"And why does he think I am interested in listening to him? I'm the mayor of this town." Mayor Duncan pointed at his own chest, raising his voice slightly.

"I'll hear what he has to say," Mr. Miller said.

"What do you want to suggest these men do, Patrick?" Jack asked.

"Well, why don't they settle it by having a contest?"

"A contest?" the mayor raised one eyebrow. Hesitation purred through his voice.

"Yeah."

Although skeptical, Craig couldn't deny he was intrigued. "What would the contest be?"

"You both wish to mine the mountain, providing jobs and revenue to the townsfolk. Why don't you each mine a small section of said mountain for a certain time period and see who can pull more gold out of it?"

"Mining's not that simple." Craig shook his head.

"You're just saying that because you know you'll lose." Mr. Miller smiled mockingly.

"Says a man who has never mined a day in his life."

"Well, I guess then you have nothing to worry about."

Craig's eyes narrowed. He didn't trust Sidney Miller any farther than he could throw him. But he also knew he had a skill that no one else in these parts had. He knew how to mine a mountain better than any man around.

He stepped forward. "All right. I'm in. Are you?"

Sidney's eyes narrowed. "All right, Mr. Harrison. You've got yourself a deal."

The stories of the residents of Featherstone Valley aren't over...

You're just getting started...

WANT MORE OF FEATHERSTONE VALLEY?

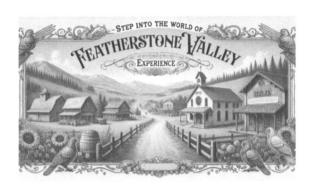

STEP INTO *THE FEATHERSTONE VALLEY EXPERIENCE*—YOUR CHANCE TO IMMERSE YOURSELF IN THE HEART OF THIS SPIRITED MONTANA TOWN! EACH WEEK, RECEIVE EXCLUSIVE EMAILS FILLED WITH HEARTFELT STORIES, DELIGHTFUL SURPRISES, AND EXCITING TOWN HAPPENINGS. MEET QUIRKY NEIGHBORS, EXPLORE LOCAL BUSINESSES, AND ENJOY CONTENT FROM THE *FEATHERSTONE VALLEY GAZETTE*, INCLUDING GOSSIP, COUPONS, AND WANTED ADS. INTERACTIVE GAMES, POLLS, AND CHALLENGES MAKE YOU FEEL LIKE A TRUE PART OF THE COMMUNITY. IT'S FREE, FUN, AND THE PERFECT WAY TO ENHANCE YOUR FEATHERSTONE VALLEY READING JOURNEY. DON'T MISS OUT—SIGN UP NOW AND START YOUR FIRST ADVENTURE!

JOIN TODAY

SHOWDOWN IN FEATHERSTONE VALLEY

BOOK #2 ~ FEATHERSTONE VALLEY SERIES

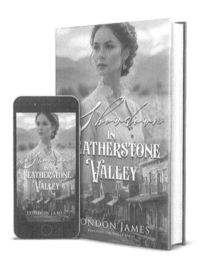

Can love blossom amid the dust and danger of the mines, or will Craig and Ava's rivalry cost them everything they hold dear? Find out in this thrilling tale of ambition, resilience, and unexpected romance.

ORDER TODAY

WANT MORE OF FEATHERSTONE VALLEY?

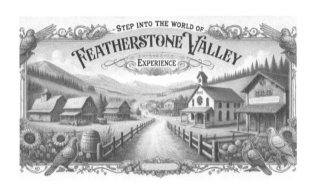

STEP INTO *THE FEATHERSTONE VALLEY EXPERIENCE*—YOUR CHANCE TO IMMERSE YOURSELF IN THE HEART OF THIS SPIRITED MONTANA TOWN! EACH WEEK, RECEIVE EXCLUSIVE EMAILS FILLED WITH HEARTFELT STORIES, DELIGHTFUL SURPRISES, AND EXCITING TOWN HAPPENINGS. MEET QUIRKY NEIGHBORS, EXPLORE LOCAL BUSINESSES, AND ENJOY CONTENT FROM THE *FEATHERSTONE VALLEY GAZETTE*, INCLUDING GOSSIP, COUPONS, AND WANTED ADS. INTERACTIVE GAMES, POLLS, AND CHALLENGES MAKE YOU FEEL LIKE A TRUE PART OF THE COMMUNITY. IT'S FREE, FUN, AND THE PERFECT WAY TO ENHANCE YOUR FEATHERSTONE VALLEY READING JOURNEY. DON'T MISS OUT—SIGN UP NOW AND START YOUR FIRST ADVENTURE!

JOIN TODAY

WAGON TRAIN WOMEN

Five women headed out West to make new lives on the Frontier find hope and love in the arms of five men. Their adventures may be different, but their bond is the same as they embark on the journey together in the same wagon train.

Order the series today

Turn the page for a sneak peek at book one, Her Wagon Train Husband.

ONE

ABBY

Everyone loves adventure.

Well, almost everyone.

Abby had to correct herself on that point. Her parents didn't like adventure much. Neither did her three older sisters. They liked being home. They liked being in a place they knew. They didn't enjoy the thrill of the unknown or the sense that the world could open up under their feet.

Of course, that wasn't an appealing thought, for surely that would mean death, and Abby didn't like the idea of that. She wanted the adventure.

Abby heaved a deep sigh as she walked along the path around the lake. It was a favorite pastime for her and one she enjoyed nearly every day. Well, every day that her parents and sisters stayed in their country home. When they were in the city... well, that was another story. She would often sneak out of the house and head to the park. Even if she had to be careful about being seen, she would still try to take a little walk in the trees and sunshine. Wasn't that what spring and summer were for? Perhaps even autumn? Winter, surely not, although she couldn't complain too much about those months, for she loved the snow too and would enjoy it until her fingers and nose turned red and her skin hurt.

Something about nature called to her like a mother calls to a child when they want them to come home or to the table to sit down and share a meal. She loved everything about it: the smell of the air, the sound of the birds, and the leaves rustling in the breeze. The feel of the sunshine upon her skin and how it felt as though her body tried to soak it all in like a rag soaks up water.

The outdoors made her feel alive.

Much like the sense of adventure did.

And the two, she thought, *went hand in hand.*

"Aaabbbbyyyy!" She heard a woman's voice call out in the distance. Her name was long and drawn out and sounded as though the woman—her mother—calling had her hands up against the sides of her mouth.

Her heart thumped. She couldn't be caught coming from the direction of the lake, and yet there would be no chance to sneak around to the other side of the stables without being seen. Her mother called for her several more times, and as she tried to round the stables, appearing as though she came from a different direction, she heard her mother's foot stomp on the front porch.

"Abby Lynn Johnson! And just where have you been?" Her mother raised her hand as if to stop her from answering. "Don't even tell me you were walking around that lake all by yourself."

"All right." Abby squared her shoulders. "I won't tell you that."

Her mother's eyes narrowed, and she pointed her finger in Abby's face. "You listen to me, young lady; you will not flitter off again. Do you understand me? You have far too many responsibilities in this house to do anything other than what you're supposed to do."

"But sewing and cooking and cleaning are just so boring. I want to be outside."

"Outside is no place for a woman unless she is out there to hang laundry on the line or in the garden. Both of which you need to be doing too." Her mother continued to wave her hands around the outside of the house, pointing toward the laundry line and the fenced garden at the back of the house. Clothes already hung on the line moved in the breeze. "Your sisters certainly don't spend any time fooling around outside."

"That's because my sisters are married and have husbands to look after."

"And you will have one too. Sooner than later, now that your father has made it official."

"What do you mean?" Abby jerked her head, and her brow furrowed.

"Mr. Herbert Miller is coming to the house this afternoon."

"Why?" Although she asked, she wasn't sure she wanted the answer, nor did she believe she would like it.

Her mother shook her head and rolled her eyes. "To finalize the agreement and plans to marry you and take care of you, of course."

Abby sucked in a breath, and spit went down the wrong pipe. She choked and sputtered, coughing several times while she gasped. "I... I..." She coughed a few more times and held out her hand until she regained her composure. "I don't want to marry him."

"That's not for you to decide. He comes from a well-to-do family and intends to provide a good life for you. Not to mention, we could use the money." Her mother clasped her hands together and fidgeted with her fingers as she glanced around the home. It was still in good shape for its age, but even Abby had seen some of the repairs it needed, and she knew her parents couldn't afford it. "I dare say he's the richest young man out of all of your sisters' husbands. You will have a better life than any of them."

"And you think I care about that?"

"You should. It's well known around St. Louis that the Millers have the means. Mothers and fathers all over the city would love to have him for a son-in-law. You're going to have quite the life, young lady."

"But is it quite the life if it's a life I don't want?"

"How can you not want it? A husband. A nice home. Children. It's all you've wanted."

"No, it's all you've wanted. And it's all my sisters have wanted."

"Oh, spare me talk of your dreams of adventure." She rolled her eyes again and wiggled her finger at her daughter. "There is plenty of adventure in being married and having children. Trust me."

"That's not the kind of adventure I want, Mother."

"It doesn't matter what you want, Abby. Your purpose in life and this family is to marry and have children. If you're lucky, which it looks like you are, you will marry a nice man with means. You should be happy. You could have ended up like Mirabel Pickens." Mother brushed her fingers across her forehead. "Lord only knows what her parents were thinking, marrying her off to that horrible Mr. Stansbury on the edge of town. He's twice her age and hasn't two pennies to rub together. Of course, he acts as he does, but honestly, I think the Pickens family gives him money." Mother fanned her face with her hand. "Now, go upstairs and change your dress. Fix your hair too. He'll be here within the hour."

Before Abby could protest any further, her mother spun on her heel and marched back across the porch and into the back door of the kitchen. Abby stood on the porch. Part of her was too stunned for words, yet the other part wasn't shocked at all. She always knew this day was coming. It just had come a little sooner than she thought it would, and although she had thought of a few excuses or reasons she could give to put it off, with

Herbert on his way to the house, she didn't know if any of them would work.

Scratch that.

She knew none of them would work.

Her parents had their eyes set on the young Mr. Miller for a while, and there wasn't any reasoning they would listen to that would change their minds.

It wasn't that Herbert—or Hewy, as he once told her she could call him—was a dreadful young man. He wasn't exactly what she would call the type of man she would hope to marry, but he was nice. He was taller than most men his age and skinnier, and he wore thick glasses that always seemed to slip down his nose as he talked. He was constantly pushing them back up, and there were times Abby wondered if he would ever buy a pair that fit better or if he enjoyed the fact they were a size too big. Like it had become a habit for him and one he liked.

She remembered how distracting it had been at the Christmas dance last December that her parents' friends hosted at their house. Every few steps, he would take his hand off her waist to push his glasses back up his nose, and he would even miss a step here and there, throwing them both off balance because he had to lead. He'd even stepped on her foot once or twice.

Her toe throbbed for days after that party.

No. She simply could not marry him. She just couldn't.

If her mother wouldn't see reason, perhaps her pa would.

She marched across the porch and into the house, making her way toward his office and knocking on the door.

"Come in," her pa said from the other side, and as she opened it and moved into the room, he glanced up from his desk and smiled. "Good afternoon, Abby."

"Well, it's an afternoon, but I'm not sure it's a good one."

He cocked one eyebrow and threw the pencil in his hand

down onto a stack of papers on the desk. "What has your mother done now?"

"She's informed me that Mr. Herbert Miller is on his way to the house to finalize an agreement for my hand in marriage." She paused for a moment but continued before her father could say a word. "Father, I know you aren't going to accept it. Right?"

"And what makes you say that?" He glanced down at the papers on his desk as he blew out a breath.

She knew where this conversation was headed. She'd seen this reaction in him she didn't know how many times in her life. When faced with a question Pa didn't want to answer, he used work as his excuse to ask whoever was asking him what he didn't want to face to leave. She wasn't about to let him do it today.

"I don't care what it is that you have on that desk that is so important, Pa. This is important. This is my future. I don't want to marry Herbert Miller. I don't love him. You've got to put a stop to this."

He reached up and rubbed his fingers into his temples. "What is it that you want me to say, Abby? I don't have time for this."

"I want you to say no and tell him that I'm not ready to marry and that you don't give him your blessing."

"You know I can't say that, young lady."

"For heaven's sakes, why not?"

"Because we've already agreed, and he's already paid off our debts."

"He's done what?" She didn't mean to shout, but she did anyway, and the look on her father's face as the loudness in her tone blared in his ears told her she should have given a second thought before letting her volume rise.

"Don't take that tone with me, young lady."

"I'm sorry, Pa. I didn't mean to. It's just that... I don't want to marry Herbert Miller."

"And I don't understand why you don't. He comes from a good family—"

"And he wants to provide me with a good life. I know." She threw her hands up in the air and paced in front of her father's desk. "Mother already told me all those things. But they don't matter. It doesn't matter how good his family is or what he wants to provide for me. I don't want to be like my sisters. You know this. You've always known this."

"Don't tell me you still have all those silly notions of adventure stuck in your head."

"They aren't silly."

"But they are!" He slapped his hand down on his desk. The force was so great that it rattled the oil lamp sitting on the edge, and the flame flickered. Abby flinched, and she stared at her pa, blinking.

Of course, she'd seen her father angry a time or two growing up. She didn't think there was a child alive who didn't see their parents in a fit at least once. It was what adults did.

But while she knew he could get that angry, she didn't expect to see it. At least not today. Not over this.

He fetched an envelope, opened it, and yanked out the money tucked inside. He threw it down on the table. "Do you see this? This is what will save this family. You are what will save this family. Abby, it's time you grow up and stop wasting your time and thoughts on silly things. You're not a child anymore. You're a woman. It's time for you to marry and care for a husband and children. I know you have never talked about wanting those things, but I thought perhaps the older you became…"

"Well, you thought wrong." She folded her arms across her chest.

"Perhaps I did. But that doesn't change the fact that we will make the wedding plans when this young man comes over this afternoon."

"Pa, please, no. Don't make me do this."

He held up his hands. "I'm sorry, Abby, but I've already decided, and the deal is done. It's what I had to do to save this house and my family. And it was the best thing I could have done for you." He moved to the office door, opening it before pausing in the frame. "Now, if you'll excuse me, I must see to the rest of my work before this young man arrives."

"Pa?"

"Abby, this conversation is finished."

Tears welled in her eyes, and although she tried to blink them away, she couldn't, and they soon found themselves spilling over and streaming down her cheeks. She shook her head as she watched him leave the office. While she knew there had been a chance he wouldn't listen to her, she hoped he might.

And now that hope was gone, leaving her with only a sense of desperation.

What could she do? She couldn't marry Herbert. She just couldn't. She would rather run away than marry him.

Run away.

That was what she would do.

That was the answer.

If she wanted adventure when no one would give it to her, well then, she would simply take it for herself.

All she needed was to pack some clothes and get her hands on some money.

Money.

She glanced over her shoulder toward the pile of cash Pa had yanked out of the envelope. She didn't know how much was there, but it looked like enough. Or she should say it looked like enough to get her where she wanted to go. It was hers after all, wasn't it? If she was the one sold like a farm animal?

She moved over to the desk, staring down at the paper bills.

She didn't have to take it all. She could leave some of it for her parents.

Never mind, she thought. *I'm taking every last dollar.*

OREGON TRAIL BRIDES

Four orphans and their headmistress set out for Oregon in search of men looking for mail-order brides. Will they find what they are looking for? Or will fate have other plans?

Order the series today or Read for FREE with Kindle Unlimited

Turn the page for a sneak peek at book one, Her Oregon Trail Doctor.

ONE

WINONA

How does the gut know when something isn't right? How does it know when something is amiss? Is it just the nature of the body and mind? Like some balance between the two that no one can understand or at least explain? Or is it just the Holy Spirit whispering in your ear, telling you what could— or would—happen if you don't listen to the strange inner voice inside your head, telling you something was good or bad?

Perhaps it's foolish to wonder.

Perhaps it's not something we are to know.

Perhaps we are just supposed to follow it blindly as we follow God.

Or at least that was what Winona was supposed to do.

Wasn't it?

Winona stood in front of the window, looking down onto the street from the second floor. The rain clouds had darkened the sky for most of the day, and now that night had begun to creep in, it made the people walking along the cobbled footpath and the horse-drawn carriages gliding down the street harder to see.

She crossed one arm over her chest, resting her other elbow

on it while she tapped her finger against the side of her cheek. She didn't want to think about the letter she'd received in the mail that afternoon, yet that was all that weighed on her mind. Of course, she knew it was coming . . . or at least had a gut feeling it was. After all, the girls were over eighteen and hardly considered children anymore. Still, though, what were they supposed to do? What did Harvey Kensington think they should do? He couldn't possibly believe that they could leave one afternoon and have employment and a house by dinner.

No, surely not.

So what did he expect?

No matter how much Winona questioned the man, she knew none of her questions would be answered. Or at least not answered in the way she wanted them. They did have an answer; it was just one she didn't want to hear.

She spun around, facing her desk once more as she spied the letter sitting in the same spot she'd left it. Although she couldn't see the words printed on the page in black ink, she had read them so many times that she could recite them.

Dear Miss Callahan,

It displeases me to write to you today as I know how you will feel after reading my letter. Please know that it is not meant to offend you in any way, nor is it meant to diminish all the work you have done for my orphanage or me. I am most pleased with your work over the years, and I hope you will stay on as Headmistress even after this letter.

It has come to my attention recently that four young ladies at Kensington have reached the age of eighteen. Two of them are even a year older. While I don't wish to disparage them or the relationship I am sure you have with them, I must ask you to enforce the policies of the orphanage and ask these women to leave the premises immediately. As you are aware, these women are no longer children according to the United States government, and as such, they are no longer allowed to be in the care of Kensington Orphanage.

I know it must be difficult for you to face; however, we are an orphanage for children and only children, and because of that, I must ask you to respect the policies and ask these women to leave. I realize what I am asking of you, and so I also ask that you give them the envelopes I have enclosed.

There is enough money for each woman to secure a room at a boarding house for a month while they inquire about employment.

I look forward to your reply informing me they have left.

Sincerely,
Harvey Kensington
Kensington Orphanage, Founder and Owner

Winona continued to stare at Mr. Kensington's letter and the four envelopes full of money. She wanted to be angry, yet part of her knew she couldn't be. He only followed the rules of his business and offered help to the young women when he didn't have to.

But still.

What were they supposed to do if they couldn't find employment? How would they pay for a room or food then? Each of the women had spent a different number of years here; however, they still were young enough that this home was all they knew.

And now they had to leave?

Winona thought of each one of them. Lark was always the high-spirited one, longing for a freedom she would never feel. Shy and prim, Grace, whose kindness melted even the hardest of hearts. Cora, the ever-helpful one who learned all she could about being a wife and mother, sometimes to the point of annoyance. And lastly, Harper, the bookworm who studied every subject under the sun, devouring knowledge like a dry rag soaks up water.

Winona had come to know and love all four of the women as she would her own daughters, and given that she never married or had children of her own, she supposed that they were her own. Sure, she felt a kinship to every one of the children that had come into and left the orphanage over the decades she'd worked there, but these four . . . they were different. They held her heart in the palm of their hands.

And now she was being forced to ask them to leave.

Her heart broke just thinking about telling them.

A knock rapped on her door, and after she turned to tell whomever it was to come in, the door opened, and Natalie, one of the maids, came inside carrying a tray.

"I have your evening tea, Miss Callahan," Natalie said.

"Thank you, Natalie."

"Oh, and I found the copy of this morning's paper. Louie had stuffed it in the kindling box again, thinking it was yesterday's paper. I'm afraid some pages are smudged with soot, but most of the articles are legible."

"That's good news. Thank you."

The maid set the tray on the desk and unfolded the paper, laying it beside the tray before she nodded and left Winona's office. The soft click echoed, and Winona looked out the window once more. She knew there had to be a solution to her problem, but she didn't know what it was.

Yet, she thought to herself.

She moved over to her desk, pouring a cup of tea before sitting in the chair, scooting it forward, and grabbing the copy of the *Liberty Tribune*. She scanned the front-page news, passing over the articles about the blockade in Odessa and the state of

Europe as she turned the page over. A few black printed words caught her attention, and she furrowed her brow as she leaned in and lifted the paper closer to her face so she could read it better.

"To advertisers! The Matrimonial News. A weekly journal devoted to the interests of love, courtship, and marriage," she read aloud.

She cocked her head to the side, continuing to read the article about men either heading out West to Oregon or already living there who were seeking mail-order brides—women who were eager to start new lives in the frontier with men who were waiting for them. All they had to do was write and take a chance.

Surely, that would solve her predicament.

Of course, it also raised another problem as well.

What if the young women disagreed?

She bit her lip and rose from her chair, fiddling with her hands as she made her way over to the door, opened it, and called the women by their names to come into her office.

It must work, she thought to herself as she paced and waited. *It just must work.*

Three of the four women came immediately, and Winona told them to take a seat while they all waited for Lark. They all watched her continue to pace.

"Whatever chore you want us to do tonight, I refuse. I don't care what it is," Lark said as she finally entered the room.

"This is not about chores."

"Oh good." She blew out a breath, and her shoulders softened.

"However," Winona lifted her hand, wiggling her finger at the petite blonde. "If I did have chores for you, refusal would not be an option."

Lark looked at her and opened her mouth like she had something else to say. Before she spoke, however, she glanced at the other women, and as Harper and Grace shook their heads, Lark closed her mouth. She rolled her eyes and took a seat next to Cora, folding her arms across her chest as she exhaled a huffed breath.

Winona moved over to the desk and sat in her chair, turning toward the women as she fetched the letter from Mr. Kensington.

"I don't know how to tell you, ladies, what I'm about to tell you, but I have no other choice."

"What is wrong, Winona?" Grace asked. Her brow furrowed, although not in anger. The tallest of the women, even though she sat, she still towered over the other three.

"Well, I'm afraid I have bad news for you."

"What news?" Lark adjusted her body in her chair. Her brow furrowed, too; only it wasn't in a concerned way like Grace's. Instead, hers was more in a flight or fight, as though she braced herself for her whole life to be turned upside down.

Winona wished the woman wasn't right about that fact.

"I received a letter today from Mr. Kensington. He is the founder and owner of the orphanage, and he was recently made aware that the four of you are over eighteen—two of you are even nineteen."

Although both Harper and Cora raised an eyebrow, Harper asked the question. "So, what does that mean?"

"Well, it means that you have to leave."

"But where are we going to go?"

Winona looked at Harper, then at the rest of the women, saving Lark for last. Lark's shoulders were hunched, and she rocked back and forth in the chair for a moment before it seemed like her anxiousness had gotten the better of her. She bolted out of the chair, crossing the room so she could pace in front of the bookcase.

"I know you all have questions," Winona said, watching her for a moment before looking at the other three sitting on the couch. "But before you ask them, please hear me out. I think I have a solution to your problem."

"And what is that?" Harper asked.

"Well, Mr. Kensington realizes that he is asking you to leave the only home you've ever known and to do so without a place to live, food to eat, or employment, so he is sending you with some money."

"How much?" Grace asked.

"It's enough for a month's board at a boarding house and food. However, I think I found a better idea for you."

"And what is that?" Lark threw her arms in the air, letting them fall to her sides, smacking her dress. Before Winona could answer, she folded them across her chest again and continued to pace, raising her voice with each step. "Don't think I don't know where women who can't find work or can't afford a room and food end up. I know exactly where and exactly what they have to do to survive. I won't go back there. I won't. And you nor Mr. Kensington will make me." Tears welled in her eyes, and Winona dropped the letter, letting it fall back to the desk as she rose from her chair and rushed over to Lark, wrapping her arms around the young woman.

"You will never have to go back there. I promise," Winona said. Lark's body trembled in Winona's arms, and she squeezed the young woman tighter. "I won't let anything like that happen to you again."

"What is the idea you have, Winona?" Harper asked.

Winona turned toward the other three. "While reading this morning's paper, I saw an advertisement."

"What sort of advertisement?"

"For mail-order brides."

Harper and Grace glanced at one another. Both of them raised one eyebrow while Cora bounced in her seat, a smile etched across her face. Lark pulled away from Winona's grasp, and her brow furrowed again.

"What is a mail-order bride?" Lark asked.

"Well, men—nice, young men who are moving out West to places like Oregon or Montana or who already live there—are taking out advertisements to find themselves a wife. Women answer said advertisements, then travel to where the man is living, and they get married." Winona glanced at all four with a huge smile, hoping her enthusiasm would help with the sting of reality in what she was saying to them.

"What kind of men are they?" Grace asked. She straightened her shoulders and leaned into the back of her chair.

"They are lovely men. Men with employment or ranches. Men who have the means to take care of a woman in a proper way."

"How do you know?" Lark asked the headmistress.

"I beg your pardon?"

"How do you know they are lovely men? If they were lovely men, why couldn't they find a woman to love and marry outside of an advertisement in the newspaper?"

"Well, perhaps there just aren't many women where they are. There is so much unclaimed land out West, and although towns are growing, they aren't like they are here or back East."

Lark dropped her gaze to the ground, shaking her head.

Winona's heart thumped. She not only wanted them to agree, but she wanted them to agree together. If they traveled together, there was a better chance they could keep each other safe.

But if one stayed behind...

"Do you have any of the advertisements?" Cora asked. Her smile was as big as ever.

"No, I don't. But I can write to the address on the advertisement and see how we would find out who these men are and how you would contact them."

"Well, count me in. I think it would be quite the adventure."

"You just want to find a husband and get married." Lark

rolled her eyes and waved her hand toward Cora. The youngest of the four, Cora was often treated as though she had her head stuck in the clouds and was always daydreaming about a life she had pictured in her head. Winona didn't want to admit that she had the same feelings toward the young woman. Still, her relentless sunshine-filled perspective had a quality about it that made Winona smile.

"You're right, Lark, I do. But what is wrong with that?" She glanced at Harper and Grace. "Don't you two want to find love and marriage? And have a husband and family? I know you both do. We have to leave the orphanage, so why not start a new life out West? What do we have to lose?"

"Do you want the answer to that question?" Lark asked.

"Not from you." Cora glared at her and then turned back toward the other two. She reached out and grabbed Harper's hands. "Don't you want a little adventure in your life?"

"I suppose I do." Harper looked at Grace, who shrugged.

"If you two are going, I suppose I will too," Grace said.

The three looked at Lark, who had started pacing again in front of the bookcase. Hesitation purred through her, and for a moment, Winona didn't want to know what she was thinking. She knew it could go either way. Lark could say yes. But Lark could also say no.

It was the no that Winona feared the most.

Lark stopped pacing, looking at them before she looked at the headmistress. "Are you going with us?"

Taken aback, Winona blinked at the young woman. She had been so focused on finding a solution for the women that she hadn't considered what that solution would entail. She hadn't thought about how they would get to Oregon or that they would have to travel alone.

Did she want them to travel alone?

She looked at the four faces, and for a moment, she saw them as little girls with bright, blinking eyes as they looked to her for love and guidance—two things they didn't get from their parents, as most children in the world did.

She wanted to say yes to Lark's question and agree to go with them, but something made her pause and hesitate. "I don't...I don't know," she said.

Cora stood from the couch, squaring her shoulders as though she wanted her stance to prove a point. "It's all right if you don't want to go with us. We can manage on our own. We are grown women, after all. If we can't find our way to Oregon, then we have no business even going to find a husband."

Lark rolled her eyes and groaned before she left the room, not even closing the door behind her. Her shoes clicked on the hardwood floors, echoing down the hallway. Winona wanted to go after her, but she didn't. Instead, she just stood by the bookcase, staring at the door. The sudden awareness that she'd failed to solve their problem overwhelmed her.

All she wanted was their happiness.

Harper and Grace made their way toward Winona, and Grace wrapped her arms around the headmistress. "Don't worry. Lark will be all right. She knows what you're trying to do to help us."

"I feel like she's going to hate me," Winona said.

"She doesn't hate you. She hates herself."

BRIDES OF LONE HOLLOW

Five men looking for love . . .

Five women with different ideas . . .

One small town where they all will either live happily ever after or leave with shattered dreams.

Order the series today

Turn the page for a sneak peek at book one, Her Mail Order Mix-Up.

ONE

CULLEN

"God never gives you what He can't carry you through."
Pastor Duncan's words repeated in Cullen McCray's mind as he glanced down at his niece. All of just nine years old, the little girl sat beside him in the wagon as they drove into town. Her small body bumped into his every time a wheel rolled over a rock, and her white-blonde hair blew in the gentle breeze. She was the purest example of what the pastor was talking about. Or at least that was what the pastor had told him when he brought her to Cullen's cabin that day, scared and sad. Her entire world had been torn apart by her father's sudden death, and he, her uncle, was her only chance.

She glanced back at him. Her eyes—his brother's eyes—stared at him. She looked more like Clint every day, and he wondered if she would grow up to have Clint's mannerisms. Would she act like him? Talk like him? Would she think like him? While he wanted her to, a part of him didn't. He wasn't sure he wanted another Clint in his life.

"What do we need from town today, Uncle Cullen?" Sadie asked.

He rolled the piece of straw from one side of his lips to the other, chewing a little more on the sweet taste of the dried stem. "Just the usual, Sadie. Did you need something else this time?"

She shrugged. "I was thinking of making a pie when we got back to the ranch."

Pie.

He hadn't thought of pie in months, hadn't thought about much of the things his late wife used to bake, actually. Because thinking of them would have reminded him of her and how she wasn't around to bake them anymore. He ate chili and stew and steak and potatoes and eggs and bacon, which made up the sum of his diet. Perhaps he would have some bread or biscuits on those cold winter nights when he needed something to stick to the sides of his gut and keep him warm, but other than that, he didn't branch out. He didn't want to. He didn't want the reminder.

Of course, he knew that needed to change now that Sadie was in his life. He had to care for her, and a little growing girl needed more nourishment than what he'd been putting into his body. She needed a garden with lots of vegetables and an orchard with fruit trees. She needed bread. She needed cakes and cookies and, well, pie. All the things his late wife would spend her days making for him. He could still smell all the scents in the house. But back to the point. Sadie needed more, and she also needed to cook and bake—or at least learn to do those things along with how to sew, read, and do arithmetic.

"Do you know how to bake a pie?" he asked the girl.

"I do. Well, sort of. It was one thing Nanny Noreen taught me before . . ." The little girl's voice trailed off. She didn't want to say before the accident. She never did. She always stopped herself when she found the words trying to come out of her lips.

Not that he blamed her. He never wished to speak of it, either. His brother and his sister-in-law were now up in Heaven with his wife, leaving Sadie and him down here on earth to pick up the pieces as best as they could.

"What kind of pie did you want to make?" he asked; a slight hope rose in his chest that the girl would say peach or apple. Those were always his favorites.

"I don't know. I guess whatever fruit I can find in town."

Find in town.

Guilt prickled in his chest. She shouldn't have to find fruit in town. She should be able to go out and pick it off her tree. It was just another thing he mentally put on his list of things to do for her—plant some trees.

"Well, I suppose we can look to see what Mr. Dawson has. If you find something that works, we can get it. Did you need anything else for a pie?"

"I don't know. I suppose if I may, I'll look around?"

"Yeah. You can do that."

She glanced at him again and smiled before leaning her head on his arm.

His heart gave another little tug at his guilt. For so many months after the accident and after Pastor Duncan brought her up to his cabin, he hadn't wanted her to stay. Not quite a burden, but almost there. He had packed her bags, he didn't know how many times, fully intent on taking her down to the orphanage where he thought she belonged. She needed a chance at a family with a ma and pa. She didn't need a gruff lone wolf like him. Not to mention, he had wished to live his life alone in his cabin. The cattle ranch. The family. Those were all things Clint, his brother, wanted. He didn't. Or at least he didn't until . . .

He shook his head, ridding himself of the thoughts of his late wife.

He couldn't think of her.

Not now.

Not today.

Never again.

He tapped the reins on the horses' backs, then whistled at

them to pick up the pace into a trot. He needed the distraction of town to ease his mind.

~

MAGGIE

"Love always, Clint." Maggie once again read the ending words of Clint's last letter as the stagecoach rolled down the lane. Her heart thumped, and she bit her lip as she leaned back in the seat and rested her head against the back.

She didn't want to think about the life she left to travel hundreds of miles across the United States so she could marry a man she didn't know. Or how she fled her parents' house in the middle of the night with her mother telling her to leave while her father slept. She only wanted to think about the life she was about to start as Mrs. Clint McCray. It didn't matter that they hadn't actually met before and had only corresponded through letters. Nor did it matter that she wasn't exactly in love with him... yet. It only mattered that in those letters, he promised her a life far away from her parents and the life they had planned for her. One where Daddy would shove her into a loveless marriage with either Benjamin Stone or Matthew Cooper—two sons of business acquaintances he'd known for years. She knew both men well, too. Benjamin was nothing but a bore, and Matthew... well, let her just say she didn't care for the way he treated women. Not to mention, his reputation in town left little to be desired, and she doubted the perpetual bachelor would even want to marry. He had more fun pursuing other tastes.

While she knew her daddy didn't think they were the best choices, he also wasn't about to have a spinster for a daughter, and she knew her time was fast ticking away. As did her mama. Which was why, when Clint's letter arrived with the plan for her to leave, they packed her a suitcase and bought her a ticket out west. Out to Lone Hollow, Montana.

"Are you headed to Lone Hollow?" the woman sitting across from her asked. Slightly older than Maggie, her hair was styled in a tight bun at the base of her neck, and she looked through a pair of spectacles resting on her long, thin nose.

"Yes, I am. My soon-to-be husband lives there and is waiting for me."

The woman smiled and ducked her chin slightly. "Best wishes to you both."

"Thank you. I'm Maggie, by the way. Maggie Colton."

The woman nodded. "Amelia Hawthorn. It's a pleasure to meet you."

"You, too." Maggie shifted her gaze from the woman to the window of the stagecoach. Nothing but mountains and forests and wilderness; Montana had been nothing like she'd ever seen before. So pretty. So peaceful. Like God's perfect place and glory was here in this state. "Where are you headed?" she asked, turning her attention to the woman.

"Brook Creek. It's about forty miles west of Lone Hollow."

"So, you still have a bit to go in your travels."

"Unfortunately. But I figure I've been this far. As long as I get to my post, I don't mind the distance."

"Post?"

"I'm a schoolteacher, and I received my post orders for the small town. I had asked for Lone Hollow, seeing as how it's a milling town, but was told it was filled at least for now."

"A milling town? Does that make it a more appealing post?"

"A little. Lone Hollow has one of the few sawmills around, and having a sawmill means more amenities than Brook Creek, like a hotel and café. There is more of a population in Lone Hollow than in Brook Creek, too, which means there are more families and children. They told me they would let me know if the teacher in Lone Hollow leaves, and if he does, then

I will move again as I'm not sure I want to stay in Brook Creek."

The name made Maggie giggle. "It's funny that the town is named for two synonyms for a river."

"Don't get me started on that." The woman rolled her eyes and exhaled a deep sigh as she slid her fingers behind her ears, tucking any loose strands of her blonde bun behind her ears. The feathers on her maroon hat fluttered with her movement, and they matched her maroon dress. "Of course, all I care about are the children. I hope they are nice and are ready to learn."

"I'm sure they are, and you will do fine." Maggie bit her lip again at the thoughts in her head. She dropped her gaze to her hands, fidgeting with her fingers. "My husband-to-be has a daughter. She is nine years old. His first wife died of Scarlet Fever several years ago when she was just a baby. I feel awful that she was never able to meet her mother."

"Such a shame she lost her mama."

"Yes, it is. I just hope I can bond with her. I don't wish to replace her mother, but I hope to be someone she can accept and love."

"I'm sure she will. It might take some time, but you will do just fine."

Maggie glanced at the woman and smiled as she nodded. She didn't know if she could talk anymore about the young girl or her concerns, for the notions brought more butterflies to her stomach than the thoughts of meeting Clint. She wanted to do right by the young girl and wanted to be someone the girl could trust, look up to, and perhaps love after time had passed. She knew how wonderful it was to grow up with a mother, and she wanted that for Sadie.

The stagecoach slowed, and with the change of pace, Maggie glanced out the window again. While the mountains and forests were still in her view, a few houses speckled what little she could see, and as more and more passed by, the stagecoach slowed as it finally entered the town of Lone Hollow.

To my sister
Michelle Renee Horning

April 3, 1971 - January 8, 2022
You will be forever missed. I don't know how I'm going to do this thing
called life without you.

LONDON JAMES IS A PEN NAME FOR ANGELA CHRISTINA ARCHER. SHE LIVES ON A RANCH WITH HER HUSBAND, TWO DAUGHTERS, AND MANY FARM ANIMALS. SHE WAS BORN AND RAISED IN NEVADA AND GREW UP RIDING AND SHOWING HORSES. WHILE SHE DOESN'T SHOW ANYMORE, SHE STILL LOVES TO TRAIL RIDE.

FROM A YOUNG AGE, SHE ALWAYS WANTED TO WRITE A NOVEL. HOWEVER, EVERY TIME THE DESIRE FLICKERED, SHE SHOVED THE THOUGHT FROM MY MIND UNTIL ONE MORNING IN 2009, SHE AWOKE WITH THE DETERMINATION TO FOLLOW HER DREAM.

HTTPS://LONDONJAMESBOOKS.COM

JOIN MY MAILING LIST FOR NEWS ON RELEASES, DISCOUNTED SALES, AND EXCLUSIVE MEMBER-ONLY BENEFITS!

Copyright © 2024

Cover Design by Angela Archer, Long Valley Designs

This book is a work of fiction. The names, characters, places, and incidents are the products of the author's imagination or are used fictitiously.

Any resemblance to actual events, business establishments, locales, or persons, living or dead, is entirely coincidental.

All rights reserved.

No part of this publication may be reproduced, stored in retrieval system, or transmitted in any form or by any means (electronic, mechanical, photocopying, recording, or otherwise) without prior written permission of both the copyright owner and the publisher. The only exception is brief quotations in printed reviews.

The scanning, uploading, and distribution of this book via the Internet or via any other means without the permission of the publisher is illegal and punishable by law.

Please purchase only authorized electronic editions and do not participate in or encourage electronic piracy of copyrighted materials.

Your support of the author's rights is appreciated.

Published in the United States of America by:

Long Valley Press
Newcastle, Oklahoma
www.longvalleypress.com

Scriptures taken from the Holy Bible, New International Version®, NIV®. Copyright © 1973, 1978, 1984, 2011 by Biblica, Inc.™ Used by permission of Zondervan. All rights reserved worldwide. www.zondervan.com The "NIV" and "New International Version" are trademarks registered in the United States Patent and Trademark Office by Biblica, Inc.™

Made in United States
Troutdale, OR
08/08/2025

33472752R00196